Since 1947 Dirk Bogarde has starred in more than sixty films. His popularity as a teenage idol brought him vast amounts of fan mail and enormous box-office success, which was to continue through the fifties and sixties. Later he achieved a different kind of success with such films as *The Servant, King and Country, Accident, Death in Venice, The Night Porter, Providence, Despair* and *These Foolish Things (Daddy Nostalgie)*.

He is now well known as a writer, having published seven volumes of autobiography: *A Postillion Struck by Lightning, Snakes and Ladders, An Orderly Man, Backcloth, Great Meadow* (an evocation of childhood), *A Short Walk from Harrods* and *Cleared for Take-Off*. He is also the author of another five novels: *A Gentle Occupation, Voices in the Garden, West of Sunset, Jericho* and *A Period of Adjustment*, which is a sequel to *Jericho*. They have all reached the bestseller lists and have been translated into a number of languages. Penguin publish each of these titles, as well as *A Particular Friendship*, a collection of letters written between 1967 and 1970 to an unknown American woman.

Dirk Bogarde, who now lives in London, lived for many years in France and was made a Commandeur de l'Ordre des Arts et des Lettres by the French Government in 1990. He has also been made an Honorary Doctor of Letters at the University of St Andrews and at the University of Sussex. He received a knighthood in 1992.

DIRK BOGARDE

Closing Ranks

PENGUIN BOOKS

PENGUIN BOOKS

Published by the Penguin Group
Penguin Books Ltd, 27 Wrights Lane, London W8 5TZ, England
Penguin Putnam Inc., 375 Hudson Street, New York, New York 10014, USA
Penguin Books Australia Ltd, Ringwood, Victoria, Australia
Penguin Books Canada Ltd, 10 Alcorn Avenue, Toronto, Ontario, Canada M4V 3B2
Penguin Books (NZ) Ltd, 182–190 Wairau Road, Auckland 10, New Zealand

Penguin Books Ltd, Registered Offices: Harmondsworth, Middlesex, England

First published by Viking 1997
Published in Penguin Books 1998
3 5 7 9 10 8 6 4 2

Printed in England by Clays Ltd, St Ives plc

For
Peter Wheeler MB, MRCP
Without whom . . .

Author's Note

This book was started in 1980 but after two chapters was abandoned on account of the prevailing 'political climate'. It was finally finished in ward 3 at the Edward the VIIth Hospital in early December 1996 with the generous assistance of my splendid editor, Clare Alexander, and Clare Harington, who helped me wrestle a cover design out of some rough sketches I did in a letter. Later in December Mark Handsley came to my bedside and together we did the copy-editing. Their patience and encouragement gave me great courage during a rather dark period and I cannot thank them all enough. And thanks, too, to Mrs Sally Betts, who has typed her fourteenth volume.

'Wolfsendorf' is entirely imaginary, although the events described there are not. I was not in Austria in the war, and when this tragic incident took place I was in Germany on my way to Berlin. But the rumours and stories started to follow me from Germany to Signapore with the younger men who had been eyewitnesses to the event. It is from their accounts that, fifty years later, my own description has been culled.

I have found both volumes of the Cowgill Enquiry report on the Cossack repatriation of May 1945, published in 1990, of the greatest value.

Sunday Morning

Loveday, sitting in the long orchard grasses, back pressed hard against the scabby bark of a tree, tears meandering down her cheeks unheeded, nose running, pulled a stalk of grass and suddenly saw him coming up through the trees, a black silhouette against the brilliance of the early morning. She wiped her nose on the back of her hand, dragged up her hair which grief had tumbled about her shoulders, and got to her feet.

'Mr Smollett? Is that you? Mr Smollett?'

The advancing figure, speckled and flecked with leaf-filtered light, made no reply.

'I can't see you. Rufus? Is it Rufus? Oh, *do* answer . . .'

The figure suddenly stopped, raised one arm high above his head. Sentinel.

'No,' he called up through the trees. 'It's not.'

Loveday stared at him for a moment, and then brushed her long silk skirt angrily, to conceal dismay.

'Well, how was I to know? I knew you were a man, because you are wearing trousers, but I thought you were someone else. You are a trespasser.'

He came on up the hill. 'I was taking a short cut to the hospice at Nether Dicker. I didn't know.'

'Well you are. Trespassing. Disturbing people.'

He had reached a patch of light a few paces from her: medium height, slight, fair hair. Pleasant-looking. He had a beard, and wore a rough cloth tunic over old jeans.

'Trespassing,' she repeated, to give herself time to consider him.

'I'm really sorry. I didn't know. Honestly.' He leant with his full weight on a shepherd's crook which he carried, a sagging haversack on his back.

'You keep on saying you didn't know! There is a sign down by the road, and it says that this is private land and to keep out.'

'I didn't see it.'

'Well, it's there. And if you try to strike me with that stick I'll call out for help and you'll be savaged by two huge dogs. Very fierce ones.'

'I wouldn't hit you. Why would I do that? That's a funny thing to say.'

'It's a funny thing to do. Trespassing on private land, disturbing people. A complete stranger.'

'Hardly.'

'Hardly what, pray?'

'A complete stranger.'

'You are to me.' She began to pull down her sleeves, which she had rolled to the elbows doing the washing-up earlier. 'I've never set eyes on you in my life. You aren't Rufus; or Mr Smollett. Who are you?'

'Jesus Christ,' he said.

Loveday fumbled with the cloth-covered buttons of her cuff. 'I *knew* you weren't Rufus. Somehow I just *knew*. Or Mr Smollett.'

'You called out those names.'

'I know I did. I wish they'd come. It may be too late . . . it may be . . .'

'Is it something serious?' he asked.

She fumbled with the other cuff. His voice, she reasoned, was really quite common. Not Sussex-country. Just London-common. Ordinary. He had even said 'someth*ink*'.

'Mr Smollett's aunt is dying. She is our Nanny actually, and we know her as Grayle because that's our name, and Rufus is my brother, Rufus Grayle, and we sent for them last night, urgently. We left messages on telephones and things.'

'I'm very sorry,' he said. 'I can understand why you are so sad.'

'Well, it's a sad thing. If you *are* Jesus Christ I think it's a pretty peculiar day to arrive. In the middle of all this . . .'

'Perhaps,' he said carefully, 'if she's going over to the other side, it's the *right* day to arrive?'

She looked at him directly for the first time. He had grey eyes and wasn't smiling. As far as she could tell.

'What do you mean by that? Going over to the other side?'

'You might call it dying.'

'I do. I already have. It *is*. That's what she is doing. And they are all sitting about in that little room of hers just waiting. It's simply dreadful . . . waiting for her to die.'

'Why are they all sitting round her?' he said. 'Death is a private thing.'

Loveday took a pair of spectacles from the pocket of her skirt, polished them roughly before putting them on, then stared at him, confirming that his eyes were grey, that he was smiling, and that he was quite young.

'It isn't always private, is it? Death? Not in a war, it isn't, on battlefields and so on, it's terribly public. And motor accidents in the street . . . that's *very* public. I think you've got it all wrong. I don't think you are who you say.'

'I meant if someone was dying, as you call it, in her own bed, she should have the right to go peacefully, not with a crowd of people sitting watching.'

Loveday pulled at a length of cow-parsley growing at her side. 'I don't know. Well, yes I do. They want to be

3

with her to the end, to comfort her. After all, she has been with them all of their lives. I've known her all of mine. Over thirty years. It's a long time. One has a duty, a respect.'

'Duty is essential.'

'I know that! Goodness, I know that. It's just that I simply detest them all sitting there, helplessly, waiting, watching her go. She was so good to me always, so kind and loving, overflowing with love.' She threw the wrenched stalk of cow-parsley into the trees. 'I was her favourite. She said so over and over again. No one would ever be foul to me, she said. She'd see to it. That's what she always said.'

'Over *thirty* years?' His voice was soft with awe.

'Yes. And already I'm talking about her in the past tense! Already! It's so dreadful.'

'She suffers no pain?'

'Pain? No. No, I don't think so. She's peaceful, just asleep. It's pneumonia, I think. I just wish she'd go if she has to. There's a nurse. Awful woman. Irish. Bossy. I hate her.'

'That is wrong; to hate.'

'She is *hateful*. There. I don't care.'

'Who are all the others, then?'

'The family. My family. Well, we're *her* family really. All she has in the world except for Mr Smollett, who hasn't come.' She pushed her long hair behind her ear, a tight, sharp, acid smile on her lips, as if she had bitten into a quince. 'If you are who you say you are you should know all this anyway. Without coming here unasked. Trespassing! Prying and trespassing! And on such a day.' Her eyes brimmed with tears. 'I expect you're a burglar really. I know. I've read about people like you. Getting people's trust and then robbing them. I know . . .'

He shook his head anxiously, adjusted the haversack. 'I'm not like that. Really I'm not. Perhaps it was destined that I should take a private short cut? Perhaps it was meant? Who knows?'

'What for, pray?'

'To help you. Comfort you.'

'You can't help. No one can. If you were who you say you are you could stop her from dying. All those miracles . . . *Do* one! Do one now! Don't let her die!'

'But maybe her time has come? We are mortal. There is a time for everyone to go.'

'She's ninety.'

'You see? She's had a long stay.'

Loveday poked a finger behind her glasses and wiped each eye, nodded her head, no longer trusting herself to speak. She turned away from the leaning figure at the same moment that a woman's voice, crisp with irritation, called through the trees somewhere beyond them.

'Lovedaaay! Lovedaaay? Come back . . . Where are you? *Do* be sensible . . . Lovedaaay? Come back . . .'

She turned and looked at him with steaming, startled eyes. He put out a calloused hand, from which she instantly withdrew.

'No. No. I must go. I must. That's Unity, my sister. She's rotten. Absolutely . . .' She turned, gathering up her long, trailing silk skirt in one hand and stumbled, half ran, up the gentle slope through the trees.

He stood for a moment, until she was lost to sight behind brambles and trees.

'Stark staring bonkers,' he said. 'Barking mad.' Then, easing the knapsack from his shoulder, he sat down and began to roll himself a joint.

Bottle Cottage, in which Nanny Grayle had lived in contented retirement for more than a decade, stood at the far edge of the orchard and looked across fields and water-meadows to the smooth, smudged ridge of the Downs.

One up, two down, a tiled roof, knapped-flint walls inset on each side of the front door by two triangles of green-glass bottle ends; hence its name. In the small front garden, surrounded by rusty chicken wire and a thicket of ivy and honeysuckle, Unity Uffington stood as upright and trim as the mast of yacht. And equally unyielding.

'Loveday! I've been yelling my head off! Where have you been? So thoughtless . . .'

'In the orchard. There's a trespasser.'

'Well, please don't float off all the time. She opened her eyes a moment ago. Quite clearly. Saw us, recognized us. Knew us. Very reassuring. Knew we were there. But *you* had gone wandering off.'

'The trespasser is quite unusual, actually.'

'What's unusual about him?' Unity moved towards the front door, her hand raised to lift the latch.

'His name's Jesus Christ.'

Unity froze, bit the inside of her lip sharply, cleared her throat. 'We'll get someone down to deal with him later. Come along now.'

She lifted the latch and pushed Loveday into the cramped little sitting-room. Nanny Grayle's bed had been brought down from the bedroom some years ago. She said that the stairs 'got to her', and that she felt more at ease with the lavatory near at hand, on the same floor, so for some time she had lived, and had slept, in what she called her parlour.

As things had turned out it was a sensible move, for now Nurse Monahan, crisp and dry as ship's biscuits and as unattractive, had moved into the bedroom above and had taken charge of the proprietor, who had had a fall on the slippery brick path in the back garden which had brought about the pneumonia now inexorably easing her towards her end.

After more than sixty-five years' service with the family (she had arrived to start work in the kitchens and gravitated, through shrewd good sense and a loving disposition, to the nursery) Falmouth Grayle had offered her a small apartment in the west wing at Hartleap or, if she preferred it, the lifetime's ownership of Bottle Cottage across its park.

She'd have accepted the apartment, happily – although it was high above the house and reached only by a number of staircases – but for providence, in the shape of a coach crash in which her sister, and only adult relative, Vera, on a trip to the Lake District, had been killed instantly. Although shocked, Nanny Grayle (who was born Ada Stephens) found it difficult to grieve for the loss of the sister whom she had never really cared for, and liked less when she had married Reginald Smollett, a market gardener at Hellingly, to become, naturally, Mrs Reg Smollett. Vera had always been exceptionally overpowering, and condescending to her younger sister 'in service'. They rarely met over the years: sometimes on a day off (which Nanny never liked taking for fear the under-nanny would get up to some mischief while she was away) she'd go over to Reg Smollett's bungalow at Hellingly and allow herself to be given tea, from the 'good' china, and to look at the snapshots of their last family holiday; for Vera, to her sister's mild surprise, had actually managed to produce a son, Robert, who had become the centre of his mother's life. But those visits were few and far between, and she found the journey to Hellingly tiresome.

However, Robert was as unlike his mother as it was possible to be, and Nanny Grayle liked him very much. As, indeed, she liked most, but not all, children. It was she who suggested that he should come to Hartleap and train under old Fred Winton, who was head gardener. This generous move proved to be a success. The gardens thrived, Bob

Smollett became one of the family, and Nanny Grayle forgot all about Vera until the death of her husband from a sudden heart attack just before the outbreak of war. After the irritating business of Reg's funeral, and the wretched salmon tea which had to follow his interment, she hurried back from Hellingly and put Vera out of her mind – until the extraordinary morning when she had read, in her *Daily Mail*, that there had been a disastrous coach crash near Windermere, wherever that was, and that her sister Vera, 'Mrs Reginald Smollett', with an address in Hellingly, Sussex, was among those listed as 'killed instantly'. It gave her quite a turn. It was gallivanting about all over the place that did it.

Vera left everything she owned to her son, Robert; but she had shown greater generosity of spirit than her sister, leaving her, in a detailed list, 'Two single beds, four good Witney blankets, a pair of Staffordshire "comforters", a mahogany chest of drawers, one brass fender and a china spittoon'. (The last had belonged to their father.) Nanny Grayle, overnight, became a woman of property for the first time in her life and, if not exactly an heiress, she felt pleasantly rich: accepting, with grace, the generous offer of Bottle Cottage which Falmouth Grayle had made her.

She retired in comparative splendour after years of loyal and happy labour, to tend her small garden with a sharp pair of secateurs and a sharper eye than most for aphids, mildew, ground-elder, and club-root. She was never lonely in Bottle Cottage: almost every day someone came across from Hartleap to see her, to bring pheasant for plucking, a puppy to school, an elbow to patch, a hem to shorten or lengthen.

At Christmas, or on birthdays or family celebrations, she was escorted through the orchard to the house and sat, stiffly upright, in her best-black, in Big Hall or Little Parlour (depending on the occasion) to eat her own home-baked Coburg cakes, which she always brought with her in a tin, and to take Earl Grey's tea with her Family.

As she grew older a telephone was installed in the cottage, so that, if she had need, she could call for assistance; but the telephone had always been a source of terror to her, and she touched it as little as she possibly could, answering only the occasional call from her nephew Bob, now a thriving nursery gardener himself. He lived in Shrewsbury, with a wide and respected reputation for the excellence of his stock, a good line in advertising ('Smollett's Seeds Succeed') and a pleasant, plump wife called May.

These calls took her often by surprise, and she was put into what she termed 'a bit of a tizz' for a moment or two, but the 'check' calls from the house were perfectly regular, at nine every morning, and she was accustomed to them. All in all her life was one of quiet contentment. She pottered and pruned; gossiped when someone called to gossip; baked sponge cakes, for she had a sweet tooth; and when the weather was inclement, she knitted something for someone somewhere: she was expert at turning a heel.

But time moved on, casting a lengthening shadow. The district nurse began to 'drop in' from time to time, and then three times a week. A pleasant woman arrived in a van and brought her meals, the family made checks more often than usual, not on the telephone but in person, and Nanny Grayle grew frail. Stubbornly independent and determined, she insisted on moving about her beloved cottage, and taking cautious walks in her garden, with a heavy stick.

And then, unsteady on her feet, she had slipped on the brick path, lay helpless for some time, until India Grayle, alerted by the fact that the telephone was not answered, hurried across the park with well-founded anxiety. Nothing was broken, but all was not well. Nurse Monahan was brought in to take charge of things and it was clear, after a very few days, that Nanny Grayle had taken her last walk through the phlox and sweet-williams in her overgrown garden.

Thus, on this hot July morning, the family had been gathered in the stuffy parlour of Bottle Cottage to be with her as she began a silent departure from their lives, and her own.

The night before she had drifted into a deep sleep which Nurse Monahan preferred to refer to professionally as 'a coma, poor old soul', and everything had been done to contact Mr Smollett in Shrewsbury, to no avail. He had gone off with May to a barbecue in Church Stretton, leaving a message with his answering service that all enquiries would be dealt with on his return in the morning.

Loveday's sudden, rather breathless entrance, followed by a tip-toeing Unity, elicited a suppressed 'Shssss!' of irritation from Nurse Monahan.

'Respect, surely?' she said in a cross whisper. 'She's almost gone, poor soul . . .'

Crushed, Loveday eased herself into a chair by the door. Unity moved to sit by their sister-in-law, India, on a tightly buttoned settee, a finger to her lips. For a moment there was silence, broken only by the whistling of breath from the small figure in the bed across the room.

'Fal's in the garden. We ought to call him in,' said India. They spoke in whispers.

'And Edward?' said Unity. 'Is Rochester with them?'

'They are all in the garden. It was getting a bit stuffy, and Sophie went with them. Finding it all rather a strain. The young do, faced with death. Somehow it is much easier for our age.'

'*I* don't find it easy at all!' said Unity. 'But duty is duty. One doesn't shirk.'

'Essential,' said India. 'Absolutely essential. Duty.'

Loveday leant forward in her creaky chair. 'He said that, in the orchard.'

'Who said what?' said India politely, although she really didn't want to know.

'Jesus Christ.'

India looked steadily back at her sister-in-law sitting hunched in her flowing Liberty silk dress with the long buttoned sleeves. She saw the reddened eyes behind the heavy glasses, the untidy tumble of russet hair. And sighed. 'I cannot see, Loveday,' she said in a loud whisper, 'why you find it essential to wear riding boots with that dress, in the middle of July.'

'Snakes,' said Loveday.

India looked down at her own hands, started to hum a snatch of song under her breath, remembered where she was, heard the crackle of Nurse Monahan's apron, and was silent.

'Some trespasser fellow,' said Unity quietly. 'We'll get the men to see him off, give him short shrift.'

Suddenly Nurse Monahan turned from the bedside. 'I declare! She's breathing a wee bit easier. Opened her eyes again – now that's a good girl! Having a little look around, are we? That's the ticket! Everyone is here, you see . . .'

Nanny Grayle raised a skeletal arm inches above the bed-cover. 'Bob? Bob there?' Her voice was as light and fragile as a pressed leaf.

'On his way, Nanny,' said Unity loudly. 'He's a little late. Probably got held up on the road . . . such a long way to come, you see.'

'A long way,' said Nanny Grayle. 'I'm such a trouble.'

'No! No!' cried India. 'No trouble at all. We are all here.'

'Trouble. That Beau. *He* was trouble. Wicked Beau. *Wicked* Beau. Bob told me. Bob told me, so I know.'

'I think perhaps it might be wise to ask the others to come back,' said Nurse Monahan. 'Would you do that, Mrs Grayle?'

India went across to the door.

'They sometimes do have these little remissions, you know, just before the end. She is quite lucid,' said Nurse Monahan, turning to the bed. 'Aren't we, dear? Quite clear-headed. Such a good girl.'

Loveday stifled a sob with her crammed fist.

'Loveday! Oh do behave, I beg you,' muttered India and went to call the others.

In the once-orderly garden, now a neglect of hollyhocks and nettles, Falmouth Grayle, his son Rochester and his brother-in-law Edward Uffington stood smoking in the still morning air. Sophie leant against a tree, some way off, plaiting grasses.

'I think you'd all better come in. Fal, dear, Edward? Sophie? Come along, Rochester, dear, Loveday is being terribly boring as usual. Come on, all of you.'

'She's being such a good girl,' said Nurse Monahan. 'Bright as a new penny.'

They shuffled awkwardly round the end of the high, narrow brass bed.

Nanny Grayle's eyes moved slowly from face to face, her fingers plucking idly at the counterpane.

'Edward, good fellow Edward,' she wheezed. 'Not one of the Family, but a good fellow.'

Loveday got up and moved to the side of the bed.

'Sweet Loveday . . .'

'Yes, Nanny.'

'Always looked after you, didn't I?' Her breathing was becoming laboured now.

'Always.'

'Bob? My Bobbie? Not come yet?'

'Not yet, Nanny. He'll be along in a few moments,' said India brightly.

'Too late . . . too late . . .' said Nanny Grayle, a trickle of saliva creeping down her chin. 'He knows. About Beau. Such wickedness . . .'

Nurse Monahan wiped the crevassed chin with a piece of cotton wool. 'Not too much talking, dear,' she said. 'You are tiring yourself.'

For a moment Nanny Grayle closed her eyes and then with immense effort she looked once again round the semi-circle of people at the end of her bed. The sunken eyes were bright, sparkling with mischief suddenly.

'India, Unity, dear Fal . . . the babies. No Bobbie. Is Rufus here? Rufus?'

'Coming, dear,' said India. 'He's coming, won't be long.'

'Tainted,' said Nanny Grayle in a suddenly strong voice. 'Like his father. You'll see Rufus has it. But none of you will ever fart in my blankets. None of you. All for Bob. In the will. He knows. Nothing for Beau's children. Nothing . . . Oh!' she said, with a little gasp of pleasure, staring at some vision of her own. 'Oh! it *is* pretty, it *is* so pretty . . .' Then her jaw slackened, there was a soft gurgle of breath, her head tilted to one side, chin buried deep on a thin shoulder, opaque eyes wide in surprise.

'She's gone,' said Nurse Monahan, taking up the shrivelled wrist. 'No pulse.' She made a swift sign of the cross, closed the eyes neatly.

Loveday clattered across the tiled floor (followed quickly by Sophie), pulling her tousled red hair about her face as if to conceal her grief.

'A good life,' said Edward with stunning obviousness.

'Ups and downs no doubt, but a good life. Can't complain.'

'She won't,' said Nurse Monahan. 'She's dead. It's all over for her now, and I've a few bits and bobs to do for the deceased, if you don't very much mind. And perhaps you would be so kind, Mr Grayle, as to telephone Dr Bell and let him know?'

Fal nodded. 'As soon as I get back to the house.'

'He'll have to pop up to sign the death certificate. Now then' – she flapped her hands before her as if she was herding geese – 'Off you all go, shoo, shoo, shoo. I've my work to do.'

They walked down the narrow path to the wicket gate, the men leading, tapping pockets for pipes and pouches, Rochester with arms clasped behind him, head bowed.

'Really gone to hell, hasn't it?' said Edward, kicking a clump of thistle.

'She couldn't manage it. Wouldn't have help, and we didn't want to fuss her, so it has just, as you say, gone to hell . . . We'll get it sorted out shortly.' Falmouth opened the gate and went through into the orchard.

Unity slipped her arm through India's, squeezing it gently. 'She managed to cram that little room pretty full of stuff, I have to admit.'

India gently withdrew from Unity's arm, refixed an imaginary hair-pin in her neat hair.

'She had a few bits and pieces, we let her have stuff from the House. And of course she was passionate about jumble sales, you know, she'd go miles.'

'Really made it very cosy.'

'Yes, she did.'

'We'll have to clear it all out, of course. It's absolute junk.'

'She didn't think so. It was her house,' said India. 'In any case, that's all Bob Smollett's affair now, not ours.'

'I must say that was made pretty clear!' said Unity opening the gate and going into the orchard.

India followed her and they went in single file down the track through the trees, the sweet scent of Edward's pipe tobacco lingering on the still morning air.

'Such an odd remark. None of us would ever, whatever it was, in her blankets! I mean, after all, who would want to! *Quite* extraordinary. And then calling Daddy "Beau" in that very familiar manner. Quite odd.'

'I don't think so,' said India. 'She was a very old lady, dying. The mind becomes muddles, that's all.'

Unity clipped and unclipped the clasp on her bracelet. India always made her nervous. 'I suppose that you are right. It just seemed strange. Disagreeable. Oh well . . .'

They walked on in silence. A bee droned up and away. At the edge of the orchard they pushed open the rusty iron gate and went out into the park.

'And then about Rufus!' said Unity suddenly. 'I do think that was a *most* ugly remark to make. "Tainted"! What on earth was that all about? . . . And Rufus not even there to defend himself . . . No, it was not at *all* agreeable. Calling Daddy "Beau" in that over-familiar manner, really!'

India came to a sudden halt in the middle of the path. 'Unity! Do *stop*!' She stood quite still. 'I am not made of cast iron, you know, and neither am I of your blood. I only knew Nanny just before my marriage, but I am quite dreadfully sad. I shall miss her appallingly, so will Sophie and Rochester and my poor darling Fal. She was a very old lady, probably raving away for all I know, but she was perfectly entitled to call your father "Beau" if she so wished. For God's sake, Unity! All England knew him as that during the war. "Beau Brave", in all the newspapers. So why shouldn't Nanny call him that if she wished?'

Unity had not moved during this moderate tirade. She

folded her hands together and looked suddenly at the sky. 'I'm sorry,' she said. 'We are all a bit overwrought. I was being thoughtless.'

They walked on towards the house, India scuffing through the swathes of drying hay.

'I'm glad we got this cut when we did. And after that frightful spring. I thought we'd be in trouble. But we might just get another cutting with luck.'

The land before them fell gently away to a wide, shallow valley, through which a brook serpentined, glinting in the sun, fringed with rushes and bushy clumps of water-mint. Beyond, across a plank bridge, the land rose smoothly upwards to join the ha-ha and the trim box hedges of the gardens, in which lay, stretched like a somnolent cat in the warmth of the sun, Hartleap: a rose-pink façade, tall Georgian windows, a modest portico, the east and west wings thrusting out like welcoming arms, the whole flanked by two giant cedars of Lebanon, backed by the softer greens of oak, beech and ash.

In this pleasant landscape the three men were walking up towards the gardens, Rochester now thwacking idly with a stick, Edward stopping to point at something, and Fal shaking his head, then continuing up. Voices carried in snatches: too vague to understand, too far to hear clearly.

'It's typical of me,' said India. 'Absolutely typical. To say "we" might get another cutting, when I perfectly well know that it isn't "we" any longer. "We" have no rights over hay, corn or mangel-wurzels. I keep forgetting, in the most convenient manner. All "we" own are the house and pleasure grounds.' She laughed a half-laugh. 'Who the hell put "pleasure grounds" into the lease thing? Whoever did never had to trim a box border.'

'Oh come on, India!' Unity struggled out of her beige cashmere cardigan. 'It's still our land. Still Grayle land. It's only leased, not sold or given away. Still ours, as it always has been.' She folded the cardigan neatly over her arm.

They walked on in silence, came to a halt in the ring of shade cast by a spread oak, one great limb, wrenched away in a winter gale, tumbled into the long grasses. India picked at a bit of bark, stripping it from silvered wood.

'Ants,' she said. 'Bloody thing is swarming with them, I shouldn't wonder. This really should have been carted off – do you see what I mean? – cut up, wood for the fires. Not just left to rot and fill with ants. I mean that's what we can't do now: we have no control over this sort of thing. It makes me so wretched. I *cared*. I do still, but we can't *afford* to care or bestow love. All leased to some business-man-showjumper with ideas above his station; the cottages rented to retired chartered accountants or solicitors with shrill wives, Home Farm occupied by some writer and his arts and crafts wife. I hate it all. I mind the changes, Unity, *mind* them quite dreadfully.'

'But the house is still there. Look at it! So shining, so soft, so sweet. Hartleap. Just as it always has been for seven hundred years. Never mind some tin-pot developer from London or not. It's *still* the Grayles'.'

'Oh, they'll take it when they want it. They'll squeeze us out somehow. Remember in the war? Commandeered for a girls' school? Rows of ghastly iron beds in Big Hall? The teachers' common room in your father's study? The smell of damp wool and powdered eggs.'

India half laughed again, a dry sound. She looked across the pool of shade in which they stood towards the glowing house on the rise beyond. 'They'll do it again one day. I've got used to the idea. Had to. It'll go. Fal can't keep it, can't run it. Rochester's really not interested. He wants to be a cook or something, he is like a windmill. It was photography last year. He doesn't really give a fig for the place. Sophie has some vague ideas about going to Somalia. Helping lepers. I don't honestly know. But she doesn't want Hartleap, and she couldn't manage it if she did. No, you see. They'll turn it into a teachers' training college, or an actors' rest home, or tear it apart and turn it into flats for "retired gentlefolk". Retired gentlefolk! London lampposts up the drive and Harrods reproductions. Cotton-damask curtains at the windows. It's not big, or famous, no royals attached for the NT, and we can't afford to endow the House.'

'You are being fearfully depressing,' said Unity and she started to walk down the slope to the brook.

'I am because I am depressed,' said India. 'I hate the threads breaking. They held the family here for years and years, bound it to that house, this valley, this land. And they start to break one after the other. Another just went "snap!", in Bottle Cottage. Nanny Grayle. Seventy years? Something like that. Eternity it seemed. Two fingers at the wick of a candle and the light goes.'

They reached the plank bridge, leant against the single rail, crystal water slid beneath them. A moorhen plodded with probing beak and flat, webbed feet among the acid-yellow waterweed which swirled and streamed lazily in the flow, like drowned hair.

'Well, as long as you and Fal are here it'll hold. And Rochester is very young yet, give him time.'

'That is exactly what there isn't. Time,' said India. 'Time or money. Both have run out.'

'Of course,' said Unity swatting a small turquoise dragon-fly, 'Rufus isn't a help is he, really? All over the place. So unreliable, I do see that.'

'Rufus?' said India, folding her arms on the single rail and leaning over the swift water. 'No, Rufus wouldn't be much help. He'd sell the place lock, stock and barrel and clear off to California or Peru or somewhere potty. I wonder if he's called the house yet? He must have got our message last night, unless he's in Paris, or Berlin, or Istanbul. One never knows.'

Unity, finding the dragonfly disagreeable, swung her cardigan over her shoulder and started up towards the house.

'Kathleen said she'd take any messages, if he did call. Coming? A good strong cup of tea wouldn't be amiss. Frankly, I'd rather have a pink gin. Oh well . . .'

India unfolded her arms reluctantly from the single rail and started to follow her sister-in-law. 'And then there's Smollett,' she said. 'Bob Smollett. He ought to have telephoned by now too. Everything happens at weekends, have you noticed that?'

'I have,' said Unity puffing slightly uphill, and deciding not to mention Rufus or Mr Smollett or Nanny Grayle again during the morning. Enough had been said for the time being. She altered course. 'Kathleen's terribly sweet, and really rather clever. For an American, I mean. She might be a bit too clever for Rochester. But are you pleased?'

'About what?' said India.

'Well, Kathleen and Rochester.'

'Pleased? Yes, I'm pleased, that they like each other and are happy . . . but that's all there is to it, you know? Nothing more. Rochester is a bit like Rufus. He likes his independence: Kathleen knows that. I mean, no one has *proposed* or is even on the point of proposing, if that's what is on your mind.'

'Well, it was rather,' said Unity. 'I thought it might be, you know, *suitable*. I gather that she is a very rich girl . . . which would be terribly useful, wouldn't it?'

'For what or to whom?' said India.

'Well – oh don't be tiresome! It would be such a marvellous thing for Hartleap, to start with: the tin-pot developer could be sent packing. Do you see what I mean?'

'Perfectly,' said India. 'And there's not a chance. I told you. It's a perfectly normal friendship, that's all. Nothing more. Oh God! It's Sunday . . . Do undertakers stay open on Sundays?'

'No idea. Ask Bell when he comes up, he'll know. He must have buried a few locals.'

'None as loved as this one was.' India turned and looked back the way that they had come, down across the brook, up the slope to the orchard, Bottle Cottage neatly tucked into its side. Her eyes stung suddenly with tears which she refused to shed. 'I don't remember what happened to my daughter and Loveday. Did they go off together?' Her voice was steady and clear.

Unity had gone ahead and not waited to look back. 'Yes,' she called. 'Went off on their own. Loveday *is* a trial. So emotional.'

'A trial,' said India and brushed her eyes quickly. 'Poor Loveday. *How* she'll care.'

'Sophie will cheer her up. Sweet girl. Right values. I saw her leave the cottage when Loveday went barging out.'

India turned and started up the grassy path towards the ha-ha, Unity's flannel-clad backside undulating, calves muscling, as she strode ahead.

'You're putting on weight, Unity Uffington.'

'Bloody unfair advantage you've got in that position. But I can't deny it. You should see me in trousers.'

'Perhaps I shouldn't.'

Unity stopped for a moment to recover her breath, looked back at India. 'I get puffed frightfully easily. Age, I suppose. Poor Loveday. Daddy's last try. He so desperately wanted another boy.'

'He had Falmouth and Rufus.'

'Oh, I know, I know.' Unity stopped speaking sharply, twisted her wedding ring in angry, distressed movements. 'Before Fal ... well, the girls of course. Odd, isn't it, how remembering them, even after all those years, still distresses?' She shrugged, pulled awkwardly at her skirt. 'Shouldn't try climbing hills in a girdle. This one is hellish. Anyway, then they had me, and Rufus. But poor Daddy. He longed for another boy.'

'And got Loveday,' said India as she arrived at her side.

'He got Loveday. Mumsie always said that God would punish them both for such unstinted love. Ridiculous really. We were a moderate family. Just six ... Some people had vast families, the Catholics for example. Daisy Lanchester was one of eleven. Eleven, I ask you! But Mumsie was convinced: that's why she showered affection on her last-born, and called her Loveday, of all things ... too silly. We all have absurd names. That was Daddy's fault.'

'Misplaced guilt, of course.'

'Oh yes. No question of that. She was dreadfully guilty. God's punishment and all that.'

'Poor Loveday! What a burden to have to carry. Mummy's guilt.'

'Oh, I don't think she realizes it, do you?' said Unity as they reached the iron ha-ha gate and pushed on into the gardens. 'No idea really. Edward once said that he thought Loveday must have had a frontal lobotomy at the age of thirteen. Amusing, don't you think? He can be. Very occasionally.'

'Not amusing for Loveday. Thirteen is a bloody awful age at which to be stuck.'

'I do think that you and Fal have been marvellous coping with her all these years. I've never said so before: didn't like to state the obvious,' said Unity.

'Hartleap is her home just as it is Fal's . . . more even than it is mine. I'm really only an outsider. I merely married the heir.'

'Nonsense,' said Unity.

'Have it your own way. But what alternative was there? She was born here, it is her home; she's a Grayle, after all. I mean, she's not dangerous, not barking. It was just like – well, like having an extra child in the house, that's all. No worse really. And when Nanny was here –' She stopped suddenly. 'You see what I mean about this box-edging? Absolutely back-breaking and I did them all not long ago. They need a short-back-and-sides already.'

'I love the way you've put a fuchsia in the centre of each bed, terribly pretty. I adore standard fuchsias, the old-fashioned ones, and with the lavender . . .'

'Nanny was a marvellous help: she gave Loveday such complete confidence and care. It was no frightful problem. She's not really mad or anything, just simple, that's all.'

They walked together along a gravel path between the neat square, serpentine and oval little beds of the French gardens out on to the long path which led up to the house.

'No sign of anyone,' said Unity. 'I wonder if Rufus got the messages?'

'Or Smollett?' said India. 'Rather more importantly.'

Sophie stood watching her Aunt Loveday peering about beneath the trees for a few moments.

'You are absolutely certain that you left him here?' she called.

Loveday, her long skirt snagged on a whip of bramble, tugged herself free, pushed disordered hair from her fore-head, removed her glasses.

'Absolutely. Under the Cox's Orange. I remember clearly.

My favourite tree, so I would remember that, wouldn't I? But he's gone. Didn't wait.'

'Did you ask him to?'

'Well, no. No, I didn't. Bloody Unity was yelling at me. I got in such a panic, you see, she does so make me jump. I just ran back to the cottage.' She stood desolate in a patch of sunlight in the empty orchard.

'Where did he come from, this Jesus Christ? Did he say? Galilee or somewhere?'

Loveday shook her head in irritation, put her glasses into the pocket of her skirt. 'Silly! I mean you *are* perfectly silly! I don't know where he came from. He didn't say and I didn't ask . . . He was going to Nether Dicker, I know that.'

Sophie hooked her thumbs into the belt of her jeans. 'And what's the big deal at Nether Dicker? Was he taking the piss?'

'I don't know what you mean,' said Loveday, combing her hair roughly with slender fingers to find her centre parting.

'What's at Nether Dicker that would attract "Jesus Christ"? That's what I mean.'

'Oh. Oh, I don't know. There's an hospice place there. St Benedict's. Monk people, you know? Men in long brown skirts. They shave their heads.'

'Ah. Perhaps he was going there. Perhaps they call him that there?'

'Want to come to the Wendy Hut? A cup of cocoa or a drink? Orange squash?'

'Nothing, but I'll come with you. The house is simply awful this morning. They'll all be shouting on the telephone for undertakers and the vicar and the doctor. I must admit that getting rid of the mortal remains of a person is a very preoccupying business.'

Loveday gave a loud wail and buried her face in her hands. '*Don't! Don't!* You've reminded me all over again.'

Sophie crossed the grass and struck her aunt a hard blow across the face. 'Loveday! For God's sake stop this business! Now stop at once. If you're going to have a fit every time someone mentions Nanny, or death, or undertakers, they'll just cart you off to a loony bin, I warn you! You are on the brink.'

Loveday lowered her hands, took a deep, and very audible, breath, her eyes tightly shut, and then shook herself like a dog leaving water. She opened her eyes, wiped her face, pulled back her hair. 'Now. I'm all better,' she said. 'They wouldn't, would they? Make me go to a "place"?'

'If you can't behave yourself they might. So watch it.'

'You are lovely to me, Sophie. I don't feel afraid and messed up with you. Not as I do with Unity. You don't laugh at me. Or scold all the time.'

'Why should I laugh? Or scold you?'

'People do. Because I'm a bit soft in the head.' She turned her head away sharply. 'Nanny Grayle said that. But she said it wasn't anything awful. I was luckier than other people because I was always so happy. And I was. Once.'

'And you will be again, you'll see,' said Sophie following her through the trees to the Wendy Hut.

'I'm always happy with you,' said Loveday. 'The young are much nicer, much kinder, than the elders. I wonder why?'

Because we're a bit soft in the head as well, Sophie thought, but she said, 'Oh I don't know. Perhaps Rochester and I have more patience. Things haven't become too serious for us yet, you understand?'

'I understand,' said Loveday and turned back suddenly. 'Did you notice? I said, you know, about Nanny just now? About her saying that there wasn't anything awful just because I was a bit, well . . . you know?' She stood quite still suddenly. 'Did you notice?' She ducked to avoid a low branch and moved on.

'Notice what?'

'That I *mentioned* Nanny? And it was quite all right. I didn't make a fuss, did I?'

'No. That's splendid,' said Sophie.

'I think I'm all right. I'll get used to it. The trouble is that I shall be quite alone now. You see, before, there was always Nanny up the path at Bottle Cottage. I felt quite safe. She was always there if I needed her. Comfort. A kiss. Anything.'

'But this is your home. You won't really be alone,' said Sophie.

Loveday nodded once or twice. 'Oh yes I shall,' she said. 'I'll be left with the elders, you see. Rochester will go back to London where he lives with that American girl. And you will go away to that place, wherever it is, Africa? It's quite far away, isn't it, where you are going?'

'Yes,' said Sophie.

'Why do you want to go so far away?'

'Well, I want to do something with my life, Loveday. I don't want to spend the rest of my youth selling Magimix blades and wooden spoons in the General Trading Company.'

Loveday stroked her hair. 'I don't know what that is.'

'A shop,' said Sophie.

Loveday sniffed, brushed her hair from her face. 'Africa seems to me a long way to go not to work in a *shop*.'

'Selling things, oh, I don't mean that. I mean I want to go and work in Africa, nursing. There's a lot of help needed.'

'There is here. Right here in Sussex. I need help, Sophie. You can't just leave me all alone here and go to . . . wherever. Africa.'

I'd better take this carefully, thought Sophie.

'You'll always have Mum and Dad. You know that. They love you very much.'

Loveday shook her hair about, swung her long skirts. 'I hope you realize that I am talking about *Nanny* and being alone and not making the least trouble. Do you?' she called over her shoulder. 'I mean, I know that she's dead and dead is dead. Like a little shrew I buried once in a matchbox. It was as dead as could be. Nothing could make it alive again. And that's the same as Nanny. She's with the angels . . . I'm thinking *constructively*, aren't I?'

'You jolly well are,' said Sophie as they came through the trees to a small clearing, bright with sunlight.

'I'll always have India and Fal. Of *course*. And here is *my* little housey-pousey.'

The Wendy Hut was built of wood, stuck on brick piers, roofed with pink asbestos tiles, and in need of a coat of paint. There was a front door with two windows on either side of it, a flight of four brick steps up, and a scraggly montana trained, in a haphazard way, round a wooden lattice porch. It was set in a patch of uncut grass fenced in by chestnut palings. On either side of the door two small flowerbeds had been hacked out of the grass which flourished as a muddle of nasturtiums and going-to-seed lupins.

Loveday fished about in the neck of her dress and pulled out a long, grubby string with a key at the end. 'I always keep it locked. Well, I mean, you *never* know. There was that Jesus fellow after all. He could have just walked in.'

The interior of the Wendy Hut smelled of stale fat, turpentine and damp. A battered leather settee, an armchair with a faded, dirty chintz cover, a small iron stove with a tin chimney which went up through the roof, an easel and a painting stool before it. On a battered bow-legged Victorian side table, a two-ring electric cooker; above it a frying-pan, black with years of fried eggs, and two greasy saucepans. A dented kettle stood beneath this still-life.

Loveday painted pictures. Of a kind.

The walls of the wooden hut were an astonishing testament to this fact. Among a scatter of reproductions of Millais, Burne-Jones and Rossetti hung a number of her own works. She greatly favoured Rossetti in particular and modelled herself deliberately on his subjects in high-waisted, long-sleeved, flowing Liberty silk gowns, with heavy russet hair, which fell well below her waist, tightly waved in glossy splendour.

It would not be unfair to have thought, as so many did, that her ideals of beauty should be gambolling kittens, faery knights on white chargers, capering cherubs wreathed in blue birds, or crinolined ladies watering hollyhocks, poke bonnets on their heads, a parasol in the unoccupied hand.

Her works were not of such trivia.

The unsuspecting viewer could be alarmed by what he saw. Geometric, abstract, angular, her images raged across the canvases in bewildering degrees of colour: magenta, viridian, vermilion, cobalt. Seductive, surging curves all at once formed themselves into angry, stabbing points, or angles sharp, and cruel, as shark's teeth.

They covered every fragment of the canvases, swirling before the astonished viewer's shocked eyes in circle upon circle, square within square, colour slashed upon colour, line crossing line.

Fury and madness were at work here, but Loveday was comfortably convinced that what she painted represented precisely, for her, what she observed about her in life.

Confusion was curiously organized: precise, brilliant, disturbing, forming a fearful mixture of sweetness, in the swelling curves; gaiety, in the colours; anguish and cruelty, in the jagged points and angles which proliferated in every square to which she applied her vigorous brushes. These were not paintings at which one could look without a degree of concern, even fear.

Loveday rustled about among junk, her boots clumping on a muddy numdah rug which had long ago worn into holes. 'It's a bit poky,' she said. 'But I can be quite alone here, only the birds and the field things come. Once a fox actually put his head round the door! Can you imagine! Cheeky fellow! He soon left.' She opened a small corner cupboard and took out a packet of Kellogg's Corn Flakes.

Sophie hunched tiredly on the leather settee. She felt that the morning, young as it was, had exhausted her, and Loveday's almost constant childish patter was wearying. But, as she had said earlier, it was less disturbing than the House at this moment. She watched her aunt hunt about for something which she had clearly misplaced and could not now remember where.

'Lost something, Loveday? Can I help?'

'Looking for a cup. I've got two or three, but sometimes, if I'm in a hurry, I clean my brushes in them. Can you smell the turpentine? It's not very nice in a cup . . . ah.' She cleared away a tumble of unfinished patchwork quilting. A clink of china. 'Got them. Quite clean. Now, Sophie, cocoa? Or something else?'

'Really nothing. Not now, but you do. Shall I put on the kettle for you?'

'Oh no!' Loveday shook the Corn Flakes box. 'Cocoa is for bedtime.' She took out a bottle of gin from the box, and poured herself half a cupful. 'Wouldn't India and Fal have a *fit* if they could see this! My secret.'

'I'm having a bit of a fit myself,' said Sophie sitting upright. 'That's a hell of a lot of gin, Loveday.'

'Yummy!'

'At this time in the morning!'

'Mother's ruin, Loveday's balm.' She sat on the arm of the chintz chair, legs apart.

'It's neat, for goodness' sake! Have some water with it, you'll be sick.'

Loveday looked at the cup in her hand curiously. 'I *might*,' she said. 'It's got a funny taste. Perhaps I washed a brush in this sometime? Most peculiar taste. Tainted.'

'Chuck it away, for God's sake.'

'Waste not, want not,' said Loveday, then suddenly froze, staring at the floor. 'That's the *word*!'

'What word?'

'*Tainted!* I've been thinking and thinking about it all morning. Ever since she said it.'

'Who said what?' said Sophie pulling a packet of cigarettes from the pocket of her jeans.

'Nanny did. "Tainted", she said. Meaning your uncle Rufus.'

Sophie got up and walked across to the cooker, a cigarette at her lips. She took up a box of matches. 'Did she?'

'Yes,' said Loveday. 'That's what she said. This reminded me. Awful. It's turps, I'm certain. What a silly-billy I am! Poor Rufus. Why would she say a dreadful thing like that?'

'I don't know. I don't remember that she said it.' Sophie lit her cigarette, threw the matchbox back on to the top of the cooker.

'She did. Ah-ha! She did,' said Loveday. 'And a *terrible* thing about my father. She said that he was wicked! Beau Grayle wicked! I mean, *honestly*, what dreadful things to say about them.'

'Listen, Loveday, she was a very old lady. And she was . . . well, you know what I am trying to say, don't you?'

'Oh yes. I know. She was *dying*. That's what you're trying to say. But I'm quite all right now. You needn't worry. Don't pretend or be polite for me.' She squinted up at Sophie over the top of her cup and laughed. It was a sweet laugh, gentle, soft. 'I'm absolutely hunky-dory now.'

'Good. But that's what she was, so you mustn't take things she said then too seriously.'

'No, I won't. What does hunky-dory mean, do you know?'

'No.'

'No. I don't either. I heard someone say it once, at the pictures.'

Sophie sat back slowly into the leather settee, cigarette cupped in one hand.

'She used to take me to the pictures, you know? At Lewes. And once at Brighton. But that was a very long time ago. Ages ago.' Loveday sipped from her cup again. 'Tainted. It's such a dreadful word. I'm remembering,' she said in a distant voice, 'I'm remembering, oh, years ago, a funny thing.'

'What sort of thing?' said Sophie cautiously. 'You mean a joke? That sort of thing?'

'No. It wasn't a joke. I remember that after Daddy was killed, she was terribly sad. She tried not to show it but she was. And then one day she wasn't.'

'You mean, just out of the blue?'

Loveday drained the cup. 'I dote on this ginny-gin-gin. Yes, wasn't sad. Quite suddenly. And she never spoke of him again after that. That's what I'm remembering.'

'Well, it was a long time ago.'

'She had such a pretty room at the house. Next to the old night nursery. It was full of all kinds of things, and lots of photographs. I used to spend ages of time with her in there. *So* kind to me. "I'll never let anyone harm a hair of your pretty head," she used to say.' Loveday got up and put the cup on the cooker. 'One day I saw that the photograph of Beau and Mumsie wasn't there any more. No more. Gone.'

'She had taken it away?'

'Taken it quite, quite away. There was a picture where it had been, with a man standing and a lady sitting, and it was just like Beau and Mumsie only I think it was the King and Queen.' She came back and sat on the arm of the chintz chair. 'Wasn't that funny? I didn't ask why.'

'Perhaps it was somewhere else.'

'Oh no. Quite gone. I looked. When she was downstairs one day, I looked everywhere. But no Beau. Just a photo of Mumsie quite alone. In her presentation dress.' She belched loudly, put her hand to her mouth instantly. 'Oh! I'm sorry. Sorry, Sophie, how rude.' She smiled, her head on one side. 'It makes one's stomach feel quite warm, gin. Wasn't that a funny thing to remember, though? "Tainted" reminded me. When I said the word I suddenly remembered what she said just now. In Bottle Cottage.'

'I'd forget it if I were you.' Sophie got up, stubbed her cigarette out in Loveday's empty cup. 'I'm going up to the House. I'll take this and wash it properly.'

Loveday sat motionless, her hands loosely in her lap. 'If Mr Smollett is there, we could ask him, couldn't we?' she said quietly.

'Mr Smollett? What about?'

Loveday got up, reached for the gin bottle, snapped on the lid and slid it back into the box of Corn Flakes. 'Nanny said, "Bob Smollett knows." That's what she said, clear as clear.'

Sophie made her way through a spill of old magazines, twists of screwed-up paper and an empty birdcage. 'I'm off now. You all right?'

'Thank you,' said Loveday primly. 'Quite all right. Hunky-dory in fact. *That's* what it means. Will *you* ask Mr Smollett?'

'Now look here,' said Sophie turning at the door, 'I

31

hardly know Mr Smollett. What could he know about Grandpapa?'

'He was our gardener . . . one of them,' said Loveday. 'We had four, you see, in those days. And then he went to the war, *with* Beau. As his servant.' She got up and came over to Sophie and leant against the doorway. ' "He knows," she said. *What* does he know?'

'I don't know, or care. I'm going up to give a hand at the house. There's the breakfast stuff to clear. Unless they've done it already.'

'*I* did the washing-up!' said Loveday. 'All the cups and saucers. I did them.'

'Well, I'll just see how things are.'

'Perhaps I could come with you?'

'You can if you like.'

'Mr Smollett might be there by now.' She winked, and nodded her head knowingly.

'Loveday, he lives in Shrewsbury or somewhere. They only left a message yesterday. He won't be here for ages yet. And even if he was you are *not* to ask questions. Understand? No questions today. Everyone is very unhappy.'

'I am as well.'

'I know you are. But don't start interfering. There is so much to do. No questions to anyone. Remember?'

'Very well. If you say.'

'Nanny would have been terribly distressed if you behaved badly. You wouldn't want that, would you?'

'No! Oh no! You *are* sensible, Sophie. I can't think of these things for myself, you see.'

''Course you can,' said Sophie going down the brick steps. ''Course you can. It was all that gin! Made you a bit fuddled, that's all.'

'Fuddled,' said Loveday with satisfaction. 'And no questions.'

'No questions. Cross your heart?'

'Cross my heart,' said Loveday, doing so with a long finger, 'and hope to die.'

Sophie closed the garden gate, turned and waved the empty cup. 'I'll wash this properly for you. Be good. Comb your hair.'

'I do love you, Sophie, my darling little niece. I dote on you.'

'I love you too.'

'When I've combed my hair and got pretty again, I'll come up to the house. Might I?'

'Of course. But remember?'

Loveday put a finger to her lips. 'Shsssh!' she whispered. 'Shssh!'

'That's right,' said Sophie and went off through the trees, dappled in light.

Loveday stood silent for a moment, twisting at a trail of montana. 'Oh! What a pretty, pretty day it is!' she said aloud. She put her fingertips to her lips and blew kisses high into the sparkling blue of the sky.

'Goodbye, happiness! Oh, goodbye . . . goodbye!'

Sunday Evening

'What I'd really like to know', said Edward pulling off his trousers, 'is when can we clear off home? I'm not rushing you, *do* understand that, but what I mean is, do we have to hang on for the funeral? I suppose', he said, folding his trousers carefully and placing them over the back of a chair, 'that's a silly question?'

Unity nodded at her own reflection in the dressing-table mirror. 'And as such deserves a silly answer, except that I'm too tired to think of one. Of *course* we have to stay for the funeral. We can't possibly leave. This is Sunday night, isn't it? I'm really rather muddled today.'

'Sunday,' said Edward, undoing shirt buttons.

'Well. Not long to wait. Wednesday morning, ten a.m. We'll clear off right after. I expect India will have had quite enough of everyone by then. But we simply have to hang on until Wednesday morning.' She patted a thick cream on her face, smoothing it carefully round the nose and the corners of her eyes.

'Stuff smells vile,' said Edward.

'Can't be helped. It's all for you. Keeping me youthful, feeding my skin full of sheep's placenta. Anyway, that's what the owl-faced girl in Harrods said. Revolting. And we've got single beds.'

'Thank God,' said Edward and padded on socked feet across to the small bathroom.

'Close the door,' said Unity. 'This place is altogether too intimate.'

'I'm *going* to close the door,' said Edward.

'Good job too. Those sudden spurts of yours are dreadfully disconcerting. Fearfully unromantic too.'

'Since when were we in a romantic frame of mind, may I ask?' said Edward, one hand on the door knob. 'I've been enduring a celibate life for the last God-knows-how-long.'

'I do wish you wouldn't be quite so vulgar. Nanny died this morning.'

'What the bloody hell has Nanny got to do with our sex life? Your family are all Nanny-ridden.'

Unity took her pink pot of night-moisture cream and threw it at him.

'Missed,' said Edward, watching, with mild satisfaction, the glutinous mass slide slowly down the door panel.

'You are utterly loathsome,' said Unity.

'And you have taken the paint off the woodwork. Stripped it to the grain. If that's what sheep's placenta does to wood, God knows what it will do to your face.'

'Go away!'

Edward began to close the door. 'Going,' he said.

'I don't know why I bother,' said Unity. 'I really don't. That stuff cost a small fortune; he complains about the smell and then says that it removes the paint from the door. I mean, what *is* one to do?' She got up from the dressing-table, wrapped her dressing-gown around her, reached across, took a hairnet from the mirror, where she had earlier draped it. 'I *try*. God knows, I *try*.' She pulled the net tightly down over her head so that the edge of it rested just above her eyebrows, and peered at her shining face in the looking-glass.

'*That* won't do,' she said. 'Separate beds or no separate

beds. Sex wears off. He knows that. You get terribly used to each other, that's one of the awful things about marriage.' She rearranged the hairnet carefully. 'However, one need not retire to bed looking like the Queen of the Willies.'

In the bathroom the plug was pulled, water flushed. Edward opened the door.

'Don't!' cried Unity.

'Nothing unpleasant, just a piddle. There's a rather jolly spray thing in here called Summer Meadows.'

'Well, spray it everywhere,' said Unity. 'That bathroom is the size of a hat box.'

'For which I cannot be held responsible,' said Edward, spraying about him. 'Your brother should have left things as they were: nothing wrong with a canter up the corridor to the lavatory. We always used to do it – why not now? Just because they decided to get these modern ideas and have everything in one.'

'En suite,' said Unity.

'Bloody unhealthy, if you ask me. Sleeping right on top of the thunder-box.'

Unity removed her dressing-gown and sat on the edge of her bed. 'Your language is repellent. I can't believe that you are trying to shock me after all these years. I suppose you and Fal got drunk, too much malt whisky after dinner.'

'Rather good, as a matter of fact,' said Edward. 'Shall I put out the light in this little hell-hole, or have you not cleaned your teeth? Ah yes,' he said with quiet satisfaction, 'you have! There they are in the glass, dear little things.'

Unity screamed, and buried her face in her hands. 'You sod,' she said through her fingers. 'Absolute sod! *Not* my teeth, you know that. My bridge! *Bridge!* Quite different from *teeth*. *Why* do you torment me?'

Edward switched off the light in the bathroom, closed the door and came quietly across the room to kneel at his wife's side. 'Now, come on, only teasing, doll. You know that. You teased me.'

'Never,' moaned Unity. 'I never teased you.'

'About "sudden spurts". It was a disagreeable thing to say. It happens to chaps at my age. Not as spry as we were.' He pulled her clenched hands gently from her face. 'Now, Unity! Don't be such a cry-baby over a little tease. You know it was a joke, nothing more.'

'I'm not in the mood for jokes tonight. It's been a hellish day. A ghastly man from the undertakers, Dr Bell and that awful hearty vicar.'

'I thought he was quite pleasant. He's got a dinghy, as a matter of fact, just taken up the sport. Down at Bosham I think he said.'

Unity, who hadn't shed a tear, sniffed, wiped her nose, slid into bed. 'Get up off your knees and come to bed. Well, no wonder you think he's quite pleasant. Anyone with a paper boat on a string sends you into transports. You go completely dotty about children sailing their wretched yachts on the Round Pond. You're retarded.' She hunched herself on to her side, one hand under her head.

Edward undressed, pulled on his pyjamas, lips pursed in thought, then he got into bed, reached for the switch on the table lamp between their beds. 'In my nature,' he said to the darkness. 'Can't help that. After all, you did marry a sailor.'

Unity grunted.

'Well, you did, didn't you? Rather fancied the Navy as I recall.'

'All years ago.' Her voice was muffled in the sheets.

'Doesn't alter the fact. Once a sailor, always a sailor. That's me to a T. Sorry and all that. I mean, if you mind.'

She shifted about in her bed, was still. 'No, I don't *mind*. This is a silly conversation. I'm half dead. What a day.

What a bloody awful day. it's so strange to think that, after all the years, this is the first night I've slept in this house feeling suddenly incomplete.'

'Incomplete?' His voice was bewildered in the dark. 'How?'

'Nanny. No Nanny. Always before there was Nanny somewhere about the house, and it all seemed secure. Mumsie, Beau – Daddy, I suppose I should say – and Nanny: the three symbols of security and love. And now she's gone. They've all gone.'

'Now listen, doll, don't dwell on it. She was a very old lady, you know, and –'

Unity interrupted swiftly. 'If you say, "We all have to go sometime," I'll brain you.'

'Well I won't say it. Just as long as you know that fact.'

'I know it. Thank you. May Smollett's put on weight, did you notice? Hardly recognized her. Plump. And hair dyed, of course . . . pity people do that. Far wiser to let it go grey, age with the face. After all, it's natural, one looks *less* old, in my opinion, with natural colouring than with something out of a bottle.'

'Pretty girl, I'd venture. Still has her charms.'

'Rather K-O-M, I'd have said.'

'*Now* where are you?' said Edward in some bewilderment.

'K-O-M. Oh, a silly word we used as children. It means "common" dear.'

'I see. Smollett looked all in, poor fellow. Hell of a drive, Shrewsbury. Did it without a stop. Well, just one, sandwich somewhere, no more than fifteen minutes. Bloody good going.'

'He was always a strong fellow. I remember him here quite well. I was about twelve, I suppose. He was in the Territorials . . . Daddy rather forced him into it. Yes, he's got older. Well over fifty now, I suppose.' Her voice had a smug, contented lilt.

There was a silence in the dark bedroom. For a few moments Edward thought that his wife had settled to sleep, but she suddenly rustled about, the bedhead rattled against the wall, she switched on the light.

Edward covered his eyes. 'Steady! Almost blinded me. What's wrong?'

'Rufus. No Rufus. He is impossible! Not even a reply to the messages we left last night. And no reply all day at his flat.'

'He's probably away somewhere.'

Unity sat forward, arms clasped about her raised knees. 'Edward? Edward, when we were over at the cottage this morning, Nanny said a perfectly awful thing. Well, *two* perfectly awful things. Did you hear?'

Edward sat up wearily, folded his arms behind his head. 'Really not,' he said. 'She was rambling about a bit. Stands to reason. Oh, I do remember something about not farting in her blankets. She said it quite loudly. That what you mean?'

'No. I can't imagine what she meant by *that*: senile dementia I should think. But she said something perfectly foul about Rufus, and also – and this is so extraordinary – about Daddy. She *adored* Daddy all his life. It was a terrible thing to say.'

'Didn't hear. What was it?'

Unity scratched her arm. 'That he was "wicked" and that Rufus was "tainted". I mean, really . . . too awful.'

'Rambling. You probably didn't hear correctly. Did India hear her? Any of the others?'

'My angelic sister-in-law flew at me like a wildcat when I mentioned it – I had said it casually of course. So I let the matter drop. I haven't asked the others – the children, or poor Loveday ... *She* was moaning anyway, so she wouldn't have heard. I wonder if Fal did?'

'I'd let it rest. Let it rest, dear. I don't suppose that she meant it for a moment and it's quite possible that you misheard.'

'I did not mishear. She spoke loudly, clearly and deliberately. I know that. Fart. Really. Too awful.'

'Well, just leave it. Wiser to.'

'She said that Bob Smollett would know. Something like that.'

Edward unfolded his arms and slid down into his sheets. 'Come on, doll, put out the light, we do need a bit of rest. Ask Smollett in the morning if you are so anxious.'

'How could I? How could I *possibly* ask Bob Smollett that sort of question? He wasn't there to hear her say those things. I just can't believe that you didn't hear her yourself.'

'Well, I didn't. Come on.'

Unity snapped off the lamp, wrestled with her sheets, was still.

Edward closed his eyes thankfully.

'Did you pull the chain in there, Edward?'

His eyes opened in the darkness. ''Course I did. You know I did.'

'Well, something's still running. Can you hear the trickling sound?'

They lay silent for a moment.

'Cistern,' said Edward crisply.

'Oh God!' said Unity. 'I shan't sleep a wink tonight.'

'Well, I'm not a bloody plumber, I'm a sailor.'

'Offensive, too. I didn't ask you to *do* anything. I just asked you if you could hear water trickling. Nothing more.'

'Well, I've told you. Yes, Unity, water *is* trickling. It will probably trickle all night and for the next fifty nights unless your brother gets a new washer, and I'm not about to go and ask him for a sodding washer at this time of night. Now go to sleep – even if you can't.'

'Lud! What courtly manners. What would our American guest think of you now? So full of Olde Worlde charm downstairs I could have fallen apart laughing.'

'Kathleen Tessier is an enchanting child. Very pretty. Deserves a bit of "Olde Worlde charm", as you call it. God, you are irritating!'

'So was she. Chattering on about her family emigrating from France in . . . whatever it was, to North Dakota . . . in 1750. Too boring.'

'Why didn't you tell her how your crew came over with William the Conqueror? That would have been a feather in your cap, wouldn't it?'

'Really not. We didn't come over with William the Conqueror,' said Unity, at last deciding to settle for the night. '*We* were already here.'

India held on to Fal tightly, arms about his neck, her head pressed against his shoulder. 'I think that if you were to let me go I'd just crumble into dust at your feet.'

'I'd hate that,' said Fal, holding her closer. 'I'd have to sweep you all up in a dustpan, chuck you out the window.'

'And I'd just drift away on the night wind. Wonderfully romantic. Never to be seen again.'

'Sad for me.'

'Would it be? Really?'

'Awful. I'd be bereft. What would I do without you in my life?'

India shrugged, rubbed her nose against his chin. 'Can't imagine. Run off with a loose woman or something?'

He moved her away from him, holding her steady. 'I'm about to make a declaration. Ready? I love you, India

41

Grayle. Did you know that? I love you to absolute distraction.'

She nodded gravely, smiled up at him tiredly. 'Yes, I know. You told me actually. Years ago, as a matter of fact. I remember just exactly where, too: crossing the Accademia Bridge. I can hear our feet clacking on the boards. You said it then; and yesterday morning; and this morning; and just now. So I know, you see. I feel very vain.'

'Why vain?'

'Well, it makes one vain to know that someone I love as much as I love you loves me so much. That's a terribly clumsy sentence, isn't it?'

'Appallingly.'

'I can't think of any other way to say it. Do you know, Fal, I'm sometimes terrified that we tempt God to strike us.'

Fal kissed her lightly, let her go. 'Why do you think that we'd be struck down? For loving too much?'

'I don't know. Perhaps. Can one love too much?'

Fal sat down on the side of her bed and began to remove his shoes. 'I don't know. I only know that I do. You are as glorious, exciting, as dear and as adored, as you were the very first time I ever saw you, long before the day on the Accademia Bridge. Nothing has changed.'

'You do talk rubbish. Honestly. I'm a middle-aged lady with greying hair and wrinkles at the elbow, not to mention one or two other places, and I think that you are just saying all those idiotic things to cover up the fact that you have a paramour.'

He looked up, unlacing a shoe. 'A what?'

'A paramour. Another lady. Very pretty and young. Pneumatic.'

'Who is she? Do you know?'

India untied her dressing-gown and went across to her

42

dressing-table. 'An air hostess. You have secret suppers with her in an Arab restaurant in Greek Street.'

'Oh God! You've found me out! What's her name?'

'Ummmm.' She picked up a hairbrush, thumped the palm of her hand. 'Juanita.'

'Juanita!'

'Yes. She flies Iberia.'

'Has she got a husband in Valencia. Or Seville?'

India dragged the brush roughly through her hair once or twice, narrowed her eyes. 'I'm not absolutely certain. Not *certain*. I haven't invented that part yet.'

He came up behind her, his shoes in one hand, bent his head and kissed her on each shoulder. 'My beloved middle-aged-woman-with-greying-hair.'

'But it is! Look! I bet you I've got a hundred extra grey ones since this morning. I can't imagine how you could still love me. I'm a raddled old hag.'

'I rather like raddled old hags. Interesting, full of character like Cruikshank's ladies. Anyway, nothing to be done now, I'm afraid. The damage was caused years ago, and I fell hook, line and sinker.' He crossed into his dressing-room.

'You know?' India half turned on the little stool. 'I never know what that means: hook, line and sinker . . .'

'A fishing term, I think,' he called.

She sat still, the brush in her lap, staring at her reflection, seeing nothing. 'God, I'm tired. I really could just crumble away. Was it wretched when you went over to the cottage?'

She heard him open a drawer, slide it closed.

'No,' he said. 'Not really. Odd. But not wretched. She was so very tiny suddenly. Amazingly young-looking, because all the lines and wrinkles seemed to have gone, and she was strangely translucent. Her hands were slender, so fine, folded on the sheet. She had a little white cap on her

43

head, with a frilled edge. It was tied under her chin. To keep her mouth closed.'

India was motionless, the brush in her lap. Fal came to the dressing-room door.

'The bloody thing about it was that her black marble clock on the mantelpiece was still ticking away Tick-tock! Measuring time. But she'd gone. I knew then, for absolute certain, when I heard the clock. Isn't it absurd?'

He turned, went back into his room. India began to brush her hair mechanically, heard him rustling about, something fall to the floor, an oath.

'*Now* what are you doing?'

'I'm losing my mind. I'm not the only one who's getting middle-aged. Men get the menopause, don't they?'

'So I'm told. Have you got it?'

He stood at the door in his underpants and socks. 'I'm beginning, I think.'

India looked at him briefly. 'Just like a heron you look.'

'You are foul. Knobbly knees and rounded shoulders, is that it?'

'No. On the contrary. Wonderful long legs, super shoulders, amazing! A flat belly. What are you breaking up the dressing-room for?'

'Dorothy L. Sayers,' he said. 'Is she in here?'

'I can't think why she should be. The last time I saw her she was by your bed, on the little shelf thing.'

'Not there now. I reckon you've had one of your tidying fits.'

'Christ!' said India and threw her hairbrush into a chair. 'If you honestly think that I had the time today to have a "tidying fit" you must be out of your sweet, addled head.'

She got up and went into the dressing-room, Fal followed her, half-naked.

'Trouble with you, darling,' said India, 'is that you just don't *look*. Honestly – here.' She held out a book.

'Where the hell was she?'

'Where you left her. Between the *Field* and the *Wine Society's Catalogue*. That's where.'

He picked up the hairbrush, handed it to her, sat in the chair and stretched his legs before him. 'I don't know what I'd do without you; I really don't.'

'I'm terribly good at finding lost books, mislaid pipes and tobacco pouches. Not to mention spectacles. I'm a dab hand, as they say, with spectacles.'

'You might easily find it within yourself to be a bit of a nag.'

'Unity's pretty terrible to poor old Edward, talking of "nags". I'd throttle her if I were him. Come to that, I'd throttle her anyway.'

'I wanted to when I was five years old.'

'She had to be our elder sister, I suppose. Got into the habit then. Loveday was a bit of a loss, poor thing.'

India removed her dressing-gown, crossed to the door and hung it carefully. 'Poor Loveday. She seemed pretty wobbly all day: not surprising. She's going to miss Nanny most terribly. We'll have to handle that with care, it won't be easy.'

Fal tapped his knees with his book. 'No. Not easy. I thought the Smolletts were very pleasant, didn't you?'

'Liked them enormously. But then I always did. May is sensible and jolly. I wish that I was like that. It was her idea that you and Bob should go over on your own: "Let them be alone, I think it would be wrong if all we women went barging over." That's sense. It was absolutely right. If only Rufus had been here.'

Fal made a gesture of extreme impatience. 'Oh, Rufus. He's hopeless. He's most likely abroad as usual.'

India opened the curtains, leant out of the window, arms folded on the sill. 'It's so still tonight. The air is soft as soft. Scented. I can smell cut hay.'

'You'll get a chill.'

'Don't spoil it for me. It's so beautiful. And we only get one summer night all season: I'm enjoying it. "Tainted" is an odd word to use, isn't it? I wonder what she meant?'

'I'm sitting here nearly bollock-naked,' said Fal. 'If you want to freeze to death on the only summer night of the year, I simply refuse to join you. I'm off.' He got up, slapped her on the bottom lightly. 'Come on. You've got nothing on. Be a good girl.'

'Nightdress,' said India into the darkness of the garden.

'That's how you get wrinkles in your elbows and elsewhere, leaning out of windows stark naked.'

India pulled back from the windows, closed the curtain. 'It was so lovely. The children are playing what they call music. I could hear the "thud, thud, thud" quite distinctly.' She put her arms round him, her head on his bare chest. 'Come to my bed tonight, would you?' she said.

'I'm almost there,' he said, and kissed her hair.

'I need a terrific amount of comforting. You can read if you want to, it won't bother me.' She crossed to the bed and pulled back the sheets.

'Have to read a bit. To send me off. A few lines.'

They lay in each other's arms.

'*Very* comforting, I find,' said India. 'Kathleen was splendid today, wasn't she? Terribly practical and put-together. American women are, I think. Washing up, carting the food about, brisk, laughing – Stella didn't even mind her being in her kitchen. I mean, she knows how to be tactful: leaves the dishes, didn't ask maddening things like "Where does this go?" That sort of thing.'

'Yes, she was good,' said Fal. 'Bossy without seeming to be, and we all needed a bit of bossing today, God knows.'

India shifted about. 'Romance is all very well, but my arm's going to sleep.' She eased herself into a more comfortable position, head resting on his shoulder. 'What do you reckon?' she said suddenly.

'Reckon to what?'

'Well, Kathleen and Rochester. He seems very keen on her. Would you mind?'

Fal laughed. 'You matchmaking?'

'Fat chance. No. But would you mind?'

'My dear. If they could be as happy as you and I have been . . .'

'Are. Are, please.

'Are, then . . . I wouldn't mind in the very least. I think she's charming, attractive, clever. I like her coolness, and the background's quite suitable, but she may have ideas of her own, you know. Ladies do.'

'Oh, I know,' said India, and yawned. 'God! I'm going to fall asleep instantly. But I know ladies have ideas of their own. May Smollett. Insisting they went all the way to the White Hart in Lewes rather than stay here: very sensible of her. I know that Bob would have felt, well, awkward somehow staying in the house. She knew too. Rochester needs a lady of that kind to love him and protect him. I think Kathleen would be most suitable. But he's so wildly unpliable.'

Fal opened his book, sought the page at which he had last laid it down, smoothed it with a long, firm hand. 'A severance. Nanny Grayle going. Distinct sense of severance. Poor Bob, poor all of us tomorrow. Coffins and strangers clumping about.'

India's voice was muffled by approaching sleep. 'In the morning? The coffin business?'

'First thing. They want to close it as soon as they can ... summer ... you know?'

India nodded. 'Ummmm. Death. Goodness. It's all so arranged and tidy this way. Did you take off your socks, I can't remember?'

'Of course I did. I'm going to read. Now shut up.' He kissed her forehead, she made a soft kissing sound with her lips, touched his arm.

'You read. Wicked Beau,' she said after a moment. 'What *did* she mean by that, I wonder?'

'Don't know,' said Fal. 'Go to sleep.'

He addressed himself to his book and discovered after four or five minutes that he had read the opening sentence six times. I'm not taking anything in, he thought, my mind is numb. Sharp fragments of memory scattered across the page, like pieces of shattered looking-glass. A writhen arm on a neat sheet, a white cotton cap with a half-inch frill, the bow under the chin, Edward kicking at a clump of thistle, Loveday's ruined face, her feet turned inwards like a penguin's, the hunting boots draped in sprigged silk. India's eyes, sad, wide, gentle. Rochester attempting adult comfort: 'Well, I suppose that's that? The end of an era.' End of an era all right. Why *wicked* Beau? Why the slur on Rufus? Why that? Like father, like son? Did she mean that? The translucent skin, unlined, unknown, unfamiliar, the soul departed leaving just a body-husk behind.

With the tick-tock of that bloody clock. Marking time which she no longer had. Tick-tock. Tick-tock.

He closed the book quietly, laid it aside, reached for the cord of the bed-lamp and pulled it. The room was dark. India moved slightly, murmured something, pressed herself against his body, her hand closing tightly on his arm.

He lay staring into the darkness.

*

48

Sophie set a platter of cold fowl in the centre of the kitchen table. 'Just fingers?' she said. 'We don't need knives and forks, do we?'

Kathleen shook her head, leant back in a wooden chair. 'God no! No more washing-up. Maybe, on the other hand, Rochester wants some chutney?'

'Well, he can get his own fork, or spoon, or whatever.' Sophie started to cut thick slices of bread, piled them on the scrubbed pine.

'I just felt so hungry. I don't know why.' Kathleen started to pull one of the cold chickens apart. 'I've washed my hands.'

'See if I care,' said Sophie as Rochester came along the passage to the kitchen trailing music behind him like a flying, tattered cloak, the sound rising and falling, dying away, as he walked, a bottle by the neck in one hand, a transistor radio in the other.

'One bottle of Sauvignon, not terribly chilled.' He dumped the bottle on the table, with the transistor. Guitars and drums thumped and whined about the whitewashed walls of the room.

Kathleen turned it down low. She stared up at the ceiling, the long irregular beams vicious with hooks. 'Why does cold chicken taste so awful *unless* you eat it in your fingers?' she said.

Rochester went to the fridge and took out butter.

'No one has told me? What are all the hooks for? In the beams. It's like a charnel house.'

'Rochester, if you want chutney, you get it,' said Sophie. 'We're fingers tonight. This room was the game larder. They hung pheasant, partridge, hares, venison, all kinds of lovelinesses from those hooks. Then, when Dad took over the place, he had it all ripped out and made into a kitchen. The real kitchen looks like Waterloo Station. It's vast, dark and dirty. And eighty miles from the dining-room.'

'I think this is great,' said Kathleen. 'Rochester? Want a drumstick or the thigh?'

Rochester was opening the Sauvignon with difficulty. 'Don't know yet,' he said. 'All I really want are the "oysters", so don't pinch them. Where are the glasses?'

Sophie, who had cut a pile of bread, took three cheap tumblers from the draining-board, and set them down on the table. 'Some people,' she said. 'Some people are so damned selfish, idle, helpless, can't-look-for-themselves – and that bottle is full of bits of cork. That OK by you?'

'Fine by me.' Rochester shrugged. 'Just don't swallow them. Spoon for the chutney?'

Sophie had taken a chair at the table end. 'Use a wooden fork, there are masses in the jar over there. Oh God! Loveday! I suppose *she'll* want something to eat. Roch, be a darling and turn that bloody thing right off, my head is bursting. And the elders may hear it anyway.'

He switched off the radio, and the room was suddenly still.

'Silence is glorious,' said Kathleen. She reached for a piece of bread as Rochester poured wine. 'Your Aunt Loveday's been out for an hour, you know? Do you think she's all right?'

Sophie was sitting slumped in her chair, elbows on the table, eating a chicken wing. 'She's a bit inclined to wander. The dogs are with her. She wanted to make sure that she'd locked up the Wendy Hut. In truth I think she wanted to go and have a look at Bottle Cottage.'

'In the dark!' said Rochester. 'Here's the fork, dig out a chunk of mango for me.'

'I don't know how you can eat this stuff at night. You'll have nightmares.'

'I've *got* nightmares. Had them all day. God! What a

day, dreary beyond belief.' Rochester sat down, sipped his wine. 'Well, not dreary, that's the wrong word. Just . . . well . . . a sort of non-day. The elders all wandering about looking *so* miserable . . . that ghastly vicar – rugger-bugger: he *would* ask for a beer-shandy. "Haven't seen you in church, sir," he said to me. I ask you! Me! In church! And calling me "sir", creepy bastard.'

'What did you expect him to call you?' said Sophie with her mouth full. 'Young man, my boy? M'lord . . . Your Excellency? You are impossible. Impossible, Kath. All his worst faults are coming out.'

Kathleen stuck the fork in the chutney jar and speared herself some pickle. 'About your aunt . . . I know it is *absolutely* none of my business, but it *is* after eleven, and there *is* a stream to cross and maybe she didn't take a torch? Listen, I'll go and have a look. I mean, if she's fallen in the stream . . .' Kathleen half rose. 'She just could . . .'

Sophie waved a piece of bread towards her, pushed her back in her chair. 'Kath, she won't fall in the stream, I promise you. She's *got* the torch. She goes off like this all the time. She knows her way by heart, and there's a moon.'

'It's just that it has been a sad day for you all . . . And, you know, if anything *else* happened . . .'

'Well, if she's not back in ten minutes I'll go and find her, all right?' said Rochester. 'Frankly, I think she's been slightly pissed all day. God knows how. But she had a distinct haze of spirits about her. Did you notice, Sophie? It was quite strong. But she didn't drink a thing at lunch or at dinner. Nothing. I watched carefully.'

Sophie shook her head, pressed her finger into a scatter of crumbs, raised the finger to her mouth, licked it. 'No. I didn't notice anything. Just one of her off-days: she is dreadfully sad, you know. Nanny was really all she had.'

'Curious,' said Rochester. 'I'm going to have this thigh. All right? I didn't feel hungry but now I do.'

'Stella is great at roasting. It's the rosemary, that's what tastes so good. She stuffs it under the skin. Do you want a bit more, Kath?'

Kathleen pulled the platter towards her, stripped off a length of breast. 'Rochester, can I ask something? You don't have to say if you don't want to.'

Rochester nodded. 'Say on. What?'

'Who were "the girls"?'

He stopped chewing, looked at his bread. 'The girls? *What* girls?'

Kathleen eased back in her chair, pressing herself away from the table with the heels of her hands. 'Your Aunt Unity said, "I suppose that you know about *the girls*. I expect that Rochester or Sophie have told you. It was so terrible. It cast a shadow on this house for many years."' She suddenly flushed. 'Oh God! I'm being tactless. I'm sorry. You don't have to say.'

Sophie laughed suddenly, and placed a hand on Kathleen's knuckled one. 'No you're not! Not a bit. Don't be silly. Aunt Unity babbles on: she is absolutely maddening. It was all a thousand years ago, before Dad was born even. We had two aunts, Angelica and Faith. They were the first-born, the Grayle girls. And they died when they were very small, three or four I think, from diphtheria . . . meningitis – I don't really know. I mean, it was so long ago that they weren't even "aunts". They were just two little girls, they had no part in our lives whatever.'

'Do you know', said Rochester taking his glass, 'that people have been dying in our family ever since the tenth century? So two little girls don't mean much, do they? I mean, just two, out of all the others? If it wasn't for Aunt Unity not one of us today would even remember, but she keeps the family "up to scratch", as she calls it, and a bloody bore she is too. I wondered who on earth you meant. "The girls". Listen! Loveday's back.'

She came clumping into the kitchen, a silk scarf wound round her head like a turban, the torch in her hand, two black Labradors colliding round her feet.

'Doggies want a lovely drinkie – are you all eating! I'm quite puffed.'

'Their water is in the courtyard, you know that,' said Sophie rising. 'Come on, Minder, Jess. Water!' She opened a door into the scullery and went with the dogs.

Loveday sat down, started to unwind her scarf. 'Have to wear this if I walk in the dark,' she said to Kathleen. 'You know why? Essential.'

'No. Why, cold?'

'Cold!' said Loveday. 'Goodness me *no*. I'm not afraid of a little cold. Besides, it's warm as warm tonight. Not cold. No!' She leant across the table. '*Bats!*' she said. 'They get in one's hair, and they can't untangle themselves, they scream, and struggle . . . It's *too* terrible!'

'It sounds awful.'

'Oh it is, it is! And you have to have all your hair cut off, shaved to the very scalp. So one wears a scarf. Rochester, pull off a chicken leg for me, I dote on cold chicky. If you are all eating, I will. It makes me feel peckish. Quite peckish.' She folded the scarf into a tidy square and smiled genially, if unsteadily, about her. 'Yes,' she said. 'Bats. Terrible things to get in your hair. Nanny Grayle knew a woman who lived over at Folkington who got one in her hair and went raving mad.' She accepted the chicken leg from Rochester with a neat bow. 'Quite raving mad! They had to lock her up, poor thing. How lovely. Thank you, Rochester. Some chutney? Where? Ah! Yes.'

Sophie came back into the kitchen, closed the scullery

door. 'In their kennels. Stella just stuck her head out of her bedroom window: wanted to know what was going on. Said not to make a mess in here or she'd give us what-for.'

She picked up the bottle of wine and poured herself a glass. 'Did you go over to Bottle Cottage, Loveday?' she said.

Loveday stopped eating, the chicken halfway to her mouth. Nodded. 'There was a lamp on. In the bedroom. Where that dreadful nurse is. I didn't go into the garden or anything. I just stood there in the dark.'

'Nurse Monahan's staying until the morning. She's got another case to go to in Hove. Dad gave her twenty quid to stay on. Old bitch,' said Sophie.

'Woman of Death,' said Loveday. 'You can always tell them. They *smell* of death.'

'Loveday,' said Rochester quickly. 'A drink? Glass of white wine? Make you sleep?'

Loveday placed her piece of chicken on the table, wiped her hand on a handkerchief which she had fumbled from her skirt pocket.

'I don't,' she said primly. 'Never imbibe.'

'All the more for us,' said Rochester.

'I'm afraid', said Loveday politely, turning to Kathleen, 'that circumstances here have quite ruined your weekend. I *do* apologize. But, you see, it was rather sudden and unexpected.' She removed her spectacles, pushed them clumsily into her pocket.

'Please, Miss Loveday, don't apologize,' said Kathleen, aware of the slightly glazed eyes and the over-careful speech. 'It is I who should apologize to you for being here at such a difficult time. I only hope that I haven't been in the way?'

Loveday shook her head rather too vigorously, steadied herself by holding on to the table edge with both hands. 'Not at all. Not at all. So useful. Sitting up here like a telephone operator. So kind.' She sat looking in a fixed manner across the room at nothing in particular. 'I quite *like* telephone operators. Such bland voices. They sound undangerous.'

'Bloody Uncle Rufus not calling. Typical of him,' said Sophie. 'I suppose he's off having a dirty weekend with that Ling-Ting-Tong-whatever-its name-is.'

'Do people still have dirty weekends?' said Rochester in surprise. 'I thought they went out in the thirties. *Every* weekend in a dirty one now. As far as Uncle R. is concerned, anyway.'

'Who, or what, is Ling-Ting-Tong?' said Kathleen.

'Oh I don't remember its real name,' said Sophie sweeping crumbs into her hand. 'It is one of those dotty names, like the ones you see on menus in Chinese restaurants. Madly glamorous but in the end it means nothing more than chunks of pork in hot pineapple jam. I expect Ling-Ting-Tong-or-whatever is really called Harry or Ernie or something.'

'But who is it?'

'A "lady" Uncle Rufus found on one of his travels. She's frankly awful. If she *is* a she. I think she, it, "wigs" the whole performance!'

'She is very what they call in women's magazines "petite", giggles behind her hand, and tiptoes about the place as if her legs were tied together at the knee,' said Rochester. 'There's no accounting for taste. Probably a knockout in bed. But I think it's male, *au fond*.'

Loveday gave a little cry of distaste.

'Shocked you, Aunt Loveday?'

'Disgusting,' said Loveday. 'Poor Kathleen.'

'Why poor Kathleen? I really didn't mind. Have you met this person, Miss Loveday?'

'I have not,' said Loveday, reaching for her folded scarf.

'And I don't want to.' She got to her feet, pushing back her chair, which clattered to the stone floor. 'So uneven, the tiles. Nothing is really steady. It's been a terrible, terrible day. Will anything, I ask myself, be steady ever again? Will it?'

Rochester was on his feet. 'Come along, I'll see you upstairs.'

'I can manage, sweet boy,' said Loveday. 'Thank you.'

'None the less I'll come with you. We've finished down here anyway. Time for bed, I reckon.' He put his arm round his aunt and guided her gently towards the door.

'Oh! Beddy-byes . . . beddy-byes . . . I *dote* on beddy-byes,' murmured Loveday.

Sophie and Kathleen started to clear up the glasses and the scattered chicken bones.

'Oh Christ!' said Sophie, lifting the platter of dismembered fowl. 'She's going to feel *terrible* in the morning. She only really got through today on gin. I didn't like to tell Rochester that he was right. Didn't seem fair somehow. She's got a secret hoard down in the Wendy Hut. Gives herself zonking great gollops. Her secret vice.' She got up with the collected glasses. 'God! I'd hate to be old, wouldn't you, Kath?'

'Is she old? Loveday?'

'Heavens yes. Forties. About that anyway. Do you want another slug of not-terribly-chilled and corky Sauvignon?'

'Yes, great. Keep Rochester company.'

Sophie put the glasses back on the table, pushed the wine towards Kathleen. 'You're so pretty, Kath. Do you mind me saying that? Lovely long legs, lovely long hair, slender, a super nose. I suppose it's all that French blood of yours?'

'I'm blushing. You are crazy.'

'I'm not. I mean it. I just think you are lovely. Obviously Rochester thinks so too. Do you like him?'

Kathleen poured herself a half-glassful of wine. 'Like Rochester? Sure I do.' She suddenly laughed. '*He's* got lovely long legs and pretty hair and a "super nose" too.'

'That's what I mean,' said Sophie firmly. 'You are absolutely perfectly matched.'

'He's like your father. Same build and everything.'

'Except,' said Sophie, picking at a small piece of chicken, 'except that he's not old.'

'But your parents aren't *that* old, are they?'

'Ages. They all are. I mean, can you imagine them all up there, snuggled up in bed. Aunt Unity probably snorting, boring Uncle Edward dreaming about his ships, Mum covered in face cream, sound asleep, Dad reading . . . he always reads in bed. I mean . . .' She waved a small piece of chicken vaguely. 'I mean to say. Mum and Dad. All passion spent. They haven't any real communication: don't know what it's like, I imagine. Got married, had babies, settled down. Finish. Awful.'

Kathleen rocked her glass gently from side to side on the table top. 'You think all passion is spent? Really?'

'Well, after all, they are all about fifty! Goodness – I mean their time is over! *That* time, I mean, if there was one? I think that there *was* with Mum and Dad, they still do sort of look at each other, you know. A special kind of look. They think I don't see. But I do. It's deeply embarrassing really. I look away. I suppose, you see, it's really because they have got used to each other. Over-familiar. There are no surprises, the juices have dried up. Does that sound awful?'

'Yes,' said Kathleen. 'Just awful. I wonder, though, if you are right.'

Sophie nodded firmly. 'Oh I'm certain I'm right. I think Uncle Rufus is probably better off with all his strange chums from Hong Kong and Singapore and stations east. He gets more fun, much more variety. He's not *used* to them. When he gets used to them he just dumps one and tries another.'

Kathleen started to laugh. 'Sophie! Honestly! I don't think that being promiscuous can be all that much fun, surely?'

'Well,' said Sophie. 'I imagine it's less dreary than just being dried up like the elders upstairs. I think I'd die if I got to be like that in twenty years' time. Which is why I'll let you into a secret: I won't get married, ever.'

'I don't believe a word. But Jesus! You paint a very depressing picture.'

Sophie leant forward, her hand outstretched. 'Oh Kath! Kath, it won't happen to *us*! *Any* of us. I was really only joking about myself just now . . . No, it won't happen to us. We're young. We are a different generation from them. We couldn't be like that, we would never make the same mistakes. Anyway, we've got years and years before we have to really worry. We are so much wiser at our ages than they ever were.'

Kathleen fished a piece of cork from her glass, held it up to the light.

'What's the matter?' said Sophie. 'Another bit of cork?'

'A crumb,' said Kathleen. 'I was just wondering what makes you so damned sure.'

May Smollett fixed the last roller into her hair, threw a blue net over her head and tied the ends securely in a knot at the front as her husband came in from the bathroom. She sat up in bed defiantly, arms folded.

'I know, I know *all* about it. You don't like these things and I look like a barmaid. But I'm sorry, Bob dear. They stay. I've spent the whole of today looking like the wrath of God and I do not intend to spend tomorrow in the same state. So there.'

'I haven't said a bloody word.'

'I know you haven't dear. But I know that you will. So I've just got in first. Had a nice bath?'

He unwound the towel from about his waist, rubbed his head with it, hard. 'Warm and wet.'

'That's what a bath should be. Comfy in here, isn't it? And those curtains: I love that shade of orange. It's quiet too: we are at the back, so you won't hear the lorries coming up the hill at night.'

'Thank God for that.' He threw the towel into a chair, picked up his pyjama trousers. 'You look like a mad rabbit with those ends hanging over your forehead.'

'Thank you. But just you wait until tomorrow, I'll look like a regular little Marilyn Monroe.'

'Somebody got a magic wand?' said Bob, pulling on his pyjama top.

'Oh shut up! You are awful to me. I don't know why I stand for it.'

'Because I'm your husband and you've got nowhere else to go.'

'I could always go to Gracie down at Folkestone.'

'Fat chance.' He did up the buttons and went over to the small television set on a pedestal in a corner.

May suddenly sat bolt upright. 'Don't you dare!' she hissed. 'Don't dare touch a button on that bloody thing.'

'I just thought –'

May cut him short, brutally. 'Too late for the news. So stop thinking! If I hear another word from Harold Wilson or Richard Nixon or that Watergate place I'll get up and put a foot right through the set. So there. I mean it!'

59

Bob looked at his wife, then his watch. 'Yep. A bit late for the news. But there just might be something: about the secret tapes, you know.

'I know. I know all about the "secret tapes" and I don't give a damn. We are dead tired, we've come a long way, and had a difficult day. I'm not going to lie here and listen to another word about secret tapes or anything. And neither are you. Come on, come to your bed, I don't give a bugger about Watergate.'

'May,' said Bob in surprise. 'That's not like you!'

'It's like me tonight, dear. So do as I say. We were far better off without politics. Managed a treat.'

'When?'

'When we were younger. No damned politics then.'

'May? Are you going bonkers? Don't be daft, girl, of course we had politics.'

'Well, I didn't notice them.'

Bob pulled back his sheet and got into bed. 'They got you into a bloody great war and bundled you into the Women's Land Army.'

'I'm quite aware of the Land Army. It wasn't all cream cakes and lemonade, I grant you, and I didn't like the war. But it was nothing to do with me! I never sat up half the day watching the telly and listening to politicians gabbling away. All those lies and so on. I had better things to do with my time, I can tell you.'

'We hardly had telly before the war –'

'That's *why* we didn't have politics! I'm not as daft as you think.' May thumped a pillow. 'Too high. Yours all right? Not too high for you?'

'Haven't had a chance to test it yet.'

'I'm dead tired but I don't think I'll get off very easily. What a day, ummm? My head's spinning. So many things to think about.' May reached out a pretty, plump arm.

60

'Hold my hand just for a minute. I feel a bit woebegone. Know what I mean?'

'Yes. I know what you mean. Exactly.'

They lay holding hands between the beds of the bright, impersonal hotel room for a few moments in silence.

'Funny,' said May. 'Being back there at Hartleap. All those years ago, seems an age to me now. Of course, I'd never really seen the house, had I? Full of schoolgirls and hockey sticks in those days. It's very pretty, a bit grand, but quite lived in, you know?'

'It's nice, yes,' said Bob.

'And they were so kind. Welcoming. Whisked me off for tea, no trouble. The American girl – what's her name? Kathleen something – was nice. "Come and freshen up in my room," she said. Funny word, "freshen". But I needed it. My poor old love,' she said suddenly, stooping to kiss his hand. 'You needed "freshening up" too. What a long drive, and I didn't help. Never could co-ordinate, or something . . .'

He removed his hand from hers gently, folded his arms behind his head, stared up at the ceiling. 'All those years ago,' he said. 'It was funny seeing Aunt Ada's feet. So little. Poking up under the sheet. I didn't know she had such little feet before.'

'Neither did I,' said May.

'She had. When did I last see her? Just before Christmas, wasn't it?'

'Yes, I think so. You came down to London with Charles and Stewart. You saw her then at the cottage.'

'Right.'

'But you never saw the family, did you?' Her voice was gently probing.

'No. Never did. I keep out of the way when I can, thanks.'

May fiddled quietly with one of her rollers. 'They are

such a nice lot, I think. Sophie's got such lovely hair, so blonde. The fair Grayles. Lovely blue eyes! Says she's off to Africa or somewhere.'

'What the bloody hell is she going to do in Africa?'

'Manners!' said May. 'Look after destitute Third World people somewhere, she said.'

'Well, that's one thing in her favour. Apart from her baby-blue eyes.'

'Oh Bob! These grudges! Those people were so kind to us both. They were wonderfully kind to Ada all through her life –'

'Nanny-bloody-Grayle. They even had to take her own name away from her.'

'They did not! It was *her* choice. She told me, years ago. "I'm Nanny *Grayle*," she said. "And proud of it. Anyone can be 'Ada Stephens' but I'm particular. I *belong*." That's what she said. I remember clear as clear. She was very proud of that name.'

'Not finally,' said Bob, and yawned.

'She had a good life and they loved her, and just you remember that. She wasn't pushed out into the streets, you know. They kept her here, in the family. She belonged.'

'Solicitors tomorrow at – what time was it?' His sudden change of mood, and clear uninterest in what she was saying checked her for a moment.

'Yes,' she said eventually. 'Jackson and Bellows. Weald Street at ten-thirty.'

'And the undertakers?'

She shifted uneasily in her bed, smoothed the top of her nightdress. About seven o'clock I think. The nurse goes off at eight something to Hove. Do you want to go over again? To see Ada?'

'No. I said my goodbye, thanks.' He laughed suddenly; more a caught breath.

May looked across at him. 'What is it?' she said.

'Those feet. So damn small. Poking up under the sheet.'

'Don't dwell on it, Bobbie. Don't.'

'I'm not dwelling on anything! I've seen a hell of a lot of dead feet in my time, May. Don't worry, I was just thinking, looking at them then, what a lot of to-ing and fro-ing they'd done over the years.'

'Yes.'

'Carting all those bloody Grayles about.'

May suddenly sat up in her bed, swung her feet on to the floor angrily. 'Now, Bob! Bob, just stop this. I know what's in your mind. I know how you feel, I do honestly. But it's simply no good harbouring grudges. It's all over and done with. These people up at the house are a different generation, they had nothing whatever to do with anything. They were hardly born when the war was on. Some of them were only born after it. They've been good and kind, they have been honourable to your aunt, they have always made us welcome here, on the few times we came down, and they were kindness and sympathy itself today. They mind as much about Aunt Ada going as we do. She was part of their lives.'

Bob laughed, scratched his head. 'What's all the pep talk for? Been converted, have we? Had dinner with the gentry? Silver candlesticks on the table? Gone to your little head?'

May hit the edge of her bed with a closed fist. 'You're talking like a silly child! Now just you stop. You know me, I'm not that daft.' She leant forward, her hands together. 'I wasn't going to mention this, but since you're in such a bolshie mood, I will.'

'Mention what, May? I'm dead tired.'

'Well, you listen to this. When you went to see Aunt Ada today I thought I'd take myself off and have a little walk: breath of fresh air, try and find some of the places

I'd broken my back weeding and hoeing all those years ago.'

Bob unfolded his arms. 'Come on, what is it?'

'I went down to Home Farm, remember? Just to have a look, and there was a fellow standing by the gateway.'

'Who was it? Elvis Presley?'

'He was very polite, young: he's the new tenant there. He writes books, but he does a thing in a Sunday paper. He's "Tom Tiddler".'

'Clever bastard,' said Bob.

'His name is Jake Wood. He's been on telly lots of times.'

'Never heard of him. You'll catch your death sitting there like that. The windows are open, you know.'

'I'm aware of that. He said to me, "Has there been a bereavement up there at the cottage?" and I said, "Yes," and he said, "I thought so because I haven't seen old Miss Stephens for a while, and there's been a lot of coming and going, and a nurse." But this is the peculiar part, Bob. He said, "Are you a member of the family?" And I said, "No. No, I'm not. I'm just visiting," and he said, "I thought not, I've never seen you here before; and I'm a Grayle-watcher."'

Bob looked at her for a moment in silence. 'A what?'

'You heard. And he had a pair of binoculars round his neck. He was watching the cottage. And the house.'

'What did you say then?'

'I said, "Oh, I thought perhaps you were a bird-watcher. Whatever are you watching them for?" And he said, "They're a very famous family, as you must know. You surely remember Brigadier Grayle? Beau Brave as he was called, a big star in the war."'

'And?'

'I said no, pretending to be a bit gormless.'

'That's not like you . . .'

'He said he was writing a book about him because he'd

found out that no one ever had. Written a book about him, I mean.'

'What did you say?'

'I didn't say anything. He said something funny: he said that two people had tried to but weren't able to. They had to abandon it.'

'Why?'

'Couldn't get anyone to discuss anything. No one wanted to know.'

'Does the family up there know about this? They must do.'

'He said he had spoken to Mr Grayle once and he said that he had no comment to make. And that was that. Very high-handed he was, he said. He really didn't know anything. All a long time ago.'

Bob was sitting forward in his bed, arms round his raised knees. 'Falmouth Grayle wouldn't know a bloody thing anyway.'

'No,' said May adjusting a roller under her net. 'Perhaps not. But then he went to see Aunt Ada. The writer chap . . . before she died.'

Bob looked across at her in shocked surprise. 'Ada? He went to the cottage? Saw her?'

'Talked to her, Bob. He said she was much more forthcoming. Even though she was a bit hazy on account of being quite an age.'

'When did he do this?'

'A few months ago. Just after he had moved in to Home Farm and after getting the brush-off from the Grayles.'

Bob lay back on his pillows. 'Did he say what she had been so forthcoming about?' he said quietly.

'No. Didn't say anything. Just that he was sorry she had died, poor old soul, and that she had enjoyed a bit of company. His, I gathered.'

'That all?'

'That's all. Except he said that she'd been very "interesting".'

'I see,' said Bob.

'I'm telling you all this because, well, we're here for another two days, aren't we? Until the funeral, and then we've got to clear up Bottle Cottage. And I think that you ought to be careful who you speak to . . . you being in such a mood. I know you. I know you'll never forget what happened, I know that you think what you did was right, but it's all in the past now. Let's leave it where it lies. No good being bloody-minded with the Grayles, they weren't responsible for that dreadful time, none of them. Not really.'

'So what do you think I'll go and do? Blabber away to him? Think I'd do that?'

' 'Course I don't. Not deliberately. But I've seen you lose your temper, Bob. Just keep out of his way. There's no knowing what Aunt Ada told him, what she remembered even. Names. Addresses perhaps. She could have said anything or nothing, so just keep out of the way of the bloke until *we* can get away. Least said, soonest mended.'

'Hard to believe,' said Bob with an attempt at lightness. 'You talk up a bloody storm, you do. You really think I'd talk to the feller?'

'No. No, I don't. I'm just warning you, dear, that's all. It wouldn't be in your interests to do that, would it?' She got back into her bed, patted the pillow. 'It's too high this thing. You must mind your Ps and Qs: no point in finding yourself plastered all over the Sunday papers one morning.'

'As what?' said Bob quietly. 'A murderer?'

May arranged herself in her sheets, threw the second of her pillows on the floor.

I wasn't going to use that word, Bob. I didn't either,' she said. 'You did.'

At Home Farm, Isobel Wood scraped the remains of supper from their plates into a Sainsbury's plastic bag, knotted it tight, shoved the dishes in the sink, took a final swig of wine from her glass on the draining-board, rinsed it briefly under the cold tap and went to join her husband, who was standing in the shadowy porch, thumbs thrust into his jeans pocket.

'Caught anything? Horrid old bogie? A secret being creeping up to murder us? Or ghosties? Going up to the house?' There was more than a hint of amused sarcasm in her voice. She shrugged the long plait of hair over her shoulder, crossed the porch to the little iron gate by the road where the dustbin stood. She squashed the plastic bag down, rattled shut the lid and stood for a moment, hands on hips, looking up at the house on the hill, scenting the night air in the soft darkness. 'Smells so good. Clean. Sweet. Hay, I suppose.' Then looking back up at Hartleap she wrapped her arms round her heavy breasts. 'All dark up there. Gone to bed. Worn themselves out, I reckon. Had a busy day, all that to-ing and fro-ing . . .'

Jake turned on his bare feet, nodded, looked up the hill. 'Light still on up there. At the cottage. Just a glimmer.'

'A glimmer. Yes. Probably the nurse. Sitting with the corpse. They do that, don't they? You have to pay extra . . .'

Jake moved to the brightness of the front door. 'Yup. A watcher at the death-bed. It's called Bottle Cottage. I told you that, didn't I?'

Isobel shrugged, turned, walked towards the door and the beam of soft lamplight. 'You told me. *Ages* ago. Right at the beginning of your "quest". Or should we say, "research"?'

'Research. Someone did come hurrying down the path a little time ago. I'd have missed that if I hadn't been watching. I think it was the loopy one. She had a sort of turban on, a jogging flashlight and the dogs. She was moaning something, went whizzing away. She wears long skirts like you.'

'Do they swish like mine?' Isobel leant against the door, smiling, arms folded.

Jake nodded. 'They were swishing then. Yes.' She saw his smile in the lamplight. He licked his lips. A pink tip. 'Swish, swish they went.'

Idly she tapped the open palm of her left hand with her heavy plait. She sighed. 'But she's crazy. They are all loopy up at that house. Barking. Amazed they let that one loose, at night, traipsing about. She's getting on in years . . . Madness. We'll find her face down in the river next, you'll see. Do a Virginia Woolf on us.' She went into the big kitchen: lamplight, whitewashed walls, a small Aga, copper pots faintly gleaming, dulled with cooking. She began to wind the long plait of hair round her head, coiling it like a snake, a hairpin clenched between her teeth. 'But you were certain it *was* her? The loopy one? Am I spoiling your line of thought, Jake? Getting in the way of your muse?'

'Yes, frankly. You're mucking me about. You distract me. I *think* it was her, she's up there often enough. Used to be. Wandering up the track. She's got a hut thing down in that orchard.' He went across to the pine dresser, got a glass and poured himself a large Scotch. 'I met another one today, another member of the house-party. I think so, anyway. Blonde, middle-aged. I hadn't seen her before ever. Dressed for town. You know: high heels and a handbag, that sort of thing? Probably down for the funeral. Didn't say her name, just that she was having a look round "the old place". Right out there, in the yard, by the dairy.'

68

Isobel, who had now fixed her plait, permitted herself a light flicker of interest in this. She was thinking of something else. 'The *old* place. She say that? What was she, some kind of milk-maid? A vet? Why would she say "old place". Was she a farm kind of person? Not their class?'

Jake took a drink, belched gently, wiped his mouth with his hand, patted his flat stomach. 'I *must* get a bit of exercise. She said she was ex-Land Army. During the war. Worked down here. Seemed to know her way around the place. Very ordinary, might have been pretty. Then. Pretty common really, but pleasant. I told her we were the tenants of the house. She said that was interesting. She thought I was familiar. Hadn't she seen me on the telly? I said yes, perhaps. What else?'

Isobel went across to the sink for her glass, then to the dresser and poured herself a stiff Scotch. 'And? And what then?' she took a drink.

'Nothing. She asked if I was a bird-watcher, on account of my binoculars, and I said, you know, as a bit of a joke really, no, I'm a Grayle-watcher. And she just looked blank. As if I was mad.'

'As well she might! What a sodding silly reply to make. Grayle-watcher! What in the name of God is that supposed to mean? That you were *stalking* them up at the house? Because that's what you are doing, but to say it! To a perfect stranger. Have you lost your wits?' Her anger was starting to rise, giving her the solid reason to do what she had already planned to do. But not without a 'reason'. You had to have a reason. 'You are losing your marbles, chattering away.'

'No! No! I just said that I was trying to write a book about old Grayle, but it was very difficult because everyone was very clammed up, wouldn't talk.'

'You were writing a *book* about them! She'll alert the

lot of them if she's staying up there. You are mad, Jake, completely stupid!'

'Everyone has clammed up, soon as I even tried to speak of the idea. I told her that. Told her that our landlord was pretty uptight and rude. "Nothing I can discuss. Sorry," when I just mentioned it. Didn't want to know, did he? I told her, this elderly blonde woman, that it was very difficult. For me. Told her how nice the old girl up the hill was. Grayle had had a very exciting, glamorous life. She agreed. Was very interesting. Told her that she'd been a big help, old Ada.'

'Tell her if you were circumcised as well?'

'Don't be so silly. I said I'd been up at Bottle Cottage a few times, "to see Miss Stephens". That's all. Neighbour after all. Helpful. I just let it slip out. So to speak. Worry them, up there, if *she* lets it slip out. She might. But she was pretty thick. Didn't know what I was talking about. Ada and the cottage. Only that I'd been on telly and wrote books. Just said, "how interesting". I mean, really. The original dumb blonde. Thicker than the Yellow Pages and not as useful.'

He was sitting, or, thought Isobel, 'sprawling', in the one comfortable chair. Sitting on the arm, legs apart, *sprawled* against the back. The word thrust into her gently, triggering feelings which were not remotely maternal. A surge of excitement began. 'My God! You are silly. Blabbing away to perfect strangers.' Her heart began to race. She was being teased. She stared at his thighs.

He shrugged, grinned across at her, one bare foot on the ground. 'Not as daft as you think. Spreading it around a little, that's all.' He was wearing the white jeans which she had bought. A size too small, deliberately. They excited her. He couldn't wear underpants, even tuck in his shirt. All that she could see, she would get. He suddenly finished his glass of Scotch, wiped his lips. 'I told her to wander about to her heart's content. But she said no thanks. She'd really seen all she wanted to, the past was the past now, wasn't it? Better forget it. Something archaic, obvious . . .' He got up suddenly, chucked the dregs of his glass out of the open door. 'Better close this, hadn't we? Lamps attract the moths, and it's late anyway.'

She made no reply, sat watching him on her favourite milking-stool, legs wide apart, heavy calico skirts flowing, bare feet planted firmly on the tiled floor. An ample lap. Inspired by Augustus John. Tough peasant.

Jake set his glass down on the windowsill, turned the heavy key in the lock of the slammed door, stooped to run the bolt home, bent down to reach the bottom bolt, grinned up at her. The tightness of his jeans was restrictive. She watched him intently. A stupid, careless, guileless boy with a muscular bum who loved playing her game. With a slightly shaking hand she finished her drink, took it over to the sink. Water ran. As he came up behind her with his glass, she took it, rinsed it.

He protested mildly. 'I hadn't finished! Isso . . . a little one?'

She rammed the hairpin deeper into her coiled hair. 'No. No more tonight. I know you, takes the edge off, and that won't do. We don't want that, do we?'

He was suddenly quite still, his smile faded, the game was beginning. 'Isobel! No, not now, I can't *now*.'

She turned to face him, slid her arms tightly round his waist. 'No can't about it. *Will*. Jake. Will. And Isobel has gone away! Madame is here now, you're in her arms, and Madame thinks you'd better come up with her, let her deal with you.'

He laughed uneasily, she held him tight. 'Madame will deal with her careless, silly, chattering little boy, eh?'

Still holding him, she spread her legs and pulled him in between her full thighs. Eased him in forcefully. He gave a half-laugh, almost a gasp. 'No! Hold it, hold it! You'll have me over.' He put one hand on her shoulder to steady himself and she, at the same time, twisted his nose viciously. He cried out at the sudden shock. 'Madame will have you over all right, over her lap, Master Wood. You deserve a good whipping for talking to strange women, talking silly things with that little tongue. Dangerous! Madame feels that a whipping is long overdue.'

She was smiling, eyes half closed, let a hand wander across his buttocks. 'A good thrashing, eh?' She felt him stiffen between her thighs. 'Madame is in a bad mood tonight, she will be very strict. Very strict indeed. No more chattering about books, about watching the Grayles as if they were some rare creatures at a watering-hole. No more talk about the old lady on the hill there. You said she was interesting! Well, *this* will be interesting.'

He half-heartedly – part of the foreplay – tried to pull away. 'I didn't chatter, Madame. I said nothing important, *really* nothing –'

She slightly pushed away from him. 'You dare to argue with Madame? *To argue?* You are not in a position to argue, young man. Really!' She leant close to him, he could smell the Scotch on her breath. 'Because you argue we shall not go over her lap. No. The cuffs! We'll use the cuffs instead, shall we?' She saw the quick flash of anxiety in his eyes.

'Don't hurt me! Please don't mark me – don't cut me –'

Isobel released him suddenly, so that he nearly stumbled over, and slapped his face hard. He ducked. 'I didn't say *anything*, really nothing. I told you what I said.' She struck him again. 'Madame is weary of your whining. She will certainly use the cuffs – you have *argued* with her! So Mr

72

Rod will deal with you. You have provoked Madame's wrath. Douse the lamps, set up the breakfast things: cups, saucers, ordinary things, just to give Madame time to prepare for you. Don't be too long. Just time to prepare.' She took up one of the lamps and went across to the staircase. 'Time, but not too much. Madame longs to see that pretty little bottom of yours again. Her sweet peach. She feels it is ripe now for its whipping . . . and so does Mr Rod! He will be severe tonight, very severe. Poor sweet peach!' She turned and went heavily up the stairs.

Jake stood in silence for a moment, head cocked for the swish, swish of her skirts until they faded and a door was closed. That sound, more even than the idiotic words of their game, excited him more than he could bear. His heart was beating. He found the tray, looked at his watch, started to lay up the cups and saucers, noticed, not without pleasure, that his hands were shaking. He smiled apprehensively in the gloom of the single lamp. The 'man of today' was about to be transformed into 'the man of secret night'. Madame's Little Man. He had mown the lawns all afternoon, done some odd jobs, and after a shower had eased himself into the white jeans she had bought him. He might have been enamelled. It was a signal which she had accepted with contained excitement.

But both ignored the overt sexual offer completely, until he had started to talk about meeting the blonde. Then 'the game' began. He heard the floorboards creaking above, stood looking up at the white ceiling, heard the drag of wood over wood as she eased the high, padded stool into the centre. He knew exactly what he would have to endure. For a moment, he closed his eyes, leant against the dresser, held its edge, overwhelmed, as he always was, by excitement mixed with fear of the pain that he expected. Then he heard the boards creak again, feet moving towards the door above, the groan of the hinges, her voice, harsh now, no affection, flat, commanding.

'Madame is quite ready. Everything is in place. She is waiting. Do not vex her further, you have been naughty enough already. Mr Rod is waiting too . . . We are both waiting.'

Jake doused the lamp, walked very slowly barefoot towards the stairs lit by the glow of a distant lamp. He started to whimper slightly.

'Come along! Don't delay any longer, you will only have to suffer much more, much more if you are vexatious. Come along, let Madame see her sweet peach, come along . . . *We are waiting* . . .'

Monday Morning

A heron swung low out of the sun over the stream, as Nanny Grayle, boxed in a plain oak coffin, was shouldered through her garden gate by four elderly men and carried without ceremony, at that hour of the morning, down the path to the road and a waiting Daimler hearse glimmering in the early light.

The heron feathered to a halt on the stream bank, shook, preened, looked about, head high, then splashed through the sedge.

Rochester and his father stood silently by the garden gate watching the small coffin rolled into the back of the car, the doors slammed, and the four men stretch themselves.

Their voices were low on the road below. A crunch of chalky gravel. Someone coughed.

'Sid nearly had us over just now. He did.'

'Bugger off.'

'You did! Going too fast. Got to keep *slow* if you're leading, told you before.'

'Wasn't no weight there, Bert.'

'No. Light as a feather she was.'

'A sparrer.'

Someone lit a cigarette, coughed and spat.

'Bloody nearly had me over. Corpse and all.'

Fal turned sharply away and looked back across the valley to the house.

'There's a heron,' said Rochester. 'At the stream.'

'At the stream? Can't see him.'

'Near the clump of meadow-sweet, by the dead alders.'

'Ah, yes.'

Car doors slammed, the hearse revved up, eased out into the middle of the lane, and moved off towards the Lewes road.

Fal stood perfectly still, shading his eyes with the flat of his hand, still looking in the direction of the house. Rochester watched him curiously, alerted by the intensity of his father's concentration.

'Your mother. She said . . .' Fal began, stopped helplessly. 'Said that I looked . . . like a heron.'

'Mum? Complimentary, I imagine?'

'I think she thought so.' He lowered his hand, thrust it into his trouser pocket. 'Thank you for coming with me.' He was still watching the house.

'I wanted to. Don't thank me. Honestly.'

'I thought we should see her off properly. Just you and me.'

'Behaviour?' said Rochester.

'That's it.' Fal turned back suddenly towards the gate and pushed through the overgrown garden, up the path to the cottage door. 'We'll have to set to and get this place cleared.'

In the parlour Nurse Monahan, capless, humming brightly, was folding a sheet.

'Morning!' she said. 'They've just this minute gone. Oh dear! What a pity now.'

'No. No. No pity. We were there. Waited at the gate. We didn't come in. Really not much room in here, is there?'

She folded a pair of pillowcases expertly, placed them on the sheets. A blanket bunched on the striped mattress.

'Now would one of you gentlemen be good enough to give me a bit of a hand with this? If you'd just take that end, like so . . . Splendid . . . And then I take this end, and we fold it along the centre. Great stuff! Done!' She folded the blanket and put it on the mattress. 'Och, Mr Grayle! You'd be a perfect nurse in no time. No, no there's little enough room here, I agree. They had quite a job with the deceased and the coffin. No damage done, just a scratch on the plaster there by the door, but the place is so full of old stuff they had the devil of a job to get her through it all.' She stuffed the sheets and pillowcases into a linen basket.

'She was a great collector,' said Fal. 'It was good of you to stay the night. I am most grateful.'

'No problem. I'm used to it, you know. Your cook – is it Mrs Duckworth? – she gave me a great lunch. We had it in the kitchen. And then I had a good book, d'you know Joy M. Rippon? Made myself a pot of tea up here, and a wee bit of a sandwich, and I had my radio. Now.' She looked about the cluttered room, hands on her hips. 'That's all done. I've packed my bag, got my mac, and the taxi should be here shortly.'

'Mr Keen is a punctual fellow. He'll take you to the station.'

'Well, that's fine. I'll just pop upstairs, get my things and get myself ready. Now, all the soiled sheets, incontinent y'see, are in this basket.' She went across to the staircase humming cheerfully, stopped suddenly. 'Ah, there's a thing I forgot. There's a little jewel case there, see it? On the chest of drawers. I'd take it away if I was you. If the house is left empty for a while there's no knowing who might, you know, come in. There's not much of value, I dare say, but it might be wiser.' She hurried up the stairs singing. '*Spread a little happiness as you go by. You mustn't weep, and you mustn't sigh . . .*'

Rochester picked up the rosewood box. Inside, a tangled

assortment of glass beads, hairpins, a Coronation badge, a tin brooch spelling 'ADA', a heart-shaped locket. Several regimental buttons. 'Nothing of any value here,' he said, replacing the box.

The only thing of value, a cameo, set in gold and garnets, was upstairs in Nurse Monahan's plastic lizard-skin handbag.

Fal had been idly sorting through a pile of books. He took up a small clasp-bible. 'I'll take this away. In case. It all belongs to the Smolletts. Give it to him when he gets here this afternoon.' He looked about the little parlour. 'They'll have a job with all this rubbish. Let's go and have some breakfast, as soon as she's gone.'

Rochester was standing in the doorway looking out into the brilliance of the morning. 'Going to be a scorcher today. Really hot.'

From the lane came three blasts of a car horn.

Fal went across to the narrow staircase and called up. 'Taxi's here, nurse.'

'I'm ready! Just coming! Could one of you gentlemen be so good as to take this little suitcase? It's on the landing here.'

'Go and get the bloody thing,' said Fal quietly. 'Let's get rid of her.'

Stella Duckworth forked ten sausages into a silver dish, garnished them with grilled mushrooms, four half-tomatoes, and replaced the lid as her husband pushed through the swing-door from the corridor. It swung to and fro with a gentle slip-slap.

'They all down now?' she said, going to the stove for the kettle.

'All bar his "Lordship" and the heir – and old droopy-drawers.'

78

Stella turned quickly, the kettle in her hand. 'Charlie! I've told you before and I tell you again! *Don't* call Miss Loveday that dreadful name. And just behave. I don't know what's got into you this morning, honestly I don't. Grumble, grumble, grumble. Nothing but.' She poured the kettle of steaming water into a jug.

'Too much to do. That's what's got into me.'

'There are Mr Uffington's sausages . . .'

Charles looked at the dish, removed the cover. 'All of them? *Ten* bloody sausages?'

'I'll knife you,' said Stella. 'He'll take what he wants and maybe the others will have one. Here's the extra hot water. And hurry it along before it cools. Now be a good fellow, do. I'm running a boarding-house this morning, leave alone what you think you're running. Go along now.'

Charles stacked his tray and pushed through the swing-door. 'They'll go to waste, you know. He'll never eat *ten* bloody sausages, everyone else is having toast and marmalade. It's just wasteful. Think of the Ethiopians.' He was standing holding the door open with his shoulder.

'What about the Ethiopians?' said Stella, refilling the kettle at the sink.

'Starving. Hundred thousand million of them,' said Charles.

'Well ten sausages won't help them much, will they? Get along, for the love of God!' She switched on the kettle as the door closed, slip-slap, and stood for a moment, hands on her hips looking through the latticed windows into the sunlit courtyard. 'Poor Nanny,' she said aloud. 'Bloody old witch.' She took a clean teacloth and began to dry the teacups which she and Charles had just used for their morning tea. 'One mouth less to feed, I suppose. Can't say as we'll miss her, it's so long since she was in this house. And I'm talking to myself. That's a bad sign.'

She stacked the cups on the draining-board, wiped the saucers. The door swung open again and Loveday came in wearing a long flowing dress of dark navy blue silk with a wide black band round her arm and a jet necklace.

'Good morning, Stella,' she said.

Miss Loveday! Well, we *do* look the thing this morning!' And then, seeing the black ribbon on Loveday's arm, she said swiftly, 'The kettle's boiling, or will be, in a couple of ticks. Like a cup? Not going to the dining-room, am I right?'

'Yes. I've got a terrible headache. Throb, throb, throb. It's agony. I couldn't face them all sitting there. Eating. On this morning, of all mornings. It's so heartless. I feel very giddy, very giddy indeed, unworldly.'

Stella took a clean cup and saucer from the dresser. 'Be a dear, Miss Loveday, will you? The tea caddy, could you? The kettle's just about to start singing. I'll warm the pot.'

Loveday found the tea caddy after a weary look about the sun-flecked room. 'Eating and drinking,' she said.

'Well,' said Stella. 'Got to keep up our strengths, haven't we, come what may? You have to eat, you know. I mean, it's not as if they were having a party or something.'

Loveday wandered across to the double sink, leant on it, looked out of the windows. 'It's such a beautiful morning. I suppose they've taken her away by now?'

'Don't know,' said Stella filling the teapot, swirling it about, tipping the hot water into the sink. 'And not knowing can't tell. Mind, Miss Loveday, you're in my way, dear.'

'When is tea *tea*?' said Loveday as if she was asking a riddle: which, as far as Stella was concerned, she was.

'When is it what, dear?' Stella opened the caddy.

'Tea is tea and then it's tea-*leaves*, isn't it?'

Stella measured out three spoonfuls. 'Two, and one for the pot. There we are.'

'Isn't it? Is everyone in there?'

'All except your brother and Mr Rochester, they are over at –'

'I know!' said Loveday quickly. 'I know where they are! They wouldn't let us go over to see her go. Too cruel! Too cruel!'

'I think it was a very nice thing to do: just the two of them to see her off. I don't see any reason why Nanny's departure should be treated like the Lord Mayor's Show. Now don't be so silly, Miss Loveday. It was a thoughtful gesture to all, and saved everyone a miserable time.'

'*I* wouldn't have been miserable.'

'I know, dear, but there are other ladies present, remember. It would have been distressing. There is nothing to be done now. Best recognize the fact.'

Charles banged through the door with his tray.

'Miss Loveday has come to have a cup of tea with us, Charles,' said Stella warningly, hoping to forestall any trouble. 'Isn't that nice?'

'Good morning, Miss Loveday ... Very nice,' said Charles, putting his tray on the table. 'Mr Edward and his wife are down, just come in. I offered them the sausages.'

'And?' asked Stella.

'He said yes ... She's having toast.'

'I'm in mourning,' murmured Loveday. 'I don't suppose that anyone else is, in there. Are they, Charles?'

Charles looked startled. 'Are they what?' he said.

'In mourning? My sister. The Honourable-Awful-Mrs Edward Uffington, or my niece Sophie, or anyone.'

'No one. No. All in black, you mean? I can't say that they are,' said Charles, pouring himself a cup of tea.

'I just washed that cup,' said Stella.

'Well, you can wash it again.'

'Temper! My word! And there are eight for lunch, I might just remind you, so I dread to think what state you'll be in by tonight, my boy. And Gloria hasn't come yet to help with the washing up and the beds.'

Loveday sat at the table, took three lumps of sugar from the bowl in the centre, stirred her tea with the handle of a fork. 'I do feel so wobbly. Quite sick.'

'I'll get you a spoon, shall I,' said Charles anxiously, in an unaccustomed mood of gallantry, but Loveday cautiously shook her head, so he sat back in his chair at the far end, blowing on his tea. 'I don't know what they was up to in here last night, I'm sure,' he said.

'Who was here?' said Loveday, vaguely aware that she might have been.

'The children,' said Stella. 'I've lost my spatula. Now where did I put it?'

'Spatula?' said Charles. '*Spatula*, did you say?'

'Now then, Charlie. No nonsense.'

'I wasn't going to start any nonsense. I just said "spatula". Nothing wrong with that, is there? Can't have you losing your *spatula*, can we?' He suddenly winked at Loveday.

Stella opened a drawer, rummaged about among a chink of knives. 'I know you, my dear.'

'I think that *I* was here last night. With the children,' said Loveday. 'We had some cold chicken.'

'Which is why', said Stella, holding the spatula which she had retrieved from the drawer, 'there is only the salmon for lunch and no alternative. Massacred they were, those birds. Couldn't set them before anyone. *Torn* to bits.'

'I think we had chicken. I remember now. It's my head-ache. *I* didn't, they did. I was too unhappy to eat. I don't know how they could. Sophie and Rochester and that American girl.'

'Never mind,' said Stella quickly. 'They didn't make a mess. I warned Miss Sophie. No mess, I said. But those chickens! Really! Dismembered!'

'Remember Heath?' said Charles suddenly.

'What Heath?'

'He dismembered his women victims, didn't he? Or was that Haigh?'

Loveday set her cup in its saucer. 'He hid bits and pieces of them all over the place, under stones and things. And one lady got pushed into a barrel of acid stuff and was quite dissolved. Wasn't it awful! Just outside Crawley. The only thing left of her were her gallstones. Wasn't that funny? Such a *terrible* thing to happen at a place called *Crawley*. Ooooh!' She shivered in delight, wrapping her arms round her thin body.

'What a conversation!' said Stella.

Loveday smothered a snort of laughter with the back of her hand. '*Crawley*,' she said.

'I think, Miss Loveday, we've got things a bit mixed up,' said Charles, wagging a spoon at her down the length of the table. Stella? Heath or Haigh? You remember?'

'I do not. It's a disgusting conversation, so stop it at once.'

Loveday sniggered, slapped her own hand. 'Behave yourself, do!' she said.

Charles watched her curiously. 'I think Haigh did the acid job. The other bloke was Heath. He was the Bournemouth Butcher.'

'Oh do stop! Charles, I warn you!' said Stella.

'Creepy Place . . . Isn't that a funny name?' said Loveday. 'They just found her gallstones in all the sludge. In the *Times*. I read it. *Sludge!*'

'Miss Loveday! Really, it isn't fitting at breakfast.'

'I have a terrible headache,' said Loveday. 'But I remember all that. I simply *dote* on murders. We don't seem to get many good ones now.'

The door, which was open into the courtyard, creaked

on its hinges and a tall, pale, undernourished girl of about twenty ambled uncertainly into the room as if she was looking for the right house. Seeing Loveday and Charles at the table and Stella, hands on hip, standing by the sink, recognition dawned slowly. She closed the door and drifted in, satisfied that she had found where she ought to be.

'Madam Gloria Bates, I do declare!' said Stella. 'We're *forty* minutes late today. We're getting better, aren't we? Yesterday it was an hour.'

Gloria Bates wore a red T-shirt, blue jeans and high heeled shoes. She crossed the room in silence, looking neither left nor right, took an apron off a hook, tied it round her thin waist with pale, tight-lipped resignation. A saint at the stake.

'Nothing to say for yourself, then?' asked Stella.

Gloria made no reply, kicked off the trodden-heeled shoes and carried them in one hand through the swing-door.

'If I was her father I'd put her over my knee and wallop her,' said Charles.

'Well, you aren't her father so hold your tongue,' said Stella. 'And don't go and upset her. If she goes we're done for: she's the third in five months and I'm on the verge, the very verge, of desperation. So watch it!'

The door slip-slapped open and Gloria returned wearing a pair of tennis shoes. 'Me mum's pregnant,' she said.

Loveday shuddered, pushed her empty cup away.

'What, again!' said Charles.

'Charlie! I *told* you!'

Gloria pushed up her sleeves and went to the sinks. 'She's been throwing up all morning. Everywhere.'

Loveday covered her ears, lowered her head.

'Tell us later, Gloria, there's a dear,' said Stella.

'All over me dad's *TV Times*.'

'Gloria! Please . . .'

'He was really pissed off.'

Loveday suddenly rose from her chair and walked in a slow zig-zag towards the courtyard door, a hand to her forehead.

'You going? Miss Loveday, want an aspirin?' called Stella.

'My head's throbbing. I'm giddy. And *now* I do feel sick,' said Loveday. She opened the door and went unsteadily into the sunlight.

'Charlie. Time to clear in there. Take your tray. Gloria, dear! Non-stick frying-pans, those! Don't use wire wool on them. There's a dear.' She took the frying-pans from the girl's listless hands. 'You scrub away at these grills: use lots of Fairy Liquid, there's a good girl.'

Gloria squirted detergent into the running water, swirled it about with a weary twist of her hand. Bubbles foamed to her elbows.

'Did you speak to Sandra, like I asked?' said Stella.

'Yeah. I saw her. Comin' about ten. She wants five quid, she says, if it's beds.'

'It's beds.'

'I said okey-dokey. You'd pay that. OK?'

'Right,' said Stella helplessly. 'Just so long as she comes.'

'Had a puncture last night on her bike. I don't know if it's mended yet.'

'Well, soon as she comes we'll have a go at the bedrooms.' Stella cleared the two cups from the kitchen table, placed them in the second sink with a couple of dirty plates. 'Now, Gloria. I've put two cups and two plates in this sink. See? So don't go jamming your hands in without thinking, like you did last week: we don't want blood all over the sheets again, do we?'

'You won't get it,' said Gloria. 'I cut meself, I go 'ome. My dad says I'm anaemic.'

The swing-door opened wide, hitting the dresser, as Charles shouldered his way into the kitchen with a loaded tray, followed by Sophie and Kathleen carrying plates and dishes.

'All hands on deck!' he cried warningly. 'I've got willing help here.'

'More than I can say for myself,' muttered Stella hurrying forward to collect the dishes from Sophie. 'Oh you are good! This is a topsy-turvy morning, to be sure.'

'I've done my bed,' said Sophie. 'Mum's done theirs, and Miss Tessier has stripped hers already.'

'I'm leaving after lunch. If that's all right?' said Kathleen.

'Of course it's all right. You shouldn't have done your bed, *really*! What is the world coming to? Guests stripping their own beds and all.'

Gloria turned her head at the sink where she was slowly scrubbing away at something in the water. 'Sandra wants a fiver, don't forget,' she said, 'if it's beds.'

India never took breakfast. Not unless, that is, she was staying in some Hotel Splendido or somewhere tremendously grand. Then she did. She reckoned that the people who brought the table to her bedside with the single rose, freesia blossom, sprig of mimosa or the daily paper and all the nonsense of breakfast got paid for doing it and thereby eased her conscience. But, she thought wistfully, staying at a Hotel Splendido hadn't happened to her for a very long time.

She'd got up early, to avoid Unity and Edward really, and all that rustle and folding of the papers, smell of coffee and scrambled eggs or whatever they would eat, and gone into the kitchen with Stella, had a cup of her 'kitchen' tea, good and strong, eaten a bit of toast and gone out into the yard with the dogs. There was no one about yet. Too early.

No sign of Loveday or the children. Probably sleeping after the music festival they had had last night.

Except, of course, Roch had gone off with his father to Bottle Cottage. She was glad it was only them. No one else had been allowed to attend at the exit from their lives of Nanny Grayle. Good thinking of Fal. Sensible. Just himself and the 'heir'.

When she thought of the word 'heir' she heard herself sighing aloud. The heir was very presently training to be a cook. He had started training eight weeks ago. How long would he last? It almost startled her, the sigh. She found that she was following the dogs down the old track to the front of the house. The morning was radiantly still at such an hour: the valley and the little stream winding through, framed in its sedge and willow, spilling away silently under a gently wandering veil of mist.

She pushed through the arched door into the paved courtyard garden before the house. The fuchsias stood sentinel in urns among the lavender in their formal beds, edged with box. She wandered down to the ha-ha, sat on its brick top, screened from view across the valley by the lead skirt of a smiling shepherdess, her legs swinging over the cropped meadow below. Some nettles, a clump of dock. How funny it is, always: nettles which sting and hurt a child, and right beside them the healing balm of the dock. They always grow together. Now I wonder why? I wonder.

Shading her eyes she looked down across the valley and up to Bottle Cottage, the still figures of Fal and Roch lounging, almost, at the gate, a window open in the little sitting-room. She felt tears well up, wiped them away, looked down the hill to Home Farm. Empty. No activity. Once there had been a herd of cows, even in her time here; there was always a straggle of geese trailing about like an unwinding bandage; usually someone clanging on some

87

metal thing, a tractor, the reaper, whatever . . . in the yard. Today stillness, except that the front door was open and the writer chap was standing in the porch. Up early? A cup of tea . . . mug of tea. It would be a mug. Why, she wondered, did he wear his binoculars round his neck? At the ready. A keen bird-watcher, perhaps? Well, there were plenty to watch, and a heron somewhere along the stream.

It was a pretty house, the Old Hartleap: she had never lived there. It was abandoned as the 'House' when prosperity flourished for the Grayles in the eighteenth century and the farm demanded a dwelling for a bailiff. So a new Hartleap, *her* Hartleap, was built. Elegant, less rustic, a house befitting a family who had made a vast fortune from tobacco in the New World. But she still loved the old house the best. The very best.

It stood this morning, as it had stood for centuries, on gently rising land, behind a hedge of hawthorn and holly, sheltered from the east wind by an immense weeping ash. It was aloof from its clutter of corn barns, the dairy, half dug into the hillside for coolness in summer, the cart sheds and piggeries. They were grouped around it, not too close. Built as needed, they did not impinge on the elegance of the house, which was a mixture of flints and pale brick, silvered beams, a diversity of latticed windows, capped with a thick roof of Horsham slab through which thrust a clustered chimney stack. It had looked like this, rather comfortably hunched behind a ragged, daisied lawn, stuck about with writhen apple trees, in one form or another, since Edward-Atte-Lepe had laid the first stone on the site sometime before Canute died. In 1035. She knew all that, had been told it often enough, and had, in her turn, told others who had come to look with delight at something so old, so ravishing.

There was a sudden flurry of activity at Bottle Cottage. A

small group was leaving the cottage doorway. She instantly turned her head away, looked down to Home Farm, at the stream; at a lone sheep wandering slowly across the meadow below, chewing. Anything, but not the sad little cortège. She couldn't watch that.

Fal had been adamant that she was not to be present. None of the women. And then the writer, or whatever, in the porch moved out on to his bit of lawn, binoculars to his eyes. He wasn't watching birds. He was watching Bottle Cottage. She stayed watching him. He lowered the glasses, and somewhere, muffled by distance, there was the sound of car doors slamming and a car, eventually, pulling away. No other sound, and it had faded quite away as the car (she would call it that) turned right on to the Lewes road and was lost. Stillness. Just the sound of the stream bickering through the fallen timbers of a long-abandoned sluice gate. We must get that mended, she thought, and remembered that it was no longer their responsibility, and looking up at Bottle Cottage she saw that Fal and Roch were no longer in sight. They had gone in. She sat there for a moment, let the tears sting, then got to her feet, called for the dogs, who had disappeared, and wandered back to the house, stopping for a moment to dead-head some lavender spikes, making the fuchsia bells jangle.

What was the chap watching out for? May had said at supper yesterday that she had met him. 'He writes books, just rubbishy stuff. But he *has* written some thrillers. Crime. I've seen him on telly once. He's quite handsome . . .' But she had said no more. A conversation-filler at an uneasy meal.

Minder and Jess came sloping up the field, stood below the ha-ha, their tails wagging, tongues lolling. Somewhere on the lane the sound of a car horn. India saw two figures start to leave Bottle Cottage and begin down the path towards her. They were talking and hadn't seen her or looked across in her direction: calling softly to the dogs she moved quickly away and went down towards the drive to Hartleap which would take her across to Home Farm, keeping her out of sight of anyone walking over the field track, to the plank bridge across the stream. She wanted no encounters. She had, of course, to pass the pair of lodges at the gates, one let to a solicitor, the other to an accountant, both there only at weekends. No one was about.

The dogs, familiar with this walk, hared off ahead of her. When she got up to the iron gate at Home Farm and the dustbin, the bird-watcher seemed to have gone. She peered over the gate, saw the door was open in the porch, and that, slightly to her discomfort, the man was just coming out again.

He didn't see her at first, so she called out brightly, 'Good morning! You are up early.'

He stopped suddenly, a pair of secateurs in his hands. 'Oh. Sorry! Good morning. Yes. Yes, we are early risers here.'

'I'm your landlady. I suppose that's what you'd call me? I live up there, at Hartleap. India Grayle.'

'Oh. Yes. I met your husband – would it be? He said he was my landlord – in the first week we arrived. Asked if all was well.'

'And was it? I hope so . . .'

'All well, yes. Is it just plain Missus? I mean, I shouldn't call you Your Grace or Lady or something.' He laughed lightly, uncertainly. He was pleasant-looking, she thought, not sinister: good eyes, snub nose, square mouth, curly hair.

'No. Plain Mrs. Nothing a bit grand. We have had rather a wretched couple of days. I hope you haven't been disturbed by it all? A funeral.'

'Ah, yes. Well, I did notice a bit of activity – extra, I mean. Miss Stephens, died did she? We rather expected it . . . she was terribly frail.'

Miss Stephens. He knew her as that?

'She's been bedridden for a while. She had a wretched fall. It's usually fatal at that age. She was over ninety, you know?'

He had walked slowly towards her. He looked about eighteen, was probably mid-thirties. 'Yes. Yes, I knew that. When we first got here, actually the day I met . . . Mr Grayle . . . she was up in her garden. We had a little chat. She must have been pretty lonely? She said she was, anyway.'

He thought that Mrs Grayle was rather pretty. Had been. A light, flowered dress, cashmere slung round her neck, short hair, fluttering in the tiny breeze which suddenly riffled down the valley.

'She wasn't all *that* lonely, you know. One of us from the house was always here at some part of the day.' India's voice was cool. 'I think when one gets as old as she was, one does rather tend to exaggerate a bit. She wasn't exactly ignored.'

He was quick to note the coolness in her voice, snapped the secateurs open and shut. 'No. I know that. She did like a little chat though. I went up once or twice, to the cottage. Before she fell over. Rather a clutter, wasn't it? My wife, Isobel, is the reverse of clutter, she's very much a minimalist.' He was smiling. 'I'll give her a call.'

India protested. 'No, really! Don't bother her, I was just passing with the dogs . . .'

But he had already called to his wife, who came to the door, drying her hands on a sacking apron.

'Good morning! I'm dyeing cotton! I'm rather a mess, up to my arms in indigo!' A handsome woman in a long flowing skirt, head in a turban.

'I was just passing . . . No problems?'

'No. No problems, thank you. So far, anyway. Come up and have a look. I've painted out the kitchen and the big sitting-room. All white.'

India shook her head. 'No, really, I have to get back.'

'Do come in. Won't take a moment. We've put all your, what do you call it, nick-nackery, away. In a small room. Locked it up for safety. I like a clear room. I utterly loathe housework! Dusting and all that stuff . . . minimalist clarity.'

They had reached the front door. India, an unwilling captive, found that she had allowed herself to be led through the gate. 'I'm afraid it was all rather spartan. We just furnished it with bits and pieces. Basics . . .'

'Well,' said Isobel cheerfully, 'the basics are under lock and key. We brought a few bits down from town. My name is Isobel, by the way, Isobel Wood, he's Jake. He writes.' She laughed. 'But you see what I mean by minimal? Suits us.'

'Lovely in summer,' said India, looking at the plain white walls and tiled floor. 'Perhaps in winter . . . ?'

Jake had crossed to the door into the sitting-room. She reluctantly followed, Isobel behind her. This room was slightly more comfortable. She recognized the stuff which belonged to the family.

'Oh! The portrait . . . used to hang on that wall there.' Jake pointed across the room like some kind of guide. 'A cartoon for a portrait, I should say: charcoal and wash.'

'Yes. My father-in-law. The portrait is up in the house, in my husband's study. Have you put it with the rest of the – what did you call it – the "nick-nackery"?'

'Quite safe. But it was foolish to leave it hanging here. I simply hate being stared at, don't you? And the Brigadier – he was a Brigadier? – did rather loom over one.' Isobel was laughing in her most girlish manner.

'Very thoughtful of you. But, as your husband said, it was just a cartoon, and there is really, as you know, nothing of the least value here, so don't be a bit uncomfortable about anything. After all, *you* live here now.'

Isobel folded her arms, splashed with blue dye. 'Jake is terribly keen to get down to a biography, of the Brigadier, but he's getting no joy from anyone at the moment.' She decided on boldness. Surprise.

'Well, truthfully, my husband did tell me that you were anxious about that, Mr . . . er . . . Mr Wood. But – how do I say it? – he's an extremely private man, we all are here. He doesn't want to have the family *invaded*. Do you follow? I should put it out of your mind. I know that my husband has.'

'My publishers are tremendously keen.'

'Are they indeed?'

'Yes. As soon as I saw that cartoon thing I realized that we were in what you might call Grayle territory. It was a terrific thrill for me.'

'Very nice. But I fear you'll get no help whatsoever from this direction.'

There was a small silence. Isobel fiddled with the knot of the scarf round her hair. 'What a pity,' she said, drily.

'Sorry,' said India. 'It's a question of family privacy.'

'That's fairly definite, then?' Jake put the secateurs on a small table.

'Absolutely definite. Not "fairly", which suggests "conditional". You see?'

Jake nodded. 'Yes. Yes, I do see.' And he moved as India went out into the kitchen.

'I've been told, Mr Wood, that you write very clever books,' she called over her shoulder.

'Just novels,' said Jake, following her out to the garden. 'No big deal.'

'Much more fun than biographies! No research, or reluctant witnesses.' India was standing in the porch. 'Someone has been working terribly hard at the mowing! You've a lawn like a pool-table.' Jake patted his belly, murmured something about keeping in trim. India pulled her cashmere over her shoulders, called into the kitchen. 'Goodbye, Mrs Wood. If there are any problems, anything crops up, do get on to the agents, Manley and Frost in Lewes, they are frightfully good. They've looked after this place for . . . well . . . literally centuries.'

Isobel came out again into the garden, stood in the warming sun, tall in her long skirts, simple bodice with buttons all the way up, the stained sacking apron, blue-stained arms.

An odd couple. She was a good deal older than him, a better class.

'Very nice to have, what do they say, "touched base"? Good luck with the mowing, it all looks very splendid.'

They watched her turn left in the lane, call to the dogs, and walk very briskly up towards the lodges.

'Cool bitch,' said Isobel. 'Anyway, my little lad, you got your answer from her. No help coming your way. No cosy chats with the son. Now you know what "clammed up" means. Like a bloody clam. They all are . . .'

Jake leant against the porch. 'Beau Grayle, that's what the old girl up there called him. I had to do all the asking, mind you. She was pretty clam-like herself. Something strange about it all. No books on him. I've tried all the local libraries: Worthing, Lewes, Brighton, so on. As you know. Nothing.'

Isobel went into the kitchen and switched on the kettle. 'I'm having another mug. You want one?'

Jake eased himself away from the beam supporting the porch, looked up the lane. It was just possible to see the gates and the lodges, and as he stood on tip-toes practically he saw India turn into the long driveway. 'She wasn't wasting any time. Got up there in a record time. What I don't understand is, why the clamming up, why the silences? He was one of the most glamorous figures of the war. Two people have tried to write books, two people have abandoned them. Hugh Ripweed wouldn't give a reason, and General Someone or other, he said it was too difficult, he was too old now – all the research – and it was "probably unwise" to stir up old memories. Why the fuck did he say *that*?'

He took the mug of coffee from Isobel. 'You'll notice I'm not sitting this morning. You dealt me some harsh blows last night.' He was smiling at her with remembered pleasure.

She sat, wide-lapped, on her milking-stool, blew on her coffee. 'Want me to put something on it? Soothing? I'd like to.'

'Don't want you to come near it. It's still burning, you and your bloody Mr Rod. And it did bleed, you know?'

She smiled up at him. 'I know. I remember. But you had been very naughty, chattering away. But the cuddles were nice, after, weren't they? It was all lovely afterwards, you really know how to – after a bit of encouragement. Make a woman happy. I can never thank the teacher who taught you.'

'Mr Tillingham. And Mr Borges. There were two of them. Both hard at work. Tillingham was headmaster, Borges took us for PT. Professionals, both of them.' Jake was leaning up against the door jamb. 'Grayle and his son, I imagine, were both up at the cottage. To see her off, I suppose. The women obviously kept out of the way, or were kept out of the way. Ah well.' He sighed, looked out, up the hill to the cottage. 'That's that. I got quite a lot out of her, but she was too far gone frankly. She did admit that old Beau was "wicked". And there was someone else I haven't seen yet. Called Rufus. Apparently he's "tainted". In some way or other.'

'Ah! I wonder *which* way? Interesting . . . The funeral's when they'll all be gathered together, I reckon. You'd better find out about *that*. No good using your binoculars for it. Try and find another elderly blonde in the dairy. Chat her up, someone must know something,' said Isobel. 'You have a way with older women.'

'You really are lovely to me, all of you. Lovely,' said Loveday happily. 'I've been working away like a busy old bumblebee all this morning; even though I had a *terrible* headache.'

'Brave of you,' said Sophie with a quick flick at Rochester and Kathleen, who were sitting on the battered leather settee. 'Courage has given you quite amazing inspiration. Right, Roch?'

'Amazing,' said Rochester screwing up his eyes at the large canvas on the easel.

'Miss Tessier, dear, do you understand this painting of mine? Does it *come* to you?' said Loveday turning round, a brush in one hand, an apron over the long blue dress, the jet necklace glinting in the shadowy Wendy Hut. 'It's symbolic, you see?'

'Oh yes. I see. That,' said Kathleen leaning forward, finger to her chin. 'I *do* see that. All those coffins. It's very . . . very . . . very . . .' She stopped, started again. 'What I am *not* certain of is the purple. All those wavy purple lines across the bottom of the canvas. I'm not absolutely convinced that I know what they represent.'

Loveday looked at her in silence for a long moment. 'The Styx, Miss Tessier.'

'Ah!' said Kathleen softly. 'Of course. The Styx . . . How dumb of me . . . and the long green spikes up on top? Those are just fascinating.'

'They are the peaks of sadness in her life, the heights and the depths. And the yellow, all this blaze of yellow, is the joy in her life. Green is for sorrow, I feel, but there is more yellow in her life than green, you see.' Loveday rinsed her brush in a jar of turpentine, wiped it on a scrap of cloth. 'It's only a rough outline, of course. But it's wonderful that you all like it.'

'Love it. Crazy for it,' said Rochester, getting up and walking towards the easel. 'I can see that in the middle of this, well, this amazing amount of yellow, there is a figure, a tiny figure exactly dead centre. Right?'

Loveday lowered her eyes, spread her fingers against the apron, head down modestly. 'Yes,' she said softly.

'Which represents?'

'Me,' said Loveday.

Rochester cleared his throat. 'Of course! Long flowing robe, red hair –'

'Russet!' said Loveday, head snapping back.

'Russet,' said Sophie quickly. 'Well, as you have heard, we all think it is simply splendid; full of feeling. Right, Kath?'

'Oh sure! I think the Styx symbol is quite wonderful. Now that I've had it explained to me. I'm so dreadfully obtuse.'

'Some people,' said Loveday, removing her apron, 'some people see things in very different ways. You were not, I believe, familiar with Nanny Grayle?'

'Not familiar. No. I came to visit her with Rochester a couple of times, not more.' Kathleen tapped an uneasy foot.

Rochester joined her by the settee, put out a hand to help her from its sagging depths. 'Time we moved,' he said. 'A little glass of something before lunch. You two coming up soon?'

Sophie eased herself out of the chintz chair and joined them at the door. 'I'll be up in a while. Loveday is staying, aren't you?'

'I'm staying here,' said Loveday. 'I'll fry an egg or something. I just couldn't bear all those faces. Not today. I want to retain serenity for this.' She indicated the picture on the easel with a flap of her folded apron.

'Shall I see you again?' said Kathleen. 'I'm going back to London right after lunch.'

'I think it unlikely,' said Loveday. 'I suppose that if I had made the Styx symbol blue, you'd have known it was the River Styx? But I've made it wine-dark – that's what everyone says it is: the 'wine-dark seas' of Greece. They *all* say that.'

'Come along,' said Sophie, pushing them out of the door. 'Off you go, I'll be up in a little while. It's such a lovely day! Goodness . . . Roch? Roch, take Kathleen up to see the Forum before you go back. It's not far, and she'd like it. See you.'

Kathleen made an attempt to say goodbye to Loveday but she had turned her back and was staring, arms folded before her, at her painting, oblivious to anything else.

'Come on,' said Rochester. 'We'll go by the Forum.'

They walked through the trees together. 'I guess I put my foot in it, about the Styx, I mean,' said Kathleen after a moment.

'She's completely dotty. All her paintings are like that. Only she knows what they really mean.'

'Well, that's reasonable, isn't it? Goes for a lot of artists, I'd say – Picasso for one? Right?'

'Picasso she *ain't*.'

98

'No . . . What is the Forum?'

They had reached the edge of the orchard and were walking down to the stream.

'Just a ruin. It was a sort of summer house. Pavilion. But it fell down in the war: a flying bomb. It's just broken columns and lumps of stone, but the view is pretty good . . . I wish you weren't leaving so soon, that I didn't have to stay on for the funeral.'

'You do have to. And I *have* to leave, you know that. Paris tomorrow and the Louvre. I wish I hadn't got to go too.'

'And I'm sorry that the weekend was all snarled up.'

'Nothing got snarled up. I just hope that I wasn't in the way.'

Rochester reached out and took her hand almost absently. 'How could you possibly be in the way? A tower of strength, that's what.'

'I'm not so certain about that. Those old clichés . . .'

Kathleen held his hand firmly as they walked in silence towards the plank bridge. A moorhen hurried through the rushes on the stream bank and launched itself into the water, flicking its tail with fussy anxiety.

At the bridge Rochester leant over the rail and spat a gob of spit into the slow-running water below. 'Pooh sticks,' he said. 'But with spittle.'

Kathleen released his hand, leant on the rail beside him. 'Pooh sticks?'

'Winnie-the-Pooh. Childhood memories. A book.'

'I know. I remember.'

He hunched his shoulders, shook his head twice. 'A funny weekend. All upside down somehow. I feel disorientated. Events are catching me up suddenly.'

'Disorientated?'

'Ummmm. I feel different. Do I seem different to you?'

'No. Not really. What is catching you up? Do you mean about Nanny Grayle?'

'Yep,' he said and spat another gob into the water. 'Death. The great leveller.'

Kathleen looked back over her shoulder up to the cottage. A dragonfly looped round her head, dipped low, soared up, a whispering crackle of papery wings. She ducked slightly. 'Do they bite? Dragonflies? Or is that a "typically silly American remark"?'

'They don't bite. And it's not a "typically silly remark". Or American. But they don't.'

She was fully aware that he was preoccupied. She knew the expression on his face very well: lips pursed, a slight frown, eyes moving slowly about in his fine-boned face as if he had mislaid an idea somewhere. After more than a year of living with him, and loving him, she was acutely conscious of each mood, of every shadow of thought or doubt which crossed his face with the clarity of cloud shadows racing across fields. She knew that she must not interrupt, but that she must wait and let him arrange the pattern of his thinking knowing that, in time, he would come to a conclusion and present it to her for her consideration. So she waited in silence, watching the moorhen scurry up the bank with spread, green-webbed feet, feeling the sun hot on the back of her neck.

'Up at the cottage this morning – when Dad and I were watching the coffin business, doing our bit of Behaviour stuff, you know? – we just stood about not doing anything. Looking across the valley . . . there was a heron, just here along the stream by the dead alders –'

He stopped abruptly, folded his arms on the wooden rail, not looking at her. 'There was the strangest expression on Dad's face. I suddenly realized that he wasn't watching the heron at all, he was staring up at the house. He was very still, odd-looking, tight with bewilderment – do you know what I mean? What he was actually doing was willing Mum to come to him. To come down the hill, across the stream, to be there. To comfort him. There was an aching sadness about him which was almost physical. I'd never seen him like that before and at that moment I knew that I was not who he needed: he needed her desperately.'

'Did you realize why?' Kathleen's voice was quiet: she had formed a statement rather than a question.

'Oh yes. Yes, I knew why. Severance. Nanny Grayle was one of the links which held him to the house, to the land, to his youth. The links are beginning to snap now. He's losing his grip, losing balance, starting to drift. A bit like a man floating out to sea on a raft in a fog, without oars, sail or paddle. Quite lost. Mum is the sail, the paddle and the oars, you see.' He looked up the stream, lips tightly closed, eyes half shut in thought as if he was watching the raft drift silently into the mists. He shook his head. 'Never mind, never mind,' he said.

'I do mind. Tell me what I must not mind.' She was aware now that she could question, that, in fact, he wanted her to help him clarify his thoughts.

'Well, I know that it sounds a bit silly to say this, but I knew . . . I knew . . .' He looked away from her, brushed his hand across his face.

'Knew what, Roch?'

'I knew that he was willing Mum to come to him and how amazingly he loved and needed her and always had, and at the same instant I knew that I felt exactly the same way about you. I'm saying this very badly. My thoughts are all tangled up like wools in a basket. But the main thread is there. Can you follow all that, untangle things?'

Kathleen was perfectly still. A light breeze rippled the water below the bridge, hurried the hair across her cheek.

She pulled it back, and when she spoke her voice was steady. 'I can untangle it. The main thread is clear to see, don't worry. It's easy. Really.'

'It's a pretty funny way to tell you that I love you. Sorry.'

'It's a wonderful way to tell me. Thank you.'

'And you?' he said. 'What about you?'

'Me? You must know that. The answer to that.'

'How can I? You have never said.'

'It's for the guy to make the first move, so I was always brought up to believe.'

'OK, I'll buy that, even in our emancipated world. Just as long as you know how I feel.'

'I know now.'

'I'm sorry that it has taken me so damned long to say it: I hadn't realized it before, or maybe I was just taking everything for granted, as I usually do.' He stopped, turned towards her, his back against the rail, his thumbs hooked in the belt loops of his jeans. 'So what about you?'

'My turn to say?'

'Yours. If you want to. Otherwise –'

'Oh no! I want to all right, I'm not shy of that. I love you quite extravagantly. I have loved you, if you must know, from the instant that we saw each other at that god-awful party of Schnoodie Steiner's. You came across the room, pushing through all those hideous people, and said that my glass was empty and shouldn't you refill it for me. And it wasn't empty at all. Someone had just thrust a brimming cup into my unwilling hand, and you said anyway it was a ghastly party and would I stay close for a while because you were being haunted by an elderly gentleman with make-up and a glass eye.'

Rochester laughed with pleasure. 'Beverly Glenn! Oh God! I remember that, I do remember that. Did it really start then for you? Like that?'

'Like that. And it has stuck.'

'And you stayed close.'

'I stayed.'

'And could you, do you think, stay close for ever-and-ever-cross-your-heart-and-hope-to-die?'

'I could. Cross my heart.'

'Thanks. I mean really. Thank you.' He smiled suddenly, rubbed his eye with the heel of his hand. 'What a glorious morning,' he said, then turned and started across the bridge and began to climb the path to the top of the hill.

Kathleen followed him, smiling, perfectly happy to walk behind him.

The Forum stood, a lone pillar like a chalk stick, in a spill of rubble, tumbled columns and invading gorse. Below them lay Hartleap, the oaks studded across the sheep meadow in the park, the sun glinting on the windows of Bottle Cottage, a little cloud of Chalk Blues dazzling over the sorrel and toadflax. In the valley the stream wound like a silver chain through alders and willows.

Rochester swept the stone floor of the Forum in an arc with his foot. Dust drifted up in the still air. 'Look. See? A mosaic. Or rather there is, under all the junk. All gone to hell now, bomb first, then frost. Can you see it?'

Kathleen knelt, brushing the dust and stones away with her hands. 'A hart. A leaping hart in a circle of oak leaves.'

'Right. My grandfather had it built for his bride. Beau Brave's wedding gift. He got some Italians over to do it, didn't spare a penny.'

'It's beautiful. Black and white.'

'They tell me he was a black and white fellow, no grey. Not like me.'

'Knew what he wanted?'

'Saw that he got it. One day perhaps . . .' He let the

sentence fade away unfinished, scuffed the crumbled stones with his foot.

Kathleen was dusting her hands, her hair tumbled about her shoulders, the smile of contentment lingering at the corners of her mouth, aware that he was uncharacteristically shy suddenly.

'One day perhaps what? What were you going to say?'

'That one day perhaps it could be rebuilt. That's all. And *then* I was about to add "we" could rebuild it. That's what I was about to say, that it could all be black and white again after all.'

'Well, we could, couldn't we? Why leave the "we" out? Is that the word which bugged you?'

'Yes. It's a sort of declaration, isn't it? A declaration of intent for two people.'

'I suppose so. Do you mind?'

'No! Christ, no! It's only that, well, you know, I haven't really declared myself, have I? Do you follow?'

'In a vague way: are you going to?'

'Ummm. Well, yes. I mean, I'm not pushing things, honestly . . . Perhaps you'd rather I didn't, you might want to change your mind in a month or something. Some huge American, with a father like a Getty . . .'

'Not me. Go ahead, try me.'

'Well. Would you marry me?'

'I would if you asked me. Yes.'

'I have asked you.'

'Not directly.'

'Will you marry me, then?'

'Please?'

'Please.'

Kathleen fiddled with the belt of her dress. She became extremely preoccupied with its buckle.

Rochester thrust his fists into his pockets. 'Well . . . ?'

She looked up at him. 'I'd like to very much indeed. Thank you.'

He suddenly kicked the top off a molehill, scattering the soil around it in a fine fan. 'There used to be an old man here on the estate called Moley Jim. He caught moles in traps. But I never met him. He died before I was born.'

They stood looking at each other in silence.

'Golly,' said Rochester and whistled softly.

'Golly what?'

'I'm winded. Taken myself by surprise!'

'Well, you know . . .' Kathleen fished about in a pocket of her skirt. 'I have, as a matter of fact, "pondered" on the idea of you asking me that question. Only "pondered", mind you . . .' She found a coil of ribbon, snapped it like a silk streamer into the still summer air. 'It was only a lazy thought, you know, I always pushed it away behind all the other bits and pieces in my mind. It was not something that I *dwelt* on. I never thought that I'd ever really hear it said to me. By you.'

'But now you have,' said Rochester. He leant forward and kissed her on the lips. 'I think I'd better sit down. I feel weak,' he said.

'I'm fixing my hair.'

'Do it sitting down.' He pulled her towards a fallen column. 'There are, of course, problems.'

'There are?' She turned towards him, arms upraised as she arranged her hair into a hasty knot. 'Problems? Couldn't we lick them? Are they very serious?'

'Pretty serious, I'd say. You're rich, and I'm poor.'

'Oh God! Hearts and flowers. Is that really a problem?' She wound the ribbon about the gathered hair, tied it in a rough bow, and sat beside him on the fallen stone.

'Well, it is to me.'

'Why? Marrying me for my money? Is that it?'

'Yes.'

'And are you?'

'No! God no!'

'So where's the problem?'

'It inhibits me.'

'Oh, dear God! *Poor* Rochester. It really shouldn't, you know. Everything is tied up in trusts and bonds and all the rest, and I'm very frugal. And cheap. But struggle on, I'm listening. You said problems, plural, right?'

Rochester nodded his head towards the house hazed in the morning light. 'There. Right before your very eyes, Ma'am. A big one, I'd say.'

'Hartleap? Is that a problem?'

'I'd say so. One day it'll be mine. I never gave it a thought, you know. Somehow it never really occurred to me that it would be my responsibility, that I couldn't just hive it off to the National Trust or turn it into Prestigious Office Space. Men from the Midlands with Mercedes in the car park, you know?'

'I know. You never had a sense of, well, tradition, belonging?'

'No. None. That was all rubbish, never gave it a thought. It was just somewhere I had lived, home, but nothing much else. Fathers and mothers, you know, are supposed to be eternal. I thought that anyway.' He pulled at a grass stalk, began to chew it. 'Until this bloody morning.'

'And now what?'

'Now I have to face facts. I realize that. It all came in a blinding flash of light when I saw Dad's face at the cottage. And in that blinding flash of light, writ large and clear in fiery letters, was the word *obligation*!'

Kathleen flicked a beetle from the hem of her skirt, folded her arms across her thighs, leant forward looking across the shallow valley to the house. 'You know, that's another thing I thought about in the still of the night sometimes: if you gave a jot for the house, for what it stood for, or if you just considered it to be your parents' house and somewhere to come for weekends in the summer?'

'Got it in one,' said Rochester. 'In one. A convenience of a place, I didn't feel a pull of tradition or whatever. All that crap. Nothing. But now – God! It's so bloody big.'

Kathleen rubbed her chin. 'Well, it's not a palace, Roch. Not a Blenheim or a Chambord or somewhere vast. It's a *house* – after all, your mother copes with it on her own, even the gardens.'

'It doesn't run on a tuppenny battery, you know.'

'I know that, idiot. But I reckon I could cope too. When, and if, I ever had to.'

Below them in the park sheep were gathering slowly in the shade beneath the oaks, the soft isolated tinkle of a bell drifted up.

'I don't exactly make a mint out of my job, trainee chef!' said Rochester.

'So I am just what you need. I actually have a father like a Getty! Isn't that convenient!'

'Oh shit.' He brushed the rubble into a little hillock with his foot.

'Listen.' Kathleen touched his arm. 'Look at me, will you? I want to say it to you very clearly, and I want you to see, as well as listen. I love you. I love Hartleap. You have your duty to do and I have my duty to do. To you. I *want* you to need me as much as your father needs your mother. I *want* to be as much a part of you as she is of him, as much a part of the fabric of that house as she is. I know that it's a hell of a lot to want, that I'm greedy, but I'm willing to go all the way with you, all the way. Will you let me try? Could we try together?'

Rochester leant forward and kissed her on the lips gently. 'You are much too good for me.'

'And you won't think that I am just "a title-hunting heiress from New York"?'

'No. Never. Anyway, I haven't got a title.'

'And you are sure, aren't you, that you want me? Because I'm a sticker.'

'I'm sure. And stunned.'

'By what?'

'My own stupidity. You've been here up close all the time and I never really noticed, did I?'

'Well, it's easy to overlook familiar things. Like your big toe or little finger, you only miss them when they have gone.'

'Well, Big Toe' – he was grinning, his eyes sharp with pleasure – 'I won't take you for granted ever again, and we'd better be getting down, it's late.'

He rose, hitched his jeans, offered his hand, and pulled her to him. 'Kate. We'll keep this to ourselves, can we? Until the funeral and all that jazz is over.'

'We'll keep it to ourselves just until I get my ring: it's customary, you know? A nice little ring on my finger.'

'Oh Lor', a ring. Of course. I don't know how you can put up with me, I'm the late developer of the century. I've discovered a wife and an obligation all in one morning, and they've been staring me in the face for ages but I forgot the ring. I am overawed by the revelation.'

'Revelations', said Kathleen, looking across to Bottle Cottage on the hill, 'are overawing. They so often come out of left field.'

Monday Noon

Unity folded her *Daily Telegraph* and laid it on her lap. She was irritated and felt useless. Not her usual habit to sit out in the sun while, it would appear, everyone else scurried about. At least, she supposed they were scurrying. She had offered help and been politely turned down. There was a strange girl in the kitchen helping with the washing-up, and another who had suddenly crashed into the bedroom, shrieked, 'Oops-a-daisy! Thought you was out,' that her name was Sandra and she had to 'do the beds'. So she had got chivvied out of her bedroom. She had generously offered to make the beds but the girl made it clear that it was her job and she'd be pleased if Unity got out from under her feet.

'All signals go-go in this house today. Ever since the old girl up the hill went and croaked.' She had laughed cheerfully and started sloshing about in the small bathroom, running taps and whistling.

So in despair, and with intense dislike, Unity had come down to the terrace with her dishevelled *Telegraph* and her glasses, and sat crossly in a chair facing over the box-trimmed beds. Across the little valley below her, on the edge of the hill, stood Bottle Cottage. Still. Deserted. Windows blind, an abandoned ruin huddled in a thicket of neglected garden and untrimmed hedge. It seemed an eternity until Wednesday and the blasted funeral. An eternity. Staying in the house when Mumsie and Papa were alive was one thing.

Now that India and Fal owned it everything was very altered. It didn't 'feel' at all the same.

However, everything had changed after that war. She and Edward now lived comfortably in a square Georgian house near Chichester and hardly ever came to Hartleap. They were dotty, she reasoned, to hang about here. Home and all its comforts were only an hour and a half away. Why sit about in Hartleap waiting for Nanny Grayle to be lowered into churchyard soil? It was perfectly silly.

Today was Monday. She *should* have been telephoning round her little flock of 'girls', reminding them that they had a meeting that afternoon. Setting up tea for twelve . . . Edward could have been down at Bosham pottering about with his 'boat'. (She always referred to it as his 'boat' even though it was 45 foot, glittering with splendours and called *Dawn Spray*.) And here they were. Stuck. The quilting party was really reaching terribly exciting peaks. They were all working hard on their individual segments of the Dresden plate pattern, and she had a pretty good feeling that they might do rather well at the County Show in the coming month, but the very thought of Edward playing about with his charts made her restless beyond endurance. He had planned to sail over to Deauville for a few days, and she always adored that: blue sweater, slacks, deck shoes and all that playing about with rope. A delicious thing to do.

But this morning wasn't delicious at all: sitting idle, Edward trotting dutifully over the estate with Fal. Edward knew as much about estate management as he knew about baking a cake – bugger all. Anyway, she hadn't even *liked* Nanny Grayle all that much: tiresome old woman, shrewd and sharp-eyed, Mumsie's pet and, it had to be confessed, the saviour of poor Loveday. Oh, yes. Give her that. Essential for Loveday. She'd probably kept her stable in the early days . . . *More* stable. Unity realized that she was getting herself into a fizz of thwarted anger and deep frustration. She picked up her *Telegraph* and read the obituaries all over again. They were usually quite good in the *Telegraph*, but no one interesting seemed to have died recently; anyway, no one she knew.

Then she saw Stella coming through the open windows from Little Parlour, the Smollett woman with her. 'Hello!' she called with as much pleasantness as she could muster.

Stella said, 'Mrs Smollett! She just this minute arrived, so I'll leave you both to it,' ducked and bobbed and raced away as if she might have to witness a dog fight.

Unity folded her newspaper, stuck it under her chair, indicated another in which May might sit. Graciousness was now in fashion. With luck the woman might not stay too long.

'I got a taxi over from Lewes, we've been to the solicitors,' said May settling herself gingerly. 'Seemed the easiest thing to do really. Bob has gone over to see somebody's gardens. I really didn't fancy that, trailing about reading all those terrible little labels in Latin and trying to be intelligent about a handful of twigs from the Himalayas. Not my thing. Especially after that journey down yesterday. I *was* tired!'

She was a little uncertain of Unity. A half-smile trembled. It was possible that Unity might bark savagely, or even bite. She looked, in spite of surface pleasantness, subcutaneously furious. But a responsive wave of self-pity and sympathy spilled out.

'*I'm* half dead myself. Hardly slept a wink, restless, uneasy. A bloody cistern dripping *all* through the night, and then "the Youth" started playing their wireless for ages. I gather they were in the kitchen, but the noise sort of permeated the house – appalling! Thump, thump, thump for *hours*. No wonder they are all half-witted – heads *filled* with that nigger stuff. Jungle horror! You were very wise to go over to Lewes, calmer, I imagine, to say the least?'

May pushed her hair about, wiped her brow, slightly shocked by Unity's bluntness, but quickly recovered. 'Yes, calmer. We got a room in the annexe. But you don't really sleep, do you? . . . Strange beds, and after that rush down here, and Bob being so sad. She was really more his mother than his own. Vera was *very* cold . . . I was half awake all night wondering where I was . . .'

Unity felt she'd done her duty well enough, so she retrieved her newspaper, folded it noisily. 'Frankly I was sitting here thinking what a damned bore it all is, hanging about. I *know* she's your husband's aunt, but it does seem rather silly to be dragged over here, at *terribly* short notice. Of course, she was a part of the family, but . . .' She finished helplessly and let May pick up the unfinished sentence anyway she liked.

She did so eagerly. 'I agree, and *we* have to do that journey again after the ceremony. That's what happens when you die at the weekend. Have to wait about.'

Unity shifted uncomfortably. 'But until *Wednesday*,' she murmured. 'Probably got a backlog.'

May smiled kindly. 'I gather it happens. Usually in the summer. Anyway . . .' She decided to relax a little, lay back in her chair. 'Anyway, it's not raining. It *always* rains for funerals. Have you noticed?'

Unity shook her head and said that, no, she hadn't noticed, and wondered helplessly what else to try as a subject. Even though she had known May since the war, when May stamped about in breeches herding the cows, they had never been what one might call 'friends'. Perfectly pleasant young woman, but not really Unity's 'type', as she then termed it. Not her type now either.

May didn't give a toss. She had a tiny, deep-seated shard

of anxiety lying in the pit of her stomach. It lay there like a lead nugget. As soon as she got Bob safely away from this dangerous place the better. She looked down at Home Farm. There were lengths of blue and yellow cloth flapping, drifting on lines strung across what she remembered as the dairy yard. She knew what it was like to blunder across those cobbles on a dark, freezing morning, blacked-out, torch waggling, boots slipping on ice, eyes still gummed with sleep.

'What do you suppose all that stuff is, down there, at the farm? Like lots of streamers blowing. Blue and yellow.'

Unity looked down towards the farm. 'God only knows. Doing their washing or something.' As she turned to make some utterly pointless remark, India came out on to the terrace. 'Just in time, India! We were wondering why all those streamer things are flying about down there. Any idea? Someone making flags? Or kites?'

India shaded her eyes with her hand. 'No idea . . . Oh yes I have. It's our lady tenant. She's dyeing what she called her "batik". An awesome woman. Very much into arts and crafts.'

Unity showed a spark of interest for the first time that morning. 'Oh Lor', I know the type. We have one near the village. Got a shop: coloured witch balls, decoy ducks, log-candlesticks and frilly gingham cushions. Didn't last a month. She your tenant?' May froze into heat-induced silence. 'You know her? I mean met her.' Unity hung on to her bone. '*Do* you, India? You *must* do.'

India wandered slowly away, began dead-heading a fuchsia in one of the big urns. 'Don't know her. Have *met* her. This morning actually, for the first time.' She fussed gently among the leaves, fiddling, uneasy. 'Said she was dyeing her batik. Covered in the stuff, yellow and blue, all over her hands. Up to her elbows. Asked me in.'

Unity leant forward, 'And you *went*?'

'I hadn't much choice really. I was just walking the dogs past and they sort of grabbed me, marched me in to see the house . . . what they had done to it.' She had a handful of petals and seed pods, threw them over the ha-ha.

Unity had got to her feet, smoothing down her skirt. 'What *had* they done? Découpage lamp-shades, Cretan pots and baskets of dried flowers? Do tell.'

India had come slowly back brushing her hands. 'No, not that sort of arty-farty. Very, very minimalist: everything whitewashed, no rugs, no pictures, some wooden milking-stools, a scrubbed pine table, you sit on a sort of convent stool . . . very long with no back. Hell in the winter, I'd say.'

Unity shook her head, collected her raped newspaper and her glasses and, grateful to ease herself away, said that she was off to get 'ship-shape and tidy round a bit. And then I'll nip down and see if there's a bit of gin going spare? Maybe a little touch of the pinkers? I expect Edward'll be back by then, they must have covered all Fal's territory by now. It's about mid-day, isn't it? Yard-arm and all that stuff.' She didn't wait for an answer, clattered into the house singing lightly, very possibly in anticipation of her pink gin.

India took her chair, sat down. Smiled at May. 'I couldn't tell you what it is, but Unity makes me feel terrible – guilt-ridden, as if I had been deceitful or something. Dreadful feeling. I just fidget when she's about. She's always the Head Girl. Bossy. Know what I mean?'

May laughed, eased herself upright, no longer looking down at Home Farm. Relief flooded her. 'I thought it was just me. She *terrifies* me, really. But of course it's different. You are all family, I'm the outsider. I bet the only person like me she ever meets is behind the check-out somewhere, or weighing sprouts. And we've known each other for years, for God's sake! She was hardly in her teens when I got this posting, in the Land Army . . . can you believe?'

They both laughed at time passed. 'She doesn't mean to be so awful and overbearing – a real embryonic memsahib, no room for her now in India, no Empire, so she takes it out on her quilting-circle, or the village council or whatever. Mind you, there is a new breed of them, brilliant replacements, in Dubai and Kuwait, rather more glitter and henna, but she'd be a wow in the Arab Emirates . . . except perhaps for the pink gins. She'd soon get round that.' For a moment or two they sat together in contented silence, liking each other.

May opened her handbag and took out a tissue, patted her forehead. 'Sweating like a pig, I am. This funeral – *such* a trouble. The sooner it's over the better. Roll on Wednesday.'

India was looking idly down at Home Farm, the flapping, billowing streamers of blue and yellow. 'You were down there yesterday, weren't you? On your Memory Lane walk?'

May put the tissue back in her bag. 'Yes. Yes, I went down there . . . spent a large part of my youth – *and* my courting, come to that – down there. Your family had all moved into it, a bit of a squash. The girls' school took over the house here . . . Seems such a long time ago, goodness! No cows in the yard now, no chickens or geese, no smells . . . just that awful stuff blowing in the wind. She was doing it yesterday as well. I didn't see her, heard her singing somewhere.' She snapped her bag shut, put it beside her. 'I think I saw him. The husband? Nice-looking, much younger, I'd say. Just passed the time of day.'

India bent down and pulled a tiny root of grass from a crack in the terrace. 'As I said, *I* saw her, this morning. She is older, hefty, big bosom, flowing skirts to her ankles, bare feet and a huge plait wound round her head. No make-up.

Very basic, Mrs Wood, I think. That is the word. Earth mother. Covered in blue stuff. Perfectly pleasant, on the surface, just doesn't believe in wasting time on the "niceties" of life, likes getting to the point.'

May felt the nugget of lead in her gut tremble for some reason. 'What do you mean, Mrs Grayle. She wasn't *rude*, was she?'

India laughed, shook her head. 'No, not at all. Not rude, direct. Look, I'm going to call you May, we can't go on calling each other "Mrs". I'm India – it's tiresome but that's where I was conceived, I'm told. It won't choke you, will it?'

May shook her head, laughing. 'No. I'll try. But what did you mean about "getting to the point"?'

India lay back in her chair, her hands over her eyes shielding them from the morning sun. 'Nothing really. Just very direct. Polite but not going to make a great effort. Not that she needed to. I'm her landlady, she's my tenant for a year, it's all quite straightforward. Anyway . . .' She sat forward and looked at her watch. 'Anyway, I didn't waste any time. I've enough to do up here today.'

'Of course you have. I just wish we weren't so many, cluttering you up.'

India got to her feet. 'May, dear, no one is cluttering anyone up . . . or if they are it's Nanny Grayle, and we really can't blame her. I'm delighted that you and I have properly met. Years do count, you know, and this place is about as familiar to you as it is to me. Perhaps even more? You worked here, you must know every stone on the land. You knew it all long before I did.'

May had got up to stand at her side, and together they looked across the gardens to the distant swell of the Downs, soft in the morning. 'I didn't know every stone, India.' She tried the word and found that it slid out easily. She folded her arms, her handbag hanging easily from her wrist. 'I never even counted them. I swore a lot. But then I got shoved into the dairy. I thought I was being done a favour! Four o'clock in the morning! Four in the afternoon! I must have been mad . . . I *stank* of milk. Even today it's black coffee for me. But I loved it, the house, Hartleap, loved it passionately. I had wheedled away at Bob to get me a place here, I mean rather here than lifting potatoes up in Ayrshire or Norfolk or some other damp place. He managed. Somehow.' She was laughing gently as they turned and walked together to the house. 'What a long time ago it all was. I was a chicken, Bob was a strapping lad. Today he's a hefty fellow, stamping about with a notebook in someone's garden taking down the names of plants he hasn't got himself, and very likely never heard of.'

They reached the windows. India smiled wistfully. 'My husband is wandering *his* acres with Unity's bewildered husband. It's a hopeless safari. My husband has had to let all his land, it's not really *his* to show off and brag about, and Edward doesn't know an acre from a furlong, although he's terrific about sea-miles and halyards. It's futile, but it's keeping us occupied until we can all go back to being normal. Normal! God almighty, what on earth does that mean, I wonder?'

'Just being on your own again, quiet, doing your own thing, I'd say.'

'I'd say you were right. That must be what I mean . . . Mr Wood, the chap you met down at the farm — you did meet, you said?' She was probing delicately.

They had reached the long windows into Little Parlour; India pushed through the voile curtains and they stood together on the polished floor in the cool room. 'At Home Farm, yesterday. You met him?'

'Yes, yesterday evening. I told you, India.'

'Yes, I know you did. Did he mention any of us, up here, ask questions?'

May's little nugget of lead flipped gently. She looked about the long, cool room. 'Hasn't changed a bit. It's such a pretty room. And all those peonies, in that big glass tank thing, simply lovely.'

'Those are the last, I fear, for this year. Did he mention Hartleap?'

'He did say he was writing a book. But you probably know that, I expect he told you when you saw him? He was very persistent, I thought. I played the idiot, didn't say anything – you know? – smiled and nodded, but when I saw the binoculars round his neck and he said he was a "Grayle-watcher" I nearly passed out. Honestly. Well, it's a bit of a shock, isn't it? I think you are all being watched from Home Farm, India . . .'

There was a silence broken only by the soft rustle of the voile curtains over polished wood. India suddenly took up a small malachite lizard from a drum table in the windows, held it up.

'Pretty? Malachite. They say it is Fabergé but I doubt it rather . . . Mr Wood said much of that to me too. Mrs Wood weighed in – what I meant about her "getting to the point". Oh, they know who we are all right: call this "Grayle territory". He's desperate to write a biography on my father-in-law. Why? Is there something I don't know? Beau Grayle? – Bravery, eccentricity, fearfully handsome, a Brigadier. But that's just it: only a Brigadier . . . there were *hundreds* of Brigadiers. What was so particular about Beau Brave that some idiot down in Home Farm wants to write his biography?'

May stood silent, one finger tracing round a Baccarat paperweight.

'I mean, others have tried to write a book, but they

packed it in. My husband refused to co-operate. Apparently they had a go at him and he rather snubbed them . . . at Home Farm. I don't know why, except that *they* too were trying to write a book. So: they've got at Fal, at you, and me and who else?' India replaced the lizard.

Somewhere in the house there was a clatter of laughter and movement, a voice called out, 'Where is she?', and May said in a quiet voice, 'Mr Wood spent quite some time up at the cottage with Ada, he sussed her out quite early. Said she'd been "very interesting indeed". It's four of us . . . And *I* told my husband. I had to . . . That's five . . .' Laughter from the hall and a girl's voice saying, 'Oh don't, no! Leave it until a bit later . . .' May folded her arms. 'I simply dread my Bob getting near him. Dread it.'

India turned quickly. 'Bob? Why Bob Smollett?'

In the hall beyond Little Parlour Roch called out. 'Mama? Mum. Where are you?'

'Bob was Beau Grayle's servant. Remember? With him when he was killed.'

Roch burst into the room, laughing, excited, dragging a reluctant but joyful Kathleen behind him. He stopped suddenly, they collided together, her hair had fallen loose about her shoulders.

'Oh! Lor', sorry, I didn't know you were talking.'

India said quickly, 'Not at all. We were gossiping only, darling. May and I' – she deliberately planted the name so that informality should register – 'were trying to think of what to do with all the . . . furniture, up at Bottle Cottage.'

May said quickly, 'There is *so* much junk really. We'll have to get rid of it. But we'll have to go through it all first in case there's something . . .' She dried up helplessly.

India came in swiftly. 'Like some marvellous heirloom?'

'Yes! Exactly that. Like the bit of whatever it was, the lizard . . .'

'Like a bit of Fabergé you mean . . . What have you both been up to?' India sat on the arm of a chair.

Roch came across, leant down, one arm on either side of his mother's slight body. 'You wouldn't have a little bit of Fabergé about you now, would you? Not an Easter egg. A simple ring?'

'No. Not "about" me, I haven't. Only the lizard there. You don't want a lizard?' Suddenly she knew, from the brightness of his eyes and Kathleen's utter stillness. She was standing apprehensively just behind him. 'I haven't got a ring, you said? What for?' She was half smiling. May clasped her handbag to her side beaming.

Roch stood away from his mother, folded his arms. 'Well, fact is Kathleen has accepted to be my wife. But she insists on having a ring first.'

For a moment India was quite still. She said in a calm, level voice. 'True, Kathleen? Have you? He's not making it all up? He is frightfully good at that. He's not blackmailing you in public?'

Kathleen moved towards Roch, a hand on his shoulder. 'No, no. I did, *do* rather, *do* accept. I only hope you'll accept me?'

India was swiftly on her feet. Ignoring her son she embraced Kathleen. 'I have never found anyone, apart from his father, so acceptable to this family. I am so glad – I do hope you know what you are doing. He's inclined to Grayle madness.' There was laughter of a modest sort and India turned to May immediately. 'May! What fun, it's like a hand of Happy Families! Have we had better news on this vexing day? I'll find a ring – it won't be Fabergé, but it'll be just as binding for all that!'

And then there followed a kind of country dance with embraces and handshakes and Roch cried, 'This is a champagne affair!' and raced off to find Charles and Stella.

Monday Afternoon

As India pushed the swing-door open with her knee, Charlie, half crouched, half sprawled at the far end of the kitchen table, looked up slowly and then began to rise, slopping the contents of his mug across the *Sun*, spread out on the tabletop. India waved a hand clutching three dirty champagne glasses and told him not to move. So he re-sat slowly and watched her carry the glasses and a full ashtray across to Stella at the sink.

'You must be half dead, Charles. I am. I just collected these up from Little Parlour, they got left behind. It's all cleared now.'

Stella was peeling off a pair of yellow rubber gloves. 'Thank you, you shouldn't have troubled, really, Ma'am. I'll rinse those glasses, just give me the ashtray. Everything seemed to go very well, didn't it? Not much left on that poor salmon . . . just as well I made a "mess" with the bits of chicken the children left from last night's feasting – a bit of curry, a few prawns, and *that* all went!' She dropped the gloves on to the draining-board, rinsed the glasses and emptied the ashtray into the pedal-bin under the sink. 'I don't care what you say, stale tobacco stinks! It really does, no other word – *stinks*. And I was a pack-a-day woman myself! Disgusting.'

India was sitting on the edge of the table. 'Goodness, I'm weary,' she remarked as Stella wiped the glass ashtray.

'You do look a bit tired, I must say. Not your usual spry

self, Madam. Well, it's been a morning, hasn't it. Go up and have a nice lie down, why not?'

Charlie pulled his mug towards him. 'Have a cup of my tea? A small tot of brandy does wonders. Set you up no end?'

India shook a weary head. 'I seem to remember that the word I really need to describe myself today is "knackered". That's exactly what I am.'

Stella looked shocked. 'He *never* said that to you? He *never*! Charlie? You never said something as shocking as that to Mrs Grayle? You are beyond the pale, you really are.'

India straightened up. 'No. No, I think it was Roch who said it. I stole it, that's all. And it's absolutely how I feel. I think we all are. I really came in to thank you both for being so splendid today. You honestly were . . . And to let you know what the battle plan will be for tonight.'

Stella was carefully drying the glasses. 'It'll have to be fish cakes, you know?' she said quickly. 'I can just get enough off the bones if I mix it up with mashed potato and some nice fresh parsley.'

Charlie set his empty mug down on the table. India sighed. 'Just four tonight. Family. Simple as can be. Miss Unity and her husband have cleared off to Chichester. I mean, really, she's quite right. There is simply no point in them both hanging about here all this time until the funeral. She's fussed about some "quilting" group she runs. Her ladies are doing a big exhibit for the County Show, and she gets very fretful if she's not there to interfere. And they are both sailing over to France next week, and he's twitching about that, so I said, "Go! and be back at dawn on Wednesday."'

Charlie stood up. 'Well, I did see the car, heard them lugging the stuff down, but no one called me.'

'No, Charles, no one did. It'll get their lunch down to have a bit of exercise. The Smolletts are over at Bottle Cottage, to check the stuff there, and my husband has driven Miss Tessier and Sophie over to the station, and Roch went with him, so all we'll need is some tea, when they get back, but *don't* do a thing! We can cope with that ourselves, set up a few cups and boil a kettle. Easy.'

Stella was drying her hands. 'The Smolletts going back to Lewes then, are they?'

'To Lewes. I think they are happier that way. Mr Smollett feels a bit uncomfortable here. I absolutely see why. So Mrs Smollett said they'd go back to the White Hart. Wiser. Then they have to arrange to have the cottage cleared, the stuff taken away.'

Charlie put his empty mug in the sink. 'The whole lot wants torching, that's what. Kindling wood.'

Stella was pulling at a knot in her apron strings. 'So that'll be four. Well, I think we'll just make it. Miss Loveday's only had an egg all day, as far as I know. She came up for some bread. I gave her some cheese. So that's supper for four, right?'

'Right. Miss Tessier won't be back for Wednesday. She'll be in Paris. Sophie comes back tomorrow morning. Just up for the night.'

'They came and showed us the ring! Quite surprised, I was, very unexpected!'

'Surprised me too. They're going to be sensible, wait a little. The ring belonged to my grandmother, didn't fit me, and I loathe diamonds. It seemed just the thing.'

Stella took off her apron. 'And it stays in the family, so to speak. She's very pretty, I must say. And helpful – don't find that often. She'll run a good house.'

Charlie suppressed a noisy yawn, apologized and excused himself with a polite bob, and left the kitchen. Stella hung their aprons behind the door. 'I suppose there's been no news from Mr Rufus, has there? We *can* manage five, I think . . .'

'No, no news,' said India flatly. 'He's probably a thousand miles away. God knows!' She hesitated at the open door into the hall. 'Stella? You met the people down at Home Farm? The Woods? She's a bit daunting, he's rather nice-looking.'

'Not *met* them, but I know who you mean, of course.' Stella took up a cloth and started to wipe down the table. 'Seen him on telly sometimes, he's 'Tom Tiddler', you know? *Sunday World*? Journalist. I never read his column, it's all about film stars and people at nightclubs, in Rolls-Royces, drinking what he calls "bubbly". Sandra and Glenda read his stuff. Charlie too, I'm afraid.'

'He's a journalist? He said he was a writer when he signed the lease.'

Stella wrung out the cloth, spread it along the side of the sink to dry. 'Journalist means writer, doesn't it? I only get a glimpse of him, mind you, through their gate. He's always mowing when I walk Jess and Minder. Wearing a titchy bit of stuff as would cover a sparrow. Only he's not exactly sparrow-size . . .' She laughed, wiped her hands on the aprons.

India smiled weakly. 'But you've never *spoken* to him?'

Stella shook her head. 'Good morning. Hot enough for you?' That's all. Not spoken to, no. Ask Charlie. He often met him up at Ada's. Nanny's, I should say.'

India was still. 'Did he now? How often did he meet this Tom Whatever?'

'Only when Charlie had something to deliver at the cottage: medicine, some fruit, papers and magazines you'd sent over. You know? Said he was very unpleasant. Used to be reading to Ada! Can you believe? Very kind he was.

Well, she did get a bit lonely, and her eyesight was failing. He had a big notebook. I expect he was reading her bits of his new novel or something.'

'*Very* kind. She was getting old. Cataracts. They come with old age.'

Stella rolled down her sleeves. 'She *was* a bit on her own finally. Miss Sophie was so good – and Miss Loveday! Well! Words can't say how saintly *she* was . . . But I think Ada quite enjoyed what Charlie called "her new boyfriend". He often used to see him – not every time, mind you. "Ada's new boyfriend was up there," he'd say. We had a bit of a laugh. It was a kindly thought, entertaining an old lady.'

'I'm only asking, Stella, because apparently he's trying to write a book about my father-in-law. He's very curious about him. He feels he's got on to a story for his paper. I am pretty sure of that now. Something his "readers would be interested in". But why? It was in the war, thirty years ago or whatever it was. Why this sudden interest, why start all this curiosity? From a stranger? We really don't want that. It's the most terrible intrusion into the life of the family. Sort of tabloid stuff. He asked my husband ages ago and got a smart rebuff, and then they started on me this morning, both of them. The wife was rather worse. I never thought they'd try to get you and Charles entangled.'

'We're not *entangled*, we just passed the time of day really, and, as I said, *I* never spoke to him.'

'Well, now that Nanny's gone they may just look around for someone else to question. Because that's what he's doing. Ferreting out what he can. So just be careful, Stella. Beau Brave was very famous in the war, he was cruelly killed, and that's that. You might just warn Charles. I feel it's better to be forewarned than forearmed. If that makes sense?'

Stella was frowning, she folded her arms. 'I do hope,

Mrs Grayle, that you don't think that Charlie or me would even dream of discussing this family with journalists? It wouldn't occur to us to do so, in a thousand years.'

India swiftly noted the 'Mrs Grayle'. There was a reprimand in the phrasing and the name. She crossed and put her hand on the folded, freckled arms. 'Stella, dear, I *know* that. But, you see, it never occurred to *us*. I was terribly shocked. My husband had never even warned *me*. So I just thought I ought to warn you, that's all. It's a wretched feeling knowing that one is being watched all the time. "Grayle-watching" he apparently calls it. He's got a pair of binoculars. Frightened the wits out of poor Mrs Smollett who went down to have a sentimental look at the farm. I don't think it's at all a serious business, but we just don't want a complete stranger, a pair of complete strangers, raking about in the family affairs. You see?'

Stella said she did, and that she'd warn Charlie. 'Is that why he rented the farm? To sort of spy? Very handy!'

'I don't honestly think so. I'm afraid it was probably entirely *my* fault for leaving a portrait of my father-in-law in the sitting-room. It never occurred to me. But they saw it and realized who he was, and that they were in what he called "Grayle territory" . . . stupid of me. But he'll probably lose interest with no Nanny to question. That's what he was doing, you know? *Asking* her questions. He wasn't *reading* to her, Stella. He was taking notes. And she was a chatty old thing, if you remember, with a mind as sharp as broken glass. Alas!'

'Yes, didn't miss a lot. Charlie called her "Old Beady Eyes", but that was really because she never let him get away with anything when she was around. Sure I can't make you a little cup? No problem, it won't take a minute.'

India felt the thread of forgiveness drifting into the question. She shook her head. 'No. Really, no. You've been

126

marvellous, both of you, it was all a bit of an emergency really. We all knew that she would have to go one day, but it always takes you so by surprise, doesn't it? One is never prepared for death, even if you expect it.' She went across to the door. 'I think she had been so much a part of this family's life that she was expected to be immortal, stay on for ever. Nannies don't fall off the bough in this family, they remain inviolate.'

Stella wasn't certain what this meant, or where it was leading. She looked at the clock on the dresser anxiously. 'My word! After four already! Sure about no tea?'

India shook her head and went into the hall. 'Absolutely certain. Off you go, and thank you again.' She closed the door and stood for a moment in a shaft of sunlight which spilled along the corridor, her hand to her head in weariness.

'I have a desperate need of you, Fal,' she whispered. 'Do come home, oh, do.' Then she straightened up and walked briskly out on to the terrace.

Fal turned right off the Lewes road up the rutted lane to the house. 'We really will have to get them to do something about this lane, it'll be like a battlefield in the winter, ruts, holes. Someone on a bike could have a dreadful fall.'

They passed the low hedge of Home Farm on the left, no sign of life. To the right, up the slight hill among the apple trees, Bottle Cottage with all its windows open, a flutter of lace curtain lazily whipping and flapping in the afternoon breeze.

'The Smolletts,' observed Roch. 'Still sorting things out, I suppose. Funny place to park, their car stuck in the bank. Only place, I suppose.' Then he hit his forehead lightly. 'Oh Lor', I forgot we've still got Nanny's clasp-bible. You didn't give it back, did you? They'd better have it before they finally glide off to Salop or wherever they live. Shropshire.'

'Look it out when we get in. Leave it in the hall. It *is* theirs, I suppose? Not from some auction somewhere?'

'No, theirs – hers rather. Stephens. Large family. Goes back to 1789 or something. Originally belonged to "Miss Sophia Stephens. Her book, 21st May 1789". They were apparently literate. Or, anyway, Miss Sophia appears to have been.'

Ahead of them, neat on a white post, a green and gold Gothic-lettered sign indicated 'North Lodge'. Fal turned and drove between the two small cottages. One was shuttered, the other, North Lodge, a riot of delphiniums; and struggling over a trim, white picket fence a splendour of Rosa Gallica threw striped petals abundantly across the gravel driveway.

'It's all a tiny bit Pinner,' murmured Fal, and laughed at his own snobbery. 'It's been a day of surprises really. You and Kathleen, which delights me, and Unity and Edward clearing off, which brought *huge* relief to your mother, and now we discover that Sophia Stephens was able to write her name in her bible in 1789. Goodness me! Whatever next?' He turned into the big yard behind the house among the carriage sheds and kennels. 'I'll put this away, shall I? Won't be using it tonight, and you won't need a car, I imagine, and right now, early as it is, I desperately need a cup of tea.' He backed the Bentley carefully into the carriage house.

Roch said, 'It's not all that early. Five o'clock. Perfect time for a glass of champagne. There *is* one more surprise to come. You'll need it, Pa.'

Fal looked up apprehensively, the engine died, they sat in silence. '*Now* what? Why will I need a glass of champagne? What's happened suddenly?'

Roch leant back in his seat, threaded his fingers. 'Well,' he said, 'what's happened is that I'm not going up to London on Wednesday after the funeral. I'm staying here, and I'm not going to be a chef, or *cook* as you call it, and I am quitting Marcus Aurelius Ltd for ever, and please will you start teaching me how to take the reins and run this estate? There.' He unthreaded his fingers and grinned at his father, who was white with shock.

'Have you lost your reason?'

'No. I have regained it really. Lost it ages ago. All better now.'

'An aberration, brought on by Kathleen agreeing to be your wife? It's male hysteria. It happens. We do go a bit loopy when we are "accepted". You'll calm down. Just keep on with Marcus Aurelius Ltd. Always vastly useful knowing how to spatchcock a poussin, or turn in a really light omelette, or whatever. Do be sensible, Rochester. No point in going bankrupt trying to be a farmer.'

'You don't really believe me, do you?'

'Frankly no, not for one moment. A pleasant idea, but unrealistic. You have never stuck with anything you decided to do.'

'Completely realistic to me. Harmfully so. I suddenly took note the other day of a number of little things, when they were all getting Nanny tidy for the tomb.'

Fal got out of the car, closed his door thoughtfully, wandered out of the coach house, stretched, found a bale of hay and sat heavily. 'I don't think I can take a great deal more, Roch. We got Kathleen to the station just in time, Nanny's out of the way, and the Smolletts will be leaving soon and I did so want a cup of tea.'

'You'll get one. I just want to get you to realize that I actually mean what I say. I've talked it over with Kathleen. She doesn't want me to run a trendy restaurant at all. I think that *I* did. I would have lost her if that had happened. She was just hoping for me to come to my senses. And I

have. She's a very patient creature but enough is enough.'
He sat opposite his father on an upturned bucket.

Fal leant forward, hands clasped, arms on his thighs.
'You do happen to remember that the estate is leased? I
have no rights over it, not yet. All we own is Hartleap,
Home Farm, Bottle Cottage, the lodges and some acres
they delight in calling "the pleasure gardens and amenity
lands". That is all I can offer you, my boy. It might seem
a lot but it doesn't bring in a penny.'

'How long does What's-'is-name have the lease for? The
horsey guy?'

'If you are talking of Major Smiley-Dawson, and I must
assume that you are, I think he's still got another couple
of years to go. End of '76. Something like that.'

'Has he an option to purchase?'

'If I default. I mean if we can't find the cash. Yes. Yes,
he has the right to purchase all the land. It joins his. He
wants to enlarge his holding. An eager businessman all
week, a dashing showjumper every weekend, cherishing the
idea of a peerage. That sort of bloody nonsense. Sometimes
they take to polo. This one has struck it rich and wants to
be a "gentleman farmer". His father was a haberdasher,
made a fortune out of vests and ribbons, set up his son,
who is *not* an idiot. He bought the Lutterals' place next
door, as you remember, ten years ago. Came across with
an offer I was too broke to refuse. In simple terms that's
all you have to know.'

Roch laughed. 'I've got to know more than that, but it'll
do for the moment. I do *mean* this, you know? And I love
Kathleen in the same way, exactly, as you love Mum. I
didn't, at least I didn't know I did. At first it was just, well,
you know, sexually amazing, and she was fun, and then it
developed and we moved in together, we've been "an item"
for over a year . . . almost two. But it was really just

130

the other morning, with you, watching the heron, that everything suddenly fell into place. Like one of those games you find in your stocking. Remember? Shake it about and suddenly, before your very eyes, it makes a picture. A clear picture. I knew that morning that if I lost Kathleen I'd probably do something mad, drink myself to death – I don't know – snort mountains of "stuff". I even asked Sophie to go up to town with her today to see she was safe, got the flight to Paris . . . Stay with her tonight. I'm completely daft. I can't bear her out of my sight now, she really means that much to me. *She* does. I was thinking, Pa, that the next time I am "with" Kathleen, if you know what I mean, I shall be as shy as a schoolboy, as if it was for the first time. I love her so much that I shall be afraid to touch her. And we have not been exactly nun and monk during the last months. I cherish her and, what is more, I know that she cherishes me. We have a love affair going here. You and Mum aren't the only ones.'

For a moment or two there was silence. Fal shredded a piece of straw, Roch sat on his bucket, looking at a chain of ants hurrying to and fro by a hole in the crumbled brickwork of the coach house. Fal was wholly unconvinced.

'You haven't *said* anything, Pa. Nothing. Not even "good luck".'

Fal looked up slowly. 'No. No, I haven't, have I? What *do* I say? Of course I'm terribly happy for you . . . I'm supposing that Kathleen knows the facts? She knows you couldn't find the change for a tuppeny ice? I mean, she does know the financial facts?'

Roch nodded. 'Knows it all, said she's got lots . . .'

Fal looked at his son in undisguised shock. 'Rochester! You aren't marrying her . . . That's *not* allowable.'

Jess and Minder came wandering into the courtyard gasping. Minder lifted his leg absently, Jess pushed his saliva'd nose under Roch's hand. 'Well, she seems to think that to start with we should mend the sluice down on the stream, rebuild the old Forum, and that Bottle Cottage will take a good deal to make it really possible, habitable: baths, wiring, damp course, so on. A few extensions.'

'For whom?' said Fal mildly.

'For us. We'll live there. I said I couldn't afford it, and she said that she could. So. Look, I'm not about to start an argument at this stage of the game. Anyway, she'd win.'

'It makes me feel dreadfully uncomfortable, Roch, really it does.'

'Well, it doesn't make *her* frightfully uncomfortable. As she said, she's got lots of money, and I haven't. She wants Hartleap and me to go with it. So what's the problem? I'm not giving her up on account of money. She's a living part of me, the essential part. Without her I'd slowly die. I know that now for certain.'

Suddenly, in a swirl of floating silk and streaming hair, Loveday was there, standing breathless in the archway between yard and house, hand on heart. 'Naughty Minder! Jess! Leaving me with that man! Where is Sophie? Oh *where*?'

She was clearly distressed. Fal and Roch got to their feet quickly.

'She's gone to London, with Kathleen. For the night. Why, what is it?' Roch went towards his aunt, hands outstretched. 'What is it, Loveday. What man?'

She pulled her hair high on her head, a brown envelope in one hand. 'He calls himself Jesus but of course I know he's not really. He's just pretending, showing off . . . He suddenly came to my studio. He gave me this and told me it was very important. I had to give it to a "grown-up" in the family! I ask you! As if I wasn't.'

She handed the letter, reaching past Rochester, to his father. Fal took it with uneasy caution.

'There you are. It's all right,' said Loveday, her breathing steadying slowly. 'I have read it. It's all about Rufus, and I don't care about him anyway.'

Tuesday Morning

At the breakfast table Fal looked at his watch, pushed his chair back, and asked Loveday for the key to the Wendy Hut. 'It's quarter to, I'd better get down there.'

Loveday fished the key from round her neck and with cautious good grace gave it to her bother. 'Don't lose it, please. And don't play with any of my things in the studio? There's a big canvas on the easel. It's still wet, so don't go and smudge it or anything? And mind flying things.'

Fal looked up at her. 'Flying things?'

Loveday nodded, rebuttoning her mourning dress at the neck. 'Well, you know, Flies, bugs, things flying about. They'll get stuck on the paint. I can't think why I can't be there, to guard it all. I wouldn't *utter*, honestly.'

Fal was on his feet. 'Loveday, the fellow says it's private, it's about Rufus, and he wants no one else present. You'd put him off. Did you come up the path last night? I mean past Home Farm? Because I'll go down through the orchard, by the old Forum. I hate this feeling of being watched everywhere on my own land. I'll take cover under the trees.'

India sighed, poured another cup of tea for herself. 'Try not to be there for ever, darling. Tell the chap you're busy. Rufus can't be all that important, I'll bet you he owes him money or something. Loveday says he works over at Nether Dicker, in that hospice. How *could* he know Rufus?'

Fal kissed her head. 'We'll soon find out. I won't be

late. Roch, Sophie said she'd be arriving at Lewes on the eleven-thirty. Don't forget, if I'm stuck there.'

Roch buttered a piece of toast. 'Sure you don't want me to come down? Just to lurk about in the orchard with a mallet, in case he's a loony or something. You could always give me a yell.'

Fal shook his head and went out into the hall. Loveday put her head in her hands. 'Going to meet Jesus Christ! And they'll have a dreadful fight or something. Bash my painting. My *Requiem*. It's inspired. I really *was* inspired. If it gets bashed about by those two I'll *really* be very vexed. I'll never paint again. It was my masterpiece.'

India set down her cup. 'Don't use the past tense, Loveday. No one will touch your painting. It's on the easel, you said? Well, people will respect that. Fal isn't exactly an oaf and I am perfectly certain that if this man works down at Nether Dicker he's all right. A gentle soul, I shouldn't wonder.'

Roch muttered under his breath, 'Suffer little children to come unto me.'

Loveday snapped a look at him. 'I heard that! Smarty-boots! You say filthy things about me! So I'll just shut up. I'll go to my room and lock myself in.'

Using as much dead ground as he could between himself and Home Farm, Fal went across the terrace, to the Forum, and from there down to the bridge and the back of the orchard. He approached the Wendy Hut, ducking through low branches, and saw Jesus leaning against the crumbling porch with its scraggly montana. The man was looking up through the trees to Bottle Cottage. Fal called, 'Good morning', which spun him round. He was pleasant-looking: fair hair tumbling to his shoulders, a thin, but not wispy, beard; he was dressed in flared jeans and a T-shirt, and was leaning on a long stick.

Fal raised his hand with the key. 'I'm not late? You said ten o'clock. And here's the key.'

Jesus shook his head. 'No, not late. I was worried that *I* would be. I walked from Nether Dicker. Took ages.'

Fal pushed open the paint-flaked door. 'Come in. We can't talk out there. I might even be able to find a kettle for some tea.'

'Just water, thanks. I'm dry.'

The studio smelled of spilt turpentine, oil. It was sour with neglect.

'Sorry about this mess. It's not mine – my sister's. She paints. I haven't been in here for years. Apparently there is a "masterpiece" which we must treat with care. Just avoid anything with wet paint.'

Jesus unslung his modest backpack and dumped it on the floor. 'I've never been in here either. I met the lady the other day. I was taking a short cut, she seemed very distressed. I think she had an idea I'd cut her throat or something.'

Fal handed him a glass of water. 'It might taste of turps. She's inclined to get a bit muddled. One never knows where she washes her brushes. That all right?'

Jesus nodded. 'It's fine. She was sitting outside. Waiting for Rufus, she said. That's who she called . . . the name.'

Fal sat on an arm of the sagging chintz chair. 'Yes, she said she'd been waiting. That you had come up the track. Your name? Are you really "Jesus"?'

Jesus laughed quietly. 'Justin Christy – J C. I got stuck with that at school, and it sort of carried on into my life, my outside life. I don't know how it got spread about. It just happened. I'm a nurse. Some people find it comforting, the name, so I just let it stay. Know what I mean? If you are a nurse in Casualty you do meet all kinds. I told your –

is it sister? – it was Jesus because she was so agitated. It sometimes sort of calms them, disturbed people.'

Fal took the brown envelope from his pocket. 'She gave me your note. I'm her elder brother. How can I help you? Is it money? Rufus owe you money?'

Jesus laughed, set the empty glass on a bamboo table, shook his head. 'It's not money, nothing as simple. I mean, you know him? Nothing is simple with Rufus.'

'How long have you know him? Long?'

'Oh. Longish. Long enough to get embroiled, as it were. Know what I mean? He came into Casualty one evening with Mai Lee Ping. You know who I mean?'

For a second Fal looked startled, recovered. 'Yes, he brought her down here a few times. To see his old nanny who died the other day. She was a moderate success, the *first* time around.'

'She was a he. OK? Depended how Rufus felt. One day the wig and giggles, next day no wig, no giggles.'

'I *am* getting this right? You aren't pulling my leg – he?'

'I'm telling you as clearly as I can. He. Him. That's what I said. Rufus had very interesting tastes. He brought him into Casualty because he had had a nasty accident. Something about walking into a lamp, or whatever. They were with their telly crew, doing some kind of documentary. And this Lee Ping had had a "fall". Nothing really serious, I dealt with it. He was a bit mashed up. Rufus had belted him one. So the other guys on the crew said. They were laughing.'

'What was he that night? Him or her?'

'Oh, him. *Always* a him on the job. No wig. Brought him back the next evening, to check the dressings. My suggestion. And the next, then he was what you call "out of the wood", and Rufus asked me up to his pad. He was very grateful. I went . . . first time I ever had champagne!

Most impressive. Nice place. And madame was there, Lee Ping, couldn't have been kinder. "Look! No marks!" "she" kept on saying. "You are a miracle man. Not a sign." Lovely wig. Then there was a lot of kissy-kissy stuff and Rufus said that if "she" was really so pleased perhaps she'd show me her little act. So she did. Quite interesting. Funny people, Chinese.'

'And my brother? He suggested this business?'

Jesus was grinning. 'Turned the lights down, he loved it all. But I wasn't shocked. After three years in Casualty you get all kinds. We made a good threesome, you see? Rufus insisting . . . all the wine . . . I didn't mind – quite exciting. I gave a good performance.'

Fal brushed his face roughly, as if he'd walked into cobwebs. You mean that my brother had hit the . . . Chinese chap? There was no accident? Rufus did it? You can be sure?'

'Oh yes! Fist marks, not metal or anything. No, he'd had a bashing. Rufus, as you probably know, had a short fuse.'

'Fuse?'

'Temper. He had a very violent temper, and he was strong. I think he quite liked Lee; sometimes he was fine. He was a Hong Kong Chinese, British passport. Rufus used him as a replacement focus-puller or something, with some film they were doing. I don't know the technical details. They were together, oh, I don't know, a couple of years maybe. I've known them for a year. They went over to Germany in May. To do a film there, Rufus producing, as usual. He telephoned me from Germany the other day. Night, I should say. I was on the ward. This message came, the night before all your shenanigans started. Was it Friday?'

'Miss Stephens died on Sunday, if that's what you mean.'

'That's what I mean. I came across here to give you a message from him. But it all seemed a bit fraught. Your sister sobbing under a tree . . . I gathered your nanny was dying. She told me. So I thought it better to keep away, just then. Today is the only day I'm free – well, more or less: you aren't ever free in a hospice. There is always something to keep you busy.' He spread his hands, looked at his fingers. 'People usually come to die in a hospice, so you have to be around.'

Fal shifted, moved from the arm of the chintz chair into the seat. 'What message did Rufus have for me? Why didn't he call me?'

'Well, two reasons. Lee Ping is dead. He drowned at sea, the Baltic, I think. They'd taken a boat with some crew people for a recce. Can't remember where now. I don't quite know what happened really. Rufus and Lee were apparently swimming and then Lee got cramp and went down. And Rufus said that he went hysterical – he, Rufus. But it was too late. When they fished Lee out it was all over.'

Fal looked flatly at the blond-locked, bearded figure sitting quietly opposite him. 'Where is Rufus now? Is he coming home?'

'Point is, Lee was terrified of water. He couldn't swim.'

There was a deep stillness. Somewhere in the orchard a magpie scolded.

'But you said they'd gone swimming?'

'Ah. Yes. *So* Rufus said.' Jesus leant back in the torn leather settee, hands folded in his lap. 'I didn't get all the details. You know Rufus? Enough is enough. All you have to be told. Lee had drowned. *Fini.* Ask no questions – you'll hear a lot of lies.'

'And nothing else. Is he coming back to the UK?'

'No, that's what I was to tell you. Apparently they finish – whatever it is – shooting Tuesday. Today, right? Then he's flying out to Uruguay, to Montevideo, the moment they have wrapped or something. We had had an arrangement to meet. He said he hoped I would not miss him too much, take a rain-check. He's off on a big recce.'

'Montevideo?'

Jesus smiled a wan smile, ran hands through his hair. 'Yeah. It's a long way off, Montevideo. People can get lost there, wouldn't you say?'

'Is that the message? What you came to tell me?'

'Well, not *just* that. He called back that evening. Late. Sunday, you said? Father Martin was on the ward, I was off duty watching telly. He came along to say there was a call again, this time from Berlin. Rufus wanted to know if I'd contacted you, so I told him, about the nanny and all, and he was a bit shocked, and then he said, and these are his exact words, as near as, "Oh Lord. Forgot her. Poor old bat. But don't forget to tell my brother there that I'll be out of touch for a while. He *doesn't know where*, if anyone asks. Oh! And don't forget to go up and collect the McDougall's. It's got to be there still. Thank God you reminded me. I give it to you. For past kindnesses. Do it soon, flour goes mouldy in the damp, and that bloody little hovel is probably streaming." That was that. Then he said he'd miss me, not to forget to tell you, and to take care of myself. Not that he really gave a tuppenny toss about me per-say. But he did worry about the flour. Especially when he realized the old girl – sorry, Nanny – had died. I suppose your people will clear it all out, right? The cottage? So I came over as soon as I could get away. It's only Tuesday.'

Fal eased himself out of the chair, sat on the arm again, swung a leg. 'What is this McDougall's all about? Flour? It's a code or something?'

Jesus shook his head, grinned across the shadowy studio. 'Nah. Well, sort of. I understand it. He told me, ages ago. It's up in her cottage, in a big enamel bin marked "BREAD".

She let him stash it there. Didn't want to know. Told him to put it on the top shelf. She was pretty pissed off, he said. I suppose it's still there . . . She may have forgotten all about it. They do tend to wander when they start the slide, get really forgetful. I see it all the time.'

'What would she forget that worried Rufus?'

Jesus twisted his hands together lightly. 'Half a pound of cocaine,' he said.

The stewardess closed the galley curtains gently behind her, walked slowly up the aisle looking down left and right at the passengers with a remote benevolent smile, a school mistress supervising her class.

That's exactly what she looks like, thought Rufus. Hair in a tight bun, neat tie at her throat, legs like milk bottles, trim, efficient, deadly plain and a Kraut. He didn't care for Krauts, although he only had a hazy idea of the war (he was eight when it finished). He blamed them for the death of his father, whom he revered. Doubtless this Kraut woman was good at her job: could get you into your life-jacket without a whisper of fuss, calm a raving drunk on his first flight to Lima, probably even deliver a premature child in the last four rows. But bloody well plain.

The days of the golden girls who once flocked to the job had long since gone. They had discovered that their chances of meeting, bedding, even marrying, a millionaire, a major film executive or a member of the aristocracy were over. The people who flew normally now were as ordinary as the lot on the Neasden line. The stink of pre-cooked food and stale aftershave, and the untidy disruptions of their periods, began to get through to them and they started scurrying off to be models or croupiers, leaving the ranks wide open for a more 'motherly' kind of woman who coped effortlessly with everything from vomit bags to a fire in the starboard engine. Airlines preferred this type of woman: they were reassuring and every passenger flew, it was well known, with a little knot of terror beneath their too-casual exterior.

But Rufus disliked age. Plain people displeased him. Even ugly people were more attractive: they almost had a strange form of beauty in their very unshapeliness. Plain people offered him nothing. They were packets wrapped in cheap brown paper unlike the ones wrapped in silver, gold and glitter. Throughout his life he had always reached out for the latter and rejected the former. Of either sex. No matter to him that the plain package might well contain a mind of shattering brilliance, an intellect to rank with Einstein's, or just pure gentleness of spirit – he had no time to chip away at the dull façades. Drabness affronted him. In any case, he disliked Jews and despised gentleness as a form of weakness. In short, he preferred the peacock to the sparrow, the hawk to the wren. Sparrows and wrens, he felt, did not embellish him.

Although he was an exceedingly handsome creature by all standards (and knew it well), he was not a pleasant one; but he did possess, when he needed it, immense charm, which he used like a double-edged sword to hack through the undergrowth of mediocrity or any poor idiot who might have the misfortune to get in his way, for his charm attracted all kinds to him. He was as aniseed to dogs. Some, of course, had to be 'quietly dealt with', in his own words.

He disliked his own family greatly, always had done. The only member he excepted was his father. Even at a tender age he began to model himself on his glamorous, dashing, ruthless parent. And the parent in his turn idolized his final son but never lived to see him reach manhood. Which was perhaps just as well.

There was, of course, a reason for this hauteur, his

arrogance, treacherous charm, and general attitude to life and its players. He was five foot five inches tall, and he cared bitterly. His sister Unity, his brother Falmouth, were both above average in height. Although he considered them to be easily ignored – Unity because she was a coward and bully, Falmouth because he was airily, poetically unremark-able – he bitterly resented their extra height, and this soured him, causing him a deep resentment which quietly throbbed away like the start of an abscess. Loveday, nearest to him in age, disturbed him. Her apparent arrest, mentally, at the age of twelve or thirteen frightened him, although he tried not to let it show. Somewhere deep in his psyche he was afraid of her inadequate mind, just as the death of the two girls secretly terrified him. But they had died long ago, out of memory. Loveday was still *there*, living, before him. He often felt, as he grew older, that his parents had loved too well and too often, and that he, with his lack of height, and Loveday, with her impaired mind, were the runts of the litter. He minded their excesses deeply and blamed his mother, Mumsie, all his life.

The stewardess came back along the aisle behind him, a slow, dreamy walk. He sensed her presence and raised his empty glass without looking round. She leant forward and took it, full-breasted, heavy scent of female, her fingers pink, neat, cared for. 'I bring you one more?'

He handed her the empty double-measure bottle. 'My empty. Famous Grouse. If you still have it?'

She smiled. 'I will see. Can I do anything else for you?'

He looked directly at her. Smashed her with his 'boyish' grin. 'You *could*. But perhaps not here . . .'

He saw her throat redden, her face flush. She went quickly back to the galley and he let the grin fade, stretched back in his seat. The man beside him slept, his head jammed into the corner of the bulkhead and seat.

Looking back, the only single person that Rufus knew he loved without question was Nanny Grayle. The late Nanny Grayle as he'd recently been informed on the telephone by JC. That was a cruel rupture in his existence; now he'd left it too late to make his apologies for Lee. She had been horrified by Lee – not that he had behaved wrongly, improperly: just that he was a foreigner and she disliked all foreigners automatically. She particularly hated the Chinese part of him, the 'slanty eyes', she said. All that 'shiny hair'. Most of all the wigs. Didn't trust him, not a bit. She was stricken when Rufus had said, calmly, that he wanted her to like him, because he liked him very much. He was a good friend and good at his job. He'd come down again with him, and she'd gradually get used to him. She had shaken her head firmly. '*Never!* I'm a good British woman. It's wrong you carrying on with Chinese people, I can't abide it. All the years I've cared for you, and now you bring me grief in the evening of my life. How could you, cherub? To your loving Nanny, who has brought you up, cherished you, stood up for you? And now you ask me to keep something valuable for you? You ask a terrible favour and hurt me dreadful.'

But he quietly persisted, and she was forced eventually, very unwillingly, to accept the 'slanty eyes'. The wigs – sometimes on, sometimes off – she could never come to terms with. Didn't try. 'If you've brought something for the bread bin, you know where it is. Just don't show me anything. Have you been up to Hartleap?'

Very often he hadn't. The atmosphere there was hostile: India uncomfortable; Fal distant, civil and usually up in his study when they arrived; the children aware, amused, casual, a knowing grin on Rochester's face that he could have willingly erased with a spade. So he kept away when he had to visit Bottle Cottage. Loveday, shocked, wide-eyed the first time she saw Lee, curious and afraid, usually kept out of the way in her hut.

A different stewardess came briskly up the aisle to his side – a thin, dark woman – a fresh glass and a couple of small bottles on a tray. 'Mr Grayle, we apologize, there is only Black Label or J & B. You like to have both? Courtesy of Lufthansa!' Polite, smiling, firm.

He accepted both.

Nanny Grayle had always comforted him. Cherished him. 'Cherub' from her was a sweet word, not absurd. He'd lie back in her arms. *You are my cherub. Perfectly formed, just a small man, dearie, won't make a policeman but you'll be a wonderful jockey.* And he was. She had sat him on his first pony at three.

'He's too little!' Mumsie had cried always. '*Too* soon!' – tender, over-loving, with a crippling sense of guilt. She would hug him to her and whisper to him how beautiful he was, her eyes filled with maternal love, dull with the glaze of bewildered amazement that she had birthed a trout rather than a salmon. 'My beautiful little one,' she would murmur, and he would hold his breath dreading the following line which she would add, stroking his head: 'Hair as black and glossy as a raven's wing.' He curled his toes, and she invariably said it.

He'd got away from them all. School was a nightmare until he decided to cash in his credits. He played rugby and cricket brilliantly, his height not mattering a scrap, he rode like a dream, swam and fenced, was moderately literate, and fairly quick to realize that his lack of height was of no consequence when horizontal.

School was, he later admitted, character-forming, amusing and 'a breeze'. After that, with useful connections made, he discovered his place in life through television. In time, his own programme, *Grayle! In Search of . . .*, became a huge success. He exploded off the screen with extraordinary force and an overtly sexual maleness which drove women viewers to mild distraction, giving them the certain impression that he was indeed 'perfectly formed', as Nanny Grayle had insisted, but at least seven foot high, owing to a series of little boxes on which he stood when he was photographed among chunks of tumbled Carthage, beside the Victoria Falls or under the oldest sequoia. When possible he was astride a mule, or squatted on a mountainside in New Guinea, straddled a fallen tree in the deep jungles of Peru. He was never photographed standing with anyone, unless he was on one of his little boxes or *they* were standing in a pit. It paid off. He had a steady audience of eight million once a month, and spent his time travelling 'in search of . . .', which kept him happily exercised, in the public eye and far away from his idiotic family.

The crowd with which he mixed, all most carefully chosen by himself, were eclectic to say the very least. They accepted him easily and never questioned his often swiftly veering behaviour. They came when he called and were perfectly contented to wait on the sidelines until he did. They easily accepted Lee and his wigs, for example. If Rufus found pleasure in an ambiguous Chinese youth, so be it. And, it had to be confessed, wigged or brilliantined, he was attractive and, as far as anyone knew, discreet. The fact that Rufus might one day switch, and produce a 'Caroline' or 'Geraldine', some vapid piece of pink and white marshmallow, blonde hair, legs like sugar tongs, and a pea-brain which rattled in her skull like a bean in a whistle, did not alarm them. He was suddenly 'into' Barbie Dolls, that's all, and one could take a bet on the fact that its father was indecently rich and its carnal knowledge encyclopedic. He never fished in shallow water.

On the other hand, after Barbie Doll there very well

might be the dark Ulrike, a blazing-eyed, leathered Valkyrie from a wild and bosky shire, who rode like a maniac, matching him across country, as if she were swooping down on the bodies of the dead to collect for Odin. She gave him infinite pleasure in every other direction, for Rufus determined to vary his diet as often as he could, and swung from Gentleman's Relish to peanut butter with easy dexterity.

Poor Lee was, however, entirely separate. He was part of both, and as such could be exceptionally useful. His little Chinese 'tricks' almost overwhelmed Rufus until he started to get used to them, and then they rather palled. The wigs began to bore, in all their vast variations. The hair, Rufus was to find quite suddenly, was without life, hung dead from the scalp; curled, or combed in a waterfall, it was lifeless. He began to imagine to himself that they carried an odour of staleness and death and he requested that they should be worn less and less. Which distressed Lee and made the entire arrangement stressful. Without the curiosity of the wigs there was no interest. Merely a pleasantly lightly muscled youth who was swiftly becoming a giant yawn — a smothered yawn, as yet, but nevertheless familiarity was busily breeding contempt.

What was far more tiresome was that the boy was a clinger. Somehow when he was wigged and skirted, bejewelled and scented, this didn't seem to matter to Rufus at first. It was a novelty he had never experienced before, and it intrigued him greatly. He adored the look of astonishment and unease among people who were, for example, like his own family: correct, routine, well-bred, courteous but wholly shattered when confronted with the theatrical truth. Their startled eyes, their lack of any vocabulary whatsoever to deal with the situation, their total bemusement, delighted him.

But gradually, finding himself to be accountable for the boy from Hong Kong at every turn, disenchantment started to rot the rather insubstantial fabric of his desire. He began to wonder just how he could shed himself of his burden, and, as with so many relationships, the disintegration was disturbing and ugly. It crumbled into little silences, shrugs, sullen looks and, almost worst of all, tear-rimmed eyes – not his, *never* his: idiot Lee's. And then one day the scene he had dreaded being played was played out, and Rufus moved through it exactly as he had moved through them all: effortlessly, firmly, cautiously.

You don't love me! Not any more! I'm just a game for you, Rufus! You've got fed up with me, you want it all to end, don't you?

And Rufus, with great regret and sweetness, suggested that perhaps the time *had* come . . . But was stopped in his well-trodden tracks by the accusing words 'Polaroid! Wigs! Savage beatings! Hong Kong and an innocent in vicious Europe! Unnatural sexual activities! Destruction of my family honour!' etc. Swiftly Rufus had to adjust: soothing, calming – infuriated and astonished that blackmail had entirely escaped his mind, he made certain that it would not, at least there and then, go ahead – his arms around the shaking shoulders, his lips smothering as many of the clichés as he could.

I thought you didn't love me. That you were going to ditch me, Rufus. I think that I'd die if you did that.

And Rufus wished wearily that he would: there had to be some way out. Quite suddenly Lee had become dangerous. Smoothing the tear-raddled make-up, he reminded his sodden partner that they must put all stupid thoughts away and now prepare for the next *Grayle! In Search of . . .*, which was, as it turned out later, to be very timely. The subject was the 'Effect of the Wall on the Ordinary

Countryman', not the *urban* man. For the 'Wall' carved Germany neatly in two parts, 700 kilometres of vicious division, not just concrete blocks, but tangles of barbed wire and watchtowers strung across the fields and through the woods of toy-town countryside, and Berlin had had all the attention. Rufus was soon off to the north, to the Baltic coast in fact, to explore the problems the 'Wall' posed for the people of Lübeck, Travemünde and the countryside. 'We'll be near the sea, so you'll have ample opportunity to learn to swim!'

Lee had looked appalled, but was a little comforted by Rufus's strong arms and his caressing whisper of 'I'll never leave you. I'll be there to take care of you. Promise!'

Smiling happily to himself, as indeed he had been through all this meandering memory of the past, he signalled, politely, to the thin, dark stewardess, who was presently attending to the passengers in front of him. She held a bottle of water in her hand, and he indicated his need for a measure for his second whisky. She was at his side almost instantly, and he handed her his two empty bottles with a modest smile of gratitude; he did it very well. The sleeping man beside him, with his head buried in the bulkhead, dragged in a huge sigh through wet lips and moaned into his nightmare.

It had been a nightmare off the elegant white yacht, hired to tack around the coast with the camera crew and a rather dull girl from Putney who had a stopwatch and clipboards and coped with footage and focus numbers. No one had really noticed him slip away with Lee to have a 'swimming lesson'. Lunch had been eaten, a certain amount of beer taken, the sun was high, people, as he had judged, were somnolent, dozing in the still hot northern light. So when he and Lee paddled off in the little dinghy, which normally clung to their stern for any emergency, no one, later on, could really remember very much.

They did remember the shouts, the scream, the desperate struggles, and seeing the dinghy bobbing happily away on the portside. Empty. By the time anyone had come to their assistance, it was, as it had been planned that it should be, too late, and an agonized, sobbing Rufus, clutching firmly his lifeless companion in arms as rigidly locked as a banker's safe, was shouting, 'He's dead! He's dead!', giving a hugely convincing portrayal of anguished grief – all the time keeping the idiot's face under water. That's all that happened, really. A vicious knee in the groin, strong arms, and the wide, astonished, breathless mouth speedily stuffed into the heavy sea, gulping and swallowing, were all it took to extinguish a very unpleasant threat. He felt not the least remorse – just relief – but gave a moving account of tragic grief when the inert body was dragged from his tight grip. He held his victim tightly – he had to be certain no one spluttered to life on the yacht. And no one did. And the coroner, or whatever they were in Travemünde, murmured about swimming on a fully belly and muttered something about 'stimulants', which for a moment alerted Rufus into a beading of cold sweat, for he had induced Lee to sniff up a couple of lines to give him courage. Anyway, 'Death by drowning and misadventure' was what was noted down, and a deeply distressed Rufus Grayle was comforted down the steps of the coroner's office by the dreary girl from Putney, who kept whispering softly, 'There, there . . . no one was *really* to blame.' Which made him so angry that he could have struck her, but he smothered his rage, and quickly summoned tears, into her shoulderpads. As soon as that shoot was finished, a couple of days later, he packed up his things and now here he was, 35,000 feet above the Atlantic.

He couldn't see outside the window since his sleeping, drink-sodden companion in the next seat had slumped

across it, but he did know that he was fairly exhausted,
that he was heading west, that Ulrike would probably be
at the airport, and that it was, as far as he could remember,
only Tuesday morning and he hoped that Jesus had found
the bread-bin. Then he really could relax.

It had all been rather a near thing when you thought
about it. So he decided not to bother.

The sun sparkled and winked on the chrome and gleaming
bonnet of a dark-blue Mercedes wedged into the side of
the little hill just below them. Fal said, in a low voice, 'Oh
blast! The Smolletts are here already, follow me,' and
pushed into Nanny Grayle's overgrown garden.

'My name is *Christy*, remember? I mean, if you have to
introduce us. I don't want the piss taken.' Jesus's voice was
low. He dodged a swinging spray of vicious, overgrown
gooseberry bush.

'You'll be Christy. They are rather nice – he's a bit
taciturn, but she's very jolly.'

The windows of the cottage were all wide open. The
door as 'open as it could be', as May said when they
clattered into the crammed little sitting-room. She was
'airing the place, smells of decay. *You're* in good time!' She
was standing in a large pile of clothing, stuffing it into black
dustbin sacks. 'This is the bit I really hate, old corsets and
petticoats and god-knows-what-else.' She turned and called
up the narrow staircase. 'Bob? Bob, Mr Grayle has arrived,'
and turning round she said, 'I'm being very rude, I don't
think we've met, have we?'

Jesus shook his head and put out a hand. 'No. I'm a
friend of Rufus Grayle. My name is Christy.'

'Justin Christy,' murmured Fal, who had just caught
sight of the bread-bin on the floor in a huddle of china
candlesticks, Staffordshire dogs and shepherds.

'And what do you do?' asked May mildly, taking his hand absently, stuffing a bundle of linen bloomers into a bag.

'I work over at the hospice, at Nether Dicker. Do you know it?'

May shook her head. 'Not *yet* I don't. There's always time.'

And Bob came down the narrow stairs, a pair of old-fashioned binoculars in his hand. There were general polite greetings all round. May continued stuffing her sacks.

'Bob's taken up bird-watching too. I mean, why not? If that sod across the road is so interested in all of us, why shouldn't we return the compliment.' She folded a plaid dressing-gown, thrust it into the sack, then squeezed in a pair of old trodden slippers and tied the sack top into a knot. 'Are you the chap who scared the living daylights out of poor Miss Loveday?' Her bright eyes were fixed on Jesus's face enquiringly. 'You gave her a letter about young Rufus. She told me yesterday evening.'

Jesus agreed. 'I didn't scare her, she just sort of screamed and galloped off.'

'She does that if she's surprised. I reckon you surprised her, Mr Christy. Only she calls you "Jesus Christ" . . . but we won't dwell on that. Now, Mr Grayle, you look a bit flustered. We're not stealing anything, you know. Everything in this house belonged to Bob's aunt or his mother. Isn't that right, Bob?'

He agreed with a sigh. 'It was all Ada's and my mother's. Mum left her a few bits and pieces I recognize. The pair of dogs there, chest of drawers upstairs, nothing worth a damn.'

Fal cleared his throat gently. 'Rufus left a package here with Nanny, for Mr Christy. He came to see your aunt more often than the family I'm afraid. He was very close to Nanny.'

Bob laughed lightly. 'Used her as a sort of – what shall we call it? Guardian for lost objects? Not a post office, she didn't have to send things anywhere. I know! Left luggage office – will that do?'

Fal and Jesus were feeling vaguely uncomfortable, which was Bob's idea. May, even though she was still stuffing another sack, wore a polite smile and never took her eyes off Jesus.

'Well, it wasn't a general business, Bob. Something really between Nanny and Rufus. We'd no idea.' Fal leant away from the wall. 'In this one case, as far as I know, Mr Christy was asked, by Rufus, to come over and collect it. I brought him over.'

Jesus decided to help out, to explain a little more fully. 'Yeah. He called the other night. To the hospice. From Germany. Said would I come over and pick up something he'd left behind here. He's gone to America. He was very shocked about Nanny. Sorry, I'm afraid I don't know her proper name.'

Bob settled himself in an armchair, wrapping the straps of the binoculars tidily, securing them carefully with an elastic band. 'Wouldn't do you any good if you did know her "real" name as you call it. Any more as it'll do you to try and pick up your package, I'm afraid. Where was it? Did he say?'

'In a bread-bin. In the larder.'

'Well, it's all in the cesspit, down the garden, now.' Bob smiled cheerfully.

Jesus moved slowly through the clutter and sat heavily on Nanny's stripped bed.

'Well, let's face it . . .' May had found a bundle of much-darned black stockings for her bag. 'Let's face it.

You don't expect to find a half-pound of cocaine in the bread-bin, now do you? Not in a respectable house anyway. You didn't mention any of that last night, Mr Grayle, when we came across to have a little drink. I hadn't begun to deal with bread-bins and frying-pans and so on by that time. But you never said.'

'Because I didn't know. Mr Christy told me just now.'

'And you work where?' Bob's voice was deep, calm, interested.

'Nether Dicker. At St Benedict's Hospice. I'm a casualty nurse, or was. Now I work over at the hospice.'

May collected up a pile of aprons. 'What do you *do* there? I mean, if it's not a rude question?'

Jesus looked at her flatly. His ash stick tumbled across his thighs and fell to the floor. He let it lie there. 'It *is* rather. Rude. It would imply that I don't work there. Right? Well, all I *do* is stay close to them. Check the dose times, morphine – we try to keep them sedated pretty well up to the end – and then . . .' He shrugged hopelessly, looked up at Fal, who was now leaning silently against the wall. 'Well, then, I suppose I just hold their hands. Everyone, or nearly everyone, needs that at the final shove-off. That's all I *do*. Apart, of course' – he reached down and picked up his ash stick – 'from pee bottles and bedpans, or changing the sheets when they can't make the bedpan. It's no big deal.'

May, who had quietly filled her black sack, started to tie it up. 'I'm sorry,' she murmured.

Jesus half smiled at her. 'Not a popular job. They are grateful for anyone. After some years in Casualty at Chiswick and Staines General I thought I deserved a little rest. Know what I mean?'

May avoided his smiling eyes, which sparked with amused sarcasm.

Bob said suddenly, 'What did you think you'd do with

a half-pound of bloody cocaine? Get a "lift"? A big "high"? Help you cope? Is that what keeps you going?'

May flashed him an angry look and Fal moved lightly away from the wall. But Jesus was perfectly prepared. 'I don't use it, Mr Smollett. Seen enough of what it does on the wards. Rufus left it to me to collect because he'd forgotten it in his hurry – he was a bit pressed – so he told me where it was and that I could have it, and I know a *lot* of people who will pay me a lot of loot for what was in that McDougall's bag.'

'A pusher?' Bob asked mildly.

Jesus stood looking at him for a long silent minute, then he said, 'Yeah. OK. I'll buy that. But not cocaine. I push cannabis to my lot, my patients. *Cannabis*, right? It calms you down, the pain *seems* to ease a bit. I've got half the ward puffing away like Hornby trains. I give them a joint just before the morphine wears off . . . seems to help. But, you see, you need money to buy cannabis. It's illegal, do you believe? So Rufus's packet of self-raising would have been very handy. I could have flogged that. Thanks a lot for fucking that lot up. Can't be helped, can it? You wouldn't know . . . unless you were on Sunshine Ward at my hospice.'

Bob looked away, cleared his throat. 'Sorry.'

May looked up from her plastic sacks in anguished comprehension.

'We are a small place at Nether Dicker. Ever seen it? We can only take in about a dozen. No one gets paid. It's all on hopeful charity. The brothers don't get a salary, you see, and nor do I. We take every penny we can get. Sure, OK, I'm a pusher when it comes to the brothers and St Benedict's. It's no secret. That's what I would have done.'

Bob got up from his chair and wandered across to the window. For a moment he stood with his back to the room, his fists on his hips. 'We've all got secrets, every one of us,' he murmured. 'It's all right, I think I know what you mean, and I've chucked the lot down the lavatory.'

'Rufus would have a fit if he knew, cost him a bloody fortune. Brought it in bits and bobs . . .'

'What do you mean,' asked May, 'bits and bobs?'

'Small doses at a time. Whenever he could. That's why he came down here so often. He had a . . . friend, a Chinese friend, who sometimes helped him out. I mean, no one moved a half-pound of coke at one go! Blimey . . .'

Bob turned from the window. 'Did my aunt know? Nanny? She know?'

'She knew. Hated it. But she loved Rufus, as you know. He was her favourite, and she was pretty old.'

Fal said in a quiet voice, 'I think she had given up loving Rufus at the very end. I heard her, here, in this room, lying on that bed. "Tainted," she said. It was very disturbing, but now I understand. My wife and my sisters were pretty shattered. Still are truthfully. It's the kind of word that hangs about, it almost has an odour, it corrupts, like rotten fish or fruit, flesh.'

Jesus got up from the sagging death-bed, banged the floor lightly with his stick. 'That's about what he is, Rufus, tainted. Nothing you can actually pin down, just . . . well . . . tainted.' He shrugged hopelessly. 'It's a sod, really, all that money down the cesspit. Oh well, I never *expected* to have it, so it's no loss really; never mentioned it to the brothers either. Just as well . . . So that's it, then.'

Fal had thrust his hands into the pockets of his jacket. 'Well, quite honestly, since that appears to be the road we are taking, it's not *quite* all. I was here at the time. Nanny said that indeed, but she also said that he took after my father, that *he*, Papa, was tainted. I don't know what she knew that we didn't, but that's what she said. And I'm bloody certain she was right about Rufus. So, Papa? You know, Bob? You think he was "tainted"? Something inside, wrong? Why did she chuck all his photographs out of this house suddenly? Stop speaking his name? It was never off her lips at once time. Beau Grayle was her idol . . . So was Rufus, who was, she said, the spitting image of the "Master". So why? You were his personal servant all through the war, close to him at all times right up to the end. So why "tainted", this dainty word which burns like acid? Any idea?'

Bob shook his head. 'None. None at all.'

And May, with a quick smile, started to smooth and neatly fold a pile of pillowcases – a witless gesture, because the next thing she did with them was to stick them in one of her bags. 'I think we should all forget about Nanny's death-bed chatter. She was dying, she was old, and time plays tricks and I've got a pile of stuff still here to get sorted out for Oxfam or whoever. Let's set all that aside, shall we? Mr What's-your-name, how are you going to get back? No buses to Nether Dicker at this time of day – *I* know that – unless magic has happened here since 1948. And I bet it hasn't.'

'I'll walk back. Walked here so I can walk back . . .'

'It'll take you a good hour, but my son is in Lewes now, meeting the eleven-thirty.' Fal was worriedly looking at his watch.

'Don't trouble. I am used to it, walking. It's a pretty morning.'

Bob suddenly rattled the lid back on the bread-bin, chucked the binoculars into the seat of the chair. 'I'll drop you over. The car's right below, won't take a moment, and if I hang about here with that idiot across the lane pretending not to keep watch, I'll just go across and hit him one!'

May quickly came round her bundle of old clothing. 'Yes, dear, *you* take Mr Whatever back. It'll be good for you to get out. Then you can come back and stick those yellow stickers on the bits you want to keep.' She came over to Jesus and put out her hand. 'I'm sorry I was so hasty. I think it's wonderful about what you're doing and I'm sorry about the cesspit. But we really couldn't risk all that powder being left about the place. The removal people are coming on Thursday, after the funeral. You know how they poke about. And in a small place . . . ?' She shook his hand. 'Now, if you'll excuse me, a few more bits of clothing and then I'll start on the cooking things.'

'Which reminds me,' said Fal, coming into the centre of the room, 'I forgot the clasp bible. Sorry.'

Bob had found his car keys, pulled on a jacket. 'Bring it to the church tomorrow, it's really not important. But bring it if you remember.'

'A church', said Jesus, 'is a good place to find a bible.' He shook hands all round with great solemnity. 'Good-bye, Mr Grayle. Sorry about the panic, but now you know why? I don't suppose we'll meet again. No need.'

'No,' said Fal gently. 'No need at all.'

Tuesday Noon

Isobel came out on to the porch, an onion and a knife in her hands. Jake sat hunched in a creaking old wicker chair, work table before him strewn with papers, newspaper cuttings, his portable typewriter; in his hands a heavy ledger; on the back of his chair the binoculars hanging. He was sucking a pencil, staring blankly into space, oblivious to the world. The ledger was half open. A tiresome, almost familiar, sight to Isobel when he had started on 'working out stuff' for a book.

'I'm doing a Niçoise for lunch. All right? A medium onion like this, or larger? Last time you grumbled I'd used too much onion.' She waved it almost in his face. 'What size, Jake?'

He didn't look at her, chewing his pencil. 'Whatever you say.'

She felt a sudden surge of irritation. 'Well, *do* you want a lot of onion this time? Or just a –' She hit the table with the fist which held the knife. 'Jake! Have the good manners to just *look*! I'm talking to you.'

Then he did look up, vaguely, as if he'd been on a journey and had suddenly returned. 'Sorry. What is it? Ah! Onions . . . I don't really mind, you choose. I'm working, you fix it, O K? Got some olives?'

She stood up, her brow creased with frustration. 'Sometimes I really wonder why I bother. You'd eat a doormat. I've got the olives.' She shaded her eyes with her hand and looked up the hill to Bottle Cottage. 'That bloody place has been a sort of fixation for you. Thank God they're clearing off. The car has gone at last. Our landlord went skittering off through the orchard as if he was expecting an arrow in his back. I suppose you'd got him in your sights.' She laughed coarsely. 'Awful to be haunted by a pair of binoculars. Maddening. I mean for them, not for you. Fun for you, I suppose.'

Jake realized that she was not going to let him free. He shook his head roughly like a dog crawling out of a pond, settling his thoughts. He'd been miles away. He placed the ledger on the table, folded his hands resignedly together on top. 'Yes, kept my eye on him. The blonde woman is still up there. The big fellow went off with a thin, bearded chap. Shabby sort, with a stick. Haven't caught up with him. But the big fellow I seem to think I *have* placed.'

He opened the ledger, the spine cracked. 'Here is the list, long list. Guesswork in places, but I think the cast is more or less complete now that he's shown up. I think he's called "Bob", or "Bobbie", or "My Bobbie" as the old woman used to call him. He's married to the dairy-maid, she'd been a Land Army girl. Came here . . . um . . .' He looked down at the open ledger, flipped some pages. '*May Smollett. Land Girl at Hartleap, end of April 1940. Married under-gardener, Robert, Bobbie, Bob, Smollett. Presently lives in Shropshire*.' He looked up at Isobel, a light smile. 'You must admit it's neat and tidy, all my info. Just can't be certain that the big chap *is* Smollett. But she is, sure as hell, May. It fits perfectly. She'd have been very pretty some thirty years ago. Funeral's tomorrow, right?'

Isobel nodded. 'Tomorrow. Then they'll all clear off and what will you do then? No one to keep watch on. How will you fill your column, "Tom Tiddler"? Who gives a toss anyway? It was all years ago. A milkmaid and an under-gardener are hardly what you might call explosive stuff. Quite spoil your "work", no "bubbly", no suites in "posh hotels" at "£250 a night" . . .'

Jake raised a gentle hand. *"Plush.* I don't use "posh" since you explained what it meant. Super teacher, you are.'

'Well, it won't be much fodder for your beastly column.'

'I'm writing a book. A full, fat book on that ruddy Beau Grayle. You should have seen the milkmaid's face when I told her I was a Grayle-watcher. Nearly had a fit – red in the face, dry-mouthed. She didn't say a word, but I could tell she was petrified. I was a messenger from the Devil, I could be dangerous!'

'She's right there, my dove,' said Isobel quietly. 'You could be a messenger from the Devil . . . but I keep it in check, don't I? You know that.' She was trying to smile at him, but he was elsewhere again entirely. She was wasting her time trying to engage him. She shrugged at his silence, looked at his hands, joined together in a sort of supplication, a heretic before the Inquisition. She absorbed the idea with pleasure.

That's how she liked to see them: slender fingers, wrists bound, him kneeling before her. But he had lost her completely, and she knew when he suddenly said, 'They give themselves away so easily. She did, the old woman up there. Talked herself into a froth of dribble. Afraid I'd leave her, afraid of the dark. So I got "Mumsie" and "Beau" until I was flattened with boredom – only I wasn't. I was prodding and probing until finally she was getting more and more befuddled and spilling it all out. In the end she resembled a sack of corn, you know, someone had torn a hole in? Stuff just trickling away. But she was crafty. She didn't go the whole hog. There were things she *didn't* say.'

Isobel was suddenly uncomfortable, irritated, despairing all at once. She knew when Jake was 'leaving' her. And he was set to do that now, immersed in his book. He was, she knew, on summer leave from the wretched 'Tom Tiddler' piece. She had expected a happy, unblemished time alone with him. She'd do her bits of work, her painting, sculpting, batik work, and maybe induce him to resume posing for her bravest attempt: her life-size St Sebastian, bound to a tree trunk, as stiff with arrows as a porcupine with quills. It excited her to contemplate it, but he was less keen, was bored with the pose. The ropes cut his ankles and wasps and insects zoomed around his naked body. It was not his favourite way of spending an afternoon and pleasuring his wife.

'Well,' she said, 'I'll leave you to your plotting.'

He was picking through papers, photocopies of old news-cuttings, he did not look up. 'Yes, do that angel-face. Leave me to my plotting. Be lovely and kind, piss off, and go and make us a super Niçoise. Be a little love.'

She almost hated him at that point, turned and went back into the cool kitchen, chucked both onion and knife with some force into the big porcelain sink. Her eyes blurred with tears of anger, but beneath the anger, leaden and lethal, lay a loitering marsh gas of fear. She leant over the sink and, as if from a distance, a distance of years, she heard like an echo in a childhood shell, her father's unasked-for words of advice: *Never marry out of your class, Isobel, you'll come to grief. And never get hooked up to a feller far younger, without money. Don't panic, just be calm. Take your time.*

Silly old idiot. There wasn't all that time to take: she was hitting forty, she wanted a man, and she planned to have Jake Wood. They liked the same things, she liked 'instructing' him, 'making him over', as she privately said to herself. When she had finished with him he'd pass unhindered through the world, every A, E, I, O, U intact, every move gracious, there would not be a flaw to detect. She knew it might be a long haul. He knew it too, but was willing. With a postman for a father and a biscuit-packer for a mother, the road would not be smooth. But somewhere a gene had escaped from the grim ordinariness which had appeared to be his settled route. He liked her domination, lusted for it, and she liked that situation. No ordinary, cosy, chintzy woman she. Somewhere in her make-up also a stray gene was whirling about wildly. They joined seamlessly. As compatible as, immutable as, pepper and salt, oil and vinegar, prisoner and gaoler. She also had all the money: a strong, comforting allowance which left him free to play at 'Tom Tiddler' and her free to summon him when needed. There was not a lot of intellectual exchange, but that hardly troubled either. Oh, she had thought, there was time for Plato, Flaubert, Baudelaire and Giotto, all that sort of stuff – later, in the autumn of their lives. Give her time to read up on them anyway. But the disturbing vapour of fear drifting beneath her present anger seemed to be growing over the years.

When they married he was thirty-one, she seven years older. On the brink, if you like, but it hadn't seemed so important then. The tremendous excitement in discovering each other, of the mad sexual experiments, of mutual lust, had eased doubts. But she knew one day he'd get bored. He was not a constant creature. On the porch just now signals had flashed – tiny winking lights rather than giant explosions, but signals of danger in their outwardly serene existence. It had been a refusal in its way, a refusal to join her, to let her join him. He had never refused her before, shut her out. She started to assemble the Niçoise.

One day. Well, one day was here. She would cease to excite him, he'd become uninterested suddenly, one day he'd cease to 'obey' her, would laugh at the idea, would even laugh at Mister Rod, and she would know then that familiarity had bred contempt, that she had become physically distasteful to him, could no longer arouse him or command. When her splendid breasts began to sag, when wrinkles corrugated her firm arms, her elbows creased, then he'd go. She would no longer be able to offer him Juno.

In order to distract herself from such distresses, she deseeded the peppers, stoned the olives, and put on the kettle to skin the tomatoes. It would be all right, just a passing cloud of despair which, unlike the vapour drifting below her heart, would shortly disperse.

On the porch Jake, unaware of his wife's anxiety, closed his ledger, shuffled his papers into some kind of order, and saw the two dogs from Hartleap race past the gate. He stood up, moved into the sunlight from the shade just as Loveday, running like a woman from Bedlam, hair and skirts flying, arms waving, came abreast of the gate. She stopped in terror, hand to her heart, trying to catch her breath.

'Good morning,' said Jake quietly. 'It's going to be a very hot one again.'

She regarded him with overt fear and dislike through misting oval glasses. She still hadn't the breath to speak.

'Did I scare you?' He moved a step towards her, she drew back with a stifled squawk. 'I didn't mean to. I'm Jake Wood. I live here.'

She nodded quickly. 'I'm aware of that, thank you.' She gulped for air. 'Quite aware. I venture to suggest that you are utterly disgusting. Standing there stark naked before me, flaunting yourself! Be off!'

'I'm not stark naked!'

'I don't know what *you* think you are, but I am certain that *I* know what you are.'

'I know, madam, exactly what I am. I am perfectly

correctly dressed for a hot summer's day. In my own back yard! That's what!'

'Are you indeed! Well, I must say . . .' Her heart had stopped racing. Calm had almost set in. She hoped that he would notice that she was in mourning, black ribbon on her arm. But he didn't seem to. He ignored the decency she expected for the victims of cruel death. She was in mourning, deserving of consideration. She tossed her head and he suddenly snapped the thin elastic band taut across his thigh. She uttered a little cry and looked desperately up the winding path to Bottle Cottage.

He was grinning at her discomfort. 'In France they wear these all the time. In the summer. On the beach. The Riviera. It's called a "thong".'

She stared him out, holding a look midway between his eyebrows and hair line, shaking for fear she might lower her gaze. 'Well, this is *not* disgusting France. This is Sussex, and the beach is absolutely miles away, and if you will pardon me I am in a great hurry. That's why I was running. I'm in a huge hurry. Please let me pass.' She gathered up her ample skirts as he snapped the elastic again against his bare flesh. She moaned softly, backed away.

'It's *all right*. Quite safe. *Secure*. There will be no sudden tumble of splendours to distress you.'

She pulled herself together, let her skirts fall, stood with her arms rigid at her side. 'You are impeding my progress. You are an exceedingly vulgar young man. Let me pass at once!'

'I'm not impeding anything. Nothing at all. I'm within my own boundary, paid for monthly, you are on the path *beyond* my boundary, free as a fart. Pray, madam, continue.'

'You are vulgar, impertinent and disgusting! You might like to know that I am an artist, I paint. I paint a great deal. I have a studio in the orchard. You don't in the least impress me, sir. I have been to Florence. I've seen the *David*, seen the *Dying Slave* or whatever it is. Very boring. But I saw them. Miss Elliott made us go. Right up close, to sketch, so I'm absolutely unimpressed, you see? Quite unimpressed by your disgusting flaunting. You don't measure up, not one bit, and if you don't let me pass, unhindered, I'll call the dogs down and they'll savage you! Make a most fearful mess of you, I shouldn't wonder. Get behind your gate and let me pass instantly, or else! I warn you! One call from me . . . !'

Jake moved deliberately behind his gate, closed it, bowed to Loveday's rigid stance. 'Off you go, madam, no one will hinder you.'

She gathered up her skirts again and started off at a staggering hobble, clambering, sliding up the narrow path. In order to catch her breath halfway up, and aware that she had set a reasonable distance between them, she turned, skirts gathered, and shouted loudly, 'You are an insolent fellow! Remember the dogs! Or Mr Smollett! He's bigger than you, much bigger, strong too. Be warned. He'll wrestle you to the ground. Helpless you'll be!' She turned and went on up, slipping in her polished boots on the chalky path. 'Mr Smollett, Bob Smollett! I'm on my way . . . wait for me . . . there is another awful trespasser . . . protect me!' She slid on upwards.

Jake stood perfectly still, clenched fists on the bars of the gate as if he was holding barbells, smiling, nodding his head. '*That's* what I wanted to hear, that's *just* what I wanted to hear. Sod me!'

In the kitchen the running tap had made the conversation incomprehensible, which irritated Isobel greatly. She could hear the blur of the confrontation as through a waterfall. She twisted off the tap in anger, went to the door. 'Who is that? Were you talking to someone? The tap was running.'

He brushed his hands through his hair, shook his head. 'Got it. The missing link. That's Smollett up there. My "Bobbie", or "Bob", the old girl's beloved nephew. That's bloody Bob Smollett! She told me, in a deadly whisper: "*He died in my Bobbie's arms*. Grayle *did*." I can't believe *this*! That loony woman has given me exactly what I needed. Called his name! All I have to do now is have a little chat with him.' He came up across the baked earth, his toes curling against the heat, his body glistening with sweat, his sex, she noticed quickly, caught in its tight thong, juddering as he stepped up on to the porch.

She said, 'I don't know what you're talking about. ". . . in his arms"?'

'Yeah. A sort of "Kiss me, Hardy" thing, know what I mean?'

She brushed her skirt roughly. 'What does that mean. "Kiss me, Hardy"? *Should* I know?'

His impatience showed. He looked at her with polite, controlled irritation. 'You're the clever-dick. I'm the thick-headed pupil. Right? Hardy, Nelson, the *Victory*? A famous legend. Right? See it on biscuit tins, tea caddies . . . Got it?'

She rubbed one foot against another. He went to his cluttered desk. 'Got it,' she agreed. 'I remember.'

He whistled through his teeth. 'Great. Good. Clever old girl. Rummage around long enough, I knew you'd remember. "Kiss me, Hardy." *Couldn't* forget that.' He had opened his ledger, smoothed the pages. 'I am now going to set down the cast as I know it. May-Dairymaid, Bob Smollett, and the funeral is tomorrow, right?'

For a long moment she looked at him across his paper-strewn table, her anger mounting, watched him fuss and fiddle, rustle about in cuttings, drag the ledger towards him, flip through pages and then, startlingly, as if she had appeared from a burning bush or a hole in the ground, he said, 'Bloody hell! You scared me. I didn't know you were there.'

She smiled coldly. 'I've been here for ages. Wondering what you are doing. But I can see. You are getting "absorbed". Absorbed in the Grayle saga. I won't trouble you any longer, *maddening* to be disturbed just as one gets into things. Yes – you asked – the funeral *is* tomorrow.'

It was heavy and hot, no air, prelude perhaps to a storm. She sensed time stopped, waiting. She watched perspiration trickle gently down his brow.

'In your hand?' he said suddenly. 'You want help?'

Startled she raised a hand clutching an oval tin of anchovies. 'Oh, how silly, I was getting things ready to make up the salad.' She swung the tin idly, like a schoolgirl. 'I can open it easily; there is a sort of pull-ring; don't bother.'

He didn't. Grunted, and ruffled through his papers again, a hog after truffles.

'If you've lost your pen,' she said gently, 'it's there, in your ledger.'

She turned and walked back to the house, unnerved slightly: unnerved by his preoccupation, rather like a door being politely shut in her face. 'Clever old girl,' he had said. Well, she'd failed herself really, forgetting the 'Kiss me, Hardy' rubbish. Not that it mattered. Just extended the age gap. 'Old girl' and 'rummage around' hadn't been encouraging. He had dismissed her, probably unintention-ally. She suddenly felt redundant, fearful, uneasy.

She thought of a garden shed, a sagging, ageing garden shed, abandoned now, vine-covered, rusted hinges. That's who I am. She set the tin of anchovies down on the draining-board, turned on the tap, picked up the knife, heard the slap and scuff of his flip-flops on the tiled floor.

'A beer! I'm desperate for a cool beer. Found the pen, it was in the ledger. We have got beer, haven't we?'

'In the fridge. Second shelf.'

He stopped to open the door. 'Hey!' he said suddenly. 'Hey! What's wrong? You crying? Crying? Why?'

She brushed a fist across her eyes. 'Onions. They do that when you peel them. Onions make you cry.'

Tuesday Evening

Without really thinking, Sophie picked up the little bible and riffled the pages. A card fell out. She picked it up, put it on the bedside table.

'This yours, Roch? This fat little bible? I didn't think you were into prayer and that sort of thing.'

She was sitting on the edge of his bed and suddenly, instinctively, winced when the first violent flash of lightning burst into the small room, throwing everything into sharp relief. It died away. The room was momentarily still, faded. In the taut silence, before the first tremendous crash of thunder, she sat hunched, head down, waiting. Roch was half crouched by the windows. Thunder exploded above them, a colossal burst of brutal sound. The bible dropped to the floor, Sophie clapped her hands to her ears. The storm, which Isobel Wood had sensed that morning, had finally broken. The rain began, slowly at first, in hard penny-shaped splatters, and then grew into a frenzy, whipped away across the valley in racing sheets driven by great gusts of furious wind.

Sophie stooped and picked up the fat little book. 'I asked if this was yours.' She wagged it at Roch, who was now peering through the rain-rippled windows with cupped hand. 'No, no, it's not yours, I see: *Sophia Stephens. 21st May 1789.* Wow! It's *ages* old –'

Another searing flash of lightning scoured the room with brilliant light and made her duck again. Thunder crashed and rumbled above, giant boulders rolling downhill in a metal oil drum. It thudded and grumbled, clattering through the pelting rain. The windows rattled softly.

Roch turned and came away from his position behind the curtain. 'No. No, that's not mine, fathead. It says Sophia What's-'er-name. Nanny's family. I picked it up before that Irish nurse could pinch it. Didn't quite trust her. I'll give it to the Smolletts tomorrow, at the church.' He sat beside his sister.

The bedsprings protested mildly. Sophie closed the bible and set it back on the table. 'I was a bit worried that you'd gone Goddy or something, decided to be a priest . . .' She kissed his neck. 'I say! I *am* glad about your news. I mean, that's simply great, if you mean it.'

'I mean it. Took me rather a long time to reach the point, that's all. I just hope I'll be able to make it. Pa said he'd help me, but I know he thinks I've lost my marbles. Doesn't believe me really. Not deep down.' He lay back across the bed, arms behind his head. 'I've suddenly got a fixation. It's what I want to do, I *know* that. I think I've always known – just let it get set aside.'

Another blinding flash, the thunder cracked and raged, the rain fell in steel curtains, like a shining fireguard. Sophie leant against the bedhead. 'Kathleen will be amazed. God, she'll be relieved! She said so. Well, I mean, she said she had a hope that you'd get it out of your system, the chef business. She had images of lank, greasy hair from the cookers and grills, and Elizabeth David and Mrs Beaton lying all over the place. She'll be utterly delighted. She didn't know, did she? You hadn't said?'

'No. No, she didn't know. I never said. Ma looked a bit mizzy at dinner, did you notice? Perhaps not so much miserable, anxious really. Her eyes had that distant look of doubt, anxiety, you know? I think perhaps they both think I'm soft in the head, about taking on Hartleap and all that. Worried about Kathleen's loot. That I'm just going bonkers because she's rich and I'll live off her . . .'

Sophie had found the small card which had slipped out of the bible. 'Well, half the landed families of Great Britain married rich American ladies: the Curzons, all sorts of Dukes and things. You had to . . . unless you had coalmines under the croquet lawn. Anyway, Kathleen won't worry, she's *utterly* besotted by you. She spent the whole journey up to Town staring at her engagement ring.'

'I think,' said Roch, scratching his arm thoughtfully, 'I think that perhaps they'd quite like it if I ran a chic little restaurant somewhere not too far from Peter Jones, or Harvey Nichols or somewhere. So they could nip in for a bit of radicchio and some Perrier water. Free.'

Sophie laughed, laid the card on his stomach, got up and wandered away to the windows. 'You are daft! Really loony. I think it was a bit of a shock for them, the idea, that's all. The old don't accept changes quickly. And, face it, you've had so many. Having you run the place is a change. And it was quick – and put that card back in the bible. It fell out. God! Look at that rain! "Good for the garden", as Aunt Unity will be bound to say tomorrow . . . Oh Lord! We've got that to get through, the funeralischer-business.'

Roch had taken the card and was tapping it against a thumb. 'This was in the bible? As a bookmark, I suppose. But it's a bit weird, isn't it? Did you take a look?'

Sophie shook her head. There was another flash of lightning, a crack and roar of thunder, diminishing now; it had peaked out. 'No. I just saw it was a crucifixion thing. Very gruesome.'

Roch sat up, the card in both hands. 'It's Calvary, that's sure: the two thieves, and Jesus Christ on His cross in between them. But someone has scribbled things on them. Over them, I mean. Come and look.'

It was a cheap, mass-produced German lithograph, with 'Leipzig, 1908' printed in a corner: robed figures crouched in mourning at the foot of the main crucifix; the thieves, left and right, had no one to mourn them; a centurion holding a spear, a riot of flying angels, haloes ablaze, blood gushing redly from ugly wounds, a storm-bulged sky.

Sophie looked at it in silence. 'What am I to look at? I mean *particularly*? I can see Jesus. I suppose that's the Virgin Mary, she's in her usual blue, and all the angels.'

'What else? Nothing else?'

'Well, the soldier. I suppose he was the one who stuck the spear . . . and the robbers, or whatever, who were crucified with him . . . What else? It's going to rain, billowing clouds . . . That it?'

'No. See the scribbles, over their heads? Look, this is "RG". This one on the other side is "BG", and in the middle, over Jesus, it's just got "RS" printed with a halo round it. It's all done in Biro, see?'

Peering at the card, Sophie said, 'I see. Yes. So?'

'So this robber is *Rufus*, RG, this one is *Beau Grayle*, BG, and right there in the very middle dripping blood in a loin cloth is Robert Smollett, RS!'

There was a moment's silence. Sophie's voice was low. 'What does it mean? *Nanny* did that? Why?'

Roch put the card back in the bible. 'I don't know why. Something curious. A dotty old lady making scribbles. Remember? She said something odd when she was dying . . . you were there, weren't you? She said that they were . . . I can't remember. Something. I know it upset the old ones, Unity and Ma. *Tainted!* That was the exact word.'

Sophie shrugged. 'An old woman with her fancies, or

whatever. She was just doodling away in her bible, that's all. Give it to the Smolletts in church tomorrow . . . And, one thing, I nearly forgot: about tomorrow, watch out for Auntie Loveday. She'll be desolate; Nanny was her whole life.'

A torch wagged thinly in the open door; Loveday followed it nervously into the darkening room. 'She will *indeed*! Where have you both been? I've been so frightened, with this terrible storm, and there was no one, no one to help me . . . You are quite correct: "Auntie Loveday" will be *desolate*. Absolutely *desolate*. Prostrate. I am prostrate now. Where can I sit down? All those stairs . . . Why do you live up in the attics, boy? I must sit down. Help me, please be so kind.'

Sophie clambered off the bed, eased her slightly dishevelled aunt into a fat, floral-chintz chair with arms, and took the torch. 'You smell like a taproom, Loveday. You've been nipping away!'

Loveday was clumsily trying to rearrange the bit of ribbon round her tangled hair. 'Don't shout, Sophie. Don't *shout*! I've had the most terrible day, terrible.'

Sophie sat back on the bed. 'Did you have any supper? In the kitchen with Stella and Charles? Is that where you were? They said you were too miserable to come to dinner . . . was that it?'

Loveday, who had finished trying to fumble her hair into the twisted ribbon round her head, nodded mutely, hands lay still in her lap. 'Too miserable. I was on the verge of weeping. I still am. And Stella doesn't nag me. I had a poached egg.'

Roch snorted, put the bible on the table. 'And a pint of gin by the smell of you. Really, Aunt, you'll do yourself a mischief drinking so much.'

Loveday buried her head in her hands. 'Nanny said that!

Oh! Don't remind me! Nanny always said that and it's raining. I *knew* it would rain for tomorrow. She always said that. Mischief . . .' She bowed her head and sobbed miserably.

Sophie lost her temper. 'Look, Loveday, we've *all* had a beastly day. I came up from London on a bloody stopping train, Victoria to Lewes, it took hours. It hasn't been an easy day for anyone.'

Loveday looked up at them both wretchedly, bleary eyes, hands clasped. 'Rufus? What about Rufus? What did that Jesus person want, bringing the letter to Fal? *They* won't say, just that it was a silly little matter. But what was it? Why won't they tell me.'

'Frightened you'll be upset I suppose,' said Roch lamely. 'Rufus. Rufus owed the Jesus chap money. Right, Sophie?'

Sophie caught on quickly, 'Yes, money. He owed him money. He wanted it back. Naturally, um, it was a *lot* of money. Well, *quite* a lot.'

Loveday pushed a straggle of hair from her cheek. 'Why did they go up to the cottage. I know they did. I went there and that woman was throwing all Nanny's clothes away. In bags. I got a pinafore. She let me have a pinafore, as a keepsake. But I know that they were there. Why?'

There was a dull silence, far away a distant rumble and tumble of thunder as the storm trailed away across the Weald. The rain hissed gently, now pattering on the gabled roof above.

'Why?' repeated Loveday.

'I think . . .' said Roch. 'I don't know, but I *think*, that Rufus used to see Nanny quite often. And, um, I think he, um, left a sort of I O U thing with her. To keep for the Jesus person. That's what I think, anyway.'

Loveday looked singularly unconvinced. 'How did Rufus *know* that awful creature? He's just a tramp, a trespasser.

What would Rufus possibly have to do with someone like that?'

'He's a nurse. He's a nurse at the hospice place, used to be in casualty in London. Maybe Rufus met him there? I mean, maybe.' Roch flailed around. He was not adept at lying, and was worse at having to lie on the spur of the moment.

Sophie quickly followed in; she started to distract her aunt by tidying up her hair, soothing her with gentle words. 'Don't fuss, Loveday. Rufus knew all kinds of odd people, you know that. Remember the Chinese person he brought here? And there must have been lots of others.' She took her aunt gently by the arm. 'Now come along, I'll get you down to bed. Where is the gin bottle? Down in the Wendy house still? Or did you have some at supper in the kitchen?'

Loveday got to her feet unsteadily, her face wan and tear-streaked. She wiped her nose with the back of her hand. 'Awful people. Rufus knew awful people, that's what Nanny said always. "Rufus knows unsuitable people, my lambie." She meant me, of course. She used to call me "lambie". I've got a half-bottle, in my bag.'

Hanging from the crook of her elbow, a woven Greek bag, tourist kitsch. Sophie found the empty gin bottle among a litter of screwed-up Kleenex, a stub of lipstick, hairpins and a jar of Nivea cold cream.

'You drink all that? Tonight?' Roch sounded amazed.

Loveday nodded bleakly. 'I'm not certain. I think I did, and it hasn't done me any good, no good at all. But I have worried all day about that man and why he gave me the letter . . . all day.'

Sophie started her on her way to the door. Drunk she was, but like some drunks she knew exactly where she was once she was pointed in a familiar direction – this time the way to her bedroom. She let herself be guided by Sophie quietly down the stairs.

'The torch. Put the torch in my bag. You *are* good to me, I will have to let you be my guide from now on. I'll be all alone, you see . . . You won't go to look after lepers in Africa or somewhere, will you? Promise?'

'I promise. For the moment. Come along.' At the foot of the stairs she stopped and called up to Roch and said goodnight.

Loveday stood like a weary old Labrador, draggled, head hanging, her tall body helpless and fightless, the bag of Greek tat swinging loosely in one hand.

'He's a darling boy. Tell him I love him too,' she mumbled, and shuffled after Sophie.

Her room was shadowy, dimmed by closed shutters, draped with chiffon scarves: in one corner a large brass bed, a table in the middle of the floor covered with opened books, a jug with dried teasels, a half-eaten cake on a forgotten plate; along the pillows on the bed, ranged in a jumbled assortment, a row of various teddy bears.

'Sit down, Loveday. I'll get your boots off.'

Loveday sat obediently on the bed, lay back, tears spilling soundlessly down her cheeks. She waved her arms slowly from side to side, like underwater weeds, her hands spread and closed. 'So kind and loving, you are, Sophie. *So* kind . . . There was a naked man down at the Farm, quite naked. Flaunting himself at me . . . flaunting himself . . .'

Sophie stopped for a moment, stared at her aunt. 'What naked man?'

'At the Farm. By the gate. I told him to be off. I said I'd been to Florence . . .' Sophie continued pulling at the boots. 'I would like to go back to Florence . . . Perhaps we could ask Miss Elliott, she took us last time . . . Or Rome? Rome would be lovely.' Suddenly she started to sing quietly under her breath. 'I'm forever blowing bubbles, pretty bubbles in the air . . .'

Sophie wrenched off one boot, slung it, started on the other. 'God alone knows why you have to wear these bloody things all day.'

Loveday drifted back slowly and spoke clearly and precisely as if to a deaf person. 'I-wear-them-because-of-snakes. And-because-of-naked-men-flaunting-themselves – I can kick them!' Her tear-streaked cheeks were sagged with tiredness. It was only then, at that moment, that Sophie remembered that her aunt was not a child.

'Come along, Loveday.' Her voice was gentle. 'There you are, no boots. Now, do you want your slippers? You'll go to bed soon, won't you? It's late.'

'I'll go to bed soon. Just have a little sip-ette. Is there some left for a tiny sip-ette? I dote on ginny-gin-gin . . . It'll make me sleep, and I *must* sleep.' She sat up suddenly on the edge of the bed, groaned loudly, clutched the bedcover with both hands. 'I'm going to be sick. Get me to the bathroom.' She reached out a shaking hand. 'Get me there, show me where . . .'

Up in his bedroom in the attics, Roch looked thoughtfully at the Leipzig card, and then slid it gently into the fat little bible.

'Wonder what that was all about?'

In Little Parlour, India unwrapped a bittermint and began to eat it. She offered the box to Fal, who was reading the *Brighton Argus* by the light of one lamp at his side. 'Want a bittermint? It's the last one.'

He shook his head, turned a page.

'But you love bittermints.'

'Not now, I'm reading.'

'I'll have it then.' She pushed the empty box into a

wastepaper basket and wandered across to the windows. The sky was clearing, evening had drifted in from the west, thin strips of yellow in the sky: watered, pale. A star hung high above the ridge of the hill, trembling diamond-bright. 'The storm has gone, it'll be quite all right for tomorrow, you'll see.' She was restless, tired, uneasy. She ate the last bittermint. 'What on earth is so fascinating in the *Brighton Argus*?'

'The IRA have lobbed a bomb into the Tower, the Turks are presently invading Cyprus . . . not a great deal.'

India was leaning against the window, cheek against the cool glass. 'I don't believe today.'

'I don't believe today either.' He folded the paper, laid it on his lap. 'My son decides to train as Squire. My brother murders a Chinese transvestite. There is half a pound of cocaine chucked down the cesspit. I meet Jesus Christ in the Wendy Hut and have a happy little chat. It's been that sort of day. Utterly normal.'

'Do you think it's true? About the Chinese person?'

'It's what I've been told. It's true about the cocaine. That came from Bob Smollett, and he did the deed. Added to which, my dearest heart, there is a mad pair down at Home Farm trying to find out just what Daddy *did* do in the war. I mean' – he threw the paper on to a chair – 'what the hell *is* all this? What do I not know? Eh? What do I not know? What am I missing out on?'

India walked slowly across from the window, her arms wrapped round her tired body as if consoling it for its fatigue. 'I don't know. I don't even know what you do know . . . *we* do know. I thought you'd heard the last of all this stuff ages ago, after that Major-General or whoever came down, remember? He said it was a . . . what was the word he used?'

'Contentious.'

'Contentious subject, and that he wouldn't want to stir things up. And then that awful man at Home Farm. *What* things?'

Fal shook his head wearily. 'I don't know. Is Rufus really in Montevideo or wherever? That's where the chap from the hospice place said he'd skipped off to. The inference being it was a nice long way from the scene of the crime. But you'd never know, would you? Rufus could be in New York or Haywards Heath, he's such a bloody liar he could be anywhere . . . if he did drown a Chinaman.'

India shuddered in a slightly exaggerated way. She sat on the edge of a chair, arms still wrapped round her body. 'Oh don't say that! Don't even say it jokily. It makes it sound true . . . It would be so terrible.' The room was growing darker.

'It probably is true. Nothing to do with us. What is so strange to me is that two days ago, on Sunday morning to be precise, all was normal in Hartleap. We were quiet, calm, it was going to be just another day, a happy, sunny day and then, splat! someone drops the tea-tray. Everything flies about. Nanny Grayle dies – I mean we knew she was ill, knew that, but I thought it would be longer before she packed it in. Suddenly Sunday was the tea-tray, the whole thing teetered and disaster was everywhere. The people at the Farm emerged into our lives, Kathleen and Roch are engaged, all this business about Rufus and the coke, the whole of our life pattern has got chucked about, scattered, people invaded. Christ! No wonder we are exhausted!'

India smiled wanly. 'So much can alter in a few days. And, oh God! Loveday! What's to become of Loveday? Are we to have an ageing child with us for ever?'

'The fact of the matter is that, yes, my darling, we are. We'll have to get her a companion or something, to live in – there's room – and if Roch does decide to go through with this wild idea and marry Kathleen, he wants to move up to Bottle Cottage. If he means it. Which I really do rather wonder.'

'I think that he's in love with Kathleen, and that Kathleen is in love with him. Sure of it . . . The rest I can't be certain about, you'd know more about all that than I do. I mean the land, the farm, Hartleap. You don't think so? I can tell you don't.'

Fal shifted uneasily, scratched his head. 'I don't know. I can't think anything now. A bit of fantasy perhaps. I think he really does mean what he said, for the moment anyway. And I won't dissuade him. Give him a year to sort himself out here, get to discover that it's not just a question of mending the sluice gates. It's not picnics under the oaks, or rebuilding the Forum. It's tough, it's draining, and I don't think he's got the least idea of what being a farmer, or landowner – and there are a thousand acres to play around with here – really means. It's a delightful, old-fashioned fantasy. I don't care how rich he thinks Kathleen is, or how generous she might be, running this place today is exactly like running water into a sieve. He'll go bust in a couple of years.'

India laughed, a light, relaxed, rather helpless laugh. 'Oh God! Poor boy . . . But do let him try, don't block him too soon. Maybe he's really sincere this time. He may have a hidden streak of brilliance. Now.' She got up and was suddenly brisk. 'Now, first things first. Tomorrow looms. Today is done. Unity and Edward arrive in the morning, Sophie has promised to cope with Loveday, who wants to wear a veil and a black hat. We don't have to ask the new rector, or vicar, to lunch: he's got another what he calls "interment, tragically" over at High Boxwood at two. Then the Smolletts will meet us at the church under their own steam and – don't be furious – I've asked them to come in for supper, an early supper. They want to leave on Thursday as soon as possible, and I want to know just exactly what that bugger down at the Farm is after. Bob Smollett was your father's servant; he's got to be faced and made to tell us. He must know something. I can tell you one thing, his wife, May, knows something and has become my friend. Between the two of them, at supper, I'm going to find out what. All right? I'd better get some more bittermints.' She stooped and kissed her husband firmly on the lips. 'It's dark now. Put out the lamp when you come up, busy day tomorrow, remember.'

Wednesday Morning

The usual sort of funeral apart from the fact that there were no wreaths – just one from the house – trembling gently on the top of the coffin. Nanny Grayle was over ninety, and no one had outlived her that she had known. Her life was the Family. And there they were: the Smolletts, Unity and Edward, the Hartleap lot, with a bowed, veiled Loveday sitting between Roch and Sophie in a wide-brimmed black hat. There were two elderly women whom no one seemed to know, and apart from Stella, who had come out of good manners and because she felt herself to be a part of Hartleap by now, that was the assembly.

The little church was cool, quiet, and rustled with its unexpected congregation. The vicar did his performance well, they had an address, the Lord's Prayer, and went off into the churchyard in a modest straggle, relieved that the whole business was at an end. No one in black except for Loveday; just black ties for the men. And in silence, broken only by an angry cuckoo miles away, Nanny Grayle was set to rest in her plot of Sussex earth while Loveday moaned softly, which alarmed everyone who didn't know where the sound was coming from, on account of the heavy veiling, and the determined strength of Roch and Sophie, who held their aunt in vice-like grips so that she was quite immobile.

And that was that. Bob threw a modest handful of chalky soil into the grave, turned and wandered, with May close beside him, down the little path among the yews to the tilted lych-gate and the village street.

'I could do with a little strengthener,' said Unity to no one in particular as they made their way to the cars. 'A pink gin awaits us at the house –' She stopped suddenly as Jake Wood came from behind Edward's car and walked towards Bob Smollett, who stopped in mild surprise.

'Mr Smollett?' Jake was correctly, neatly, dressed, smiling.

'I'm Mr Smollett, yes.'

'I'm Jake Wood, from Home Farm. I wondered if I could have a word . . .'

Bob Smollett almost raised a fist, pocketed it instead. 'I don't talk to the Press,' he said and moved quickly, with an anxious May, down to his car.

'I'm not from the Press. This is personal. It's a private matter.'

Bob Smollett turned slowly. 'Just sod off, will you? Before I give you a proper belting.'

He continued on his way to his car. There was no question in anyone's mind that he would do exactly what he promised.

The four cars left St Luke's Church and began the journey back to Hartleap, Fal and India leading, with Loveday crushed mournfully in the back. She had wanted, had implored, to be let travel with Roch and Sophie, but Sophie's Mini had proved impossible to contain the length of Loveday plus the width of her hat and veils, so with some gentle persuasion, tearful protestations of a muted kind, she was not shoved into the Mini but dragged into the back of Fal's Bentley. Unity and Edward followed, a subdued Edward on account of giving Stella a lift back. Stella clutched a handkerchief to her lips all the way and kept her eyes tightly closed. She was car-sick at the sight of an

AA badge. However, all was well. The Smolletts brought up the rear, relieved that Shropshire was almost in view.

Fal and India were relaxed because the stifled moans and hiccups from the wealth of black weeds were almost at an end, as indeed was the whole grisly weekend. Edward and Unity were quiet, slightly occupied with charts, shoals and anchorage, and it would *seem* that everyone had forgotten the sudden appearance of the glittering-eyed man who had sprung on Bob a few moments before. 'Tom Tiddler'.

'What did that sod want? How did he know me?' Bob was crushing the steering-wheel in suppressed fury.

May pulled off her gloves nervously. 'Don't know, darling. He's quite certainly after you. He's got a line on to something. Watch your step, dearest.'

'I'll break the bugger's neck if he comes near me again.' Bob wrenched the car into a half-turn and bounced after Fal up the bumpy drive.

May's soft Shropshire accent was blurred instantly by the overlay of the genteel voice of Hartleap she chose to affect when she remembered. 'Do take care, my beloved. Take care.'

Suddenly the little convoy slowed down, almost colliding. Fal made frantic signals. Ahead, moving like a stately hippopotamus, was a white van, inching and bouncing carefully over the ruts and puddles, 'Heather's Pantry' in gold Gothic lettering on the side with an address in Lewes. It was obviously in no hurry.

Eventually everyone reached the stable yard and parked, to the acute relief of Stella, who, adjusting her hat, sticking her handkerchief into her pocket, leant out of the window and shouted, 'Heather Sands! You're late *again*!'

The white van had parked outside the kitchen door. Heather Sands was a stocky woman with close-cropped hair like a boy, bare legs thrust into yellow ankle socks and Jesus sandals. She brushed her divided skirt quickly, buttoned herself into a white chef's jacket.

'Don't lose your rag, old girl. We'll make it. Puncture – just my luck – at Maple Cross. Sorry and all that but don't blame me, blame sodding Mr Dunlop. We'll be ready in a jiff, just want to see a hot oven for a couple of ticks, maybe ten mins. Not more. All right, Stella? Can do? Where is our glorious Gary Cooper? Your amazing husband, chuckling Charlie? He can help out. Give him a yell.'

Stella marched into the kitchen calling for Charlie. Heather, who had been a formidable officer in the ATS some years before, still retained her speech pattern from those days, of a war in which she had never taken part, but knew from others who had. She barked with laughter. 'Tikh hai? Bang on!' and then buttoning her white jacket she roared, 'Valerie! Where in the name of God have you got to? Valerie? Come along, show a leg, stand by your bed! We're late on parade: get the trays out, take 'em to the kitchen and don't spill the vol-au-vents. Jump to it, girl!'

Valerie, in contrast to her boss, was a froth and frill of cotton floral, hair ribbons fluttering, patent leather ankle strap shoes, a tinkle of silver charms at her wrists, clink and wink of Gipsy coins at her throat; she might have been thirty. She bobbed politely to the uneasy company getting out of their cars and wound an apron round her skinny waist. Together she and Heather started the unloading.

Fal put his arm lightly round Edward, nodded to Bob, not quite managing the familiarity of his Christian name, and led the way round the side of the house to the terrace and the open windows of Little Parlour. The two great cedars sparkled still with raindrops from last night, puddles on the flagstones were already starting to steam gently, the hot sun was breaking through at last.

'Come in and have a glass, they'll be hours yet.'

India called out that they'd have the 'feast' in the summer dining-room and where was Unity.

'Gorn for a pee,' yelled Edward in reply. 'Don't use up all the gin. She loves her pink gin.'

India apparently hurried after Valerie because she was chattering about 'bringing the basket of bridge rolls'. Then her voice was cut off by the closing of a door.

Sophie meanwhile was helping Loveday to untangle herself from pins and yards of black chiffon. As the russet hair cascaded wearily in a crumpled mass round Loveday's shoulders, she started quite deliberately to move away in the direction of the terrace and the ha-ha. Knowing what was in her mind, Sophie screeched, 'Loveday! You're *not* to. Come here, *come back*.' She was left holding the large flat hat and yards of veiling, her voice thin with impatience. Loveday made no reply, simply took off like a black rocket, trails of streaming Liberty's silk flowing behind her, with a desperate Sophie hard on her heels.

'She's off! *Stop her*, someone! Oh! *Do* catch her.'

But no one did.

Edward, stepping out of Little Parlour, was moderately interested as the two wild figures crossed the terrace, clambered down the ha-ha, and streaked off towards the orchard and the Wendy Hut. 'What's that? A race?' His interest grew slightly since Jess and Minder, released from their kennels by Stella, joyously joined in the game and howling with glee, baying as at a pair of foxes, streaked after the two women. 'Know what it is, Fal?'

Fal, opening a bottle, said, 'My sister, I believe. My daughter behind her.' He was as usual occupied in what he was doing, and being quite used to the sight he hardly looked up. 'Loveday has taken Nanny's death brutally. And now we'll *all* have to cope with her on our own. It's going to be bloody hell, let me tell you. Poor Sophie! The sooner she goes off to her lepers or whatever they are, the better for her. Otherwise, she'll be trapped for life here.'

India and May came in as Bob turned away from the hysteria outside.

'That Loveday?' said India mildly. 'Well, we'll have lots of that to cope with presently. Got the champagne open, darling? I'm parched . . . *They* can scream and caper; and let bloody Heather and Valerie sort themselves out. Poor Charles is outraged. He hates them at the best of time and this is for him the worst. But they *are* useful. They do these little ceremonies very well, saves the cooking. Stella calls this a sticky-fingers-and-paper-napkin-job and is just as disapproving. But she has got us for dinner tonight. She'd far rather have us all sitting round the table in black having a good old "mourn".'

Edward handed her a glass of champagne. 'All getting deliciously sloshed, terrific idea.'

India took her glass with relief. 'I was thinking of this all through the dire lesson about "Dearly Beloveds gathered here to celebrate the life of our sister in God Ada Stephens" – oh Bob, I'm sorry, but really, the rubbish they talk. May, dear, you must have a glass to pull you together, a sparkling glass to revive flagging spirits?'

May looked across at her husband. 'All right if I do, Bob? I mean, why not? We're not leaving here until tomorrow, are we?'

Bob Smollett, who had been talking to Fal about taking a branch off one of the cedars, turned to his wife suddenly. 'What say?'

May nodded. 'A glass of champagne? I'm not driving anywhere today? All right?'

Bob smiled, his dour face suddenly radiant with charm when he saw his wife. 'No, you go ahead, my duck, take it when it's offered. You'll only get Babycham up at the Craven Arms.'

For some reason, although it was not in the least funny, Bob's remark cracked the awkward mood which had drifted into the room. Everyone laughed, Edward poured her wine, May cried that she'd get tiddly, and the odd burst of laughter set the few people present free from whatever restraints had been imposed on them.

Edward, who had taken over as bartender, put his hand on Bob's arm. 'You don't want this stuff, it's cat's piddle with bubbles. There' – and with a wide sweep of his arm – 'we have English beer, Dutch, and Swedish, and French beer or, better still, a luscious black bottle of *Irish* beer! A glass of Guinness will suit you as well as it suits me! Join me?'

Bob laughed and gratefully accepted. 'But I'd still get those two lower limbs dealt with. On the cedars there? They really do need attention. You get a heavy snow next year . . .'

He had started to open his bottle as Roch, slightly out of breath, skidded into the room apologizing. 'Sorry I'm late, I've been trying to get Air France, or *anyone* at bloody Gatwick, trying to get seats for tomorrow for Paris. God! They take their time: *We'll put you on hold. You are in the queue.*'

'Have a glass,' said Bob. 'Off to your lady there, eh? Know the feeling very well. Can't wait a moment longer, right? Feel you'll bust! We've all been there long before you, my boy.' He grinned across the room. 'Torment, eh, May?'

May, laughing, raised her glass. 'All been there before, yes indeed! *Torment*. Some of us *did* have to wait a bit longer than others, some just waited in vain alas. I thought I was waiting in vain after the war when Bobbie was coming

189

back from Austria . . . You *were* a long time.' A little, unexpected silence fell.

Bob suddenly looked uneasy. 'Torment all right. I'll say that. But I made it in the end. Eventually.'

Just for a second May's jolly face lost its smile. Remembering something wretched had given it the appearance of a kind muffin, but she nodded and looked brightly around her. 'Well, never mind. All over now and here we all are.'

'The other reason I'm a bit late', said Roch, 'is that I almost forgot this. It's yours, sir. We collected it from the cottage when that nurse was there. She had a pinched, holy face. Thought it wiser. Your bible, sir.' And he handed the little fat book with a flourish to a surprised Bob.

'Mine? *I* never had a bible in my life! Not ever. Sure it's mine?'

Fal took a large swig of his wine. 'Your name's inside. Millions of Stephens! More than you ever knew you had probably.'

Bob opened the cover, read aloud, '*Sophia Stephens. 21st May 1789.* Who the hell was she? Never heard of her. Not ever.' He closed the cover and the bookmark fell out.

'This is a part of it too,' said Fal. 'It's got Nanny's name in *her* handwriting on the back. *Ada Stephens, her book.* But look what someone has done to the sacred figures.' For a second they looked at it together in silence.

India and May came closer, looking over his shoulder.

'The crucifixion,' said India. 'But look at all the initials! How strange. Look, May.'

Fal came across from the windows. 'Know what it means? Any idea? There's a large R G – for Rufus? – over one of the thieves, a B G – presumably Beau Grayle? – over the other, and *you* seem to be in Christ's place. Right in the middle, with R S in a Biro halo round your head? What do you make of that?'

Bob tapped his lip with the slim card. 'Did *she* do this? Are we sure?'

Roch took the card slowly, reversed it. 'Same blue Biro that she wrote her name in, and date: July 1945. Same as the haloes. I just wondered if you knew any reason for her doing this? I mean, *if* she did – and I'm sure she did.'

Bob took back the card, slid it into the little bible. 'I haven't a clue,' he said. 'Not the vaguest. She was playing a bit of a game, I reckon. Instead of knitting.'

He slipped the bible into his jacket pocket. 'People do all kinds of daft things when they get lonely. Dwell on themselves too much. I reckon she was lonely.'

Unity came out of the little bathroom, closed the door firmly, wandered in a vague way towards a bed, dragging her silk Harrods shirt behind her. She sat down slowly on the edge of the bed, staring at her own reflection in the wardrobe mirror, pulled the shirt over her knees, screwed up her eyes and began to weep soundlessly. After a moment of this indulgence, she wiped her nose quietly and said, 'Oh shit! Bloody well shit! *Now* what?'

She had found the small lump under her breast yesterday evening in the shower. Her fingers slithered through soft soap suds, found it, paused, moved on, stopped and went back. The size of a hazelnut? Perhaps not as big? A dried pea? Had she always had it? She had not noticed it before. Been too busy perhaps, rushing about getting packed and ready for Thursday. Well, ready for today, Wednesday, and this wretched funeral, and then Thursday, the joyful sailing to France. And now? She vaguely hoped it had gone away. What do you do when you find a small lump anywhere in your body, even if it is just the size of a pea? God knows I've read the phrase in a thousand women's magazines, I should know. But I always rather skipped over the details. I wish that I hadn't now. But come on, old thing, it's just a little lump. Doesn't hurt.

She felt it again with tentative fingers, cautious, politely, afraid to anger it and discover that its anger induced pain. But it did not. She sat and looked at the wreckage of Unity Uffington before her. It took a hell of a shock to do so much damage to a face. She got up quickly, dragged on her shirt and cleared the tears away from her eyes, with a Kleenex, at the frilled dressing-table. First things first. I don't mention this to Edward. We don't stop the trip to Deauville, he's been longing for it for so long. We won't be gone long, a week, ten days? I couldn't bear to have him disappointed, not do the trip, cause all the worry and panic and then, I hope, find it's all nonsense and old Unity over-reacting as usual. Don't want that.

She started to button her cuffs. I'll just keep quiet – keep aware, of course. If I feel any changes I'll have to cave in, but I can't think much will alter in ten days. Really. I mean, it seems too cruel. When we get back I'll go up to Town and see someone, top chap, quietly, no fuss. But for the moment think Deauville. Enjoy it. Try to, anyway. And don't let Edward even have a suspicion of anything. It'd knock him for six. Oh, he'll cope. If he has to. He'll cope. Just let's see if he *has* to, that's all.

She ran a brush through her greying hair. Well, you look all right. Eyes a bit red. Neat and tidy. No one would ever know the terror which holds your heart in an iron grip. And no one must. Yet. Just wait a bit, be patient. Now . . . She looked right and left at her reflection, tucked away a loose curl, nodded with satisfaction and went down to Little Parlour whistling (she always whistled, so they'd know she was on her way: 'The Surrey with the Fringe on Top'. She didn't know why. Perhaps one of her 'team' of stitchers had been singing it – Oh God! The quilting ladies! That was another thing . . . She whistled louder.

Loveday fiddled about at the neckline of her mourning-dress, found the key to the Wendy Hut, rammed it into the door and lurched across the threshold. She reached out to the leather settee, eased herself into it and slumped there, head hanging, gasping for breath. She'd run very fast. Sophie had started to walk. She clambered up the four brick steps, pushed into the frowsty gloom and found the chintz chair. For a moment or so the untidy hut was silent except for the two gasping women.

'You really *are* dotty!' said Sophie. 'Dotty. Running off like that. I must be a bit dotty too, running after you. Good riddance. Just let you go.' She chucked the flat hat and the tattered veiling on to the floor. 'Daft. What's to become of you?'

Loveday lifted a haggard face, brushed her hair roughly with a claw-like hand. 'Daft? A boy called me that once. I've never forgotten. In Woolworth's, with Nanny . . . Brighton. There were hundreds of goldfish in a tank thing, and there wasn't enough room for them, and they were struggling and gasping, and I started to scream. Nanny told me to hush up, and then this *awful* boy came up and said, "Oh, she's soft in the head. Daft." Just like that. And I got dragged away. Nanny said I wasn't daft at all but you had to expect that from village boys. So I did. I mean, I never forgot him saying I was daft, but I didn't know what it meant really, but when Nanny said what it was I was ruined. I wept and wept and wept. Honestly! It was too awful. But' – she shrugged and got up stiffly – 'I got over it. Nanny said "daft" was just a very common, villagey way of saying I was different, and that I was, and so I had to expect that sort of thing from low people. But I remember

it made me weep, because I knew she was being nice to me.
Do you want a drinkie? I do.' She got hold of the Corn
Flakes box, shook it roughly.

Sophie moaned softly. 'Loveday, *don't*. Don't drink that
stuff today, we've got to go up for the lunch, the wake
thing.'

Loveday lowered the box, and her head. Started to weep.

'Now don't do that, Loveday. *No snivelling!* You
promised. It's all over now, Nanny is free and up with
the angels. Be glad. *Don't* snivel and I don't want any
gin.'

Loveday braced herself. 'The last time you were here,
my dear, you gave me a completely poisoned chalice.'
She wiped her nose with the back of her hand. 'Do you
remember? I'd used it for turpentine? Too awful. Well, I
shall not ask your help today. I will drink it as I see fit,
from the bottle.' She tilted her head back, raised the bottle
and swigged a hefty mouthful.

Sophie uttered a scream and smothered it. 'You'll be
sick! Now *no more*!' She got up and took the bottle from
her gasping aunt's hands.

Loveday, tears welling from the harshness of the neat
gin, sank into the settee again, coughing and dribbling.
Sophie stuck the cap on the bottle and put it high on a
shelf, out of reach.

'Loveday! The painting! That wonderful canvas of the
. . . whatever . . . the Styx: where is it?'

Loveday wiped her face with trembling hand.
'Destroyed!' she said. 'Destroyed, because *you* all laughed
at it. Destroyed with a chopper!'

Sophie stared at her aunt. 'Loveday! You didn't!'

Loveday nodded, wiped her eyes and chin. 'I did. I really
did. Like Lizzie Borden. Do you know about her? Gave her
father forty-one whacks! Isn't that funny? I did that to the

painting. Gave it forty-one whacks!' She fiddled with her tumbled hair. 'I know what you were all doing. Being kind to the "daft" old woman. I just *knew*. That odious girl with Rochester, didn't know that the wavy lines were the Styx! The purple, wine-coloured waters . . .'

Sophie sat on the arm of the settee. 'Now you really are being daft! We loved the painting, all the colours –'

'I know! Cheering on the old idiot. People who don't understand a painting always praise the colours, Sophie. I'm not *so* daft. I remember! I remember that haughty American girl. "Now that I've had it explained to me," she said. *Odious* creature! So when I saw it this morning, when I came to arrange my veils, I thought, no! I thought, don't let them laugh at your homage to Nanny. Philistines, the lot of you! So I didn't do my veils right away. I got the chopper and did that instead. Chop! Chop! Chop! All gone. Quite ruined, no one can laugh at it now.'

'I think that it was a disgraceful thing to do! Disgraceful. It's desecration!'

'Your sneering, even if it was in secret, was more of a desecration, sweet girl! Don't speak of desecration, you all did that yourselves. You are all culpable!'

Sophie got up briskly. 'Come along, get a brush and do your hair, it's like a crow's nest. I'll give you a hand, you can't go up to the house like that.'

Loveday gripped the arm of the settee, shook her head vigorously. 'Not going to the house. I'm *not*! A terrible feast, wine and food and Nanny only in the earth an hour ago. How *dare* you! Leave me with my memories –'

Sophie grabbed her aunt and pulled her roughly to her feet. 'Now get up! At once! You are coming up, you'll pay your respects to Pa and Ma and to the house which gave Nanny her shelter and its love. It's the last thing you'll ever have to do for her. You have the rest of your life for your memories, but today you bloody well behave! For the family.'

Loveday suddenly collapsed full-length on the settee, sobbing and moaning. Sophie stood for a moment, hands on hips, biting her lip. Loveday's hands were like lizards' claws on the tired leather.

'Nanny *hated* this family! She did. She said it was cursed, that she had put a spell on it. And she did. She showed me the photograph I'd known for so long, her most favourite picture of Mumsie and Beau. She *spat* on it! There! Spat! Stuck a bodkin right through his eyes. There!'

There was a shattering silence in the Wendy Hut, broken only by Loveday's moans and hiccups. Sophie just stood perfectly still. She had never really had to face a totally mad person before. Whatever they said about her aunt being 'backward' or 'lobotomized', she had seen enough this morning to recognize the thin skein of pure madness which lay among the tangled silks of a deeply disturbed mind. One clear single thread. Silken, secret, terrifying.

'Very well,' she said quietly, 'I'll leave you to it. You stay here. Better for everyone. I'll say you are too sad to come. All right?'

Loveday slowly sat up, her hair cascading, falling over her face, hiding her eyes. She picked frantically at the side of her thumb. 'Yes . . . yes, say that. Sad. Please. I'm sorry. *Dreadfully* sorry. It's my sadness which makes me cry, and the desecration of my homage. Say I'm too sad.'

Sophie started towards the door. 'Don't do that, Aunt, picking your thumb. Don't! You'll be bleeding like a pig. You'll make a terrible sore place.'

Loveday suddenly slapped her own hand. 'I went up to the cottage and *stole* the picture. I knew where Nanny hid it: in a copy of *Woman's Realm*. I knew which one. And the awful Irish nurse was rummaging about, in *her* jewel box! I caught her! She screamed and said I'd frightened her, and she was so upset she didn't notice me take the paper, so I just ran away.' She pushed her hair from her forehead. 'I ran away here. With Minder and Jess . . . walkies . . . and then I came on up to the house. You were all in the kitchen. Eating chicken. You didn't know what I'd done, did you?' She wiped her eyes with a fist. 'Didn't know. Daft, silly old woman, I've been cleverer than any of you. I've got the photograph here. Safely here.'

Sophie looked through the open door. 'Do you know *why* Nanny did such a terrible thing? The cursing and the bodkin, and the spit? Why did she do all that? What terrible, terrible thing had Grandpapa done? Did she say? She must have said?'

Loveday shook her head firmly from side to side. 'Oh no! She didn't say why. No, she didn't say. Just that she hated him, and she hated Rufus. We are all tainted, she said. Remember? I was so shocked! Tainted!' She sat upright, like a piece of driftwood wreckage, with blazing eyes. 'That was the word. Tainted.'

Sophie turned at the open door. 'I'm going. You are on your own now, Loveday. You do realize that? I shan't come back after the . . . after the wake. You find your own way from now on, for the rest of your life. I'll just remind you that India and Fal are having a farewell supper for the Smolletts . . . if you have a shred of good manners left . . . They leave for Shropshire tomorrow after the moving-men have stripped Bottle Cottage. Unity and Edward won't be present because they leave for France tomorrow early, and Roch and I fly over to Paris in the afternoon. So it won't be a late evening. But you do just what you like: I have no influence over you, Loveday. Tomorrow Hartleap will be empty, more or less, which will make you happy, I should think.' Sophie peeled a strip of faded paint from the door.

'So, in case you don't come to the wake, and can't face the supper tonight, I'll say goodbye now. I have my own life to live. Goodbye.' She ran down the four steps with Jess and Minder lolloping alongside, hurried away under the trees of the sodden orchard.

Loveday watched her go, stock still, watching the flicker of Sophie's dress through the tree trunks, amazed, appalled, unable to take charge of the wild basket of tumbled silks, all the more disturbed by this conversation, which passed over her head. She started to moan, cried aloud, reached out an imploring hand. When she saw that Sophie's figure had finally disappeared she sat upright, clutched her tangled hair, shook her head, wiped her eyes and, staring out of the open door past the seeding lupins and the muddy path leading through them, stuck out her tongue.

'Now! That's what I call spiffingly pretty, don't you, Stella?' Heather stood back from the table where she had placed the last platter of asparagus and smoked salmon, in neat little bundles, and shoved her hands in her pockets. 'Good enough to eat! Tempting. That's the ticket.'

'Taken long enough, God knows,' said Stella setting a pile of plates at the end of the table. 'They'll be half pissed in there.'

Heather smiled brightly. 'Then they won't be too discerning, will they? Hardly notice the difference between your cooking and mine! Valerie! Just put the napkins in *two* neat piles, one here, one there. We aren't feeding the multitudes, only nine people. I do think this is a simply wizard room. I always love arranging the table in here. The Gothic room. Lovely.'

Stella cast a quick eye over the table. 'It's called the Summer Room, on account of the ceiling: summer skies, lots of swallows flying among the angels.'

Heather looked up. 'Hadn't noticed that. Just over-whelmed, Stella, by all the Gothic whiteness. I always am. The views through the arches – so clever! Looks absolutely real, only all trompy-loile! Amazing. Clever boy who did it all. Killed in the war, I understand?'

Stella, irritated because she did not understand, smoothed the tablecloth, rearranged a dish and said, 'Well, now you're all ready, I'll call Charlie to get them in – must be half starved, it's taken long enough. And you losing your wheels and all!'

'Not *my* fault, old dear, told you.'

Stella called through the door into the hall for Charlie, came back into the room, removing her overall. 'Mind you, no offence really, but there isn't much here as would staunch a hunger, Heather. Not a *hunger*. Not a real sit-down-after-grieving sort. A few tiddly vol-au-vents, some scraps of asparagus – tips only, I notice! Well! I don't know, I *really* don't know.' Stella picked up an empty basket and pushed the tinkling Valerie out of the way.

'It's what was ordered!' said Heather. 'I obey orders. This was what they wanted, nothing elaborate.'

'You've made sure of that! Elaborate! Crikey!' Stella snorted and went to the door, held it deliberately open.

Heather stroked her large bosom thoughtfully. 'I *could* have done my coq au vin, or the paprika chicken . . . I've had a lot of praise for that . . .'

Stella leant against the door jamb, taping the empty basket against her knees. '*Praise!* I'll say! Never forget that Hungarian Evening, never. Nor will they – half dead the next morning, the lot of them. Five heaped dessert spoons of that red powder! Five. You used enough paprika that night to breach the walls of Windsor Castle! Come along, now, do hurry.'

Heather thought for a moment that she might take a

quick punch at the tall figure grinning at the door, but suddenly broke and choked with laughter, covering her face with her hands, leaning her head against Stella's unyielding shoulder. 'Oh my Lor', Stella. That *was* a dreadful time! I remember Charlie said they had had to cart poor Admiral Buller Delderfield off to Hartfield Hospital in the night. The whole house was flushing like Niagara. What a silly billy I was . . .'

And so laughing, together, they went out into the hall, passing a hurrying Charles buttoning his white jacket, who scowled at them: 'It's all right for some, late is what we are, and dinner for this lot tonight. Bloody hell!' – making them laugh even more, so much so that a bell-tinkling Valerie started to snigger in a kind of hypnotized terror.

Heather stopped instantly. 'Nothing for *you* to laugh at, girlie! You don't know the joke!' She stamped across to the sinks and set the sausage roll tins to steep. 'Don't know the joke, my dear! Wouldn't laugh if you did.'

Isobel was ironing her batik squares in the converted dairy. She heard Jake's car swing into the yard and stop, a door slam.

'That you?' she called loudly.

'It's me. Back from the church.'

She started singing over-cheerfully. It was good to have him back, but, apart from that, she was determined not to be 'feminine' today and let him see any signs of anxiety or wretchedness. Tough, today: that would alarm him more. Yesterday's weeping and wailing were not to be repeated. She set the iron on a brick, folded her cloths. 'All done? The funeral? Got her buried?'

He muttered something but she didn't hear. She switched off the iron, looked at the pile of batik squares.

The dairy had been converted into a playroom, years

ago. It was empty except for a couple of wooden chairs, cobwebs and the large green plywood table at which people had, at one time or another, played table-tennis, when the weather was inclement. Now she used it as an ironing-board or simply a work table in general. There were packets of dye, boxes of paints, jars of brushes; against one wall a stack of canvases, against another the life-size portrait of Jake at St Sebastian – unfinished and, from what she was beginning to realize now, unlikely to be finished for some time. She'd lost him to his wretched book.

She gathered up the batik squares. It had been coming along quite well. Good detail, that was one thing she had worked hard at in her life class, detail: bone and structure; balance; muscle. She tilted her head to one side, regarding her unfinished work critically. Yes, it was good. She hadn't painted in the arrows, had merely marked their points of entry into the muscular flesh with little dots, to give her an idea. And she would leave it undraped, she decided.

Who would have draped it 'daintily' with a napkin at such a brutal moment! That was done to preserve the modesty of the viewer. A few judiciously placed leaf shadows just to break up the *absolute* form, that's all that she needed. And there would be Jake, stark naked lashed to a post. She felt certain that it would be a post and not a picturesque tree. They would have roughly bound him to a post. Besides, a post, or stake, was easier to paint than a tree, with bark and branches and all the rest. She wanted this to be vivid, vicious, truthful, a painting of pain and submission, the curly head thrown back defying the agony of the arrows' penetrating pain . . . the blood trickling gently from the wounds . . . it would not gush from the point of an arrow . . . unless an artery was hit . . . She'd got a good head, it was exactly like him: Jake half awake, or half unconscious, as she so often had seen him, head slightly tilted back . . . against the pillow . . . cradled in the crook of her arm, against her breast . . . sprawled across the bed, satiated after punishment.

She clutched the batik cushion covers tightly, shook the images away and went out into the yard, lifting her heavy swinging skirts away from the damp cobbles and little puddles from last night's storm. She swirled herself into the kitchen. No sign of him. She set the batik down and went into the sitting-room. He was at a table with a pad of writing-paper. 'I wondered where you were. Did it go all right? All the family present, I suppose? Anyone else?' She leant against the door, arms folded.

'All there,' he said, not looking up. 'No problems. Except for that bastard Smollett.'

She unfolded her arms, stuck her hands in the large pockets of her skirts. 'What about him? What did *he* do?'

Jake looked up patiently. 'I asked him, perfectly politely, to give me a few moments. He nearly hit me, I swear! Said he didn't speak to the Press and just made off with that pink-faced wife. So I'm writing him a note to explain *why* I wanted to speak to him. That's all. Can I finish, please?'

Sensing hostility Isobel wisely eased away from the situation. 'Of course. Just be very careful what you say. You know how you fly off the handle. He's a nasty bit of work. It's too late to post it, they'll be leaving as soon as they can. The removal men are coming tomorrow at dawn. The man from Lewes was here this morning, just to check around: size of van they'd need, where to park it, that sort of thing. How are you going to get it to Smollett? They said, because I asked them, they'd be finished by ten in the morning. Cottage would be stripped.'

Jake took up the pen he'd set aside to explain things to his wife. 'If you will *allow* me,' he said, 'I'll just finish this and take it up to the Cottage myself. By hand. One way or another it'll get to him. He may even feel tempted to give the place one more little look. Know what I mean? So go away, Isso, go away, so I can write this.'

'Just don't write him a book, that's all. Leave that for another time,' she said, and with a swishing of skirts and a burst of happy song (she hoped it sounded a happy song – she had no idea what it was) she turned and went back into the kitchen.

'Funny!' she called. 'To see you all dressed up in a suit. Depressing!'

'Barking. I mean really barking. I don't know how they'll cope with her here, now that Nanny's gone. She was a stabilizer, didn't do much but she was there. Kept some sort of control. Well . . .' Sophie lay back in her chair. 'It's not going to be me who copes. I'm damned if I'm going to be my aunt's bodyguard. Not me!'

Roch laughed shortly. 'No one's asked you, have they?'

'No one's asked me and no one *is* going to ask me. I have my life to live. There is always a time to start it. It's time for me.'

They were sitting out on the terrace. The sun had broken through the low clouds and the day was going to be hot again.

In Little Parlour someone rattled coffee cups, and Unity came to the windows. 'Ah! There you are, sneaking away from the party . . . We'll be sneaking away soon. Edward is fiddling about with the car. As soon as he's all together we'll clear off. I've got my class, my "quilters", to just check on . . . and a bit of . . . oh, a few bits to pack still.'

Roch got to his feet. 'Off tomorrow?'

Unity nodded, tucked her shirt into her skirt. 'Off tomorrow. Dawn. We have to catch tides and things. Very nautical.'

Sophie swung round in her chair. 'We'll all be in France tomorrow. Very exciting, as long, that is, as Roch got the seats? You did, Roch? I'm not going to be downcast with a negative?'

Roch laughed and said he had the tickets and Unity kissed them both, and there was a general wishing of luck for the journeys and she stepped back into Little Parlour and they were alone again. 'You know that Kathleen works at night on this *Vogue* job? I mean, they can't shoot in the Louvre until it's closed. Six until six a.m. You *did* know that?' She looked at Roch slightly anxiously, but he nodded. 'So that's all right then. I wondered if you knew. I'll just go straight to Jean-Claude's flat, he'll be there. I hope you'll like him – be rather a bore if you don't.' She pleated a bit of her skirt with nervous fingers.

Roch grinned. 'I'll like him, don't worry. I suppose I'd better like him if you do. I didn't even know about the man until yesterday. You kept your cards close to your chest. Is he a doctor?'

Sophie shook her head. 'Medical student, he's joining this team. I mean, he *nearly* is a doctor, but just wants to get a bit of what he calls "field experience". That's why he's coming out to Somalia . . . how I met him: he's a friend of a friend of Kathleen's. I like him, so we fixed it up definitely when I took her to the airport. He's a bit shy, but so am I really. I expect Somalia will cure that, don't you?'

'I reckon so. But you wouldn't do something loony, would you? Like falling for the guy, this Jean-Claude? You wouldn't?'

Sophie laughed shortly. 'I've really hardly met him. A couple of times, that's all. I mean, you don't get romantic leanings with a glass of Dubonnet and a pretzel in your hand. Anyway, I didn't.'

Roch wandered over to the edge of the terrace, leant

against the lead shepherdess. 'People can get quite faint, sometimes, over a glass of Dubonnet and a pretzel. Or even a glass of ginger beer. Or nothing. You sort of go "Wham!" and that's it. I did, quite suddenly, up there at the Forum, with Kathleen. Sudden as that. Crash. God knows I'd had her under my bloody nose for months. We made a pretty pair, but I didn't get "the feeling", or whatever you call it, until the other day up there. We didn't have any Dubonnet or ginger beer either. So be warned! It can happen, and it is devastating when it does, changes your whole outlook . . . your will, everything. Changed mine.'

Sophie got up and went to join him slowly. 'Well, I don't think that's going to happen to me. You had the great advantage of knowing your subject in detail. In depth, shall I say? I have only got to the Dubonnet stage as yet. It was a sort of gentle click, like a switch going on. I know he felt it too, his hand was a bit shaky. It was *very* slight. So don't bother to fuss, my darling bro'. I just don't *see* me as a doctor's wife, honestly, but I am bloody determined that I won't look after wretched Loveday. I'm not going to end up like the only daughter in the family. Expected to cope with the elders. She'll be raving mad one day. She's tripping down that road now. But *I'm clearing off*.' She patted Roch comfortingly.

'To Somalia?'

Sophie nodded. 'I tell you, after this awful week I'd happily be off to a polar cap.'

Roch kissed her lightly. 'Which one? North or South?'

Sophie kissed him back. 'I think the South. It's rather near New Zealand, of course, but I'd have to put up with that. I doubt she'd make it to New Zealand. Anyway, not in that bloody hat with all the veils. God!'

They took hands and wandered slowly back to the house as India came on to the terrace.

'All over! Unity and Edward are off to their boat, or whatever he calls it, and they're clearing up in the kitchen. You were both very dear and sweet and loving. More I cannot ask. *Can*, but wouldn't expect to get. So now it's just supper, not difficult. The worst, my darlings, is over. Sophie, I should have asked before, but where are you actually staying in Paris? With Kathleen?'

Sophie, on the brink of a lie, blushed. 'Yes,' she said briskly. 'I'm staying with her, or with some friend who's got a sofa, or something.'

India caught the blush on her daughter's face, smiled to herself and said, 'Did either of you notice that poor Heather Sands sports a jolly good moustache? Must be so difficult, I'd think.'

'She might enjoy having one,' said Roch. 'We'll be back by the weekend. From Paris, I mean. I may bring Kathleen back with us? If she can come. If the job is over, I mean.'

The white van with Gothic lettering suddenly started to inch down the drive. Valerie waved frantically. "Good-byeee! I hope it was all right?' Her light tinkling spilled over into the still afternoon. She was waving a thin brace-leted arm as far down the track as Bottle Cottage, and just as they reached the shade of the orchard Bob Smollett's blue Mercedes spun out between the lodges and went past them all rather quickly.

May waved. 'Back soon! Up to the Cottage . . .' And in a skitter of gravel they went on down.

Roch looked surprised. 'Now where are they off to? Not leaving?'

India folded her arms across her chest. 'Well, if they are, they didn't tell me, and I think they would . . . It seems to me such a fearfully long way to go, Sophie. Mogadishu, or whatever it's called? Right across Africa . . . the east coast. *Must* it be so far?'

Sophie shrugged. 'That's where the base is, Médicins Pour Le Monde. In Baraawe, actually. Mogadishu is the capital.'

'I just meant it was a frightful way to go to help the poor disadvantaged, or whatever they are. You could do quite a lot in Cardiff or Liverpool, even in London – lots of disadvantaged people there glad of your assistance.'

Sophie looked slightly sullen. 'I haven't been *asked* to go to any of those places.'

Roch laughed cheerfully. 'But you *have* been asked to go to Mogadishu?'

Sophie nodded, prodded a beetle on the terrace with her foot. 'I have, and it's a jolly long way from bloody Loveday! I can't just nip back on the train when I'm summoned.'

India quickly got the point and defused the situation. 'Yes, where *is* she? I don't mean "Go and find Aunt Loveday", Sophie. I just asked, but it was a silly question because your father's gone up to the Forum with the dogs to stretch his legs. You know how he hates these gatherings. Said he'd peer into the Wendy Hut. See she was functioning all right.' She came towards her daughter and kissed her. 'You go to Mogadishu, my darling. As soon as you can,' she said.

Fal sat easily on the arm of the leather settee. 'Just came to see if all was well. I'm taking the dogs up to the Forum. All well?'

Loveday, sitting upright on a rush-bottomed chair, turned with great elegance and draped an arm over the back of her chair, a long paintbrush dangling. 'I'm perfectly well, as you can see. I'm working away, like a busy old bee.' Her eyes were puffy and red.

Fal leant forward, hands clasped on his walking-stick. Minder and Jess snuffled about in the orchard. 'Another painting? You are indefatigable. But no lunch, eh? You didn't come up to lunch.'

Loveday shook her head gently, smiled sweetly. 'No. Loveday hates those terrible things. People, all laughing, after a funeral. I have some lovely choccie biccies. Plenty left. Want one?' Fal shook his head. 'So . . .' She continued setting the brush in a jar of blue liquid. 'So I had some sustenance. And if you notice the Corn Flakes box up there? Do you? So you see I've had something in my insides. Nanny always said . . .' She dried up quickly, took a piece of stained rag and scrubbed her hands.

Fal nodded kindly. 'But you'll come up for supper? It's just the Smolletts and the children and India and me. Family. It's a send-off for the Smolletts. They won't be back again I have a feeling.'

Loveday wiped her fingers one by one. 'No, Fal, dear, I won't come up for supper. Thank you for the suggestion. I'll probably go and have some soup with Stella and Charles. They don't mind.'

Fal sighed. 'You *are* difficult, you know, Loveday? Stella and Charles will be busy with our supper.'

Loveday got up suddenly. 'Not *my* fault! I didn't ask the wretched Smolletts to supper! I don't see why you had to. I'll sit as quiet as a mouse, I won't be in the way. I've had enough, really quite enough unkindness from this family for today! Your daughter, that Sophie, was rude as rude to me! She had not an ounce of sympathy for me. Said she had no *control* over me, and I must do just what I liked. She actually' – she started to remove the paint-stained overall – 'said "Goodbye"! She physically shook me! Pushed me! She was vile! So I won't come up this evening. *Vile* she was. Ugly and cruel. I've been abandoned.'

Fal prodded the dirty dhurri rug at his feet with his stick. 'Don't be silly, Loveday. She was probably a bit tired too.

We all are, it's been a distressing few days. You aren't abandoned. Don't be daft.'

She suddenly turned on him, threw the screwed-up overalls on to the floor. 'I am *not* daft. I am "different", that's all, "*different*"!'

Fal instantly saw the welling tears, the trembling lips, backed off quickly. 'Well, you do as you like, my dear. Don't give it another thought, you are quite right. You *are* different, and if you want to have supper with Stella in the kitchen, then why not? It's no great deal, as long as you keep out of Charles's way when he's got a loaded tray.' He tried a mild laugh, saw the tears fade away, the lips cease to tremble.

'Corks!' said Loveday. 'Wouldn't it be simply too awful if I banged into him with a loaded tray! He'd kill me, he'd have my "guts for garters" – that's what he says. He's really quite vulgar.' Laughter bubbled, she wiped her lips. 'You do cheer me up. Really, Fal, you are sweet to me. Shall I show you a deadly secret? Deadly, deadly secret? Only you must swear not to say anything to anyone. Swear?' She was riffling through a pile of old pre-war dance records in brown-paper covers.

Her swift mood changes discomfited him as usual, but he was pretty well used to them by this time. He'd think of 'the future' a bit later on.

Loveday had found what she sought: a battered copy of *Woman's Realm*. She proffered it cautiously. 'I stole this, from Bottle Cottage, from right under the very nose of that hideous nurse creature. Stole it. You'll see why. Go on, open it.' She covered her mouth with both hands, eyes wide with the amazement which she expected Fal to show.

But he didn't show anything . . . a mild interest . . . 'Oh yes! Papa and Mumsie. I remember this photo. I love her corsage or whatever it is.'

'But look,' said Loveday anxiously. 'Hold it up to the light. Then say what you see! Not a silly old corsage.'

Fal dutifully held the cardboard photograph up to the light of the open door. He was still for a moment. His stick fell between his legs and clattered to the floor. 'Who *did* this, Loveday? Did you do this? To Papa's eyes?'·

She shook her head vigorously. 'No! Not me. It's a bodkin. Nanny stuck the bodkin right through his eyes. His pretty blue eyes, *and* I think she spat on him, she actually spat on it! And she hid it. After that rotten Bob *Smollett* came to see her from the war, oh, years ago . . . after that she hid it quite away and never mentioned it again. But she used the bodkin. Isn't it awful? Just so awful and vile? I don't know why, and she wouldn't say. Never ever spoke of them ever, ever again. Wasn't that terrible? She hid it away, but I remembered where and stole it while that dreadful nurse was there. Stole it. So I don't want to see the *Smolletts*, thank you. I'm not *daft*, just . . . well, as you said, *different*!'

Fal got up slowly, handed her back the *Woman's Realm* with its ugly contents, found his stick. 'I must start off, get the dogs up to the Forum. When did all this happen?'

Loveday slid the magazine back amongst the Deccas and Parlophones. 'She was still in her sweet little flat up in the house, next to the Night Nursery. Oh, it was long before she came here. You did that, didn't you? Gave her Bottle Cottage, I mean? And that Smollett had just come back from the war. She was so pleased, she cried and cried. It was lovely. But I never liked him after she did the thing with the bodkin. All the little pictures of them, Mumsie and Beau, banished. Banished!'

Fal was at the door. 'I wonder why she did that? Did you ever see her bible?'

Loveday was still, blank. 'I didn't know she had one.

She never showed me one. Oh! I could have had it today! How *suitable* . . . But no. Will you speak to Stella, I mean about supper? You are angelic.' She hurried forward, hugged him, kissed him. 'I'm quite better now, thank you. Hunky-dory in fact! But you won't say, will you? About the photograph? Because I stole it. I'm a thief: isn't that fearful?'

'I won't say, and I'll tell Stella. And you never saw a bible? With scribbles all over the . . . the . . . ummm . . . bookmark? Never saw?'

Loveday shook her head, her long tresses flew about with joyous abandon. 'No, never saw. Oh, sweet doggies! Minder! Jess! Off for walkies with Papa.' They went to the door together. Fal went heavily down the red-brick steps. Loveday turned and went back into the Wendy Hut, singing mindlessly.

He collected the dogs, climbed slowly up the path towards the Forum. He dimly remembered Smollett coming up to the house. Remembered because he came alone. Beau was dead. Killed, as they had been informed, in action, deeply regretted, at somewhere or other. Where? *Wolfsendorf.* Somewhere in Austria. Mumsie received the letters and all the bumf . . . and crumbled. She retired into widow's weeds about then, started to die: slowly. Never spoke of it again, never even saw Smollett. I remember that. Refused to see him . . . he was here for only a day.

How old would I have been then? I think that coming to terms with being the heir to Hartleap rather took over. I can't remember. I wish to God I could. I must face up to him at dinner tonight. I really must. This absurd inner panic of mine can't go on. I'll just come out with it. Over a stiff whisky: 'What actually happened to my father at Wolfsendorf, Smollett? Can you tell me?'

*

Looking round the stripped-out little room, the pile of furniture stacked up in the centre of the floor, May said, 'Well, that's the lot. I've got the Staffordshire and you've got your bits, and the keys to give to Stella. So, let's go. I hate this place now. She's gone, it's all finished. Come on.' She started out into the narrow hallway leading to the front door.

Bob stood for a moment in silence, holding his cardboard box. The black marble clock on the mantelshelf, he realized, had finally stopped. The silence was singing. 'We couldn't have carried all this stuff down that path, not without the car. We can make a quick getaway.'

He rustled his way through sheets of old newspaper, beside the empty ticking-covered bed, four blankets neatly folded on the top, two pillows tied round the middle. So that was that, a final severance. He heard May call him in a low voice from the hallway.

'There's something in the letterbox, Bob. An envelope. Hand-delivered. For you. It's from that bugger down at Home Farm . . .'

India was crossing the wide hall when May arrived, hair rather dishevelled, face flushed.

'Tea!' said India. 'It'll be ready directly. I seem to have lost Fal and *all* my children. My dear! Don't stand there! Go up to Unity's room and have a wash, you must be covered in dust and printer's ink from all the newspaper.'

May raised an unsteady hand. 'India. India, dear, we aren't staying. We'll just go right on, to the White Hart, to Lewes. We'll leave first thing tomorrow for home. No tea or dinner, please. *Please* understand.'

India was rock solid, still, frozen by May's intensity. 'I'll understand if I knew what it was that I had to understand. What *is* it? What has happened?'

May's eyes had unaccountably filled with tears. 'I'm going to say this, perhaps I shouldn't, but it's got to be said sooner or later, and I'm the best one to do it.'

India suddenly clutched her fists over her belly, as if to ward off the blow which she knew, instinctively, would come. 'What is it, May?'

'India, dear, it's . . . well: Bobbie killed your father-in-law.' Helpless tears welled and spilled down her cheeks.

Wednesday Evening

Standing at the window in Little Parlour, hands in his trouser pockets, Fal, tall and apparently perfectly calm, looked down across the valley. Sheep quietly cropped, the late afternoon sun lasered across the polished floor.

'I suppose that's what you meant when you said, "We've all got a secret"?'

Bob looked up quickly. 'I said that? When did I say that?'

'Up in the Cottage. The day I brought that Jesus fellow up. "We've all got a secret." Were you thinking of my father?'

'Perhaps. Yes. Suppose so.'

'The Jesus chap had explained about Rufus and half a pound of cocaine. I think you meant something else.'

'I meant something else. Yes. Yes, I did. Did you know he was called "Bluebell"?'

'My father? No, I didn't.'

'Well, he was – not to his face. But they called him that.'

'Why on earth?'

'Those eyes of his. Astonishing. And he was tall and thin, looked like a bloody bluebell, languid, elegant. When he wasn't being the other thing.'

'What other thing?'

'He was noted, shall we say, for his amazing bravery. For his courage and his violence. He was no bluebell in the desert. Those strange blue eyes were killer eyes. He enjoyed killing, gave him a turn-on. There were six Jerry prisoners, hiding in a dip in the sand. He told them to stand in line, hands raised, then about-turn and march away from him, into the sands. And then he shot them all in the back with a Bren gun.'

'I see . . .'

'I don't think that you really do. He said we were an attacking Brigade, on the move, we couldn't cart prisoners around with us. Didn't know where the nearest casualty-clearing place was. So he shot them. It was perfectly logical to him.'

'How did his men feel, did it matter?'

'No. No, it didn't matter. He was making life easier for them. No prisoners to worry about. We got the idea. Anyway, "C" Battalion did. "C" Battalion were happy with the information. Very happy. He knew his men.'

India and May came quietly into the room, closed the door. India sat down in an open window, her back against the jamb, hands clasped. May found a tight little silken chair.

Bob said, 'I was saying that we used to call him Bluebell, Grayle, I mean.'

Fal leant against the jamb of the middle windows, hands still in his pockets. 'Who, or what, was "C" Battalion.'

'I suppose it had a number, I can't recall, I've wiped it out. Bluebell had collected together the dregs from every battalion around. They were his particular bunch of bully boys, even their officers were frightened of them. Bluebell bashed them and they worshipped him. They'd do anything for him. Just a knack he had.'

'He sided with the rough, that it?'

'He enjoyed thugs. He knew they had nothing between their bloody ears except killing or maiming. They were just what he wanted. Most of them were illiterate, tough, miners, steelworkers, labourers, physical creatures. They'd kill without question, and most especially if it was "legal". Bluebell and the war made it legal.'

'And you shot him? That it? My father?'

'In a manner of speaking. I killed him. Yes.' Bob was staring blankly out of the windows.

'Was the war over by then?'

'Ha! *We* thought so. The day you were dancing in the streets in London we were moving up from Italy into Austria. Peacetime job, no problem. It wasn't over for us. Just a matter of "clearing things up". You know? No, of course you don't.' He clasped his hands together, looked at his feet. 'We were to assist in the repatriation of "a few Cossacks and Yugoslavs" back to the Russians. They *said* it was a few. And then the Russians would repatriate our prisoners of war back to us. That was the idea, very simple: we sent the Cossacks back to their Russian masters, and got our blokes back in exchange. Agreed at Yalta. All easy and above board. A simple job of repatriation. Going on all over the place. Displaced Persons crawling around everywhere. We had to help tidy it all up. They had reached a place in Austria, Wolfsendorf. There were about seventy thousand of them altogether. A few more than we expected, just a few. Bluebell called all his Battalion commanders together, with some odds and sods, for a briefing in the schoolhouse. *We* had about twenty thousand of the buggers to get back, across the river below. There was a wide bridge down there. Across the river a pole was flying the Red Flag, hammer and sickle job, so we knew we were fairly close. Our Allies, Bluebell called them. Job was to shove them, in trucks, across the bridge to the Russians, disarmed of course, and without using force! That was the daftest order I had ever heard in my life. Daft. Twenty thousand in our area to get across the river and use no force! Very honourable. They were frightened that perhaps if we used force, or whatever, there would be trouble for our boys the Russians had taken prisoner.'

'How did *you* know all this? Were you at the briefing or something?'

Bob sighed, wiped his face with his hands, wagged his head. 'Bluebell, as a very ordinary Brigadier, was not entitled to an ADC, or a personal servant. Only he was *not* any old Brigadier. He was this famous Beau Grayle, noted for his dashing bravery and bloody daring, for his duties under Monty, for his DSO and Bar, his medals and God-knows-what. So he *had* his ADC in fact. Me. Brought me with him from the UK, determined to keep me. Trained me. We were together in the TA before the war. I carried the maps and his bedding roll, his whisky and all his papers. I blancoed his bloody gaiters and webbing – white. *Not* khaki – white. His brasses and badges and things shone like a Christmas tree. "When I'm on duty, Smollett, I want to look like Asprey's window, got it?" I hadn't; didn't know what Asprey's was. I learned. And I stayed. He was a real shit. And I loved the bugger. Couldn't tell you why, just did. Admiration, perhaps? His amazing cheek! Courage.'

'And use no force?' Fal eased his hand from his pockets, brought the conversation back on tack, found a chair and sat. 'That was the rule all through, was it? No force?'

'Throughout. We all knew that. It didn't go down all that well with 'C' Battalion, I remember their CO at the briefing saying that. "It'll be OK as long as they aren't provoked, my lot. They don't fancy those buggers." And there were a lot of women and children up there. All muddled together.'

India crossed her ankles, rested her head against the window. 'What were women and children doing in a battlezone? Surely –'

Bob cut her short with a weary wave of his hand. 'Things

get changed in war, you know. These were refugees from the Russians: wives and daughters, mothers, grandmothers, Russians, and some were Yugoslavs. Displaced Persons officially. Crawling with them. When we moved into our area they had all settled in for life, I think. They didn't want to go back to Russia. Campfires, tents, there were goats and horses, the women seemed to give it all a settled sort of look. Children, too: it was not a good sign. I told Bluebell and he told me to hold my tongue, we'd obey orders from higher up – orders from Yalta, in fact – and to think of our chaps who were prisoners of war. But when he said that he had a sparkle in his eyes. He was just laughing really. Wanted a good show but didn't give a damn if we used force to shift them or didn't. Only we *mustn't* use force, he said. Remember that. Orders. *Very strict orders.* He thought.'

May hadn't uttered through this story. She'd heard it all before; she also knew what was to come. She shook her head, as if ridding her mind of ugly things, brushing them metaphorically from her hair like insects, her eyes still puffed with weeping.

'The other thing was that we were not to tell them where we were sending them. If they asked we had to say they were being taken to Italy. It wasn't that far, and there would be camps for them there. We'd just come up from Italy, it was fairly bashed about, I knew. But if that's what we had to tell them, then we would. No mention of the flag across the river. I mean, it was daft! You could see the Russian sentries down at the bridge, near as near. That's what we told them anyway. Made me feel a right shit. One old man, really old, came up to some of us on the first morning. Sort of bobbed and bowed, took out a crushed pocketbook and an old, creased postcard. It was, you know . . . sepia . . . brown? He was very proud of it. It was of

Queen Mary, our Queen Mary, tiara and all. He took off his cap and kissed it again and again. He was saying something, I don't know what. We turned him round and sent him back again to the main camping place. I wondered why. I mean, why Queen Mary? He wasn't English . . . But that's what it was like just at first, they trusted us – that's what was so bloody awful – trusted us to keep our word and send them to Italy. We were respected. We were, before the war, but it stopped there in that big meadow up by Wolfsendorf. Stopped there. Just a small place, end of the line, buffers and old sheds, some houses, the school, a church in the middle with that onion dome. No one about, the local people had all gone. Just as well. We took everything over for billets. Wolfsendorf. Sort of burned into my brain. I've carried this secret about with me like a hod of bricks you couldn't see. Just May knew, and Ada – you call her Nanny – but Ada knew. I came right down here to *her*. Not my mum, she never really figured in my life. It was always Ada . . . Soon as I was demobbed, soon as I was clear, I came down here. Alone. To be with Ada. To tell her about Wolfsendorf. Get it off my chest.'

'And . . . ?' Fal was interested, ankles crossed, appearing quite relaxed . . .

Until Bob said, 'Listen. I've tried to forget all this for thirty years. I've faded it out, you could say. I don't *want* to remember. You'll have to poke about. Ask me questions.'

'We never met. Or did we?'

'Sometimes, distantly. I was on the land. You used to ride past. Acknowledged each other, that's all. You were still at school. College.'

'I did come home, when we heard. For Mumsie.'

'I don't know about that. I went up to Ada's place, top of the house. Back stairs.'

'So we never met.' Fal put his fingers together. *This is*

the church, this is the steeple . . . 'How long did it take, this, umm, tidying up? Twenty thousand people?'

'Some days. Can't speak for the whole Corps area, but quite a time, for us. It wasn't what we were used to, really. With women and children all mixed up.'

'My father enjoyed all that?'

'Not enjoyed, I didn't say that. Not enjoyed. He just liked being at war, with his Brigade. Toy soldiers. Enjoyed doing the things we did in the Territorials. But for real.'

'Did the people just go? They didn't sit around waiting to be sent off, did they?'

'No. God no! We had told them, or someone had told them, they were going to be sent off to Italy. To camps we had made in Italy for them. I told you. That's what they thought.'

'So?'

'So they were, more or less, accepting. Until they saw the train.'

'Train?'

'Yes. There was the little single line, ran right past their camping area, where they'd set up camp. Buffers. The village, or town, was the end of the line. I told you . . .'

'What happened? I mean, what did they see that alarmed them? The train?'

Bob stretched a leg before him. 'Well, what they first saw was the train, right? And it stopped. And the people in the train – it was all cattle trucks and they were shut in – started hammering and yelling, because they had no one to open the doors for them. They had realized something was wrong, and then, from out of the woods and from some storage sheds and things by the railway, a whole crowd of Yugoslavs in uniform suddenly appeared. A warning. They were the loyal ones, loyal to Tito, and the people in the train realized they had been shunted into a trap.'

'By us? By the Allies, you mean?'

'That's what I mean. Exactly. It's better if you ask questions. I see things a bit clearer.'

'I'll try. Don't know what to ask . . .'

'It was the signal for them, when the Yugoslavs came swarming up. They opened the trucks – big iron handles sort of slotted across the doors – dragged the "prisoners" out.'

'Where had they come from? The "prisoners"?'

'I don't know. We never knew. Somewhere down the line, they'd been collected up.'

'And then?'

'All hell broke out. It was suddenly crazy, they lost control, completely lost control. We got mixed up in it by that time. Especially "C" company – went in to assist, I suppose. The people went wild. Women were screaming, the men were screaming, shouting "Italia!" all the time because by then they knew they weren't going to Italy. Not Italy! They were being rounded up and sent off across the bridge to the Red Flag.'

'Returned to Russia?'

'Repatriation we called it. Without force being used. What would you call a swipe across the face with a rifle butt? Gentle persuasion?'

'Not the women?'

'You looked surprised.'

'I am surprised. I'm horrified.'

'Well, hold the line. There's more to come. The women crawled to us. Hands and knees stuff, trying to stop us by holding round our legs. Some had babies and some were pregnant . . . they were holding their children up, high, above the screaming and fighting, they kept on howling, and crying, showing us their children.'

'And my father, in all this? My father?'

'Your father was shouting above the din, "*Don't use force*, get the sods into the trucks, but *don't use force*." He was actually firing his Sten gun above their heads. And laughing. He'd never had such a thrill. It didn't trouble him like it did us. Some of our blokes were crying. Really crying. Tears. We didn't expect this to happen to us. And then the trucks backed into the crowd and we started trying to get the old people in, the ill ones, the disabled. There were all sorts, the whole mass went bloody mad, screaming, crying. Women actually came up to us. One came to me and begged us to shoot their children. My woman, young, had one in arms, one in her hand. Know how she asked?' Bob's eyes were flat with shame.

Fal shook his head. 'No. How?'

'Well, she grabbed the stock of my rifle, shoved it against the kid's chest, then she stuck it hard against the other one, in her arms. That's how she asked.'

'Oh God . . .' Fal looked at the floor, unable to hold Bob's intensity.

'He'd got bugger all to do with it, God had. He was off duty that day. He was off duty all the time we were down in Italy. Not a *sign* of him. I sometimes felt sorry for the padres. They were calling on him in vain. He just didn't give a damn. Not a damn. Everyone asking for Him, yelling out for Him, and He didn't ever hear! Didn't hear a sound from us. Didn't hear a sound from the priests the repats had with them that day, wandering about chanting, wagging their beards, waving their wooden cross, all the black robes and fancy overalls. Didn't hear them either, not a bloody sign.'

May, in an effort to staunch this tirade, laid a gentle hand on his arm, but he brushed her off roughly.

'Next time some well-meaning idiot comes up to *you* and says "Jesus loves you. God has got his eye on the sparrows. *He cares*," just to say He hadn't got His eyes on about seventy thousand of them around Wolfsendorf on May the 14th, 1945. He was bloody stone deaf and blind. Both Jesus *and* His God, if they are different. Where did they wander off to during our war? Where were they when they were most needed?'

'Don't! Bob, don't! You must say that the colonels were worried, weren't they? You said that. They were distressed, asked him to ease up . . . you said so?'

Bob simmered down a little. 'Yeah. The colonels from our Brigade came up to him, said they couldn't "guarantee the mood of their men". They were all "deeply distressed". He exploded, Bluebell. Stood there, hands on his hips, furious, but he heard them out. They said the men hadn't joined the Army to beat the living daylights out of helpless civilians, and he just said, calm as you please, "No!" He said they came into the Army because they were bloody well conscripted into it! "They didn't come willingly, didn't volunteer. They are fighting the enemies of our country. *They* are the enemy, the King's enemy. All those cringing creatures, those Cossacks and Yugoslavs belong to the Russians, and the Russians want them back! They deserted! Now they've been beaten, so they crawl and apologize! You tell your men, each and every one of them, that they are the enemies of our Allies, the Russians! *They* want 'em back, we'll send 'em back, and then we'll get our *own* boys safely back. Tell 'em that! Tell them!" They all shifted about, sitting up there in the schoolhouse, didn't know how to reply. One of the IOs, a decent man, a Captain Adams I can remember, was braver than the rest. He just said, "Well, sir, it is a very distasteful job," and Bluebell blew his top. "Distasteful! Bloody distasteful! In the middle of a world war, to send the deserters back to our Allies! Distasteful! Christ almighty, they, and you, have been given

223

a job to do and however bloody *distasteful* you find it, you bloody do it! Right! Got that?" And he chucked all the maps and papers on the table right across the room. I remember that very well because it was my job to get them all together. He went bashing about among the crowds, yelling and firing his Sten gun over their heads, to hurry them on. He got the priests moving, I'll give him that. Pushed them into a group with their crosses and their flapping banners, vestments, and made them march to the top of the road leading down to the bridge. Then he fired his Sten just behind them, at their heels, you might say, and they started to shuffle down slowly, started some chant-ing and singing, then people started to follow them – the Cossack lot anyway – and in the end they were sort of marching, a bit straggly, singing down to the bridge. Some of the young men broke away, ran off up into the woods. I saw them . . . They were followed by the uniformed Yugoslavs, lots of yells and shots fired. They were just being hunted, hunted in the woods. No, I'll give Bluebell his due, he got the priests moving, and once they started off, carrying their banners and the wooden cross, people seemed to follow and our lot went on bashing the ones who wouldn't or couldn't, never was sure, get up and go for the trucks . . . It was a lovely spring day.'

India slowly folded her arms across her chest, stared down across the terrace, to the oaks and sheep in the meadow. She was weeping soundlessly, making no movement.

Fal cleared his throat. 'And then? What was next?'

Bob looked up at him slowly. 'Next? Oh, don't remember what was next. Seemed to go on for ages, all day, into the night. There were a lot of people to deal with . . . There were still a lot of people to deal with next day. They were still trailing away after the trucks. Dogs ran about . . . I took Bluebell some hot water in a mug so that he could shave. Very fussy he was, even then, at that moment, that morning. And when he came out of the schoolhouse it was just like the day before. The train kept bringing in more and more. Soon as we got rid of one lot down to the bridge others arrived, and the yelling and shouting started all over again. I never thought I'd be ashamed of being British. I'll never forget their screams of "Italia", and them drawing a finger across their throats. They knew where they were headed, knew we'd lied. We have a strange habit of doing that. I didn't realize at the time. I do now. We just wriggle out of things. Evade, I think is the word to use, but suddenly there were two God-almighty explosions. I wasn't looking at Bluebell at the time, he had been up on a bank across the road firing away into the air. When the smoke blew away, the clods of earth and stuff fell, someone started to yell and I could hear it over the terrible din. It was a clear shout, English and near me. It was the young IO, Captain Adams. He just yelled out, 'They got the Brigadier,' and we ran through the panicking crowds. Some of them had caught hefty splinters, everyone was screaming and yelling. I couldn't see him at first, and then it cleared, the crowd and the smoke, and there he was. On his back, looking very surprised.' Bob stopped, wiped his face roughly, swallowed.

Fal prodded. 'And . . .'

'And . . . and he'd completely lost his left arm. The grenades had been chucked from his left – that's what they had been, two grenades. Between his feet. On the bank. Right between his feet. His left leg was bust, torn wide open. You could see the bone. Bluish. Shiny.' He stopped and looked haggardly at Fal. 'They got him in the guts. Castrated him. That's what.'

May bowed low in her chair, head in her hands. India had closed her eyes.

Fal just stared ahead. 'Was he dead then?'

Bob shook his head, raised his voice, drew strength from somewhere. 'No. No. He wasn't dead then. He was looking at me. Those wide blue eyes full of surprise. Bluebell. He was frothing blood, bubbling all round his lips. Making a whining noise. Like a dog. I found his revolver in all the mess, stuck it in his mouth.' There was a stretched silence. 'That's all. That was what you wanted to know?'

Fal got up and walked away. He stood lost, unable to move, in the middle of Little Parlour.

Bob sat back in his chair, took May's hand in his, held it tightly. 'Captain Adams and his Colonel . . . Wintle, I think, Colonel Wintle . . . were crouching there with me. They were bleeding too. Some of the lads had gathered round, people were milling past, yelling and shouting. It was Wintle, I think – yes, Colonel Wintle – who looked at me. He leant over Bluebell and shut his staring, amazed eyes. Slowly. Then he said, "We close ranks here. Right? Just remember that. All of you." He had to shout it, almost, because of the row. Later we buried him up in the little church. We never found the bits . . . Much later, in the evening, it didn't get dark until . . . oh, about eight or nine, it was May . . . we buried him, and there was a big meeting up in the schoolhouse. I had to be there. Naturally. 'Course I did. They all agreed that nothing should ever be said, apart from the fact that someone, some "dissatisfied person or persons" had chucked two hand-grenades "in his direction". Not *at* him – "In his direction". No one witnessed it. They closed ranks tightly. Nothing more was said. Nothing. I don't know what was written to your mother. Obviously she got official notice from the WO. But *they* didn't know for certain. And no one ever told her the truth. Not in this house. This is the first time it has been told. Here,

today. Because you asked me. So I *did* kill him, yes. That's
how it was.'

The late sun flickered through the trees in the orchard as
Jesus followed the dirt path to the Wendy Hut. As the
steps, and the slightly battered wooden building, came into
view he stopped and called loudly, 'Miss Loveday Grayle!
It's Jesus. I've got another message for your brother. Miss
Grayle?' He felt it was prudent to warn her, unless she went
into a fit or something. She quite easily could, and he didn't
want any fuss. He knew she might be in the hut because,
although the sun was dipping low, there was a light on,
and the door was open. Just as he reached the seeding
lupins and the trodden little beds, the two dogs, Minder
and Jess, came leaping and jumping out, down the brick
steps, and frightened the wits out of him. He waved his
stick at them. 'Fuck off,' he yelled. 'Miss Grayle! A message.
It's Jesus.'

Loveday appeared at the open door. She might just have
woken up, he thought, and then realized that, indeed, she
had.

'Could you call these bloody dogs off . . . please?' She
looked at him cautiously. 'Please, Miss Grayle, I'm not going
to attack you or anything. Just a message to give you. Rufus,
your brother, telephoned me at the hospice again.'

Loveday called to the dogs, who stopped leaping and
baring their teeth and looked, resentfully Jesus thought, at
her before wandering off into the orchard. 'What does the
message say?' Loveday made a motion which indicated,
uncertainly, that he might come nearer, join her on the
little wooden verandah. 'Yesterday you said that Rufus was
in Argentina. I think you get it all muddled.' Loveday led
the way into the Wendy Hut and sat in her chair by the
easel.

'He was in Uruguay. That's where he actually was. But he just now called and said that he's moving on, in a couple of days, to New York. Can I sit somewhere? Just for a moment?'

Loveday waved an indifferent arm about the hut. 'Sit where you like. I was asleep when you came, on the sofa. It's been a terrible day, a terrible, terrible week. You first came here on Sunday!' She turned accusingly in her chair, a paint-stained overall bunched on her lap, her hair a wild tangle.

'Yes. Right. Sunday. And now it's Wednesday . . . so?' He nodded.

She turned back to her painting. 'You were here yesterday too. They buried Nanny this morning. It seems so long ago. So long . . . Where's the message?'

Jesus fumbled his backpack off his shoulder. 'He called me, Rufus, because he had just arrived in his hotel, and he was anxious to know what had happened up at the cottage. I mean, he had something he'd left with Miss Stephens and I was supposed to go and get it, before the removal men arrived. Understand?'

'Very well. Of course I do. You were supposed to collect some silly old IOU or something. The children told me all about it. I remember very well.'

'Well, that's why he telephoned. To see if I had got it.'

'And had you?'

'No, I hadn't.'

'Oh. Was he furious? I bet he was angry. I bet. He's always angry.'

Not wishing to disturb her general air of calm he didn't tell her just how angry Rufus had been. He slid away from the subject: searched his backpack, found a small notebook. 'He said he was sorry to hear about Nanny, but sorrier to hear about the ... IOU being lost. He won't be back on this side of the Atlantic for the foreseeable future. That's what he says: *foreseeable*. I'm to put that on a piece of paper. Send it up to the house. Have you a piece? Of paper?'

'Some people!' said Loveday. 'Some people take advantage. Give them an inch and they take an ell. That is Nanny talk. She's dead now, so I talk it. Here, a piece of paper. I suppose you want an envelope too.'

Jesus shook his head and said no, no envelope. Perhaps she'd take it up herself?

Loveday looked at him sourly. 'Well, I might. If I go up to the house. If I take my supper there. I won't go up particularly, but if I do go, yes, I'll take it.'

'That would be very kind.'

'They have visitors, for dinner. I can't, myself, understand such callousness, on the funeral day. The Smolletts are having dinner. *Wine* and everything. It is so very uncaring. Thoughtless.'

'If the Smolletts have that smart blue Mercedes, they've gone. I passed them on the road, roaring off to Lewes. They could have given me a lift, but I had to come here with this message. The "*foreseeable*" part seems to be important. It's all there. I'll just fold it in two. You won't drop it, will you?'

'You will take the short cut, I suppose, down to the village?'

'Yup. I'll get the evening bus at the King's Arms. On the hour, I think.' He got up and hitched up his backpack. 'Thank you. I won't be troubling you again, I'm sure. Now that I have told Rufus there isn't ... that the IOU was lost in the muddle, he won't call me again. Anyway, he's moving on. And I'm moving on too.'

Loveday wandered slowly across to the door and watched

him walk down the path to the road. He turned at the bottom and waved goodbye. She didn't move.

Jesus heard Rufus's furious, then despairing, voice in his head. *Chucked it! Chucked the McDougall's packet! You realize what it was worth, I suppose? You do know its value? Christ almighty!* Then he said he was moving on, as soon as he'd had a rest – New York, probably – and he wouldn't be back. *Tell the stupid idiots up at the house. Tell them that. Chucked down the cesspit! I won't be back. Say for the 'foreseeable future', that'll keep them silent. Don't even say New York. I may not land up there now. I've closed the job with the BBC. Need a break. All finished. Did you get the papers? As I asked you? Nothing about me?* And Jesus had said no, nothing, German local news was hardly important stuff, and anyway *his* ratings had been slipping badly. It was a wonder, he thought, that the BBC hadn't dumped *him*. But he'd bought all the what he called 'nasties' and gone through them: nothing, and nothing in any of the broadsheets. Sunk without trace, he'd said, and wondered as he got into the village what he'd do with so many newspapers that no one seemed to want. He heard the bus snorting along behind him and hurried to catch it at the King's Arms. He bitterly regretted the loss of the flour, but that was too late to regret now. He'd lost a fairly healthy cut. All down bloody Nanny's cesspit. Oh well . . . It would have been very useful just at present, tided him over . . . paid the rent for a few months somewhere nice . . . new shoes . . . Sod it.

He started running towards the bus-stop. At least he'd delivered his note, they'd get the idea. Foreseeable future was pretty definite. What will they make of McDougall's? He swung on to the bus and it pulled out into the traffic of the main street.

*

'Do they X-ray luggage at the airport? I was thinking of my travelling-clock. Roch? Roch, did you hear? My travelling-clock?'

Roch wandered from his room down the corridor, a pair of shoes in his hand. 'You do ask potty questions. The IRA have just bombed the Tower of London and you ask if they X-ray luggage! Of *course* they do. Place crawling with bloody IRA and Customs everywhere. It'll show up and then you'll be carted off and strip-searched. Stark naked. Awful.'

'What is strip-searched exactly?'

'They will examine every orifice in your body. And that's not just ears, nose and mouth: other places too – with a torch. And then you'll miss the flight.'

Sophie shrugged. 'You really do try to disgust people. In my hand luggage, then they can see it.' She dropped it into a green canvas holdall. 'God! Dinner was a bit gruesome, wasn't it? Poor old Mum. No Smolletts – pissed off to wherever they pissed off to – Papa was wretched as could be.'

'Well, I would be too, if I heard that someone had killed *him* like that.'

' "Helped him out" – that's what we have to remember. He was "helped out". It wasn't a murder or anything. And *we* have to close ranks.'

'I won't find that hard to do. I didn't actually know Grandpa, just the "legend". I didn't know either about that bloke at Home Farm. Never even seen him that I can remember. Have you?' Roch looked at his two shoes. 'I haven't room for these. Have you met the people down there, seen them?'

Sophie sat at her dressing-table, started to wipe her face with a cream. 'No. Seen them: she's rather fine, tall and very arty – hair in a turban thing, huge skirts, bare feet, that sort. He's quite pretty, much younger, I'd say. But I don't honestly see why the elders are in such a fuss about them. They don't know us, don't know anything serious about Grandpa, do they? The chap's a journalist or something, Stella said so. I don't know why everyone is in such a fizz. It was thirty years ago! People get killed in war. Soldiers. I rather thought that was the entire point? Bang! Bang! You're dead, so we've won. No?'

Roch sat on a wooden chair, looked down thoughtfully at his shoes, one brown, one black. 'I haven't even got a pair here, so I'll just leave them. Can't get them in, so leave it. That's my answer to everything irritating. We'll be back on Monday so that's all right. Does your medical student know how long you're staying?'

'Yes, I told him. Does Kathleen know how long *you* are staying?'

'Yes, told her too. Her assignment finishes on Friday. Tra-la! I just hope she'll come back. It's not sure yet – I mean come back here, with us ... me. Are you going to get closer to the student? I mean closer than with a pretzel and a glass of Dubonnet, that's what you said. Am I prying?'

'Yes, bloody rude. He's Jean-Claude Berrichon – don't call him "my" medical student. It's more than you are anyway. He's dedicated.'

'I'm your brother, and I'm dedicated too, to this place. I've got a slight worry about Kathleen. I mean, I'll tell her my decision. Which seems to have fussed Papa, about money an' all, and her being "used".'

Sophie started to wipe off the cream which she had stringently applied. 'You will remember what Papa said at dinner, keeping things to ourselves? Not even Stella and Charles, and, above all, *not* Loveday. He was most particular about that. Can't think why. She'd never take it in.

232

She's so damned scatty she'd let it all wash over her, after a good cry.'

Roch fidgeted, stroked the shoes on his lap like an ill-matched pair of guinea pigs. 'I am to tell Kathleen when she "joins the family", according to Papa. That means when we are married and she swaps names and becomes a Grayle. Then I can tell her. Frankly I don't think she'll give a fig. Years ago, it's not her sort of thing. She simply wouldn't be interested. Why *should* she be curious about what happened to Grandpa years and years ago? I think they are all taking the whole thing too seriously.' He decided, stroking his shoes, that he might change plans and wear the brown ones instead. They were almost new after all. A pleasing feel.

Sophie chucked a bunch of soiled paper into the bin beside her. 'Apparently they, the people at Home Farm, *have* got a clue about him. Want to write a book about it all. No one ever has: forbidden land. Mama blames herself for leaving a portrait of the old man down at Home Farm. They saw it and the guy recognized it somehow and started off on some research. Apparently he got keen when people all clammed up. But that's the trouble with the elders, they all live in the past – haven't got enough to do, frankly, so the idiots start digging up their past, looking for worms, like blackbirds on a compost heap.' She turned and laughed. 'I say! That's quite good, isn't it? Is it an analogy or a metaphor?'

Roch snapped his mind away from his shoes. 'How would I know! When did Mama leave a portrait of Grandpa down there?'

'When she was tidying it up. It's a rough. Not the real thing, we've got the real thing here. It's in the drawing-room. Those blue eyes staring . . . I rather hate it. She loves it. So does Papa. I do remember that Nanny would never go into

233

the drawing-room because of it. She sat, when she came down here, with the kitchen crew, or in Little Parlour. Funny, I have just remembered that. She simply hated his portrait. Said it gave her the creeps. Exact words: "Gives me the creeps," she said. I wonder why?'

Roch sat in silence for a moment or two. 'Of course, we have to remember that Pa said that he was actually murdered. Smollett said that someone, on *our* side, had quite deliberately chucked those grenades at Grandpa. He was killed by his own side. Have to remember that. Smollett, if he's telling the truth – and I see no reason why he'd lie at this stage of the game – did, as you say, "help him out". He didn't deliberately mean to kill him, someone else did that. And although there was all kind of awfulness going on, no one apparently was actually chucking grenades about, until those two, at that one figure . . . between his legs. Remember that, Sophie.'

She looked worried, screwed up another piece of paper and cotton wool. 'Yes, I will remember that. God, how awful . . . never occurred to me – I mean at dinner. I was wondering about this: packing, tomorrow, Jean-Claude . . . Golly, I do see why the man at Home Farm got interested. It's obviously been leaked. I mean someone knew. Said so. Why would anyone want to deliberately kill someone on their own side in a war? She dragged her hair up into a knot on top of her head. 'I quite like my hair up, what do you think?'

Roch got up and banged the shoes together. 'I have some decisions of my own to make. I like your hair anyway you like to wear it. He was called "Beau Grayle", Grandfather – fearfully brave and daring, and I should imagine a real bastard. Someone didn't like him enough . . . It would make a good story, wouldn't it? "Golden Boy Brutal Killer At Heart", something like that, we now reveal! Shoving all those people back to the Russians – prisoners, women and kids – was not very popular, I gather. Something we British didn't do. Only we did.'

Sophie sighed. 'I wasn't even *born*, no one ever spoke of it!'

'I never knew about it either, until tonight. I remember at college we heard murmurings but they quickly got squashed. Something about a near mutiny as well.' At the door he turned back into the room. 'I have made a huge decision. I'll take the brown pair and not the black and that means I'll have to take a light suit, not the charcoal . . . Repacking . . . Shit!'

Sophie got up impatiently. 'Honestly! As if it mattered! Wear your flares and sneakers, why not? You won't have time to dress up. Kathleen works at night.'

Roch waved a brown shoe at her across the room. 'I don't know what you and your medical student Berrichon will do, but I'm going to take Kathleen somewhere very chic for dinner where sneakers and flares simply won't do. OK?'

'Good luck,' said Sophie. 'I had better go down and see if bloody Loveday has made it from the kitchen. It's her first night completely on her own, so I suppose I'd better just check.' She tied her dressing-gown round her waist and went to the door just as Stella reached the far end of Nursery Corridor.

'Stella! Stella, I was on my way. Is she all right?'

Stella, heaving to get her breath, pushed a fall of greying hair from her forehead. 'She is now. Heavy as a log of wood. Got her into bed, or on to it. She'll sleep till morning. She hasn't been off the bottle since God knows when.'

'You are an angel, Stella. Thank you. I was just coming down.'

'Well, we will have to take stock tomorrow. We can't

go on like this, Miss Sophie, we really can't. We'll have to have a few words when we are all less tired. But it won't do, it really won't. I know people don't have a funeral every week but this has been a back-breaker, a real back-breaker. She needs a daily companion, that's what. And it won't be me and for sure it won't be Charlie. He's chewing the carpets and bringing up blood. So beware!'

And she turned and hurried, silently, down the stairs.

Roch came to his door, leant out. 'I heard all that. I do see. We'll have to discuss all this. Do it in the morning . . . Oh Lord . . .'

As Stella reached the bottom of the stairs, Charlie, in his white jacket, came out of the Gothic Room with a loaded tray. 'Got her up there, did you?'

Stella took the tray from him and went through the baize doors into the kitchen. 'I did. Get her there. God! She was a weight. *Dead* weight.'

Charlie had followed her in. The door click-clacked behind him. He shucked himself out of the jacket, hung it behind the door with the aprons. 'Drunks usually are. They just go limp. She's getting hopeless. I mean, what kind of a life is it for us with her sitting in a heap all through supper, snivelling? I'd have chucked her baked beans at her!'

Stella had stacked some glasses ready to wash, too deli-cate for the dishwasher. She ran water. 'I don't know what we're going to do now. I did have a sort of "airing of our views" with Sophie, but it's not her fault . . . We'll deal with it tomorrow. They'll all have gone by then, the children are off to Paris . . .'

Charlie cleared the rest of the tray, swiftly and expertly. 'I wouldn't really mind, not if I were paid to look after her and did *nothing else*. It's just when she starts invading our

236

space – and God knows we don't get much of it – when she starts whining about a "poached egg" and just the corner of the table! That's when I go spare. Corner of the table! What are we supposed to be doing? Watch her eat on her corner? We need a bit of privacy ourselves. I thought I'd do someone a mischief when that God-awful Heather and her lady friend were here this morning. I mean, no peace . . . bashing about with our ovens . . . and leaving it all for me to clean.'

Stella rinsed the glasses in a bowl of soapy water. She remained perfectly calm. 'I don't *want* to give in our notice,' she said, 'not after all these years. But if it comes to having to deal with Miss Loveday, not to mention the dogs – they never leave her side – we'll have to have a *serious* think about things. We won't do better, as far as money and kindness and all that . . . not to mention accommodation and holidays . . . but having to deal with someone who is missing a box of screws in the head is something else again.'

'Look!' said Charlie grimly. 'Bloody mud – those dogs! She just tramped it in, when she came up from her sodding Wendy Hut. And the *dogs*, feet all over everywhere.'

Stella rinsed the glasses, stood them on the draining-board. 'It was the rain last night. The lane is full of ruts and puddles.' She took up a teacloth, started to dry the glasses. 'She could hardly help muddying the floor.'

Charlie had filled a bucket, found a mop, was furiously sloshing water across the black-and-white-tiled floor. 'At this time of night! We've been at it all day. For days. You are too willing and kind by far, my girl – even going to the funeral! I reckon that if they get some sort of companion for Loveday that'll be another mouth to feed. And another set of beds to make, and you can't get that Gloria every time . . . well, not permanently. We'll give in our notice, that's what. Or at least we can, say, suggest it? It's too much . . . Mind your back, I want to empty this bucket. Come on, old dear.'

Stella leant on the edge of the sink. 'Look, don't "old dear" me, Charlie, I am not finished. If you are, chuck it into the yard, now go along. Don't be so irritating.'

Charlie looked at his wife with anger. 'Irritating! After twenty hours' slog! You block up the sink! *You're* the irritating one, you are.' He yanked open the door to the yard and chucked the muddy water across the cobbles to the stables.

Stella said thoughtfully, 'At the funeral, Charlie, that chap was there. You know? The one from Home Farm.'

'So? What if he was?'

'I just thought it curious. No one knew him. He just jumped up from behind a gravestone thing, jumped up and accosted Bob Smollett. Quite a surprise, you could see that. I don't know what was said – not much, I assure you. I really did think Smollett would hit him. He was furious! Now why, tell me, should that bloke down there want to speak to Smollett? No one else, just Bob Smollett. It's odd.'

Charlie hung the mop in a cupboard, the bucket beneath it to catch the drips. 'I don't know if it's so odd, Stella. You know he's watching them all up here? Binoculars. I think he's so busy watching them come and go on the terrace and in the car and so on that he doesn't notice *me* watching him back. I've got an old pair of binoculars, loaned them to Smollett. He was curious. The guy spent so much time up at Ada's, at Nanny's, especially in the evenings . . . cheering her up. Saw him going in, five or six times, with a Sainsbury's bag. Probably fruit or something.'

Stella placed the dried glasses on a tray, covered them with a clean cloth. 'Yes,' she said, 'she liked her fruit. As long as it was soft. I didn't know you were bird-watching that lot down there. I've just said hello when I was out in the lane. Funny woman. He's quite good-looking. What could he find to interest him in Bob Smollett, for heaven's sake? I mean, I know the kids say he's someone called "Tom Tiddler", gossip person, journalist – Gloria knows them all, it's for people like Gloria and her mum and dad that they make those dreadful papers. But why should he find Smollett interesting? Spend so much time up there with Nanny? I think it's a bit weird. But Smollett was really furious today. Furious. Come on, lock up – let's go up.' She kissed his forehead and took off her apron.

India pulled herself in from the open window of the dressing-room, closed the curtain. 'They've just put out the lights. Down there, at Home Farm. I'll leave these windows open, shall I? It's wonderfully warm still.' She passed Fal, lying flat in his bed, touched his feet lightly.

'Yes, leave them open, I'll close them if a storm starts. And get to bed! I'm absolutely filleted.' He opened his book.

India sat on the edge of his bed. 'I think that was the longest weekend I've ever spent. The very longest. It seemed to go on for days and days. Amazing how many things can get crammed into a day. Just a day.' She sat slightly hunched in her nightdress, arms folded across her thighs. 'Poor May Smollett, she was a ruin. She'd never have made supper. Not even an omelette. Never. He was no better, poor man. You *were* good. Very good, darling. And then having to tell the children. You were *so* good, thank you. Shall I go away?'

Fal laid his book on his chest. 'Yes, go away – not very far away, just to your bed, so that I can see you, hear you breathing. Don't go any further.'

She leant down and kissed his lips. 'I won't, promise. I'm too weary to go very far. I love you.'

He lay for a time staring at the ceiling, heard her turn down her bed, busy about doing something, and then her light snapped off and he was in the half-light from his reading lamp. He tilted it down so that it would not leak out and perhaps disturb her.

So that's how it was. That's how he died: brutal, messy. I hadn't expected that. Bloody brave of Smollett to come out with it. Not much alternative, really. Still, he need not have been quite as ... what? Graphic. Helped him on his way ... Yes, I see that. Pa would have been useless minus an arm and a leg. And his balls. He couldn't have lived anyway. Riding out with him at dawn, how I hated it. God! When I think! Everything absolutely correct, boots polished like bloody glass, collar and tie – no jeans and sneakers. We didn't have jeans and sneakers then. I didn't do things as he wanted: funked the jumps, hated gallops. He said I was useless. I was. I always have been, I suppose. He was *very* disappointed in his eldest son. Me. He had lost hope with the girls, Angelica and Faith. Dead from meningitis. The first-born, a pair of *girls*! That shook him. Tried for a son, got me. That was all right – to start with. Then Unity – He went at it, Pa. Poor Mumsie, a sort of breeding oven – He never cared for Unity really, a "throw-back" he called her ... Rufus made up for it, at the start. Until he didn't grow. Christ! A short-arse for a son! – His words ... Mumsie weeping quietly, sorrowing with her short-arsed son. Then Loveday. Oh God. The despair when it became apparent. That was the final indignity. He was furious, Pa. Puzzled ... Two runts. The seed's running out, he said. I remember that. It's a punishment from God! Losing his potency, as he called it, was the thing he dreaded most. He never seemed to think it could have been Mumsie's fault. He just, more or less, turned his back on her, on us all, from then on in. No more hurly-burly. Mumsie no longer crawled about now with a large belly, brow furrowed with anxiety, longing to please. She was a silly woman. I have come from a silly family. Which is why I'm silly too. I must be. I haven't run this place correctly since I took over. It's overtaken me. I have a pretty daughter whose highest ambition is to go and help lepers in Somalia and a son who changes his mind so often he's like a windmill . . . and just as loose, swinging in any wind that blows. Perhaps the girl, Kathleen whatever, will last. She might be a help. If they do get hitched. Women are so often far stronger than their men. Except for Pa. Who was strong in a bullying way. His life was made absolutely perfect by the war. His big ta-ra-ta-ra! Here I am, world! He bullied and battered the world, and that doesn't go down very well. The world has a vile habit of hitting back when it gets fed up with you. Got fed up with him. Started right from the beginning, with the girls. Give you two females, golden as corn, corn-flowers and poppies, and just when they are starting to break into bloom — bosh! Take 'em away! Punishment! And all the rest of us were more or less bloody failures. Anyway, in his eyes. Loveday and Rufus almost did for him. He really liked Robert Smollett and made it obvious, anyway to me. He did all the things brilliantly that I was a failure at: felling trees, riding hard, physical, strong, unafraid. Unafraid of Pa, didn't give a damn. Excellent with every-thing from peaches to sheep, splitting logs, gutting pike, laying bricks, pruning roses. Pa said I was "too bloody bookish — wouldn't put it past you to write poems!" I did. And eventually *he*, Smollett, helped him out. Would *I* have been able to do that? Would I? I might have been brilliant. I'll never know now. And what does that sod down at Home Farm want with this sorry little tale? What can he make of that? Everyone will protect him, Pa. He was so admired by those who didn't know, he used the war to make up for the awful failures in his family. As he saw it. The weakness of his structure. He played the Golden God! Beau Grayle! Roughshod he rode over everyone. And some-one, one afternoon, didn't like it all that much, disapproved and topped him finally. What a way to go. God almighty!

He closed his unread book, put it aside. People have come down here to try and 'do' a book, as they said. Gave it up in the end. Too complicated, no true evidence, the W O not at all helpful – that was some Major-General . . . remember that. Wrote books about shooting elephants and rhino. Odd choice to make: picking Pa. The W O said any facts at all about 'the repatriation of the Cossacks' could be 'detrimental to public interest'. Of all bloody silly things. Why? It was thirty years ago, and if Smollett was right, allowing for time and memory, I suppose, it did seem un-British. Not something that would stand exposure. And now that idiot at Home Farm is picking at the scar. It's healed! Why not leave it all alone? Let it rest.

He reached up and snapped off his light and India said suddenly, 'I've had thoughts tumbling and racing through my brain . . . silly things. But I suddenly remembered: you know when we were all in Little Parlour just before lunch, the wake. Edward was doing the drinks?'

Fal turned on his side, stared blearily into the darkness. 'Yes.' He heard India ease up in her bed.

'Well, do you remember that Unity had gone up to her room? We were sort of waiting for her, really.'

Fal remembered, nodded in the darkness. 'Unity? Yes, remember very well. I thought how very hearty and "Unity" she was being. Singing some show song. Not altogether appropriate for a gathering like that. Yes, I remember it well. Why?'

'I do too. She wasn't as jolly as her song. She'd been weeping.'

'Well. One does that at funerals. Normal, surely?'

'Unity didn't give a fig for Nanny. Called her a wicked old bat many a time. In all the muddle of things today, I suddenly realized that Unity had been weeping. For herself.'

Thursday Morning

Her strong fingers curled round the smooth pottery of the mug: both hands to gain warmth, for this moment, her favourite moment, was still chill from the night, and the dew lay like frost across the lawn. She thought that, perhaps, it was her *most* favourite time of the day. That moment just after dawn, as the light began to seep into the dusk, throwing no shadow, for the sun had not yet risen and the sky lay above her like the interior of a pewter spoon, grey, shiny, unwarmed. From far down in the valley, modest though it was, she could hear the bicker and whispering of the little stream as it bubbled and swept smoothly through the reeds and bulrushes to spill over the broken sluice gate.

If she stayed just as she was, if the *time* stayed just as it was, a new day about to be born, her toes curled against the cool of the stone slabs which supported the porch, the scent of coffee in the air from her pottery mug – if it all stayed quite still, petrified, silent, she would not have to face the new day. She didn't at all want to; she knew that it would be hateful and that she would be the loser in the battle. Well, hardly a battle. No point in trying to fight the inevitable. That had been explored in detail yesterday – crushing, brutal detail.

'Look, Isso, I'm going to go up to Town, just for a bit, I'll stay at Frank's. Frank Heffer? He's got room, won't be there anyway, he's off to Budapest doing something on the reconstruction. I don't know what. Something. But he says I can have his flat in Belsize Park. It's small, quiet, undisturbed. I can write there. Get myself sorted out. And, if I need to, I can nip anywhere I have to, to interview whoever. I don't know who, but I can check up on things. It's difficult from here. If I am settled in Town, as it were, I'd feel closer to things. Understand?'

She was hemming the squares of batik: cushion covers. The buyer at Liberty's had said they'd take a couple of dozen, to try. She did her best not to look up at him. 'No, frankly, I don't understand. What am I supposed to understand? That you are taking Frank Heffer's flat in Belsize Park to get on with your bloody book? Is that what I am to understand? I fail to. Quite fail to. Surely this is the best place to be? To write? You are undisturbed, it's silent as the grave, no one to interrupt your muse. And everything you are writing about – as you have been for weeks now, as far as I am aware – everything you need, is right here. No? You are in the heart of it all, the Grayle heart.'

Jake laughed. 'That's the problem. I'm too damned close. Can't see straight.'

Isobel took off her thimble. 'You realize, don't you, you'll probably destroy a lot of totally innocent people, up there, at the house, destroy their lives? They had nothing to do with Beau Grayle. Apart from being born.'

'That's enough, isn't it? Same blood. I hate that class. They hand it on. All those lunatic names! Falmouth, Rochester, Unity – God!'

'It's my class, as you call it, too.' Isobel replaced her thimble, took up another piece of material.

Jake said, 'Well, I'm getting you sorted out, aren't I? And that daft thing you made me do, St Sebastian – just an excuse to get me tied up and stark naked. You enjoy that. Warped!' He was grinning, she knew by his voice, but still she did not look up. 'That's why I stopped fart-arsing about. I mean, it's all right now and again, but it's warped. Your class all is. What was Grayle doing dying in his head gardener's arms, eh? That's what the Nanny told me. "He died in my Bobbie's arms," she said. "Bobbie helped him out." Helped him out! What other bit of rubbish did he do? Give him a lollipop? Did he ask Smollett to give him a kiss? Kiss me, Hardy. Smollett? It's all bunk, isn't it? Went too far, Isso, someone topped him, end of story – except it isn't. I've got the story put nearly together. Nanny was very interesting, a great help. Said more than she meant to, I reckon, and I'm going to write it down.'

'Well, leave it. Leave it. A silly old woman. Rambling, half dead. I'm sorry about the St Sebastian, I didn't know you hated it, no idea ... Thought you got a kick from cavorting about. Anyway, leave the Grayle thing, do. She was a very old woman, a dying old woman, rambling ... Let it go. Please?'

'Don't be so thick, Isso. Be sensible. I've got a hell of a lot of work to do. I have a big story here.'

'I know that only too well. I just don't see why you have to clear off and rent a flat in London to write, when you have a perfectly good place here in the country. All paid for! It mean that I'll be stuck here on my own all summer. I suppose you realize that?' He had grunted, and she'd finally looked up to bite through a thread and tie a knot. 'That porcine grunt means that I am right? It is something that doesn't trouble you too much? Me being here alone?'

'It won't be for ever. I'll come down some days maybe. When the flow dries up, or I lose my way, you know? Anyway, weekends, I could get down at weekends ... Or perhaps you could get up to Town, have a break, see some chums ...'

She looked at him coolly. 'What "chums" are you speaking of? How many "chums" do I have? We didn't exactly collect a congregation, you and I, we were enough for each other once. You might have forgotten. "Chums", as you call them, didn't figure, and our relationship rather precluded making chums. Age difference, other differences . . .'

'I know what you're getting at. Don't spell it out: difference in ages, difference in class, I didn't *speak* as well as you'd have liked.'

'I was thinking about our little sexual peccadillos, not how you spoke.' Isobel was collecting up her work.

'Anyway, I don't have to pay Heffer rent. He said I could have the key, that's all, go up there when I liked. Bloody decent of him, honestly.'

Isobel had gathered up a pile of finished cushion covers. 'Bloody decent. Kind as kind. When do you plan on making this momentous move?'

He was rattled suddenly. 'It's *not* momentous, *not* even a *move* really. Well, a move, but more a settling in to start a work rhythm. I want to get this down on paper. Just get the first chapter set. I can't settle here, honestly. We've spent our time painting, gardening, getting the place the way you wanted it to be, and now I want a place to work. I'll go up at the weekend. Simple. Away from any kind of hassle or interruption . . .'

She had stood clutching her cloths in one hand, the small basket which held her scissors, threads and needles in the other. 'And I hassle you, do I? Interrupt? Disturb the magic flow?'

He ran his fingers through glossy curls; even in her anger she was aware of them: the sheen, the tumble. She rather longed to pull his head to her breast; instead she stood white with anger and heard him say, 'Well, frankly, yes. At times. Like yesterday. Banging on about how much onion to use. I don't *care* how much! *Some* onion, that's all!'

The snapping and sniping began to turn into a full, furious row, the sort of row during which energy is expended and things better left unsaid are said. It was trite and silly, just to start with. Then it became wounding and she had realized that he had absolutely set his mind on Belsize Park, turned his back on Home Farm – on her, to face facts. On her. The fears of yesterday were hardening. Behind the house, quite suddenly, the first crack of true dawn split the greyness, and as the sun rose above the rim of the silent earth, the first birds started, calling and scolding, the light grew stronger, drenching the still-damp fields. A golden haze grew in brilliance. She moved out from the shelter of the porch, felt the dew-drenched grass spring beneath her feet and, as silent and swift as a paper dart, the heron swooped down to the brook, flurried to a stop in a fuss of feathers, collected his wings, shook his head. He preened and nibbled, looked about himself, began to tread with long-legged steps along the weedy banks, brushing through the meadow-sweet, his eyes, bright as golden coins, seeking darting shadows of roach or perch in the smooth-flowing water. As if his majestic arrival had signalled the start of a new day, the valley was all at once glowing with sunlight, rang to the sound of the birds in copse and wood. A lark went bulleting into the now opal sky and the new day, however much she had hoped to delay it, had arrived.

She threw the dregs of her coffee in a wide arc before her, trod straight-backed over the trimmed wet grass, her enormous skirts billowing and dragging behind her, sweeping all beneath them; a confection, the dressing-gown, which she had made herself: Paisley-pattern silks in viridian and carmine, the sort of thing that Edith Sitwell might well have worn, mandarin-sleeved so that she could shelter be-ringed hands in them, frail as ivory, like a folded fan. She was handsomer, of course, than Miss Sitwell. She was still a 'fine figure of a woman', her father would have been able to reassure her, hair flowing, a shimmering cataract, over her shoulders and down her back. This was the one time in the day that she permitted it freedom from the tight bonds in which it was usually restrained. Her hands – she looked down at them thoughtfully – were *not* ivory. They were not Edith Sitwell hands stuck about with bulky topaz and aquamarine. They were tough hands, working hands: they could gut a rabbit, pull a bird, split wood, bake bread and mix cement. They had been useful to her, and had delighted others. Thinking of others gutted her: another, not others.

Standing slightly stooped by misery, mug hanging loosely in her hand, she looked over the hedge which marked their boundary. Up on its hill, still and shuttered, Bottle Cottage: blind windows, overgrown garden, sagging fence. Hateful place, a witch's house. They'll be here shortly to cart away the furniture and the place will be empty. What then? Who will follow the witch? Wicked old woman . . .

Then she shrugged, turned on naked heels and walked back through the cropped grass to the farm, still, asleep, its huge brick-cluster chimney glowing rose madder against the blue. If she had been less distracted, less woeful, she would have stopped to admire the glowing beauty of centuries; instead she ignored it, merely glancing upwards, hearing the dragging of her wide silk skirt across the spangled grass.

'Hassle. Hassle. Hassle.' The word nagged along with her. So that's what she did? A cause for irritation? For distraction? A splinter run in at the side of his thumbnail. Distraction, not comfort. Jangling, not soothing. He's leaving me. That's what will happen eventually. Belsize Park will please him, especially if his work goes well. He'll be back in the milieu which spawned him. Where I found him. He had never wanted to come into the country. Never really wanted a bucolic life, only for a time, until it lost its charm. Until she lost her charms. He'll leave me. Not directly – gradually, and that will be bloodier. The gradual disintegration of my life. Because that is what he has become: my life. Without him I'll wither away.

At the porch she set her empty mug on the table where he worked, pushed wet feet into a pair of flip-flops and sat wretchedly in the rush-bottomed chair. A thin vapour was rising from the valley where the little stream caught the warmth of the rising sun. The heron suddenly spun like a dart, plunged into the water, surfaced with a gleam of wriggling silver in its stiletto beak, flew heavily up into the alders. Her fists, curled tightly on the table, had shining white knuckles: a sign of stress? She pushed herself up, took the mug and went in to put on the kettle. It was just five o'clock.

Belsize-bloody-Park. Well, he can go. She couldn't stop him. But there would be a price to pay. Freedom didn't come free. She smiled bitterly at the accuracy of her thought.

'Well, that seems to be the lot. This box of books, that to go as well?'

'That as well. Everything. Sell it or dump it or give it to a charity.' Fal leant against the wall by the open door. 'It's mainly junk, her family kept the things they wanted.'

The removal man, a thin, wiry creature with a baize apron, hauled the black marble clock out of a box. 'If that's the case, perhaps you won't mind if I take this? Personal, I mean? Nice piece of marble is this, got brown veining in it. Give it a proper clean-up, it'll be as good as new. If I may?'

Fal nodded almost too willingly. 'Lord, yes. Take it. I think it rings a bell at the hour. Strikes the hour. It used to. Take it, do.'

One of the other men – there were three – shuffled in, looked about. 'That's the lot then, Fred? And this box of old books?' He carted them away, and Fred, who had collected the black marble clock, said, 'Well, we'll be off, Mr Grayle. Nothing left, nothing upstairs, the scullery is clear – bit niffy, but that's the oven: cooker *very* greasy.'

Fal went to the door with him. 'She was very old, Miss Stephens, couldn't quite manage it all in the end.' He watched the van reverse slowing into the driveway, and ease out into the lane. They were friendly with the pound note each had been handed by Fal. One of them had even made a vague motion towards sweeping up the little sitting-room until sent away with thanks and assurances that the whole house was to be stripped out anyway.

'That *is* right? You want it gutted, don't you?'

Roch came down from the bedrooms, grinning. 'They gone? Yes . . . yes, all absolutely gutted, as you say. It's a bit small. Smaller than I thought really . . . but we can build out into the garden, can't we?'

Fal hunkered down on the raised hearth. '*You* can. I don't want anything to do with that part. All I do beg is that you don't alter the . . . well, the style. Don't stick on a whacking great glass and steel bit. It may be elegant in Town but it won't do here.'

Roch laughed happily. He had a notepad and Biro and had scribbled a vague design. 'Very rough, Pa, but this sort of thing: enlarge the sitting-room, two or three bedrooms above, and a bathroom, and enlarge the kitchen space. See? And all in brick and knapped flint, like the original.'

Fal looked at his son's scribble. 'How much, dear boy, do you think this will cost you?'

Roch rubbed his nose. 'A lot. Quite a lot. But it'll be worth it. Anyway, Kathleen would have a serious crisis if we tried to slosh some paint around in here and settle in as it stands. God! Chilling!'

'Yes. "Chilling". I wonder if you really know just how "chilling" it is all going to be? Running the place. I mean, Roch, do you actually *know* just how much land you have to cope with? There's a tenanted farm, Marsh Farm: I didn't let that go with the rest of the place. Kept it for us, for Ma and me, if things got to be too difficult one day. They might. It's quite small, thirty acres, a smallholding. But it would do. The rest – apart from Bottle Cottage and Hart-leap, then the lodges, 'Pinner' and 'Stanmore' as we call them – short leases for all the rest, just in case. But it won't be easy, Roch. It beat me. That's being clear and honest.'

Roch squatted beside his father on the hearth, put a hand on his arm. 'Pa? I *do* know about all this. I've done some homework. I'm not just leaping into this as if it was a boardgame, you know? I'm not quite as thick as you seem to feel. Only, this I am *counting* on: don't die suddenly! I shall need you around for a bit until I think I can take the reins. Or perhaps one rein at first. It's like driving a coach and four, right? Not being macho in a red Ferrari . . . I know that.'

Fal poked a bit of stick into cracks in the hearth bricks. 'No Ferrari . . . but it'll swallow money just as easily. It's arable land, some cattle, and now he's grazing sheep, the present tenant . . . but there is no chance of Ferrari-living. It won't be vroom-vroom. More clank-clank.'

Suddenly Minder crashed into the room, Sophie called out to Jess, swung round the door. 'Wow! Doesn't it look titchy! With no furniture? I can just see Miss Tessier cleaning *this* place up.'

Roch said sharply, 'She won't have to. I'll get in a firm,

strip the walls, tear out the cupboards, that sort of thing. Why are the dogs with you?'

Sophie sat on a low windowsill. 'Awful stink. Phew! these curtains: years of fried plaice and chips . . . The dogs are with me because Mademoiselle Loveday is "trying something new with her hair".'

Roch said, 'probably dying it black, to go with her broomstick, that's what she's doing. Jess! Jess! Sophie *stop* him, he's peeing everywhere!'

'Marking his territory. He remembers this place, don't you, treasure? You remember this smelly room and smelly old Nanny . . .'

Fal raised a hand. 'Enough, Sophie, enough. Roch and I have been talking about him taking over.'

Sophie nodded. 'I thought you might be. Farmer Roch . . . But not immediately?'

Roch got up and stretched his legs. 'No, not immediately. Pa has promised to hang on and teach me a thing or two. And we'll wait for you to cure your first four lepers. How's that? Not until then.'

'You are putrid to me, Rochester, putrid.' She fumbled about in the pocket of her jeans. 'Pa, this is for you. Stella gave it to me. She found it in Loveday's pocket yesterday, when she was carting her up to bed. She was pissed out of her mind, Stella said, and as heavy as a block of Stonehenge; solid lump, but she got her up. Can't understand it, but it is addressed to you and she thought perhaps you might.' She handed the crushed note to her father, screamed again at Jess. 'Jess! Stop *doing* that! Go outside at once! Outside, both of you!'

Fal took the paper written on the back of an old bill. 'Reeve and Hanse. Artists' Materials'. The message in thick pencil was in Jesus's slightly uneven handwriting. He had scribbled it on his knee. *Dear Fal, that was the most expensive Victoria sponge ever shoved into a cesspit. You may just regret it. I won't be back in the foreseeable future.* It was signed simply 'Rufus'.

He handed the paper to Roch wordlessly.

'What does it mean? You know?' asked Roch.

'I've got a shrewd idea. If either of you find an old McDougall's flour bag in the garden, don't lick the paper.' He stuffed the bill into his pocket. 'One of your Uncle Rufus's little jokes. This time rather an expensive one.' Seeing two blank faces before him, he straightened up and, with the blue-eyed smile all the Grayles were noted for, told his children just what had happened when Bob Smollett found the cocaine in the bread-bin.

Sophie started to laugh. 'Half a pound! How did he get half a pound *past* Nanny?'

Fal picked up the big front-door key. 'Oh, she knew, disapproved, hated the Chinese bloke who seemed to be the carrier, but there wasn't a lot she could do, was there? Not really . . . Down the cesspit.'

Roch wandered across to the open door, looked down the weedy gardens. 'No wonder Rufus is staying away. He'll be pissed off. Christ! Half a pound of coke! That's one hell of a lot to chuck down the lav. No wonder we won't see him for the "foreseeable future".'

'Unless,' Fal cut in mildly, sticking the key into the door, 'we do, at the Old Bailey one day? Never can tell.'

'Did the Jesus chap know where he was? Why call *him* at the hospice?'

'Knew the number, knew that Jesus would be there. Jesus was a partner in crime, you see. Nice enough chap. But a wanderer, friend of Rufus. There you go.'

They were in the garden, standing among seeding poppy heads and dying wallflowers.

'It's pretty outside,' said Sophie. 'Apart from the awful

man down at the farm. Can't resist a look, can he?' Sophie waved to Mr Wood so that, at least, he'd know he'd been observed. Startled, Jake hurriedly went indoors. 'He's seen me, isn't lingering.'

Fal turned the key in the door, joined the others on the path and they started down.

'When you said that Ting-Tong-Tang, or whatever, the Chinese creature, was probably the carrier, you mean he brought the stuff in?' Roch was curious. 'How would he do that? In small portions, over a period of time? How?'

Fal smiled gently. 'Swallowed the stuff in condoms I gather. So Jesus said coming up here; *thought* that's how they managed it. Came here to get rid of them. Hence Nanny's intense loathing. There was a colander in the lavatory at the ready. That do?' They walked on in silence.

Roch suddenly laughed aloud. 'Doing your business in a colander!' He hurried on. 'Sophie! We leave at one-fifteen. OK? Be ready.' He ran down the path, laughing, the dogs beside him.

Sophie slid her hand into her father's. 'Pa, listen. I'm not going to go and marry this boy, this Jean-Claude. Don't be fussed about that. I'm not. I just like him. He's part of the group going out to Somalia and I'd like to go with him.'

'I'd be perfectly happy if you wanted to marry him. Really *wanted* to. But it seems a bit sudden, and you hardly know him, do you?'

Sophie kicked a molehill, scattered the muddy soil. 'No. No, I don't really. He's a friend of Kathleen Tessier's, we all met at her place. You see, it's Loveday . . .'

Fal released her hand, looked bewildered. 'Loveday? What about Loveday?'

'I'm not going to be the lonely spinster in the family who'll have to end up as her bloody companion. That's "what about" Loveday. It usually happens. Spinster daughter gets lumbered with ailing mother or father. Well, I'm not. Sorry, but I am not.'

Fal laughed, hugged her to him while they walked. 'My darling girl, of course you're not! What nonsense you do talk. I wouldn't let that happen to you. Neither would your mother. We'll manage Aunt Loveday somehow. I don't know quite how . . . Nanny was hellish useful . . . But we'll find a way. You go off to your lepers or whatever they are. But don't feel that you are driven out of your home because of a slightly unstable aunt! Because you aren't.'

Sophie took his hand again. 'No, I know. I do love you and Ma, I really do. But sometimes I feel a bit terrified. Roch and Kathleen will probably make it, and I'll be left. And I don't want to sell dried-flower arrangements or pots of make-up in some glitzy shop. So it's lepers. At least it'll be a new country. Something different to do?'

Fal nodded. 'It'll be a new country all right . . . and we can't get you back suddenly to look after Auntie if she gets stung by a wasp!' They laughed together.

'So that's what Jean-Claude is for. Mind you, he is rather a dish. I wouldn't mind, and he's rather keen. Not on marrying me, just . . . rather keen. You know?'

They had crossed the little stream. Fal started up the hill towards the house. The cedars were still, silver in the morning sun. 'Know exactly. Good luck. By the way, my child, remember. However caught up you become in landing your fish, or romance perhaps, it's still closed ranks. Not a word. Remember? No one is to know.'

Sophie looked back over her shoulder to the ancient scatter of barns in the valley. 'No one ever *will* know. No one.'

They walked up through the ornamental garden with its box hedges and fuchsias.

'That's a good girl. And just remind Roch from time to time. He's a bit vague . . .'

'We have a few little problems. I've come to have a talk about them.'

India swung herself up on to the edge of the kitchen table. Stella pulled off her rubber gloves and set them to dry out on the draining-board, two bright-yellow hands trembling in Fairy Liquid. She wiped her own hands, sticky from condensation, on her apron.

India poked about in the sugar bowl. 'Miss Loveday and money. That's what I want to have a talk about with you both. I don't want it to go lingering on. You see?' She found a sugar cube, stuck it in her mouth.

'Your teeth! It'll rot your teeth!' said Stella sitting down at the table.

Charlie was leaning up against the dresser, thoughtfully. It took him a long time to get to the centre of things usually, and he had to consider well, but he knew why India was there, knew why they were all relaxed. He was just curious to know when to join in, because Stella was the one, he knew, who would be in charge. He'd leave the women to it: jump in when he realized there was something he could contribute. He didn't want to interrupt the conversation. He was just bright enough to know that if he said the wrong thing at the wrong time he could bugger up the whole morning.

'The main thing, I know,' said India, 'is the vexed problem of Miss Loveday. I am right? Now she's on her own?'

Stella nodded wearily, rolled down her sleeves. 'Yes, I suppose it is the *main* thing. Funny how we all expected Ada Stephens to pop her clogs, well, for ages really, and how we none of us seemed to realize that when she went

Miss Loveday would have to have help. I mean, we were warned, weren't we? Took no notice. Given plenty of warning.'

India nodded tiredly. 'Typical, really. We never really believe in awful things happening to us. Always put them aside. They happen to *other* people, not us. Anyway, it's happened to us . . . Now you know very well Miss Loveday is *not* raving mad?'

Stella looked up from rolling down a sleeve in shock. 'Oh no! Not that . . . she's just, well, what she is, is a . . . a liability. A dreadful liability. There, I've said it. She's a liability, Mrs Grayle, and we can't run this house the way you like it, not with a liability as well.' She was made breathless by her own wisdom. Charlie looked away, crossed his ankles.

'Well, I can see that, Stella. She needs someone fairly close by to keep an eye on her, that's it, isn't it?'

Stella nodded. 'That's it exactly. I mean, you can't be certain where she's got to! She just disappears suddenly. Might be down at her Wendy Hut or get as far as the King's Arms in the village even. Charlie found her there, didn't you, Charlie? At the King's Arms?'

Charlie realized that by the question, he had been given permission to speak. 'Yeh. That's it. King's Arms . . . bold as brass, she was, looking for one of the dogs. Minder, I think, he'd gone on a bit of a wander. Bitch somewhere, you know?'

Stella interrupted him with a quick look. 'We *know*. But that's the problem, Mrs Grayle: you've got to have eyes in the back of your head. And another thing: she likes to take her supper, or even her dinner, with us, sitting at the corner, there. But it's not fitting really. It's not convenient either. This place is his and mine. I don't mind her coming here for the odd cup of tea or cocoa or something, but sometimes we do want to be on our own. Charlie can't abide strangers in his kitchen.'

Charlie thought this was a reasonable moment to speak again, and did so. 'That Heather Sands and her barmy girlfriend! I could have throttled them, and leaving the oven filthy . . .'

Stella said flatly, 'Charlie, I think that Mrs Grayle understands.'

India slid off the table. 'I understand very well. But it was really just during this awful week, surely? Only while the funeral and so on was being arranged?'

Stella and Charlie shook heads. No, it often happened. Not that they *always* minded – it was just irritating and, of course, she was often, well, tiddly. Did Mrs Grayle know that? Mrs Grayle apparently didn't. Fully. So she got filled in quickly. Charlie had had to carry her up to bed on a few occasions.

'I didn't do anything else. Just dumped her on her bed. Heavy as a load of bricks. Got to my back, that did. Stella did the rest, put her *in* bed. Had to have a lie-down myself. Right, Stell?'

India traced a finger through a spill of sugar on the table. 'You mean that she gets drunk? I mean properly drunk? Incapable?'

Stella swiftly rose to her feet. 'Oh no! Not drunk, like in a pub or somewhere. Not that exactly. I mean . . . tiddly, like I said, and then she'll be laughing and a bit woozy and she'll just go plonk! Plonk! On the floor. Right out, like a plank. Mind you, it doesn't matter to me – I've been married to Charlie long enough to know when someone has had one over the eight, but that's what worries me about Miss Loveday: when she falls. One day she'll fall on the fire, or on the table with the oil-lamps – think of that! In that hut of hers down in the orchard! All wood. Who would ever know? I mean, Mrs Grayle, if she does that down there it'll be her funeral pyre. By the time any of us saw it she'd be an eggcup of ashes. Miss Sophie had a good idea of what's what. But now she's going away, I mean . . . But drunk she is not – incapable she often has been, but tiddly, just silly, is what she is. *Most* of the time.'

India said, 'We do have a problem. I knew about some of the drink . . . not that she actually passed out. Oh Lord. I *am* sorry. No one told us.'

Stella pushed her chair into its place under the table. 'It would have felt like sneaking. I *do* forget that she isn't a child. She's a grown woman. But it's difficult . . .' She sighed hopelessly. 'It's been a troublesome few days, I will say.'

India went over to the kitchen door. Charlie still stood leaning against the dresser. He swung a hanging cup with a prod of his index finger.

'Well, what I came along to suggest is that you both go off and have a complete rest. When it's quite settled down here, perhaps on Sunday, just get away from us all: Hart-leap, Miss Loveday, everything. Somewhere fun, different: go to Paris? Why not? You can go from Gatwick, just up the road, see a different world, different people. It would be a complete change. Don't worry about money, I'll settle that . . . as long as you don't go mad and stay at the Ritz or somewhere. And the other thing I wanted to say is that we'll bump up your salary. It's about time – and now that I realize what you have had to cope with with Miss Loveday. I hadn't, quite honestly, fully realized just how much she intruded into your lives. I'm sorry, terribly sorry.'

Charlie fiddled quietly with a Spode cheese dish on the dresser top.

'I would just ask you to bear with us for a little, until we can find someone to help with her, a companion, something like that . . . I can't really think straight yet. Sophie is going away, as you know. Miss Loveday will have to have someone with her.' She sighed, stood round-shouldered, folded her hands.

Stella shrugged slightly, looked across at Charlie. 'Well, no use denying we could both do with a break. A couple of weeks somewhere. I don't think it'll be Paris though.'

Charlie leant away from the dresser, replaced the lid on the cheese dish gently. 'Not Paris. No. More like Kempton Park or somewhere, handy for the races. My cousin's got a nice little pub near Leatherhead. Very handy.'

Stella looked up at him in surprise. 'Ben's place, you mean?'

'Ben's place. Near to Epsom, Ascot, Lingfield . . . not too far from Brighton. That's what we'll do, Mrs Grayle. We'll go off Sunday to my cousin. He'll put us up, it's a good idea. Come at just the right time this has. We'll be off Sunday.'

India nodded. 'Good, fine, do as you like, Charles.'

He faced her full on. 'We'll do that. And we won't be back. Not ever. I'm giving you our notice, here and now. Final.'

Stella smothered a scream. 'Charlie! Whatever are you saying!'

'That we are leaving, that's what I'm saying. Time's up. Sorry, Mrs Grayle, given you a bit of a shock, I shouldn't wonder.'

India nodded, leant against a wooden chair. 'Just a bit, Charles, just a bit.'

'We *can't* do that, Charlie, not so sudden!' Stella was in anguish.

'Oh yes we can. I'm doing it. Done it. Sorry to have taken you by surprise, Mrs Grayle, but it's been in my mind for quite a while now. We're off.'

India unclasped her hands. 'I didn't realize that you were

so unhappy. After – what? – twenty-something years.'

Charlie started to unbutton his white jacket. 'Twenty-odd years. About. Took over from Stella's mum and dad. I've had it, we both have. Twenty years is twenty years. Smothered. We have reached the finish now.' He hung the jacket on a hook behind the door.

'Is this because of Miss Loveday?' India was bleak.

'Not entirely. Not her alone. She's had a hell of a lot to do with it, but we're getting on, Stell and I. Not young any longer. We don't have children, we just look after a fully grown child. I'm not about to haul Miss Loveday up the stairs like a felled ox no more. Nor is my wife. She's being polite when she says your sister-in-law is just tiddly. Well, your sister-in-law is often as pissed as a fiddler's bitch, Mrs Grayle. Crashes down like a great chimney stack. Crash! bang! wallop! Down she goes. Seen it too often.'

Stella cried out, her eyes wide with shock. 'Charlie! Whatever are you saying! Watch that tongue of yours, I've told you often enough. Don't listen to him, Mrs Grayle.'

'Do listen, Mrs Grayle. It's the truth I'm telling you. You wouldn't want us to give in our notice, not after all this time, without telling you absolutely why?'

India, holding on to fraying dignity, shook her head. 'Of course not, Charles. Say on.'

He leant on the table. 'Well, it was bad enough when we had that mad old bat creeping about in this kitchen, Nanny whatever. Then when she mercifully got retired off to the cottage that wasn't the end of her. Oh no! Who had to run the little errands to her place? Take her the papers, rolls of knitting-wool, pheasant to pluck, a basket of fruit? Who? Me. Muggins. Trotting up and down that bloody path – it's a long haul, and me still with the Summer Room to Hoover, the banisters to polish, all the rest. I don't *want* to cart Miss Loveday about, I don't *want* my wife to either, and most of all I don't want her to sit here, at my elbow, at my table, blowing on her bloody soup! No peace. Stella has worked her fingers so they look like an X-ray. To the bone. Well, I've finished looking after other people and other people's things. I want my own things to care for. So, thanks for your suggestion, we'll go off to Bournemouth, or Swanage or somewhere – sea air, peaceful – then we'll go to Ben's, sort ourselves out. But we won't come back to this place. Hartleap holds no future for us now. Too old. It's not on my agenda.'

He folded his arms and stood solidly facing the women. India said nothing. Stella, who had wrenched a handkerchief into a sodden roll, mopped her eyes. Charlie's tirade had shaken her. 'Have to agree with him, hearing him saying it aloud. What kind of future *have* we left? At our ages? You've all been very good to us here, it's just that it seems that this week has, as it were, brought everything to a head. She was an old tartar, that Ada Stephens. She stirred things up here all the time. An old mixer. Old people on their own do tend to behave like that, mixing, stirring. It hasn't been a happy time, I'm afraid. Not for some few years.'

Charlie ran his hands through sparse hair. 'It's just got to me this week. I'm a slow-burner, just smoulder away quietly. People say, "Oh! Good old Charlie!"', but good old Charlie is burning away underground, like an old sack smouldering: when a little wind comes along up it goes. Well, that's me. I'm slow to catch, but when I do I fair blaze. Blazing now. Work it out for yourself, Mrs Grayle. After twenty years' service, and at our age, what have we got left? A few savings and a mobile home on a caravan site with all mod cons and bugger all future. No kids, no family except Ben, just each other. And the last few years here at Hartleap have been like laying up the first-class breakfast trays on the *Titanic*. Futile! Nothing ahead but blankness . . . So, thanking you, we'll go off Sunday, take it easy. I'll help Ben out in his bar, Stella can fiddle about in the caravan making curtains or something. That's our future. He lifted two large plastic bowls from the draining-board. 'Minder and Jess, dinner-time! Another little chore I won't look back on with any affection.' He pushed open the door into the yard calling, 'Dinners! Dinners!'

The dogs started howling and barking. Stella buried her face in her hands. India moved to her and put an arm round her shoulders. 'I think he's right, Stella . . . Please don't cry. I didn't notice, didn't see. But he's right. We'll have to start again here from scratch, somehow. Charles has just saved what remains of your future together. Just in time. Lucky you.'

'Fair stands the wind for France!' Edward yelled marching up the deck, having thumped her on her bottom.

Behind Unity the ensign whipped and tore, above her the sails bellied, grew taut. She hung on to the helm, the wheel tight in her fists.

He never even got a quotation exactly right. She was rather surprised that he knew the quotation anyway: never seen him in a book, apart from *Jane's Fighting Ships*, or some sort of handbook on sailing, and one or two on MTBs. (He'd been in MTBs during the war – the *last* stages, he always pointed out. Didn't want to appear too aged – he *was* vain.) He'd once read some novel about the D-Day landing but chucked it away when he got to the part in which he should, or his MTB should, have been noted but wasn't. But he was right about the wind, about the day, the sea, and the absolute splendour overhead of the gulls wheeling and dipping on the way to France.

France lay low and hazed along the far horizon. She

could, if she squinted against the wind-brought spray, see the thin line of beach, the huts or tents, the varied gabled villas stuck along the gently rising shore. Somewhere a small church spire raked the blue sky.

Edward looked at his watch, smiled happily, raised a thumb. This clearly meant that they were either on time, or that he had not miscalculated, or that they would get in before dusk. He had been so anxious to depart exactly on time that she had raced through *her* duties. But Deauville was where it ought to be, where he had expected it to be. As if it could perhaps have drifted off and attached itself to another part of the continent altogether. He seemed amazed with joy, and without saying a word he pointed ahead, nodding his head happily. It was there. *Just* as he'd expected, and he felt triumphant that he had got them across. Even the fact that they had done the trip a hundred times did not diminish his delight. It was still a tremendous, wild adventure, and he was, except for a little help from his wife, in sole charge! He hadn't felt quite so triumphant, in a perfectly orderly manner, since the war.

At the first voyage, their honeymoon, Unity hadn't been absolutely certain of its delights. She was secretly terrified that they would hit a tanker or a fishing boat, or get caught up with some leviathan steaming slowly down-Channel to wherever. They looked dauntingly big from where she clung to a stanchion. They'd be whirled away in little bits, no traces left. No one would have noticed *Dawn Spray*.

But it had never happened, and she had grown happily complacent and enjoyed herself, as best she could; even took the helm from time to time, because it gave Edward such enormous pleasure. He wasn't the kind of man, really, to dig potatoes or prop up rain-sodden delphiniums, or dead-head the Albertine. He was, and always would be, she thanked God, a sailor. And she made allowances for that. She had married a sailor willingly and so a sailor's wife she would remain.

What was so particularly ship-shape about her husband was that he did it all absolutely correctly, even to the same room in the same hotel, the same table in the restaurant. At their slightly cluttered arrival, deck shoes, jeans, sweaters, a clutch of canvas bags, coats slipping over shoulders were instantly grabbed by familiar, and delighted, old hands. *Certainly* they were expected! Certainly their room was ready! Certainly the weather had been perfect for the voyage! The champagne cocktail awaited them in the *petit bar* where M. Guy, as he always was, attended them. *Et voilá!* After that the bath! The menu, Madame Fils assured them, was already in their room. The speciality this evening was a particular crab soufflé, but first the wine.

Sitting in the beamed and polished bar, with its murals of various watering-places in Normandy and the Pas de Calais, with the sweet scent of Gauloises, and the soft laughter or mild explosion of amused banter from a laughing group over on her left, brought enormous comfort to Unity; and seeing Edward charge his pipe, a fat packet of his treasured charts on the table, almost brought her relaxation. Well, as near as she was about to get now. She'd have another little look in the shower. She mustn't become neurotic. It will hardly have grown since Tuesday. And it won't have gone away either.

And it hadn't.

Well, one could hardly expect it to have disappeared just like that. I'm getting senile. I only found it on Tuesday evening. But I suppose if you simply long for something not to be there, you can imagine it away, *try* to imagine it away. But that is not so easy when it snags at your memory all the time. I shall wear my new Fenwick's outfit for dinner. He won't notice, of course, he never does . . . However . . .

266

It's so odd because I believe that if I arrived to sit opposite him tonight in a cambric bust-bodice with baggy drawers and a bit of blue ribbon, all he'd really notice was the bit of blue ribbon.

'Doll! You've twisted your ribbon, where it goes through the lacy bit. Want me to straighten it for you?' He was adorable in his perfectly honest ignorance. He just wouldn't imagine that I'd dine in a pair of cambric drawers, so he wouldn't see them. And I'd never do it to him, so what am I wittering on about? She laid out the shirt-blouse with its sprigs of cornflowers, and hoped the zip on the new skirt would hold. Well, wouldn't suddenly get stuck, as so often they did, a bulge of flesh bursting through like a ripe fig.

They had their usual table in the corner. Madame Fils hovered about like a benign hornet, hissing for a glass to be changed because of smears, to remove the little pink lamp, to reset the cutlery to accommodate the crab souffle; and, after that, the meal progressed competently and deliciously, and M. Jacques brought their wines, chosen with his assistance earlier in the bar and opened so that they could breathe: civilized, comforting, spoiling. Madame Fils suggested, and they agreed to, fresh raspberries, with cream from her sister's farm near Pont l'Eveque, whence, *par hasard*, the raspberries also came. The total triviality of all this was joyful to Unity's ear. Far better to discuss raspberries and cream from a farm at Pont l'Eveque than Harley Street next week. They were set before them, in a blue and white bowl, the cream in a pitcher, golden and thick as butter.

Edward helped her to raspberries. 'Too much? All water. Won't make you fat ... Of course' – he indicated the pitcher brimming and solid with heavy cream – '*that*, on the other hand, will. Put on pounds. Two spoonfuls of that and you'll look like a lump of lard in no time. The orange juice, I am informed, will cut it, the fat content . . . Doubt it, but let's have a splash, eh? Recommended. I say! Isn't this fun, doll?'

Unity felt the bubble start, just below her heart, she felt it grow, matching the one in her head, two bubbles slowly expanding, growing larger, blotting out raspberries, the murals of watering-places, the pitcher of yellow cream. As if from the bottom of a well she heard her voice, saw Edward's look of non-comprehension.

'I've got a lump, Ned.' The bubbles had joined and burst.

'A what, doll?'

'A lump. Under my arm. Mind! You're dripping raspberry juice on the cloth.'

'I don't think I'm following, doll?' He set aside the spoon. His guts had torn into a jumble. He felt his heart leap, miss a beat, carry on again. He was playing for time. He'd perfectly well heard, and understood, what had been said.

'I'm sorry. I shouldn't have said anything. It just, sort of, burst out. I did try not to say.'

Edward picked up the spoon. 'Well, where is it? Under your arm? Usually are. Big, small, when did you discover it?' He poured orange juice on the raspberries, topped it with a heavy spoonful of cream, offered her the plate.

'My dear! Ned, I'll be enormous! I found it on Tuesday. It's the size of a lentil . . . well, a dried pea. It's nothing, I'm sure. Nothing for this week anyway. I was a blithering idiot to say anything. I *am* sorry. Spoiled everything.'

Edward shook his head, he had calmed down inside. His guts had more or less settled. More or less. 'I knew, doll, when you called me "Ned" it was something not altogether pleasant. Ned is a very personal name, isn't it? You don't use it often.'

'No. I don't use it often. I needed to this time. I've felt terribly frightened.'

' 'Course you have. To be expected. You want to nip off home? Go back? We can, it's perfectly easy. Cross tomorrow if you like . . .'

Unity shook her head, ate a single raspberry. 'We'll do no such thing. I've looked forward to this little jaunt for ages. My 'quilting' bee would be thrown into a frenzy. They don't expect me back until next week, and next week I'll go up to Town, see a good chap. You'll come with me, will you?'

Edward took her hand. ' 'Course, you silly Doll, of course I'll be there.'

Unity nodded gratefully. 'Good. I feel *much* better now. I just don't want to be taken away from you yet.'

Edward put more sugar on his raspberries: a reflex action, they didn't need it. 'No one is being taken from anyone. I love you far too much to let you wander off with some snotty medic in Harley Street. Far too much.'

'Just say that last bit again, Ned. Leave out the "snotty medic". Just say the rest.'

He looked at her smiling. 'Boys and girls stuff? I know what you mean, not stupid. It must be Jacques's wine selection. Gone to your head.'

'You still haven't said it. Even if you aren't stupid.'

'I love you. That it?'

'And the other part, "far too much".'

'I love you far too much. So, presupposing that your lump won't have become a boulder by tomorrow, we'll keep to the agreed itinerary, right? Trot along and see Sword Beach, where I landed. All right?'

'Perfectly all right,' said Unity and found that she could possibly manage her dessert.

Friday Night

She sat on her favourite milking-stool, legs wide, calico skirts flowing, bare feet planted strongly on the uneven tiles of the floor, shadows all about her, from one oil-lamp. A frivolity really, the oil-lamp: the house was wired, she just had to touch a switch. But the lamplight was kinder, more seductive. It had always been a part of their 'games', shadowing detail, keeping mystery. Now, no more game.

She poured herself a large glass of red wine, set the bottle on the scrubbed-wood table, noted, hopelessly, that the bottle was empty. Hopelessly, because whatever she had drunk – and through the evening she had had a good deal, two bottles at this rate – had done nothing, had only plunged her deeper into the dull gloom which had permeated her all day. The word hassle had struck hard, bruised her, and a sense of impending loss shadowed her like the dark wings of a giant bat. A bat of despair, failure.

He would leave and never return. Simple as that. He would go to Frank Heffer's flat, start to work, perhaps come back once or twice. Gradually the visits would become fewer, less attractive. He would be immersed in his 'history', immersed in a war which he had never experienced, excited by events which had already collected dust, the dust of familiarity. He had spent the whole day in the large sitting-room, which they hardly ever used: papers, books, photographs, files of selected information from the Imperial War Museum, who had been so helpful – to an extent; an extent.

That's what seemed to happen all the time. People were not anxious to discuss May '45.

That's what always happened. It would start off with some vague sense of promise. People had died, then their sons, or wives, would appear willing to talk, and as suddenly as a door slamming pull out. It was as if they had first of all had to clear it with someone, or some Department, and the response had been strongly negative. No one was really prepared to go into the whole sorry disaster, in detail or in the main. He was going to find life difficult trying to piece all this together, even if the silly old bitch up the hill had been so obliging. At least he knew who the Grayles were, had seen the Grayles, followed and watched them. Surely to Christ he would realize that it was going to be hopeless as long as any of them existed? They had closed ranks on him. He was ignored. Even the very pleasant people at the Imperial War Museum suddenly drew back: not *that* period. They were *so* sorry, there was nothing that they could do, about *that* period. It was still, at the time, restricted. Maybe papers would be released one day? But not today, this day.

In the meantime their own partnership was undergoing strain. Holes were appearing in its fabric and she was facing a negative, empty life ahead – not immediately, but it was on its way. She had spent most of the day stuffing the batik cushions with kapok out in her studio to occupy her mind and time, and then realized that she'd never get them to Liberty's in that state. Two dozen plump cushions would need a van. Better to disembowel them all and send them up packed flat. A useless day, irritating, ill-conceived, exhausting, kapok everywhere, frustration turning to anger and anger to a dangerous rage, banked down like a boiler-fire, but ready to burst into flame at the first whisper of a breeze. They had eaten a frugal supper in that state.

Jake had started on the Scotch early. She made an

omelette and tossed a salad, afraid to utter a word about ingredients. He had murmured at some point something about the tumble of her hair. He'd been used to seeing it bound and wound round her head. She explained that she had washed it, it was drying in the sweet air. He accepted it, didn't care anyway, and she was lying. *She* didn't care anyway: couldn't be bothered to coil and bind it. What for? It had excited him once, and his excitement had driven her to joyful exhibitionism. But no longer. No one there left to excite.

Wearily she had cleared the table. 'I'll just tidy up in there,' he had said. His voice was whisky thick. She noted it, looked up at him, holding his bottle. He made a little bow and went unsteadily into the big room, leaving her to stack plates and open another bottle of her own red wine, the wine which did so little to comfort her, to lift the despair. She thus sat facing the open door out beyond the porch and watched the dying of the day, remembering that she had walked out barefoot to greet its birth only a few hours before. Not bloody worth it. She heard Jake slam a door, whistle uneasily, walk away, his tread heavy on the wooden stairs, leaving her desolate with her wine and the velvet dusk. Why was it always called 'velvet'? Balls, it was as thick as felt: suffocating, black as black.

She felt tears of acute self-pity prick her eyes, brushed them roughly away. They were tears of fury. Her father's voice, kind, considered: *You are older than he is, my dear, don't be foolish, don't think that the pleasure of a young man will stay with you. They want to find fresher grazing after you have taught them the tricks and the rules. Remember! An older woman is the teacher. When taught he'll slip away to find something younger, virginal, someone to impress with his huge new knowledge, someone who won't know the difference between Then and Now. Be warned!*

And, to give her her due, she had taken heed of the warning, had played the game as it normally was played at first: balding younger sons, cufflinks gleaming – 'Come up and have a coffee? Something stronger perhaps, why not?'; or podgy-bellied men in pinstripe suits who never revealed their ugliness until they were stripped, and then did it wearing their socks. There were the younger group – she seemed to attract them because she was stronger, bigger, tough, heavy-breasted. Motherly, they called it. They wrestled sweatily in a sprawl and then reached for a cigarette or opened a bottle, grinning blearily. 'Great! Good for you, was it?' It was true – that dire phrase, men actually did ask that. A quick bash, maybe fifteen minutes, and then plod, plod down to the bathroom. Singing. Sour breath drifting. Never asked about you. If you would like to wash *them* from out of your body. She had tried it the normal way, waited almost half her life for one moment when some perfect creature would take her hand in a crowded room, a firm, hard handshake, a questing look in the eyes, amusement on his lips, and she would know, as he would know, that yes, she wanted him. But at her price. And he would *want* to be at her mercy. Dominated. How could she tell? An instinct merely. She could. And she did. Jake Wood had known in the noisy crowd.

'I'm called "Tom Tiddler". A columnist. Don't let that trouble you.'

'I won't. I never read gossip things. I suppose that's what you mean?'

'Yes. I *ride* pretty well. Good on a horse, all the leather and boots and the smell, you know? Excites me, I rather get a kick out of that, being *astride* a horse. A big horse, in *control* of me. Know what I mean? I think it's *very* thrilling. To be like that.'

And she had smiled, nodded – she remembered that

273

vividly – and said, 'I'd like to see you on a horse . . . like the ones they have in the gym . . .'

And with this absurd conversation, which both played secretly together in the braying crowd at some party in a studio off Abbey Road, their fate was sealed. No one, overhearing them, would possibly have made any sense of the sexually coded conversation. Only they would understand. Only they would have thudding hearts.

'Do you know anywhere? There's a big settee in my place. It would not be a . . . gym . . . or a horse . . . but it might help?'

It did. She found herself smiling lightly at the memory, raised her glass, saw a shadow lengthen across the tiled floor and, looking up, saw him standing in the doorway, in silhouette, the corridor behind him, his legs and arms wide apart, a bottle held by the neck high, half empty. He moved gently backwards into the light. Wearing the white jeans. Slowly she rose and faced him.

'I've been a naughty boy, Madame. Been very cruel to you. All day. Haven't I?'

She was motionless. He had started the game.

'You have indeed. Madame is extremely vexed with you. Your behaviour has been quite inexcusable.'

He stood perfectly still. 'Inexcusable. Only a severe punishing will make up for it, Madame. I am prepared for your punishment.'

She walked slowly towards him, her skirt deliberately swinging as she moved her heavy limbs. He murmured softly, eyes half closed, 'Swish, swish, swish . . .' Giggled.

Reaching him, she said in a low voice, 'You like that sound, eh? Swish, swish of Madame's skirts. Swish, swish of the whip? You shall be whipped for your wickedness today. Such brutal cruelty to Madame deserves a thrashing. You have made her so unhappy.'

I'll be whipped! Madame will thrash me because I have been a wicked fellow! Because I am going to London, because I don't like the class she comes from. Hey! Hey! Whip away.' His hair had tumbled into half-closed eyes. He thrust his pelvis lewdly towards her, arms on high, whisky bottle clutched. He was very drunk. She watched him with mounting hatred, tempered by a swelling of lust for the heavily packed groin before her. He was swaying about, legs twisting, bottle wagging. 'Hey! Hey! I've come to beg your pardon, Madame. That's what I've come for, to beg pardon for past sins.'

He was giggling, took a swig from his bottle, and suddenly she threw her charged wine glass into the sink. It shattered, scattering red wine like gouts of thin blood. Jake cringed slightly; it had surprised him but he equally knew that he had to cringe at this point. It suggested humility, fear and submission. He knew the rules. He bowed his grinning head, heard her commanding voice order him to give her the whisky, shook his head and held the bottle close to his naked chest. 'You defy Madame?' Her voice was low. He nodded and began to tremble. This was part of the game. It would drive her to the limit: his submission, the trembling, the helplessness. He was quite unaware that he had driven her to the limit already. Only when he peered up at the still figure before him, through the fall of his hair, did he realize that the anger in her eyes was suddenly not quite a part of the game: pitiless, flat hatred.

He straightened up uneasily, took a swig from the bottle, watched her as she turned away, slammed the front door, rammed in the bolts. She walked slowly across the kitchen and stood before him. He started to tremble again, took another quick swig, wantonly thrust his hips towards her as she started to unbutton the long tight bodice and the wide skirts of her dress, let it fall open in full display before him. Her naked body glimmered in the lamplight, ripe, heavy breasts, firm thighs, legs apart. He laughed, a high excited noise. 'Oh! What beauties! What beauties! All to be cuddled, eh? All to be cuddled. I'll serve you well, Madame, *serve* you very well.'

'I shall serve you first, so that you are fully prepared for Madame. She is very demanding tonight. She will use the cuffs and use Mr Rod. Go up!'

He stood, legs astride, bottle at his side, worry flickering in his eyes like summer lightning. 'You'll make me ready, I can't serve you until you make me ready, Madame, but no Mr Rod, don't use the rod, don't cut me.'

Brusquely she pushed him. He staggered and fell up the stairs backwards, turned and began to crawl. 'Don't cut me, please don't cut me. Remember our word? Pax. When I shout pax we stop . . . ?'

Her voice was harsh with irritation. 'Get up, go on up. There will be no pax. You are to be punished, controlled. You like that, don't you? Madame to control you?'

He scrambled up the stairs to the landing. 'I like that. But don't hurt your boy . . .'

She noticed, from the corner of her eye, the open door to their room, two suitcases strapped and packed. Fury mounted. 'Get on up, get on.'

He clambered up the final flight to the attic. 'It's all prepared as you want it, all ready. The horse is shiny and waiting . . .'

She shoved him ahead. The attic was a wide-open space, lit at the far end by a single glow of lamplight, in the centre of the room the great chimney breast cut into the gabled roof. There was a clutter of old furniture, a rocking horse, boxes. Beyond the brick chimney stack lay the playroom, their secret place. Dead centre, gleaming in the oil-lamp light, the horse: smooth leather top; from each leg hung the cuffs, swinging slightly.

He nervously patted the smooth top, took a sudden swig from his bottle. At this moment, as always, his heart began to race, his excitement grew. The punishment this evening, he knew, would be severe. She knew that he was about to quit. She took a thin, mean whip from its hook on the wall, swished it with a cutting motion above his head. He ducked, drank again, whisky dribbled down his chin. 'Don't cut, remember? Don't cut me, please . . .'

Silently and frighteningly deliberate, she removed the bottle from his hand, pushed him towards the horse. 'Saddle up! Get astride, you little shit!' and with fury she struck him viciously, twice across the face. He cried out, cupping his jaw in his hands. She had cut his lips and he bled. He was half stooped with shock and pain and hardly felt her start to unbutton him. 'You have betrayed me. You are a cheat and a liar.' She tugged at a button. He made an inept move to assist her and was once again struck across the face, so suddenly and so roughly that he fell, sprawling at her feet, fear leaping. This was no longer the 'game'. He lay staring up at her with shock.

'Get them off. Pull them off!' Her voice was harsh with impatience.

'Too tight, Madame . . .' He struggled desperately. 'Too tight . . .' He was like a beetle fallen on its back, legs helplessly flailing as he tried to peel down the jeans. She struck a light blow with the whip across his naked chest to hurry him, and when he had got rid of them she kicked them aside. He lay on his back, supported by his elbows, staring up at her, hair wild, eyes wide with apprehension – he had never seen this fury before. She stood naked above him, her heavy cambric robe falling from her shoulders like a great cloak.

'Isso? Isso, pax . . . enough . . . no more . . .' She struck him harshly across the shins. He yelped. 'No! For God's sake, stop now . . .'

She kicked him, rolled him over on to his belly, struck savagely across his naked back. 'Get up, get up, get on the horse, get on the horse.' His terror was mounting, the whisky-binge fading, a sickness filled his mouth. Chivvied by the teasing flicks of her whip he blearily staggered to his feet, fell against the horse, and without being fully aware realized that he was face down, shackled at wrist and ankle and that she had moved away. Through half-closed eyes he watched her shadow, saw just below him, on the boards, the thin whip and began to whimper. To whimper was all a part of the game, but this was from sheer terror. Somewhere in his muddled head, in the blur of drunkenness and half-sobriety, he realized that she had lost control and that she was going to use the rod on him.

He tried to lift his head. 'Isso, stop! Do anything else you like to me, anything, but don't use the rod. Don't . . . Pax, Isso, *pax*!' But the first swinging blow across his buttocks was so vicious that he screamed out with pain, and tears sprang from his tightly closed eyes. 'Oh don't, no don't!'

She thrashed him, beat at the bucking, heaving body, her hair flying, his body straining against the cuffs, bucking, twisting, hooping. She slashed until the skin split and his blood spattered her breasts, and quite suddenly, with a terrible strangled cry of agony, Jake was still, his body slumped down on the leather-topped horse. He had passed out with pain. She pulled his head up, eyes closed, sweat running. The blood from the weals trickled down his thighs. Slowly, almost deliberately, she shrugged the heavy robe from her shoulders, bunched it into a thick bundle, and crushed it over his ashen face. She lay across it, pressing with all her weight against his mouth and nose, stayed there, hunched over him, her legs braced, until she felt an odd slackening in the body beneath and realized that she had smothered him. Peeling away slowly she saw a smear of vomit, and pulled the bundle off. There was a dried trickle of blood at his nose and mouth. His heart no longer beat. She slowly dragged the fouled dress round her body, turned and walked unsteadily towards the boxes and stacked junk, and on a chair by the rocking horse she sat down and started to weep bitterly. Later she rose and, without looking at the fearsome tableau behind her, started down the stairs, switching on the electric light as she did so. In the big room on his desk, neatly piled, the folders and files with 'GRAYLE' printed on them, each with a number, his homework; beside the desk an empty canvas holdall. She took each file and emptied it, throwing handfuls of paper all about the room. A blizzard of paper. Then she found the telephone book. A male voice, husky with sleep. 'Bell here, Dr Bell.' She gave her name and address clearly, no anxiety showed. He cleared his throat, said she was quite sure it was urgent? Couldn't it wait until daylight? She said it was very urgent. A domestic situation had ended in sudden accidental death. Perhaps he would alert an ambulance? And the police? Dr Bell was fully awake now. 'Home Farm, Hartleap?' She nodded. 'And suddenly I am *terribly* hungry. Do you think you could bring me a sandwich? Something light at this time of night: egg and cress perhaps? If you can . . .' Wrapping the soiled dress round her, for she had suddenly grown cold, she wandered out on to the porch, found the wicker chair, curled up in it, covering her feet. Waiting for them. They wouldn't be long. She longed for the sandwich. Did she order in the plural? Or just a single? She couldn't remember. Moths bashed away at the hanging lamp, zooming in from the night, fluttering on the table. She hugged her feet in the creaking chair. Egg and cress . . . how delicious.

The barking of two dogs slowly filtered through the layers of misery which crammed Loveday's brain. She had fallen asleep weeping hopelessly and now awoke to the frantic, if distant, howls of Minder and Jess. She recognized them instantly. With a face bloated by tears, and two eyes like stuffed dates, she hauled herself upright in the bed and tried to come to terms with the barking and what had caused it. Then she thought, Sophie! It's Sophie come back to save me. She's changed her mind, and here she is, all the way from Paris. She knew she couldn't leave me. A car was coming up the drive and that was Sophie. Clawing the matted hair from her face and fumbling on her glasses, she clambered out of bed. A car had turned into the drive, headlights isolating dock and nettles, scurrying clouds of little moths into the still warm night. But it wasn't Sophie. The car turned into the dairy yard. Perhaps there was a party at Home Farm. All the lights blazed. Those hideous people were having a party. A car door slammed and a torch wobbled hurriedly down the path to the gate. She heard the squeal as whoever it was pushed it open. No music? There was always music at a party, wasn't there? But all was still, and up on the hill the dogs stopped barking, suddenly, as if they had been bidden, and from the Lewes road, at the end of the drive, a convoy of vehicles arrived, inching slowly into the tracks, on to the field beneath Bottle Cottage. Doors slammed, voices were muted, men started to move across to the farm, hurrying. Suddenly a wide shaft of lemon-light fell across the terrace below her, a silhouette of a man standing. Fal. She could tell by his long legs and the way that he ran. He ran jerkily over the rough grass, a torch bobbing in his hand, and joined the people with the cars. It was all quite pretty, like a fairground, flashing lights, torches, people moving, and then the ambulance eased up to the little iron gate and nothing happened for a while. Moths flew, an owl hooted. It was just getting boring when a shape with a blanket over it was carried from the house and pushed into the open doors of the ambulance. Slid in. Like Stella with her fish pie. *There. Now we give it a good thirty minutes. Keep an eye on that clock!* She folded her arms on the windowsill as the ambulance began to move down the drive and then a figure, wrapped up in a blanket, was pushed and hurried into a car which had drawn up, blue lights flashing. Fal was talking to someone with a cap and silver stripes. They hadn't been very gentle with the thing in the blanket. She watched the car drive quickly away. A blanket . . . how odd. Covering someone in a blanket? On such a very warm night? How odd! She watched intently the manoeuvring of the flashing blue lights on the cars as they began to inch down to the main road. A slow trundle. When they reached the road they each paused for a second and then raced away towards Lewes. Fal waved farewell to the driver of the last car and then started to walk slowly back towards the house; and just about when the last car had filed out on to the road, all the lights in the house went off. Even the porch was suddenly dark. It was so sudden and so intense that it appeared as if Home Farm itself had quite disappeared. There was just a huge black hole where it had been. That's how it seemed, but gradually, as her eyes grew accustomed to the night, it faded in again, the giant chimney, the long bumpy line of the roof. Fal was clambering up on to the terrace. Down in the field there was one car parked under the hedge of Bottle Cottage, tucked into the bank. Someone came across from the farm. She heard the iron gate clang and a rattle of chain, then the man lit a cigarette. She saw the sudden yellow flare, his pink face. He got into the car, switched off the blue light, and very faintly, in the dark, she heard his car radio playing the 'Blue Danube'. It faded into the air softly.

Fal was just below her, starting to shut the windows of Little Parlour. He looked up to her. 'Go to bed, Loveday, go to bed. It's all right.'

She sucked a length of hair. 'What has happened, Fal? Is it awful.'

Fal shook his head. She saw him clearly in the light from the room. 'All over now. Don't worry, there is a chap on guard down there.'

She nodded. 'I can hear his music. So pretty.'

'Go back to bed. You promised to be good, remember? All is very well.' The ranks are closed. He was half smiling as he slammed the long windows. The ranks are firmly closed now.